The Summons
Legacy of the King's Ring 1

MaryLu
TYNDALL

The Summons
Legacy of the King's Ring 1
by MaryLu Tyndall

© 2025 by MaryLu Tyndall

ISBN: 979-8-9896046-3-0
E-Version ISBN: 979-8-9896046-2-3

Library of Congress Cataloging-in-Publication Data is on file at the Library of Congress, Washington, D.C.

This book is a work of fiction. Names, characters, places, incidents, and dialogues are either products of the author's imagination or used fictitiously. Any similarity to actual people, organizations, and/or events is purely coincidental.

Unless otherwise indicated, all Scripture quotations are taken from the King James Version of the Bible. New King James Version®. Copyright © 1982 by Thomas Nelson, Inc. Used by permission. All rights reserved.

Cover Design by Ravven
Editor: Louise M. Gouge, **Honorable Mention Editor:** Nicole Robinson

RANS⚓M
PRESS

For we are his workmanship, created in Christ Jesus unto good works, which God hath before ordained that we should walk in them.
Ephesians 2:10

Chapter 1

T he *Ring* swayed over Slippery Crock's grime-encrusted waistcoat, winking at Captain Blake Keene in the lantern light. The bloated cockerel slammed yet another shot of rum into the back of his mouth before running a sleeve beneath his nose and snorting like a pig in heat.

The Ring.

Blake should tear it from the snake's neck, but the pirate's three over-sized mongrels he called a crew stood behind him, eyeing the card game with black scowls, clearly itching for a fight.

He glanced at his cards and then at the pile of doubloons glittering in the center of the table. Thus far, he had proven his skill at Piquet, earning more winnings than he thought old Crock possessed. But the blasted maggot refused to give up, insisting louder and louder with each glass of rum that he would rob Blake of his ship, his coins, and his clothes before the night ended.

Crock's belch roared over the clamor of a concertina in the corner, along with the shouts, insults, and slurs of a punch house full of pirates deep in their cups. A barmaid slammed another bottle of rum onto the table, winked at Blake, and sashayed away. His gaze followed her swaying hips. It had been a long while since he'd indulged in female company.

Four dark figures in the distance caught his eye—olive-skinned men dressed in black from their tricorns to the dark cloaks cast about their shoulders, down to their silver-spurred boots. Not pirates. Blake could spot a pirate blindfolded. Nay, these men did not fit in this place. Neither were they drinking.

Instead, Blake found their glances oft landing on him. Or was it Slippery Crock they sought?

Cursing, Crock tossed down a card, snapping Blake's gaze back to the game. Standing behind him, his quartermaster, Finnegan Wix, chuckled. The sweet scent of tobacco emanating from the man's ever-present pipe showered down on Blake, bringing an odd comfort.

Crock shot him a seething look.

Finn was right. Blake would win this round, the entire pot, and an extra ten pounds' worth of silver ducats Crock said he was good for. Finally, he would have the slippery cur right where he wanted him.

Blake laid out the final card. Its snap against the crusty table sealed Crock's doom as the sight of the ace narrowed his dark eyes and tied his already crooked grin into a knot.

"That'll do it then. Pay up, you swag-bellied toad!" Blake's bosun, Claude Maston, shouted in his ever-so-slight French accent from behind him. One of only two crewmen Blake had brought. Would they suffice should fisticuffs ensue?

One of Crock's henchmen sneered and spat to the side.

Slippery Crock seemed to be having trouble breathing. Sweat beaded on his forehead, and he blinked uncontrollably as he stared at the fortune he had just lost. "I've got nothin' left, ye thievin' barracuda! Ye cheatin', lyin' son of a whore! I'll 'ave yer throat fer this!"

Crock's henchmen gripped the hilt of their blades as their captain started to rise.

Blake heaved a weary sigh and raised his hand. "Sit down, Crock. Hear me out. I have a proposition."

The old pirate, whose scaly skin resembled his name, swayed on his feet, gripped the edge of the table, and slumped back to his chair, uttering curses that would make a slattern blush.

One of his men drew a pistol. Before he could cock it and point it at Blake, both of Blake's men drew their weapons and leveled them at Crock.

A few nearby patrons glanced their way in anticipation of a fight.

"The Ring around your neck." Blake nodded toward the jewel. "Add it to the pot, and I'll play you one more game. Winner takes all."

A slow grin coiled the knave's thin lips. "All?"

"Aye. You win, you get everything, including the Ring."

Crock snorted. "I'll play ye one more game, but I'm not puttin' the Ring in." He poured more rum into his glass.

"The Ring goes in, or I take my coins now and leave."

Crock's dirt-encrusted forehead wrinkled as he fingered the ancient jewel. "What's got ye so fired up 'bout this Ring? It ain't worth that much, save fer the gold it be made of. Don't even know what these strange etchin's and words mean."

Blake grinned. "Let's just say I collect artifacts."

Slippery Crock snorted, wrinkling his over-sized nose as if he smelled something foul. "Why would ye give up so much fer a blasted piece o' jewelry?"

One of the henchmen—the larger one who resembled a bull—hmphed. "We had nothin' but bad luck since ye got that Ring, Cap'n. Get rid o' it, says I."

Crock shot his crewmen a scathing look. "I'm the captain, an' it'll be me who decides!" Turning back around, he pawed the Ring again. "An' I jist ain't sure."

"Fine by me. I'll take my winnings and go." Slowly rising, Blake drew a pouch from his belt and began gathering the pile of coins. "Good day to you, gentlemen."

Crock growled. "All right, all right. Hold yer squid. Winner takes all it be." He yanked the Ring from the cord and tossed it on the table.

Finn chuckled.

Blake smiled.

The game began. He knew he could easily beat Crock in his inebriated condition, but he found his eyes constantly wandering to the Ring. He'd been searching for the artifact for a year, ever since the old Jewish pirate had told Blake about it right before he died. And now it was so close, *so close*, he had but to grab it.

He would do just that, if it weren't for the bloodthirsty look on Crock's crew—and the men in the shadows staring his way. No doubt Crock had more allies in this punch house than Blake knew about.

A group of sailors took up a ditty to the screech of an off-key fiddle. A fight ensued to his right, and a parrot squawked overhead, but Blake paid the noises no mind. Instead, after several agonizing minutes of trading cards and keeping score, he laid out his final card while slipping his hand to the hilt of his cutlass.

Crock would not take the loss well.

'Twas an understatement, for the man leapt from his seat, grabbed the table with the ferocity of the Kraken itself, and overturned it. It crashed to the floor, sending doubloons flying. But not before Blake grabbed the Ring and jumped out of the way.

He slammed into a man as wide as a barrel, who cursed him, his mother, and the day he was born, and then shoved Blake so hard, he tumbled to the floor. The *crack* of a pistol sounded, and the shot whizzed by his head, missing it by inches. His men drew their blades, and before Blake could rise, Crock's henchmen rushed forward, cutlasses in hand. Crock, however, dropped to his knees and scrambled over the sticky floor, gathering up as many coins as he could.

Shoving the Ring into his pocket, Blake plucked his blade from its sheath and took on one of Crock's men who stormed his way.

Several pirates and not a few barmaids, scrambled across the floor like cockroaches, grabbing coins and ignoring Crock's threats to gut them if they stole a single one.

Blake cared not a whit for the money. He had what he wanted. Now, to dispatch Crock and his men and be on his way. But the mongrel swinging his sword toward him was not so easily done away with.

Leaping out of the way of a thrust that would have sliced him in two, Blake spun and brought his cutlass to bear, clipping the beast on his massive thigh. The man seemed not to notice. Not a scream, screech, or shout did he utter amid the growls and barks pouring from his lips. And Blake began to wonder if he wasn't part mongrel, after all.

The brute rushed blindly toward Blake, sword raised and teeth bared. Blake met his thrust with a counter-parry that pushed him back. But the man would not relent. Snapping his blade quickly to the left, he rammed it at Blake.

Blake veered to the right—just as the curvy barmaid who'd delivered their rum slammed a pitcher over the beast's head. Eyes rolling back, he folded to the floor.

"Thanks, love!" Blake winked at her as he spun, blade raised, to face the next pirate.

Within minutes, more pirates joined the fight, swords slashed, pistols fired, tables crashed, and all the while someone continued playing the concertina in the background.

Quickly disposing of his current enemy, Blake sought his crew.

He found Maston parrying with a pirate who held a mug of ale in one hand and a cutlass in the other. Grabbing his bosun by the sleeve, he dragged him over to Finn, who had just sent his opponent flying over the top of the bar into a row of bottles that crashed to the floor.

While Crock's two remaining henchmen were swept up in a brawl that grew larger by the minute, the man himself was nowhere to be seen. Perfect time to make an exit. Blake gestured toward the door and then led the way, shoving pirates aside as he went.

Sunlight, far too bright for the late afternoon, stung his eyes, along with a stiff salty breeze, and he blinked as he headed down the busy street. Finn and Maston came alongside him and chuckled.

"Haven't 'ad that much fun in a while, Cap'n," Finn exclaimed.

"*Mon dieu*, you left all that money!" Maston shook his head with a sigh.

"Yet, gentlemen, I have in my possession something far more valuable."

Before his men could comment, the door to the *Siren's Revenge* squeaked open, and four men dressed all in black emerged.

They glanced toward Blake and started for him.

Grabbing a basket of fruit, bread, and cheese, Emeline Hyde approached the woman who had been standing in the distance staring her way for over an hour. Two young children, faces dirty and eyes vacant, clung to her stained and torn skirts. The closer Emeline drew, the more she could see that the woman wasn't much older than her own age of one and twenty. Yet she was as thin as a mast, her cheeks sunken, with dark circles framing eyes that once must have had the luster of a turquoise sea but now were a hazy blue. No doubt she was a beauty in days past, but the ravages of hunger and poverty had wilted her bloom.

Grabbing her children, the woman started away.

"Nay, come back," Emeline called, hastening her pace. "I have food."

Hesitating, the woman glanced her way, a look of shame and desperation on her haggard face.

"It's free," Emeline added. "Stop, I pray."

"Emmy!" Her mother's shout drew her gaze over her shoulder where Juliana Hyde stood beside a wagon distributing sacks of rice and baskets of bread to the most bedraggled souls Emeline had seen in a long while. The look her mother gave her was one of "don't go too far," and Emeline nodded in return, a knowing exchange between them that she would be cautious.

Yet she was no more than ten yards from where her family was—her mother, father, sister Esther, and brother Caleb. And even though Nassau was fast becoming the new pirate haunt of the Caribbean, it was late afternoon and not yet dark. Most of the nefarious sorts had not emerged to their nighttime revelry.

Still, her father, Alexander Merrick Hyde, looked up from where he knelt to aid a crippled sailor, his penetrating eyes latching upon her.

Safe. She always felt safe when her father was around. The son of the infamous Captain Edmund Merrick, Alexander was next in line to be Earl of Clarendon, but he was also the fiercest ex-pirate who ever sailed the seas. The *Pirate Earl* they used to call him. Though no longer a pirate, but now a missionary of sorts, he still caused men to cower in his presence. He was a man not many dared to challenge, nor would they dare to harm any of his family.

Which is why Emeline always felt safe when he was near.

She waved and smiled, and he gave his nod in return. *Aye, safe.*

Turning back, she crept toward the timid lady. "Some food for you and your wee ones, Miss."

The woman swallowed, her eyes shifting between Emeline's before they lowered. "What d'ye want in return?"

"Nothing at all." She held out the basket. "Please, take it."

"Ain't nothin' free in this world, an' I won't be beholden to none."

"But you're wrong. There are at least two things free in this world. This food and the love and salvation of God through His Son, Jesus."

The woman frowned as her eyes moistened with tears. She inched toward Emeline, took the basket, and dipped her head. "I take the food, Miss. Not sure Jesus cares 'bout the likes o' me."

Emeline smiled. "Of course He cares. 'Tis because of Him I am giving you this food."

The woman looked down, turned, and headed down the street.

"We come here every month," Emeline called after her, lifting up a prayer for the poor lady. Something terrible had happened to her, something she was ashamed of, something that had no doubt put her in this state of poverty.

Turning, Emeline started back to her family, wondering if there was something else she could have said or done. She stepped onto the street. The grind of wheels and clomp of hooves on the cobblestones jarred her from her thoughts, and she looked up to see an out-of-control horse and wagon barreling toward her.

Fear strangled her. She stared at them, unable to move.

The horse reared.

A man dove for her, grabbed her by the waist, and hoisted her out of the way. He stumbled to keep his balance but finally settled her back on her feet as the wagon careened past.

"What were you thinking? Be careful, Miss!" he shouted, clearly angry at having to save her.

Flustered, she raised her gaze to the most striking green eyes she'd ever seen. Almond-shaped, dark and mysterious, they seemed to harbor a treasure-trove of secrets. Capped by dark eyebrows in a strong, chiseled face with a Roman nose, thin black mustache, and dark stubble on his chin, her rescuer exuded an authority that belied his common sailor attire. Hair as dark as coal hung to his shoulders while a matching black pearl pierced his right ear.

And Emeline's breath fled her.

At the sight of her, the harshness in his tone instantly softened, and the deep, soothing voice that emerged from his lips spiraled warmth through her.

"Forgive me, Miss, but you really should look where you are going." One side of his lips quirked in a grin that only completed the entire mesmerizing dream—for surely that was all it was. No man had ever looked at her the way this pirate was doing now, as if he could see deep within her soul.

Ludicrous.

Another pirate yanked on the man's sleeve and nodded down the street, tearing her rescuer's gaze to a group of men in the distance. His demeaner changed, and he grabbed her skirts and began fluttering them about this way and that as if he were wiping away some invisible dirt.

The enchanting spell instantly broke. "How dare you!" Moving aside, Emeline batted him away.

But instead of an apology, he winked, grinned, and, before she could stop him, he drew near, kissed her cheek, then tore down the street with his two friends.

Heat swamped her face, and she lifted her hands to the spot his lips had touched. Heart racing, her emotions raged between outrage and something else, something she was too ashamed to admit.

Her father stood before her, peering into her face. "Are you all right, darling?"

"Aye, Papa. I nearly was run over by a wagon, but a man…" She looked down the road, but the enigmatic stranger was gone.

Three to four. Not good odds. Not great odds since the four men in black already had blades drawn. Sabers, if Blake was correct—longer swords with strange engravings on their silver hilts and a slight curve to the blades.

"The Ring." The man who appeared to be the leader held out his palm. The accent. *Spanish? Italian?*

The last vestiges of the sun sank below the horizon, absconding with its golden light. But not before Blake saw the man's face. If ever there was a sinister looking face, his was it. Not uncomely with his high cheekbones, deep-set eyes, and hawk-like nose, but evil nonetheless. Hair the color of dirt was tied behind him cavalier-style, matching his pointed beard. But his eyes…an indescribable color, empty and devoid of life.

"What Ring?" Blake answered, nonchalantly.

The fist struck his face before he could defend himself. Finn and Maston started forward, but the press of four blades kept them at bay.

Pain radiated across Blake's cheek and spiraled down his neck. "Ah, *that* Ring," he said playfully, stretching his jaw.

"You have five seconds to give it to me, or you and your friends are fish bait."

Blake raised his hands. "I don't have it. I lost it in the fight. You were there. You saw how that reprobate Crock tipped over the table."

Though he could no longer see the man's eyes in the shadows, he felt them piercing into his very soul. A shiver ran down him. An *unusual* shiver.

"Search us." Blake held out his hands.

The man snapped his fingers, never taking his eyes off Blake. And he got the impression he didn't give a care whether he searched them dead or alive.

One of the men approached him, sheathed his blade, and began touching and patting his shirt and breeches. It took everything in Blake not to shove him to the ground. The humiliation, worse in front of his men, was not to be borne!

"Careful there," Blake said. "Sorry, mate, but I'm spoken for."

The man huffed his disdain.

Maston snorted out a chuckle.

Two other men searched Maston and Finn but came up empty.

A ship bell rang in the distance. Wind ripe with the scents of roasted pork and ale wafted over them as seconds turned into minutes. Still, the leader of this pack of wolves merely stared at them.

Finally, he breathed out a sigh. "I should kill you and be done."

Shrugging, Blake inched his hand to the hilt of his blade. "Ah, but what a mess that would make. We have no quarrel with you, Sir. We are but lowly pirates trying to earn a dishonest living."

The man snapped his fingers once again. Blake gripped his cutlass, prepared for the fight of his life. But the strange villain spun on his heels, his cloak swirling about him, and marched away, his lackeys following in his wake.

Blake allowed himself to breathe.

"Odd," Maston commented, as if they'd just had tea with the gentlemen. "Guess you aren't the only one after that Ring, *Capitaine*."

Finn huffed and scratched his head beneath his ever-present gray bandana. "Good thing they left when they did, Cap'n. Me fingers were itchin' t' blast them all t' the wind."

"And a fine fight it would have been, my friend." Slapping him on the back, Blake started back the way they came.

"Aren't we going t' the ship?" Finn asked.

"Nay. We're going after the Ring."

Maston laughed. "There's more of a chance to find it in the sea than on the floor of that punch house, *Capitaine*."

"It isn't in the *Siren's Revenge*," Blake responded. The only problem was, how would he find that enchanting lady again?

Chapter 2

"You did wonderfully today, Emmy," Emeline's mother said from beside her as they placed empty crates onto the wagon. She cast her daughter a look of pride that made Emeline smile.

"I wish we could do more." She glanced about the town that had instantly transformed into a foreign place with the descent of the sun. A young lad hoisting a torch atop a tall pole ran from streetlamp to streetlamp, setting them ablaze. Yet the modicum of light offered by the lanterns did naught to dispel the shadows that crept out from hiding as soon as the day ended. Even the poor and downcast scattered away as if they knew the evil that lurked in the night.

"We can only do what we can, my darling." Her father hoisted a barrel onto the wagon bed with little effort. "Then we pray God does the rest." Removing his hat, he raked back his dark hair, approached his wife, and took her in his arms. She gazed up at him with a love that had been tested and tried for many years but seemed only to grow stronger. At least in Emeline's eyes. She never grew tired of hearing the story of how they met twenty-five years ago in Port Royal, the year of the great quake that sank that wicked city into the sea. Her father had played the dual role of the Pirate Earl and Lord Munthrope, the town buffoon, in order to win her mother's heart.

"Cease you two!" Caleb sauntered toward them, a huge grin on his handsome face. "You act as though you are newly wed."

Alex tenderly brushed hair from his wife's face and kissed her forehead. "I feel as though I am."

Caleb shared a glance with Emeline and rolled his eyes.

"You would be lucky to find such love, Caleb," Emeline retorted. "With the way you flirt with anything wearing a skirt."

He spread out his arms. "Can I help that God made me handsome *and* charming?"

"And arrogant," Esther added as she set a stack of clothing in the wagon. Looping her arm through Emeline's, she grinned. "We have our work cut out for us, dear sister. Keeping our brother humble."

"We'll let our Lord take care of that," Juliana said as she approached her children. "He has His ways of humbling us when we need it the most." She shared a glance with her husband, who returned her smile.

Warmth filled Emeline's heart. She loved her family. Though they had their quarrels now and then, they were united with a bond of love for each other and for their Savior. These outings wherein they shared the Gospel, helped the poor, and even healed the sick when God ordained, were such blessed times.

But Caleb was right about one thing. He was the spitting image of his father, all charm and manly good looks. Both of which attracted much female attention. In addition, he possessed the gift of miracles, a rare power from God that he oft used for His glory.

A group of sailors sauntered down the street, pirates by their attire, their lustful eyes fastened on Esther. Who could blame them? With her golden hair, lustrous sea-blue eyes, and curvaceous figure, she was a rare beauty like her mother. But 'twas her heart that shone the brightest, a heart filled with love for the weak, feeble, and sickly. God had gifted her with the power to heal, and Emeline had seen the lame rise and walk after Esther prayed for them.

In truth, where her siblings were exceptionally pleasant to look upon, Emeline was rather ordinary. Where they were brave and outspoken, Emeline was quiet and timid. Where they possessed mighty gifts from God, Emeline had no such gifts, no special talents. She was definitely the runt of the litter. Oh how she longed to be more like them, to live the exciting life her parents lived and to have a storybook romance just like they had.

The eerie sound of a violin spiraled on the salty breeze, followed by a shout and the chime of blade upon blade. Movement deep in the shadows of a storefront porch across the street caught her eye. A group of men crowded before the closed mercantile, their attire as dark as the night.

"We must get back to the *Ransom*." There was an urgency in her father's voice that sent a spark of fear through Emeline. Perhaps they had lingered too late in this nefarious pirate haunt. He slammed the back of the wagon shut and gestured for them to climb aboard. Both he and Caleb drew their blades, if only to discourage any would-be assailants, as the women hoisted themselves into the seats.

"Wait," Emeline said. "There's that poor woman and her children." She pointed to a lady in rags standing in the distance beneath a streetlight.

Reaching behind her, she grabbed a leftover sack of food from the wagon bed and hopped down the other side.

"Wait, Emmy, wait for your father," Juliana said, but Emeline ignored her. Her father and Caleb were close by and well-armed. Obviously, this woman needed help. Perhaps more than food this time. Perhaps she wanted to know more about Jesus.

Finding the lovely lady had been easy. Getting close enough to retrieve the Ring was quite another task. Especially with her father and another man, whom he assumed to be her brother, beside her the entire time. Aye, Blake knew who her father was. There wasn't a pirate in all the Caribbean who didn't know who Alexander Merrick Hyde was, son of the infamous pirate, Captain Edmund Merrick Hyde, Earl of Clarendon. And there wasn't a pirate who was foolish enough to cross him.

Except Blake. If only to get the Ring.

Why, oh why, did he have to hide the Ring in the skirts of the daughter of Captain Alexander Hyde?

Though he had bigger problems at the moment. The four foreign strangers dressed in black also had their eyes upon the lady. How did they know? They must have seen Blake tussling with her skirts earlier but hadn't realized what he'd done until they couldn't find the Ring on him. *Hang it*! What to do now?

The foolish lady hopped off the wagon and made her way toward a lone woman and two children standing several yards away beneath the light of a street lantern. Unaware, her father and brother remained on the other side of the wagon, adjusting the reins of the horses with one hand while clinging to their blades with the other.

Across the street, the men in black eased out from the shadowy porch.

Blake had no time.

"Meet me at the skiff," he whispered to Maston and Finn, who stood behind him around the corner of a warehouse. Before they had time to protest, he made a dash for the lady.

Emeline smiled at the woman, saying a prayer that God would give her the right words to help her.

Yet unlike before, when the lady could barely look at Emeline, this time her wide eyes screamed at her in terror. Unease snaked across Emeline's back as she continued. But she continued, nonetheless. If only to help the poor woman. Was she hurt? Were her children all right? Emeline glanced down at the two little ones just as a tall man dressed in a black camlet suit stepped from behind the lady, the sharp end of his knife pointed at her back.

He shoved her and her children aside and started for Emeline.

"I'm sorry, Miss," the woman squealed as she gathered her children and stumbled away.

Shock stole all reason from Emeline's mind.

The man glanced behind her, and she followed his gaze to a group of men heading her way. "Pa—" Before she could call for her father's help, another man who smelled of rum and the sea grabbed her by the waist, swung her up on his shoulder, and dashed into the darkness.

She couldn't speak. Couldn't breathe. Couldn't even fight as each bounce crushed her lungs against his hard shoulder. She heard her father's roar in the distance.

Surely he would come for her! A dozen terrifying thoughts rampaged through her mind. What did the man want with her? Who were those other men? What would happen to her?

Oh, God. Please help. Why is this happening?

The man was strong. He kept up a fast pace, leaping over crates and fallen logs, twisting and turning around buildings as if she weighed no more than a feather.

Bootsteps thundered behind him, followed by shouts, some in a foreign language she didn't know. A pistol fired. Her cheek slapped against the man's leather waistcoat, and she finally built up the strength to pound him with her fists.

"Let me go, you beast!"

It neither stopped him nor slowed him down.

"Emeline!"

Her heart lurched. 'Twas her father's voice.

"Pa…pa!" Her scream came out a mere whimper.

Her kidnapper only ran faster, darting down alleyways, circling warehouses, crossing streets and then back again, no doubt trying to lose his pursuers.

Blood rushed to Emeline's head, threatening to knock her unconscious.

God, please?

Finally, the man burst into a wooded area, leaping around trees and hopping over rocks. Thorny branches reached for her between shafts of moonlight spearing the canopy. The scent of the sea engulfed her, along with the man's sweat as he emerged onto a small beach where two men waited by a boat.

Breath heaving, he slowed, waded through the incoming surf, grabbed her waist, and plopped her on the thwarts beside a third man. Then, jumping in after her, he took a rope and tied her hands behind her.

"Shove off!" he shouted to a man on shore who promptly heaved the boat and leapt in, nearly toppling it.

Emeline could see none of their faces. The starry sky spun above her. What was happening? Before she could scream, the man who had taken her tore a scarf from around his friend's neck and promptly stuffed it in her mouth. A putrid, salty taste sent bile down her throat.

She moaned as loud as she could, but the sound came out muffled, and she doubted anyone would hear. Her mind spun, seeking a reason for this madness. Terror numbed every inch of her as the men took up oars, and the small craft sped through the water of Nassau Harbor—black, choppy waters capped in silver by a half-moon. The men said naught until they were away from their pursuers.

"Didna think ye were that desperate fer a wench, Cap'n." One of them laughed.

"She's not a wench," the man who took her responded. "And I had no choice."

The third man swung the oar, sending them sailing over the dark waters. "Ah, that's where you put the Ring, *Capitaine*," he said in a slight French accent. "Clever."

Emeline could make no sense of their ramblings as she numbly stared at the inky waves rippling against the boat. She should jump. She knew how to swim, but could she with her hands tied and her skirts dragging her down? *Don't be a coward, Emeline!* What if she drowned? What if a shark ate her? What if she couldn't make it back to shore? Fears assailed her. But wouldn't any of those be preferable to becoming the mistress of a filthy pirate?

The boat thudded against the hull of a ship. The moment of her escape had passed. She cursed her cowardice as the pirate took her arm and once again tossed her over his shoulder like a sack of rice, then climbed a rope ladder.

At least a dozen men crowded the main deck, some whistling at her while others fired questions at their captain. The stench of unwashed bodies, rum, and tobacco pinched her nose. Her heart rammed against her ribs.

He finally set her on her feet, keeping a firm grip on her arm as his two companions leapt on deck.

She wanted to ask what he wanted with her, but she gagged from the grotesque scarf crammed in her mouth. Tears filled her eyes, and her knees nearly buckled beneath the horror.

Chattering sounds rang out, and she glanced above to see a monkey swinging down the ratlines.

"Cap'n!" one short pirate shouted from the railing. "There be a cockboat headed straight fer us." He lowered the scope. "An' they don't look friendly."

"Hang it!" The man dragged her to the railing and took the glass, pressing it against his eye.

Emeline allowed a seed of hope to plant in her heart. It must be her father and brother. *Oh, Lord, let it be them!*

The man uttered a curse, then spun and issued a slew of orders that sent his crew scrambling to lift the boat aboard, weigh anchor, and raise all sail.

They were leaving? She tugged against the man's grip, moaning her complaint, but he handed her to another sailor and ordered him to lock her in his cabin at once.

Chapter 3

The pirate warned her to stay put. The door slammed, echoing Emeline's fate through the cabin. Darkness invaded. Not only the cabin, but her very soul. She blinked, her eyes finally focusing on a shaft of moonlight penetrating the stern windows. It landed on a desk covered with maps, navigation instruments, quill pens, and empty bottles. She should pray, but her heart continued to thrash wildly, her breath blasted out her nose, and her mind refused to accept what was happening. Perhaps this was all a nightmare, and she'd soon awake and find herself safe on her father's ship, the *Ransom*.

Did people feel pain in dreams like the burn she felt around her wrists from the tight ropes? Did people smell the stench of sweat and blood and rum that now filled her nose and seared her lungs? Everything was so real—the steady rock of the ship, the pounding of bare feet above her as the pirates rushed to do their captain's bidding, the crank of the anchor chain as the anchor was hauled up from the seabed...

And the shouts of the man who had stolen her from everything she had ever known.

She swallowed down a lump of terror. Nay, this was no dream.

Father God, You know what's happening. Please, please send my father to rescue me!

A whimper caught in her throat as loosened sails thundered above and the deck shifted beneath her. Stumbling, she slammed against a chair bolted to the floor. A dozen terrifying thoughts taunted her at what these pirates intended to do with her, but she shook her head in an effort to scatter them away.

She must be strong. She must stop whining and do what her siblings would do, what her parents would do. They would not cower in fear! They would look for a way of escape. They would fight to the death, if need be, against such villainy.

Struggling against the ropes that bound her wrists, she approached the desk and sought something sharp with which to cut them. But no knives, swords, or blades of any kind could be found. A pistol stared tauntingly at her, but what could she do without her hands and a flame to light it? Not that she didn't know how to prime, load, and ignite a gun as her father had taught her.

Her father.

Oh, come for me, Papa!

The ship jerked, sails snapped, and the rush of the sea against the hull blared through the cabin. She gazed out the stern windows. The lights from Nassau grew smaller and smaller, malevolently winking at her—mocking her dire predicament.

The door swung open, startling her, and in marched four pirates, one carrying a lantern. He set it upon the desk, then sparked a match from the flame and lit two other lanterns, including one hanging on the deckhead above.

Emeline thought to retreat into the shadows but remembered her father instructing her that regardless of the terror she felt, she must never show it to her enemies. Hence, she stood her ground and raised her chin.

A monkey scampered in and leapt onto the desk, grabbed a piece of fruit from a bowl, and began chomping on it.

The captain drew his cutlass and laid it on a sideboard before spinning to face his men.

Emeline blinked. 'Twas the man in the market who had rescued her from the horse and wagon. Two chains hung about his neck. An onyx cross dangled from one and from the other, an emblem that looked like a sun. Dark hair hung in waves to his shoulders while a black pearl glistened from his right earlobe. Upon seeing her, his lips curved slightly beneath a thin mustache that matched the black stubble on his chin.

Every nerve tightened in both anger and fear at his insolence.

She recognized two of the other pirates as those who had been with him at the market. The fourth was an older man with gray hair and beard, who carried a satchel.

"What ye goin' t' do wit her?" The man with a gray bandana on his head plucked a pipe from his mouth and gestured toward her.

"Yes, indeed," the older man huffed with disgust. "Are we to add kidnapping of innocent women to your list of crimes?"

The captain shrugged, staring at her as if examining a new toy. "Possibly. Though I have no intention of keeping her."

Emeline gulped. Was she to be freed or killed? Or worse, sold? Young white women brought quite a large sum from the right buyer.

"Let's see to that, then?" The older pirate gestured toward the captain, and only then did she see blood on his waistcoat. So, one of the shots *had* struck him. Good. He deserved it.

After shrugging out of his waistcoat, he tore his shirt over his head and plopped down in a chair. Blood trickled from a wound on his shoulder, but that wasn't what drew her gaze. 'Twas the powerful muscles that rippled over his chest and arms, much like those of her father and brother. Yet *their* strength was contained within a case of honor and humility that kept the power in check. This man's apparently had no limits.

Shifting her gaze away, she examined the other pirates. The one with the slight French accent and dark features wore a blue doublet richly embellished with gold braid, over which tumbled a ruffled cravat. The other pirate—the one with the pipe dangling from his lips and the bandana around his head— bore so many weapons that 'twas a wonder he could walk at all, while the third man was missing an arm below the elbow and looked as though he hadn't bathed in years. A charming lot, but what did she expect?

The monkey finished his fruit and smiled at her. At least it appeared to be a smile before he leapt onto his captain's shoulder.

Her mouth ached. The rag had soaked up all her spit, and she started to gag. But no one paid her any mind.

The older pirate finished wrapping the captain's wound. "Shot went through. It will heal nicely."

"Thank you, Sam." The captain stretched his shoulder back and forth. Rising, he grabbed his shirt and flung it over his head. "Rummy, set a course south by southwest. Maston, all canvas to the wind. Finn, you have the helm. Alert me if you see any sails in our wake."

"Aye, Cap'n." The man he called Finn gave a salacious wink. "An' jist what will ye be doin'?" he asked on his way out.

The older gentleman packed up his satchel and left, shaking his head, while the Frenchman, Maston, gave her a flash of brows above a lecherous glance as he headed for the door.

Leaving her alone with the vicious kidnapping pirate and his grinning monkey.

A lump of terror formed in her throat. She'd swallow it down if she had any saliva left. The captain stared at her a moment, assessing her as one would a slave he'd just purchased. He slowly approached.

She wanted nothing more than to dart into the nearest corner, scoot under the cot she now saw clearly in the light, or dive into the massive oak chest and slam the lid shut. Instead, she remained still. As still as she could on the shifting deck.

"Let's get this out." He stood within inches of her, his smell of blood and the sea filling her nostrils as he reached up and carefully pulled the cloth from her mouth.

Emeline bent over, coughing and hacking and gasping for air. This seemed to upset the monkey, for he started to squawk loudly from his spot on the back of a nearby chair.

"Apologies for the rough treatment, Miss." Plucking a knife from his belt, he spun her around and sliced the ropes around her wrists.

"Is that what you call it?" Emeline managed to squeak out as she gripped her throat.

Moving to his desk, he grabbed two glasses and filled them from a nearby bottle, then returned and handed her one. "This will help soothe your throat."

She rubbed the sores on her wrists as the sting of rum bit her nose. "I do not partake of spirits."

He cocked his head, a look of surprise traveling across his emerald eyes. "Pity, that." Then with a shrug, he gulped down both glasses and set them on his desk. Spinning around, he held out his hand, palm up. "Now, the Ring, if you please?"

The monkey mimicked his master's gesture and held out his paw, grinning at her.

Had the world gone mad? Emeline could only stare at them both, confusion joining her fear. "I beg your pardon?" Forcing back tears, she lifted a silent prayer for strength. "Please, Sir, return me to my home. I am of no value to you."

"Indeed. But you have something of great value to me."

"I have nothing you could possibly want."

At that, a licentious grin raised one side of his lips as his eyes traveled over her in delight.

She took a step back. "If you intend to ravish me, Sir, I *will* put up a fight."

He chuckled. "As terrifying as that threat may be, that is not my intention."

"You are pleased to taunt me, Sir."

"Captain. Captain Blake Keene at your service." He gave a mock bow. "The Ring is all I want. As to the ravishing, I have no need to take from you what so many freely offer."

'Twas true. The man surely had no trouble acquiring female attention. A brief wave of relief swept over her.

Until he stormed toward her. "Enough of this! The Ring."

Oddly, a vision of an ancient Ring hiding in her pocket appeared in her mind for but a second, and then it was gone. "I don't know what you are—"

Grabbing her skirts, he groped through them, taking no care to be virtuous.

"How dare you! Do you know who my father is?" She pounded fists on his back, but he seemed not to notice.

"Be still, wild cat." He uttered a curse but continued. "And aye, I know full well who your father is."

Terror seized her. If the man knew who Alexander Hyde was, then he must be more than mad to kidnap his daughter. Shoving him as hard as she could, she started away, but he yanked her skirts and wrenched her back. Fabric tore. Did the fiend intend to rip off her gown?

"Ah ha!" He withdrew his hand and held something up to the light, immediately releasing her.

Breath heaving, Emeline retreated. 'Twas a Ring. Just like the one she saw in her vision. But where? How? Memories returned of him rescuing her in the market square and oddly shifting her skirts around.

"You put that in my pocket!"

He grinned, walked back to his desk, and picked up a magnifying glass to examine it.

The monkey scampered over to his master. "This is no toy, Bandit," the captain said, slapping the animal's paw away.

For the first time, Emeline allowed herself a deep breath. Perhaps 'twas only the silly jewel that this pirate wanted. Perhaps now he would release her back to her family.

Oh, Lord. Please!

"Why would you do that?" she asked.

He glanced at her before returning his gaze to the jewel. "Let's just say I needed a hiding place, for there were others after it as well."

Emeline swallowed, eyeing the door. She could slip out while the scoundrel was absorbed with his Ring. But where would she go?

"Others?" she asked, replaying the scene in her mind. Ah, the men dressed in black! That's why they were after her. "You steal me from my family and drag me aboard your ship for a silly Ring? Why did you not ask me for it? I would have gladly given it to you."

One eyebrow rose. He snorted. "There was hardly any time. Kidnapping you was not the plan. It merely became unavoidable. But *silly*? This"—he held it up to the lantern light again—"is the Ring of King Solomon."

"King Solomon. From the Bible?" Now she knew he was utterly and completely mad.

Blake studied the lady. Strands of chestnut-colored hair had fallen from her pins and tumbled over her shoulders and down her back. A modest blue gown molded nicely around her feminine curves. Eyes as golden as the sunset sparked with both fear and fury as they glared at him. Yet there was strength in them. A strong jaw, slender nose, and full lips completed a lovely face. Here was a true genteel lady, and he suddenly regretted causing her so much torment. "Is there any other?" he retorted.

Her delicate forehead crinkled. "You expect me to believe that Ring was worn by King Solomon from the Holy Scriptures."

He smiled. "I have no expectations of you, my lady."

Frowning, she hugged herself and looked away, and he found himself staring at her, studying this delicate flower, who by all attempts, pretended to be a warrior.

Bandit snagged the Ring from his grasp.

"Come back here with that!" Blake charged after him, but the thieving monkey leapt onto the lady's shoulder with a fiendish screech.

She leapt back, swatting to dislodge him. But before Blake could reach them, the churlish monkey gave her the Ring and scampered away. He would deal with him later.

For now, he faced the lady. Their eyes were but inches from each other. Shock and dismay sparked across hers…and something else he couldn't place. She started to take a step back, but he grabbed her wrist and brought her hand up, the one clutching the Ring.

Her lips curved slightly. "Seems your monkey believes this belongs to me."

He laughed. "My monkey is a thief."

"Says the pirate."

He grinned. "Touché, love." He reached for the Ring. It began to glow. *What?* Halting, he stared at the odd sight. It definitely glowed—a crimson light pulsated from the jewel in the center. No doubt he'd consumed far too much rum.

The lady followed his gaze and gasped. Nay, not too much rum.

"Take it, Captain." She flipped her hand, tossing it in the air. Blake caught it, smiling at her insolent antics.

"And if there is any decency in you," she continued, "return me to my family."

"I fear I lost all decency years ago." The Ring felt warm to the touch, but when he opened his hand, the glow was gone.

A shout preceded Finn barreling through the door. "Cap'n. Newt spotted two sets o' sails off our larboard quarter. Headin' straight fer us."

Blake cursed. "Hang it all! I knew they wouldn't give up."

"Who?" the lady asked.

"The Jesuits."

Chapter 4

E meline knew very little about Jesuits, but there was no time to ponder the odd statement as Captain Keene, if she remembered his name correctly, stormed from the cabin, the monkey on his heels. The door was left open with no guard outside. An oversight? Perhaps not. What harm could she possibly do to the ship or anyone on it? The opposite was more likely. Regardless, Emeline followed them at a distance. If they were to engage in battle, she'd rather be on deck than cowering below where shots would be aimed.

She emerged from the companionway to a blast of hot night air and the scent of gunpowder, sweat, and the sea. Pirates dashed across the deck, some carrying shot to be loaded into guns, others carrying weapons—axes, muskets, blades, and pistols. One man was pouring sand over the deck. Shouts bellowed like grapeshot, sending men into the ratlines to adjust sail for maximum speed. A young lad of no more than twelve, who carried a bucket of powder cartridges, glanced her way and smiled. No one else paid her any mind. The captain stood near the helm, spyglass to his eye.

Emeline inched her way to the starboard quarter and followed the aim of his scope. In the light of a half-moon and splattering of stars, Emeline could make out the dark outlines of at least two ships, large ships by the looks of them, perhaps frigates or galleons. Their fore-lanterns bobbed up and down as the ships rounded each swell, engaging in an odd dance of lights like fireflies she'd once seen in the Carolinas. What she *could* determine, even in the shadows, was that 'twas not her father in pursuit. That fact alone caused her heart to shrink.

Had he been able to follow close enough to see what ship she'd been taken to? If not, how would he ever find her?

Even as she entertained such terrifying thoughts, peace welled up within her. Her father might not know where she was, but God did. Surely, He would lead her father to her. *Won't you, Lord?*

"They's comin' up fast, Cap'n," the man with the gray bandana shouted. "We'll be within range o' 'er guns soon."

Captain Keene lowered the scope and frowned, then spun and spewed orders to his crew. "All hands to the braces! Two points to starboard, Rummy. Bear up and keep her full!"

"Beat to quarters!" the man wearing the bandana shouted.

"Run out the guns!" The voice of the master gunner snapped Emeline's gaze in that direction. Pacing behind two guns on the main deck, the man continued shouting orders. But nay, 'twas a woman's voice, though powerful, that emerged from the figure.

Long brown hair fell from beneath a cocked hat as she leapt up on the foredeck to instruct the gunners in their tasks. Though she wore the same attire as the pirates, the slight sway of her hips gave her away. A female master gunner? In all her years at sea, Emeline had never seen such a thing.

Nor did she have time to ponder it when a boom thundered across the sky, sending her heart leaping into her throat.

"All hands down!" someone bellowed, but she was already on the deck, covering her head with her hands.

Rarely did ship battles occur at night. Then again, everything about this night was odd.

The shot splashed into the sea, and only then did she allow herself to breathe. They had missed. Or perhaps 'twas merely a warning shot.

Growls along with cheers blared from the pirates as Emeline struggled to rise. She'd been in ship battles before but always with the assurance of her father's expert skill. She had no idea if Captain Keene knew what he was doing. Especially against two such mighty ships.

"They are separatin', Cap'n," Finn said. "Comin' along either side o' us."

"*Mon dieu*! We don't stand a chance against both of them!" Maston raged. "They'll sink us for sure."

Captain Keene gazed toward the enemy ships, only then noticing Emeline. At first, he seemed surprised to see her above deck, but then he fished something out of his pocket and held it up to the lantern light. "We shall see," is all he said as he gripped the Ring, marched to the railing, and lifted it up toward the sky. His lips moved, but she could not hear what he was saying.

Regardless, she remembered how the Ring had mysteriously glowed. Did this madman believe the ancient fables that told of its powers?

"Orders, *Capitaine*?" the dandy with the French accent asked, spite in his tone.

Pounding his fists on the railing, the captain returned to the helm and began issuing orders, "Shake out the reefs! Hoist the stays! Set royals and topgallants!"

The brig veered to larboard, sails flapping and blocks creaking, and Emeline clung to the railing as the deck tilted. A spray of sea water misted over her. Blinking it away, she gazed back at the ships heading straight for them. Should they be allowed to surround the brig and loose a broadside from both sides, they would be done for.

Mist. A puff of white smoke appeared over the water. So small at first, she barely noticed it. As she watched, it grew rapidly into a cloud that began rolling over the sea like a curtain, ending the act of this heinous war play.

But where had it come from? Emeline had seen no clouds, and 'twas far too warm a night for fog.

She glanced back at the captain, who only now noticed it, a slow grin forming on his lips.

"Wha'? I ne'er seen the likes o' that," the one-armed helmsman exclaimed, slurring his words.

All the pirates, in fact, stopped their battle preparations and stared at the odd sight.

Odd indeed, as the cloud continued growing larger and thicker until it formed a moving, undulating wall of white between them and their pursuers.

Captain Keene chuckled and slapped his helmsman on the back, then issued orders to trim sails and adjust course north by northwest.

Though shock still froze many of their faces, the pirates obeyed their captain, and soon the brigantine sailed through the dark waters without a care in the world. Within minutes, no sign of either the cloud or the ships could be seen over the dark expanse of the sea.

"Stoke the galley fire. Have Cook prepare a feast in my cabin," Captain Keene ordered before making his way toward her.

Emeline's nerves tightened.

He gestured behind him to the companionway. "To my cabin, Miss. We have much to celebrate this night."

Celebrate? Her tightened nerves knotted. "You may celebrate without me."

"Scads! Without the woman who gave me such power? You saw it!" he whispered as he gestured toward the sea. "The Ring caused that cloud."

"Ludicrous. Surely, you can't believe such nonsense." Even as she said it, she recalled seeing far greater miracles than that in her life. But those had been wrought by the hand of God, not by a trinket in the hands of a madman.

"How can you deny it?" He studied her, shifting his stance on the heaving deck.

Still clinging to the railing, Emeline flattened her lips. "What are you going to do with me, Captain?"

He huffed. "I haven't decided. Though for tonight, I wish you to be my guest. 'Tis been a long time since a lady graced my dinner table."

She would wager it had been an eternity. "And if I don't wish to come?"

He grinned. "Then you may stay here on deck with my crew."

Emeline glanced at the slovenly, rapacious men going about their duties, some casting her hungry grins.

She gave a dainty smile. "I believe I will accept your invitation, Captain."

"I thought so." He extended his elbow.

She pushed past him, heading toward the companionway, surprised at her boldness while also nervous that it might very well cause her demise.

Back in his cabin, the captain all but ignored her as two of his crew busied themselves setting up a long table, complete with silverware, pewter plates and cups, candles, and lanterns. The young lad she'd seen above deck entered with bowls of fruit he placed on the table.

"Good evening t' you, *señorita*," he said in a Spanish accent, dragging off his floppy hat.

Captain Keene spun from where he'd been holding the Ring and staring out the stern windows. "Miss Hyde, this is Pedro, cabin boy, powder monkey, and pirate in training."

The boy grinned at the last statement and dipped his head before her.

"A pleasure," Emeline said. "And just how old are you, Pedro?"

"I'll be thirteen next month, *señorita*. Old enough to be a pirate." Streaks of coal lined his youthful face where barely a whisker grew, but there was a spark of innocence in his blue eyes that drew her in.

"There are far better things than pirating, Pedro. Far more *honorable* things."

"Wha' could be better than bein' a buccaneer?" The pirate with the gray bandana strode into the cabin, casting her a disparaging glance before tussling the lad's tuft of red hair and popping his pipe back into his mouth.

Pedro grinned.

"Finnegan Wix, my quartermaster, Miss Hyde." Captain Keene crossed arms over his chest.

"Mr. Wix," she said.

"Ah, call me Finn, Miss. Everyone does."

The monkey scampered in after him and leapt on the table, grabbed a banana from the bowl, and began peeling it. Scaring him away with a brush of his hand, Finn took a seat. "Filthy beast," he growled.

Emeline nearly smiled at the irony, for she wondered when the man had last bathed.

"Ah, *mademoiselle*." The slick voice drew her gaze back to the door where the Frenchman strolled in. Removing his plumed blue hat, he dipped his head. "Claude Maston, at your service."

Without her offering, he took her hand and raised it to his lips for a kiss.

"Maston is my bosun." The captain snorted as he grabbed a bottle and poured a glass of rum. "And you've met One-Armed Rummy, my helmsman." He gestured to the tall man who ducked as he entered the room. His dark eyes scoured over her before they landed on the bottle the captain was holding. Licking his lips, he made his way over to pour a glass.

Thankfully, none of them, save the Frenchmen, seemed overly interested in her. Especially the older pirate who wandered in next, the ship's surgeon who'd attended the captain's wound earlier. His glance took in the cabin with a frown before he wandered to the stern to stare out the windows.

Behind him, two pirates entered with steaming platters and bowls, which they slammed onto the table, filling the cabin with scents of boiled fish and fresh biscuits that teased Emeline's empty belly.

"Out with you." The captain waved them away.

The Frenchman pulled out a chair and smiled her way. "*Mademoiselle?*" He was not a tall man and rather slender, but he might be considered handsome with his wavy black hair and deep-set eyes were it not for the dirt that encrusted his skin and permanently stained his otherwise elegant attire.

"She sits beside me." The captain's tone brooked no argument as he took his seat at the head of the table and nodded toward the chair to his right.

Inching her way over, Emeline sat, her stomach in so tight a knot, she doubted any food could pass through. But what choice did she have? Her mind spun with a myriad of horrifying possibilities of her future. Nay! She must trust God. He knew her predicament, and though, at the moment, she felt not His presence, she knew He was with her.

Finn grabbed a platter of salted fish and began piling food onto his plate.

"We wait for Charlie," Captain Keene said.

"Women ain't nothin' but trouble." One-armed Rummy sneered at her.

"Come now, Rummy. Charlie has saved our skin more than once." Maston took his seat and poured wine into his glass.

"Sorry to be late." A female voice drew Emeline's gaze to the door, where the woman master gunner sauntered in with a grin on her face and the authority of any pirate. Her gaze brushed over Emeline, and a tiny smile lifted her lips before she pulled out a chair and plopped down beside Finn.

And the meal commenced. If you could call it that. 'Twas more like watching pigs at the trough—drunken pigs that was. Through it all, the monkey traveled down the table, plucking any morsel of food he wished.

Aside from an occasional glance from the captain and Monsieur Maston's constant prurient stare, no one paid her any mind. 'Twas as if kidnapping innocent women were a common occurrence aboard this ship.

The woman gunner kept up with the rest of them in both drink and boasting, and the pirates treated her as one of their own. Though Emeline had encountered a few women at sea in her voyages with her family, she'd not seen the likes of this one. A vision…a thought, perhaps, filtered across her mind of this woman with a baby in her arms, but Emeline cast it aside. No doubt she was so benumbed with fear, she was imagining things.

The older surgeon, introduced to her as Sam Goode, said little, drank more than he ate, and stared off into space as if he were somewhere else. Or perhaps he wished it to be so.

She could see where Rummy got his name, for the man never ceased from his rum. The more he drank, the louder and more belligerent he became.

Finn spoke mostly of gold, conquests, and battles, the same bodacious bragging Emeline had heard from many a pirate over the years. He was a thickly muscled man with a cropped beard and tiny slit-like eyes full of greed. She got the sense he'd grown up poor, *very* poor.

"You haven't eaten," Captain Keene finally spoke to her, nodding toward the lump of fish, biscuit, and mound of peas she'd placed on her plate.

She shook her head and gave him a look of bewilderment. Did the man expect her to enjoy a meal that very well might be her last?

He stared at her with those penetrating green eyes, studying her, and she longed for his assurance that he had no depraved plans, but instead he looked away and grabbed his drink. Her gaze dropped to the cross and the odd emblem hanging upon his chest, and she wondered at their significance.

The surgeon drew a deep breath, as if it took a great effort to speak. "Quite the fortunate weather we had this evening, Captain."

Blake shared a glance with her. "I have a pirate's luck is all—the luck of a buccaneer."

"Or be it that Ring that's good luck?" Finn belched and, having finished his food, lit his pipe. "The one ye gave the lady."

"A Ring?" Maston laughed and sipped his drink. "How could a Ring create such a thick fog?"

Finn puffed on his pipe. "Then why did we follow ole Slippery Crock around the Caribbean so's ye could take it from him?"

"It's a king's Ring, and I'm a king. That's all you need to know." Captain Keene leaned back in his chair, a smug look on his face.

Rummy shifted his glassy eyes over everyone. "If that Ring 'as power, then scupper, sink, and burn me if I don't quit me rum an' live the rest o' me life sober as a nun."

The pirates chuckled.

Charlie pointed her fork at him. "What's in your head, Rummy? We all know you can't do nothing, least of all steer this brig, wit'out your rum."

"Here, here!" Maston raised a glass, joined by his compatriots. "To Rummy's rum!"

Sam snorted, eyeing the lot of them with disdain. "Only the ignorant believe in fairy tales and myths."

"Who ye callin' ignorant?" Finn shoved back his chair and shot to his feet, hand on the hilt of his blade.

Emeline stopped breathing.

"Stand down, Finn," the captain ordered, his tone akin to one swatting away a fly. "Ignorant or not, I'd say you are all too far into your cups."

The captain included, by Emeline's assessment.

Finn uttered a growl but obeyed his captain. "Jist because Sam 'as some fancy learnin' don't mean 'e can look down 'is nose at the rest o' us."

Charlie cleared her throat as if to assuage the tension in the cabin. "So, this is your new paramour?" She nodded toward Emeline, her tone playful. "She's different from your usual."

His usual?

"I beg your pardon." Emeline huffed. "I am no one's mistress!" she managed to say, though her voice squeaked like a frightened mouse.

Charlie's eyes widened. "For shame, Captain. Did you kidnap this poor woman?"

The captain seemed to take no offense to her question. Instead, he cocked his head and studied Emeline yet again.

She shifted in her seat, longing to dash from the cabin and this dangerous, quarrelsome band of miscreants.

"Nay, I plan on returning her to her home soon," he finally said.

Emeline allowed a spark of hope to ignite.

"*Non, Capitaine,* I say we keep her." Maston raised his brows in her direction. "We need something pleasant to look upon."

She shot a spiteful look toward the Frenchman.

"Women's bad luck," Rummy slurred. "I says we toss 'er overboard."

Anger stormed through her veins at the brazen audacity, uncouthness, and wickedness of these pirates, chasing away the fear. She glared at the one-armed man. A vision of a large crocodile flashed across her eyes.

"'Twas a croc that got your arm," she blurted, instantly silencing everyone at the table. Everyone, save the monkey, who screeched from his perch on the stern window ledge.

"How would ye know that, missy?" Rummy growled, narrowing his eyes.

Even the captain stared at her as if she'd grown horns.

"She's a witch, says I." Finn stood and plucked a knife from his belt. "I say we 'ang 'er from the yardarm!"

Chapter 5

Grabbing the hilt of his cutlass, Blake uttered a growl and rose to his feet. The cabin spun, and he blinked to clear his vision before firing a scathing gaze at his quartermaster. "Stand down, Finn. There'll be no hanging tonight!"

Finn's eyes darkened as he stared at Blake, his grip tight on the knife. And for a brief moment, Blake thought his good friend would defy him. But, with a huff, he sheathed his blade, grabbed a bottle of rum, and stormed out of the cabin.

Maston chuckled and glanced her way. "How could such a lovely lady be a witch?"

The surgeon, Sam, rose to his feet, brushing crumbs from his waistcoat. "Witches are but a figment of uneducated and demented minds."

Rummy, who had yet to take his suspicious glare from Miss Hyde, shook his head. "But she *were* right about the croc."

"A good guess is all," Blake said, glancing at the lady. Terror streaked across her lustrous eyes. Still, she said naught to defend herself. As if sensing her dismay, Bandit leapt from his perch on the window ledge, scrambled over the table, and jumped into her lap.

At first, the lady shrieked and jerked back, but when Bandit remained, chattering to her softly, she began stroking his fur.

Charlie plopped one last piece of biscuit into her mouth and stood. "If Bandit approves o' her, then so do I."

Odd sight, that. One Blake could hardly tear his eyes from. "Good, then you can take her to Barnacle's old cabin." He waved a hand of dismissal at Charlie. "See to her womanly needs for the night."

"Me? What do I know of womanly needs?" Charlie winked at him but finally moved to where the lady sat.

Blake turned to dismiss the rest of them, but Rummy was already stumbling toward the door, muttering unintelligibly, Sam and Maston on his heels.

Clutching Bandit, the lady slowly stood and, with trembling hands, gave him the monkey. Their eyes met and, despite his alcoholic haze, he saw something in them, something deep, meaningful, kind, even? *A peace he'd been seeking his entire life.*

All in one glance. Pish! Blasted rum! He took the monkey, and Miss Hyde turned toward Charlie, instantly breaking the spell, and followed the master gunner out the door.

Finally alone, Blake set Bandit on the table, fished the Ring out of his pocket, grabbed a bottle of rum, and dropped onto the stern window ledge. Moonlit diamonds sparkled across an endless sea of ink that oscillated in and out of view with each rise and fall of the ship. The waters were tempestuous this night. Much like his soul.

The woman baffled him. Why? He'd grant she was not the usual strumpet who graced his cabin. Here was a lady of means and education, her grandfather an earl, her father next in line for that prestigious title. Yet she bore none of the pompous snobbery of her class. And though clearly offended by the mannerisms of his crew, she did not give off an air of insolent contempt, but rather one of pity. Perhaps due to her fears? Still, he did not sense the normal terror he'd expect from a lady in her predicament, but rather a natural unease, accompanied by the oddest sense of peace.

Aye, peace.

But what to do with her now? She was not difficult to gaze upon with her silky hair the color of chestnut, her delicate face, strong chin, and shimmering golden eyes. Not to mention her womanly curves. Though nothing like the buxom beauties he was accustomed to, she had an intelligence about her, a knowing, and a treasure he sensed deep within her that he longed to discover—a treasure he'd felt when he first laid eyes on her at Nassau.

Hang it all! What was he thinking? He could not keep her. He'd committed many sins, but never kidnapping and ravishing women. Besides, the last thing he needed was an encounter with the infamous Captain Alexander Hyde.

Even *with* the Ring…

Aye, he finally had the Ring! He held it up to the moonlight, wondering if it would glow as it did in the lady's hands earlier. Nay. But its beauty was still evident in the lantern light—the twinkling of gold, the lustrous red jewel in the center, and the ancient inscriptions along the edge. The legends were true! It had command over the weather. Which meant it must also possess the power and wisdom of one of the greatest kings on Earth.

He smiled. And it would give the same to Blake. Then the world would know his true value, and those who had insulted, abused, and rejected him would pay a heavy price.

Wind whistled against the stern windows as the brig creaked and groaned over a wave.

Lifting the bottle to his lips, he took a deep draught. Bandit jumped beside him and swiped at the Ring.

"Ah, ah. little one." Blake closed his hand over it. "You won't be stealing this again." He shook his fist at the beast.

Bandit cocked his head and scolded Blake, pointing his hairy finger at him.

"Off with you!" He shoved the pesky animal away. Why he kept the filthy monkey defied all reason. He took another sip of rum, his thoughts drifting to the mysterious cloud that had saved him from a difficult battle.

"It controls the weather," the old Jewish sailor had told him. "Wind, wave, and storm."

And indeed, it had. Grinning, Blake slipped the Ring onto his finger. A perfect fit, as if it was made for him.

"It also has other powers," the man had added as they sat chained in the hold of a Royal Navy ship.

"As in…?" Blake had asked, barely able to speak for lack of water. He'd expected to die within days anyway from thirst, starvation, or at the end of a rope in Jamaica, where they were heading. Listening to the mad ravings of the Jewish pirate took his mind off the throbbing pain from his recent flogging.

"Wisdom and the ability to command demons they say." The Jewish man chuckled and scratched his thick flea-infested beard. "Some say the wearer can speak with animals."

Blake had laughed at that last one.

"But the most important power it holds…" He had leaned closer, the chains around his feet rattling, his voice a raspy whisper… "is the power to rule the world."

Rule the world. It sounded as good a goal as any. Which is why he'd asked the madcap sailor the whereabouts of this mystical Ring.

As it turned out, he'd managed to escape the clutches of the British navy a week later after they'd dragged him ashore. That was a year ago, and he'd searched for the Ring ever since.

"I finally have you." He fingered it as he gazed out over the dark sea. "And the world is now mine for the taking."

Though Emeline was glad to leave one of the most vulgar displays of barbarity she'd witnessed in quite some time, despair quickly returned when she was escorted to a tiny cabin overrun with rats, all of whom scattered as soon as Charlie entered with lantern in hand.

"Sorry 'bout the vermin." The woman kicked one out of the way. "Ole Barnacle Ben, God rest his soul"—she made the sign of the cross—"weren't the tidiest, as you can see."

A stench as if something *or someone* died stung Emeline's nose, and she covered it with her hand as Charlie hooked the lantern on the deckhead. Plates of moldy half-eaten food lay across a table, on the bed, and along the floor, accompanied by grime-encrusted attire tossed hither and thither in abandon. In the corner, a bottle of rum lay on its side, shifting with each sway of the ship. A leather baldric hung on a hook, and a single stained and shredded coverlet lay crumpled on a swinging cot that hung by ropes from the deckhead. Beside it, a sliver of starlight forged through the darkness from a tiny round window on the hull.

"Ain't nothing left of any value," the woman said, lifting a hand to her nose as well. "The crew came and took what they wanted." She finally looked at Emeline, a spark of pity in her eyes. "I'll have Pedro fetch this rotten food, Miss, an' bring you some grog to drink an' water for washing."

'Twas the first kindness Emeline experienced aboard this bucket of brigands. "Thank you."

"Jist doing the cap'n's bidding, Miss." The woman studied Emeline. "You're a proper lady, ain't you? I can tell by your speech and mannerism." Her tone grew instantly hostile.

Emeline swallowed, wondering at the sudden animosity she felt pouring from the woman. "I have been educated, if that's what you mean."

"An' raised in a proper home, wanting for nothing." Planting fists on her hips, she snorted as if it were a crime. Save for the slight mound of her chest, the smooth skin of her face, and a tumble of brown hair, no one would guess a female lurked beneath the stained white shirt, leather waistcoat, tanned breeches, and myriad of weapons stuffed in her belt.

"I wouldn't call us wealthy," Emeline replied with caution. This was no woman to cross. "But aye, I've been blessed by God to have all I need."

"God, bah!" Charlie turned to leave.

Emeline touched her arm. She didn't know why. Perhaps out of desperation for company. Perhaps because she wanted to know more about her captor. Perhaps because something about the woman tugged at her heart. "Please stay a moment."

The lady's brows collided. "What for?"

"I'm curious. I've never met a lady master gunner."

"First of all, I ain't no lady." She pursed her lips, her eyes narrowing. "An' I earned my post. I'm one of the best gunners in all the West Indies."

Emeline smiled.

"Does that surprise you?" She raised an impudent brow as she balanced her boots on the tilting deck.

"Not at all. It pleases me to see a woman capable of doing a man's work and proud of it."

"And why not? Women can do most jobs better than men," Charlie said with confidence.

"I quite agree. You should meet my grandmother. She once captained a pirate ship and won battles on her own."

Surprise flitted across the woman's expression, an expression that seemed to soften. A tiny smile lifted her lips. "I should like to hear that story one day."

"I'm happy to relay it to you.... Charlie, is it?"

"My real name is Charlotte, but I prefer Charlie on board the *Summons*. No need to remind these lusty pirates I'm a woman." She winked at Emeline.

Indeed. "So, that's the name of this brig?" Emeline stored the information away in case she needed it later.

"Aye, named by the captain. Something about a new call on his life." She gripped the handle of a pistol stuffed in her belt. "You're not like most fine ladies I meet, all hoity toity, looking down their noses at me."

Emeline nearly laughed. "Nay. I was raised on a ship."

"Humph." Suspicion furrowed Charlie's brow as the brig careened over a wave.

Emeline pressed a hand on the bulkhead to keep from falling. "May I ask you something?"

Charlie merely stared at her.

"Does the captain kidnap women often?" Since it seemed this lady was a champion of women, perhaps she'd not agree to one of her gender being mistreated.

"Kidnap, nay. But aye, he's had his share of wenches aboard."

Of that Emeline had no doubt. "Do you think he means me harm?"

She shrugged. "Who knows wit' him. He's a reckless type, that one. Both his moods and actions none can predict."

Wonderful.

Emeline drew a deep breath and lowered to sit on the cot. The cold bars chilled her through the threadbare mattress.

Charlie started to leave, then spun back. "But never fear, Miss. You ain't his usual fare. Besides, he's not a cruel man, not as evil as some pirate captains."

With that she left, slamming the door, leaving Emeline alone with her rats and her fears and no more assurance of her safety than before.

As promised, the young lad Pedro soon arrived. He greeted her with a boyish grin and shoved plates of rotted food and what must have been poor Barnacle Ben's clothing into a huge burlap sack.

"Thank you, Pedro. You're a good lad."

The boy stopped short and stared at her. "I'm no lad, *señorita*, I'm a man already." His voice deepened, cracked, then raised again as if to prove his point.

She smiled. "Of course. You're right."

"And I'm goin' to be a pirate captain just like Captain Keene one day." He continued his cleaning.

"I know it sounds adventurous to be a pirate, Pedro, but most of them shorten their lives at the end of a rope."

He chuckled. "Not the good ones." But a frown soon stole his joy. "Not the smart ones like the captain. An' he's teaching me everythin' he knows."

She wanted to say, *that shouldn't take long* but thought better of it.

"I only hope I can learn." He picked up a pair of breeches that remained stiff in his hands. Cringing, he did his best to shove them in the sack. "And be as brave as he is. But I don't know."

The ship canted to larboard as a blast of salty wind swept through the small porthole.

"Don't know?" Emeline asked, sensing the boy's sudden sorrow.

He shrugged and glanced her way. "They say I'm not too smart, don't have any particular talents."

Oddly, she found she could relate, especially when she compared herself to her family. "I doubt that is true."

A glimmer of hope sparked in his eyes. Then it was gone. What had happened to this lad to make him believe he was worthless?

The boy soon left but returned with a basin, a pitcher of water, and a clean coverlet, if you could call it that. Despite her efforts to keep him talking, he begged off with an excuse of many duties to attend.

She didn't like being alone. Even at her family's estate in Kingston or on her father's ship, *Ransom*, she preferred to be around others, particularly those she loved. In both places, she shared a room with her sister, and they oft stayed up half the night talking and dreaming. Esther dreamt of opening an apothecary where she could use her herbal knowledge and healing power to help the sick, while Emeline longed only for a romance similar to her mother and father's and a wonderful, godly hero who would steal her heart. Then together they'd sail away to great adventures as they raised a crew of wee ones.

Now that she thought about it, her dreams seemed rather selfish compared to her sister's.

Another strike against her.

A rat scampered across the deck, sniffing at the places where plates had been. She thought to scare it away but for what purpose? More would take its place. Just like the rats aboard this ship.

The brig rolled over another wave, sending the lantern swinging above and spinning a web of light and dark over the tiny cabin. A chill prickled her skin, and she hugged herself. It was in the loneliness that the accusations arose, the taunts, the reproofs that always contained a sprinkling of truth. During those moments she'd always sought out her family, confessing her fears, and feeding off their words of faith and hope until all the voices of censure dissipated. But she could not do that now.

"Oh, Lord, where are you?" She'd get on her knees if it weren't for the rats. As it was, she bowed her head and clung to herself, longing for a hug from her father, who always made her feel safe.

Of late, she'd been asking the Lord for a romantic adventure. Was this His answer? Could Captain Keene be the man she'd dreamed of? Nay! The man was a pig, a libertine, a greedy, power-hungry pirate with the manners of a goat. That he had not ravished her yet was to his credit—the single decency she could point to. But what now?

"Lord, forgive me." Tears burned in her eyes. "I've been selfish. Asking only for things to please myself, to make my life happy." Sniffing, she wiped her face.

No wonder God had not given her any talents. No doubt she would only have used them for her own joy. "Forgive me, Lord."

A sigh deflated her. He had answered her prayer for an adventure, but not the one she sought, for Captain Blake was no godly hero.

And that meant she was in a tremendous amount of danger.

Chapter 6

B lake was sure his eyes were open, yet he saw naught but black. Not a normal darkness. Nay, this darkness was alive, pumping and pulsing like the beat of a massive black heart. He could hear it breathing, feel the fiery-hot puff of its breath on his face, shiver from its intense hatred. Heart racing, he peered into the black void, hoping to see a spark, a speck of light. Anything but the thick blackness threatening to choke him.

There. In the distance, a red glare. He stared at it, afraid to move. It grew larger, brighter.... orange, yellow, and red flames reaching upward. A fire? The darkness around him stretched, moving toward his left and right, spanning the scene like a toxic curtain. Until something sharp cleaved it asunder, and it separated into black figures, some tall, some short, some round, some thin—all swaying as if they were on a ship at sea. *Or under a spell.* He could not make out their faces, but he knew they hated him.

Knew their contempt could not be quenched by anything but his eternal damnation.

Pushing the phantoms aside, a man emerged from the heinous specters. Dressed in a fine suit of violet taffeta with a silk cravat bubbling about his neck, he halted before Blake with a vile grin and a supercilious stare that resurrected memories Blake had long since buried.

"Father?"

The man snorted. "Who else, little mongrel?" He circled Blake, fingering the manicured beard on his chin, assessing him, scrutinizing him like he used to do. Right before he would pummel Blake over and over with his fists.

A plethora of foul curses and insults spilled from the man's mouth, each causing the ghouls to grow more agitated. *Or was it excitement?* Their groans and grunts grew louder, their bodies undulated more violently.

Terror clambered up Blake's throat until he could hardly breathe. Where was he? *Hell?* Was the place real after all? Of a surety that would explain his father's presence.

"Nay!" He crushed fists into his eyes, rubbing away the vision, nightmare, whatever it was, demanding he wake up.

His father appeared before him. "You never could do anything right, little mongrel." His favorite pet name for Blake.

Ignoring him, Blake searched for a way of escape. There had to be a way out! He wasn't supposed to be here! He knew it.

His father gripped his arm, his eyes wide with shock. A trickle of blood spilled from his lips. The shock transformed into a maniacal loathing, a hatred that infected Blake's very soul. His father looked down, aghast. Blood oozed from a wound to his belly. Releasing Blake, he gripped it and backed away.

"You killed me!" he seethed. "You…killed….me!"

A monkey's jabbering rang through the darkness. Turning, Blake dashed into the ghoulish mob.

Light swallowed him whole, dispelling the shadows. His head throbbed.

His stomach vaulted.

The monkey kept chattering.

He pried open his eyes. His cabin formed around him. The same fiendish dark shadows swayed across the deck.

We will do your bidding. We will do your bidding.

The words, dark and malevolent, repeated over and over.

"Be gone!" Spotting an empty bottle of rum, he grabbed it and threw it at them.

Instantly, they vanished. The bottle hit the bulkhead and splintered into a dozen pieces, glittering in the rays of sunlight floating in from his cabin windows.

Bandit leapt up and down on his desk, screeching in terror.

"Hush now," Blake mumbled as he attempted to rise from his bed. The pain etching across his skull and the sour bubbling in his belly halted him. He hadn't thought he'd overdrank. Finally managing to rise, he stumbled to last night's empty bottle of rum on the window ledge. Must have been some bad spirits, for he'd not so much as given a thought, *nor a dream,* of his father in years.

But those devilish apparitions? *Here in his cabin.*

Bandit finally settled and leapt onto the ledge, quietly staring up at Blake.

He patted him on the head. "Just a bad dream, nothing more."

Rubbing the Ring on his finger, he leaned back against his desk. Outside the windows, morning sun dappled gold over an azure sea. He would not allow a nightmare to stop him now. Not when he had the Ring and all the power that came with it.

Renewed excitement chased away the memories of the night as he grew anxious to test those powers. He didn't have long to wait as one of his men knocked on his cabin door and alerted him they'd spotted a sail.

Shaking off both the throbbing in his head and the nightmarish dream, he emerged onto the quarterdeck to a torrid breeze and spray of salty mist.

"Four points off our starboard bow," Finn shouted and gestured to his right.

Plucking the scope from his belt, Blake leveled it in that direction where the sails of a schooner puffed like cotton against a cerulean sky.

"She sits low in the water," he said to no one in particular as he spun and began flinging orders to set all canvas to the wind. Low meant she had cargo, valuable cargo. It also would slow her down. Marching to the helm, he touched the Ring and grinned. Though he'd captured and plundered many a merchantman without it, 'twould be good to see what other powers it possessed besides creating a foggy mist.

"She's a fast one," Maston shouted from the main deck. "Even with all our sails set to the wind, she keeps her distance."

Leaping down the quarterdeck ladder, Blake marched to the railing, examining their soon-to-be prize. Indeed, her smaller size aided her speed. At this rate, and with the contrary wind and current, the *Summons* would be hard pressed to catch her.

If he could but shift the wind a mere two points toward the west and alter the current ever so slightly, he could run her aground on the shoals near that cay in the distance.

He clasped the Ring and made his request, a whisper that was soon swallowed by the wind. Pivoting, he found Maston. "Ready about! Ease down. Let go the foresheet!"

"But *Capitaine*." The Frenchman stared at him quizzically. "The wind?"

"'Twill be in our favor soon. Do as I say." He knew it. For some reason, he knew the Ring would grant his request.

Shaking his head, Maston uttered a curse but continued shouting orders. "Helms alee, rise tacks and sheets!"

Turning, Blake glanced over the turquoise sea. The *Summons'* sails flapped and then dropped like old garments for but a moment, a *painful* moment, before they sprang to life again, bloated with wind. The brig jerked to starboard. Blake grabbed the railing as white foam crept up the hull, clawing for his boots.

But his eyes remained on the merchant schooner. Sails that had been round and full just minutes ago now hung limp. Men scrambled across her deck, springing into the shrouds, as the ship headed straight for the cay.

Unusual sounds and a stench Emeline could not deny lassoed her unconscious mind, dragging it from a blissful slumber she'd only fallen into moments before. Nay! She clung to that peaceful state wherein troubles dissipated and sweet

dreams brought hope. *I don't want to go back. Leave me here!*
But the sounds transformed into vulgar slurs, the thunder of
sails, and the crank of guns being run out. And she knew
yesterday had not been a nightmare. And she was not safely on
board her father's ship.

Her cabin jerked to starboard. She flew over the mattress
and struck the bulkhead, the pain jarring her into a reality she
could no longer deny.

The brig righted itself. With great effort, she rose and leapt
from the shifting cot, getting her balance on the heaving deck.
The vaulting beneath her feet, along with the loud crash of
water against the hull, told her the *Summons* was racing across
the sea. To what purpose? It could only be one of two reasons.
Either they were being pursued or they were in pursuit.

Stumbling to the sideboard where Pedro had left a pitcher
of water, Emeline poured some into a basin and splashed it
over her face. A wonderful thought dared intrude upon her
despair. Perhaps her father was after them, intent on her rescue!

Oh, Lord, let it be so.

Taking no care for the state of her gown or her disheveled
hair, she flung open the door, made her way down the hall and
up the ladder to the main deck, where instantly a dozen
prurient gazes latched upon her. Ignoring them, she cast a
furtive glance at the captain standing at the helm before
moving to the bulwarks and focusing her eyes upon a schooner
in the distance. The poor ship was in dire trouble, for she had
run aground in the shallows of an islet. Sailors dashed across
her deck, some attending limp sails, others casting trunks and
barrels overboard in an attempt to free themselves from their
rocky prison. But to no avail.

Captain Keene blared orders for main and fore sails to be
lowered and for the one-armed helmsman to bring the
Summons to a halt off the schooner's stern outside the aim of
her guns. Regardless, Master Gunner Charlie kept her gun
crew at the ready on the bow chasers and the nine-pounders
mounted on the starboard railing should the merchant ship be

able to maneuver. The gun crew were quick to follow her orders, never once grumbling at having to take commands from a woman. Charlie looked up and gave Emeline a tiny smile before she spun back to her duties. Perhaps Emeline had found a friend on board after all.

"Musketeers to the tops!" the captain ordered, and a dozen pirates scrambled above, muskets in their hands.

"Stop 'em from tossing our booty into the bay, Cap'n!" Finn shouted at Captain Keene. Other pirates glanced at the merchants still hauling cargo to the deck and grumbled curses of complaint.

The captain ignored them. "Fire when ready, Charlie!" he commanded, and in moments one of the bow chasers boomed, shaking the ship from stem to stern. The railing quivered beneath Emeline's hands even as the deafening roar thundered in her ears. 'Twas nothing she was not accustomed to on board her father's ship, but the power of these guns never failed to unnerve her.

The warning shot flew over the schooner and landed off her larboard side as intended.

Captain Keene held a speaking trumpet to his mouth. "Good quarter will be granted if you lay down your arms and open your hatches!"

"You should move to safety, *Mademoiselle*." Claude Maston's tug on her arm startled her as he grinned at her like a snake would a timid mouse. "We cannot predict whether they will put up a fight."

Tugging from his grip, Emeline glanced up at the topmen preparing to fire and then over at the schooner, where sailors were armed with muskets and blades. Would she be forced to watch a bloody battle? Thus far, her parents had kept her from witnessing such a gruesome scene. *Lord, let none die this day,* she prayed silently, then moved to stand beneath the quarterdeck. Why the libertine cared whether she was blown to bits she could not fathom. Surely the captain took not a care either, for he'd not once glanced her way since she'd come on deck.

Thankfully, the merchantmen did as Captain Keene demanded. Begrudgingly, they tossed down their weapons and withdrew from the guns lining their bulwarks. Cheers and chortles rose from the pirates as preparations were made to ease the *Summons* close enough to the schooner without running aground and then to lower the boat to haul all their ill-gotten treasure on board.

Emeline had seen enough. Not only had she no desire to watch the theft—and perhaps murder—of innocent merchants, but the pirates, having disarmed their enemies, now seemed as interested in her as they were in acquiring their plunder. Therefore, since the threat of a cannon blast below decks no longer existed, she started for her cabin, the rats infesting it preferable to the ones on deck. She could only hope that after Captain Keene satisfied his lust for treasure, he would remember her and put her ashore at the nearest port.

"May I escort you below, *Mademoiselle*?" Sweeping off his tricorn, Maston appeared beside her yet again. Black curly hair waved about his face in the wind, while sweat and the distinct scent of some kind of spirits circled him.

"Nay, I'm sure you have duties to attend." She offered a tight smile.

He glanced over the deck. "Not at the moment. It would be my pleasure."

Emeline's nerves tightened. She must not allow herself to be alone with this libertine. But what to do? She had no champion aboard the ship. No one would come to her rescue. With the pirates busy boarding their latest victim, who would even notice?

"I must refuse you, Sir." She stood her ground, daring to lock eyes with him. His were a brown so dark, they could barely be distinguished from black. A lusty gleam lit them, and yet something lurked beyond it, a loss, an emptiness. Lashes any woman would envy framed their perfect shape, and along with his aquiline nose and strong jaw—if he were bathed and dressed in clean finery—he would pass for a nobleman.

A dark-skinned woman, lovely in form and face, flitted across Emeline's vision. The scene switched to a white columned estate with an extended portico upon which an elderly nobleman stood, smoking a cheroot.

"Is this bilge-licking jackal bothering you, Miss?" A woman's voice swept away the visions as Charlie marched up to them, her pointed gaze directed at Maston.

"Stand down, *Charlotte*." Maston snorted in derision. "Best get back to your guns."

"Gladly, *monsieur*," she retorted in a feigned French accent. "An' you'll see them pointed at your maggot-infested hide."

Emeline took a step back. Best not to get involved in whatever quarrel existed between these two. Beyond them, Captain Keene stood at the starboard railing, ordering several pirates down into the boat that had just been lowered.

Maston plopped his hat back atop his head and gave a lecherous grin. "Thinking of my hide, are you? I offer it freely to you any time."

"I'd rather be skinned alive and tossed to the sharks." Charlie spat to the side, casting a glance at Emeline. "Leave her be or answer to me." She snorted in disgust. "Must every woman who dares cross your path endure your vomit-inducing advances?"

"I've heard no complaints."

Charlie stabbed his chest with a finger so hard, he nearly stumbled backward. "Not until you leave them wit' a babe in their womb an' not a shilling to live on."

For a moment, Maston merely stared at her, then he shrugged. "Such accusations, Mademoiselle Charlotte!"

Charlie gripped the hilt of her blade. "Call me that again, and I'll gut you where you stand!"

Emeline's breath caught in her throat. She took another step back, glancing at the hatch that led below to her cabin.

Maston arched his brows. "If you refer to the woman in Barbados, it was her choice. I am not a man to force myself upon a lady." He adjusted the dirty lace on his cuffs. "The babe was an unfortunate consequence."

Plucking a knife from her belt, Charlie charged him and leveled it at his throat. "You unrighteous cad. You left her with nothing!"

Emeline's heart seized. Would Charlie kill the man right where he stood? And over what? His was a crime many a pirate committed across these islands.

A wave of fear traveled across Maston's face, quickly scattered by a fury that narrowed his eyes and pulsed a vein in his neck. He grabbed Charlie's arms, spun her, and shoved her back against his chest, then forced the knife in her hand to point at her own gut.

Emeline's throat went dry. Before she could ponder her next action, before she could consider the sanity of it, she grabbed the hilt of Charlie's cutlass, pulled it from its sheath, leapt behind Maston, and pointed the tip at his back. "Let her go, or I'll slice you in two!"

Chapter 7

Blake had kept one eye on the surrendered merchantman and one eye on the ensuing altercation between Maston and Charlie. He knew there was bad blood between them, though he knew not the reason. But of all the times for them to cross blades! He had a ship to pillage, and he needed his men to be on the alert should the merchants entertain a reckless thought and pick up arms. He was about to order them to cease their foolishness when Miss Hyde did something so astounding, Blake had to blink twice to ensure his eyes did not deceive him.

The high-bred woman—the little timid mouse—grabbed Charlie's sword from its sheath and pointed it at Maston. Blake would laugh at the shocked look of indignance on the Frenchman's face if he had time for such tomfoolery. As it was, his men called to him from the cockboat below.

"Are ye comin', Cap'n?"

One glance at the merchant schooner told him the crew remained unarmed and ready to be boarded, kept under submission by the twenty muskets in the *Summons'* shrouds and the nine-pounders mounted on her starboard railing.

He marched toward Maston and the girl, plucking his cutlass from his belt, and intending to fling a multitude of curses upon them all when Charlie elbowed Maston in the gut. His bosun bent over groaning, released the knife, and leapt out of the way, cradling his stomach and laughing. *Laughing?*

"Well met, ladies. Well met!" the Frenchman managed between moans.

Charlie picked up her knife and stuffed it back into her baldric, casting Maston a seething glance.

Miss Hyde remained frozen, the sword leveled mid-air, and her bottom lip quivering.

"Enough of this!" Blake shouted, halting before the mad trio. "Back to your stations!"

Wind blew a strand of hair into Charlie's face, and she swept it away, scowling. "It were his fault, Cap'n."

Maston raised his hands innocently. "I merely asked if the lady wished an escort to her cabin."

Charlie inched to Miss Hyde's side and carefully pried the sword from her tight grip. "I thank you, Miss, for your help."

The lady finally released a breath and nodded. The *Summons* rolled over a wave. Blake reached out to settle her, but she balanced herself well enough.

Turning to Charlie and Maston, he growled. "I should have you both flogged for such antics during a raid! Now back to work before I dock your portion of the loot!"

"Aye," they both grumbled as Blake turned to Miss Hyde. "Best get below, Miss."

Her eyes met his briefly, etched in fear, aye, but also with determination and a strength he'd not expected, before she nodded and descended the hatch.

There was no time to ponder the enigmatic woman as the next three hours were encompassed with boarding the merchant schooner, keeping their crew subdued, and hauling up what turned out to be quite the impressive load of goods from their hull.

Their captain, a giant of a man with a bulbous nose, receding chin, and grey hair that resembled a porcupine was none too pleased to see the wealth he hoped to make stolen by a band of cutthroats.

Blake swept off his tricorn and bowed before the man with a flourish. "I do thank you, Captain, for your generous donation to our cause."

The man merely scowled and spat to the side. If his eyes were armed, they'd have killed Blake a thousand times over by now. As it was, Blake spun on his heels, descended to the jollyboat, leaving the poor merchant crew alive and well and their schooner still aground on the shoals. With the tide now going out, they'd be unable to free themselves for some time. Curses were hurled at him and his men as they rowed back to the *Summons*, but Blake could only smile at the plunder they had acquired. 'Twould keep his crew satisfied for quite some time. Yet for Blake, 'twas more than the wealth. A mist of seawater sprayed over him as the boat leapt over the waves. He twisted the Ring on his finger. Once again, it had proven its power—power over tide, waves, and wind. He couldn't wait to discover what other gifts it held. Gifts that would put Blake in control of not only his destiny, but over the destiny of others as well.

"What is the sum of it?" Blake asked Finn as he entered his cabin several hours later. After he'd gotten the ship underway, he'd been waiting to hear the value of the loot they'd plundered.

Rummy slouched in a chair to the left of Blake's desk, bottle of rum in his hand, while Maston stood to Blake's right, fluttering the feather of a quill pen over his cheek.

Finn's eyes sparkled with greed. He wagged his brows and drew the pipe from his mouth. "A good catch, says I, Cap'n." He held up a piece of parchment. "Five pounds o' spices: pepper, nutmeg, and cinnamon. Ten pounds o' sugar. Eighteen bottles o' rum."

At this, Rummy shouted with glee.

"Several bottles o' some fancy wine, twenty muskets, thirty blades, fifty pounds o' gunpowder, two trunks full o' fine clothin', all velvet an' lace, dried beans, coffee, salted meat, tobacco. An' the best part?" He grinned. "A chest full o' pieces of eight, silver coins, and gold guineas!"

"Quite some haul, *Capitaine*." Maston laid down the pen.

"Indeed." More than Blake had expected on such a small ship.

Bandit obviously agreed as he leapt up and down on Blake's desk, squealing with enthusiasm. Behind him, a sinking sun spread a rainbow of colors across the horizon, announcing the end of a productive day.

Finn scratched his thick beard and uttered a deep sigh. "Ye'll get yer five shares, Cap'n. Maston an' me gets two, an' the rest o' the crew gets one, 'cept Pedro gets half a share." As if summoned by his name, the lad bounded into the cabin, his admiring gaze on Blake.

Finn growled. "Don't see why this French popinjay gets as much as me, Cap'n. Don't seem fair."

"French what?" Maston fingered the hilt of his cutlass.

"Sink me, I meant no insult. Jist makin' an observation." Finn settled his pipe at the corner of his mouth.

"You agreed to the code when you signed on with me," Blake interjected, gesturing for Maston to stand down.

Pedro stepped forward. "We shouldn't complain. Captain Keene is the best pirate captain on the Spanish Main! I'm happy wit' my half share."

"Cause yer just a silly lad." Finn mumbled through his pipe, then glanced back at the parchment in his hand.

Something in the way he stared at the list of plunder gave Blake pause. In the five years Finn had sailed with him, he'd become a trusted friend. Still, the quartermaster had taken no pains to hide his lust for wealth. During many a night when they'd both been far too deep in their cups, he had shared with Blake how he'd grown up poor on the streets of Portsmouth and watched his mum and younger brother starve to death. Could Blake trust him with so much wealth?

Could he trust any of them? They were pirates, after all.

"I say this calls fer a celebration." Rummy attempted to rise but plopped down into his seat again.

"Indeed," Maston agreed.

It took no further convincing for Blake to open the cabinet and pull out several bottles. He pointed one at Finn. "See to it that the crew gets extra rations of rum this night. We have much to celebrate."

The sun dipped below the horizon, dragging warmth and light over the sea, leaving dark waters in its wake. Emeline turned from the porthole, struck flint to steel, and lit the single lantern left to her in the tiny cabin. Along with the darkness, unnerving sounds rose around her—the eerie whine of a fiddle, a chorus of ribald shanties, shouts, curses, insults, and boasts.

Hence, when a knock rapped on her door, she was hesitant to answer it. When it opened and Charlie's face appeared around the edge, Emeline breathed a sigh of relief and gestured her inside.

Charlie shut the door behind her and leaned back against it, crossing arms over her leather waistcoat. "You are full o' surprises, Miss."

"Please call me Emeline." She gestured to the chair, but Charlie remained at the door.

"I came to thank you for stepping in today, though I can handle meself wit' that froggish rake." Her lips slanted.

"I have no doubt." Emeline lowered to sit on the bed and hugged herself. "I couldn't just stand there and let him…" She sighed. "I should be thanking you for coming to *my* rescue. In truth, I had no idea how I was going to put him off."

Charlie waved a hand through the air. "I don't 'xpect he would have hurt me, an' he's not one to force hisself on a woman. Just remember you must ne'er cower before him." She gave a mischievous grin. "Next time, mention his Negro blood. He hates that."

"Negro?"

"Aye, word is his father were some wealthy nobleman on Martinique who sired Maston with one of their slaves. When the man's wife discovered it, she tossed young Maston to the wind."

Oddly, Emeline suddenly felt sorry for him.

Charlie shook her head. "Don't you go feeling bad for him," she said as if reading Emeline's mind. "He's no innocent."

"I heard what you said. How he left that poor woman with child."

A gust of wind barged in through the porthole, stirring the lantern flame and sending shadows over the bulkhead.

Charlie's jaw hardened. "She's not the first either." She pushed from the door and strode to the window. "Men think they run the world...think they can whisper sweet words to any woman, make promises to love them forever, an' then leave them wit' a swelled belly an' not a coin in their purse."

Wind tossed Charlie's hair as she stood at the window, staring out upon the sea, her thoughts seemingly elsewhere. Instantly, her belly swelled like a bloated sail. It looked so real, Emeline sucked in a breath and was about to dash to her friend to help her with whatever malady had come upon her so suddenly.

But the vision—for surely that was all it was—vanished as quickly as it had come. Charlie had been with child. What else could it mean? Confusion racked Emeline's already rattled mind, for she could not fathom why God showed her these things. "I've seen many women left destitute with young ones to care for."

Facing her, Charlie slammed a hand to her waist. "And jist how would you have seen such things?"

"My family and I,"—sorrow burned behind her eyes at the mere mention of them—"we help the poor."

"Hmm." Charlie cocked her head. "Like I said, ne'er met any lady like you, Miss."

The stomp of footsteps thundered above, accompanied by a fiddle and shouts that grew louder by the minute.

"I must go. You should stay in your cabin tonight." Charlie headed for the door.

"Why are you not out celebrating with them?"

"The more men drink, the more they turn into dung-souled fools. Best to stay away." She offered a gentle smile, quite in contrast to her manly demeanor.

"Thank you, Charlie. 'Tis good to have a friend on board."

At this, one of the woman's brows lifted. "I will aid you where I can, but I would ne'er defy the cap'n. He's been good to me."

Emeline's stomach sank, but she nodded nonetheless. All hope of asking Charlie for help to escape soared out the window with the evening breeze.

Grabbing the bowsprit, Blake lowered to sit on the bow and swung his legs over the bulwarks. The *Summons* leapt over a swell, then sank into the trough, flinging foamy saltwater onto his bare feet. He shook it off and raised the bottle of rum to his lips, taking a large gulp. Well past midnight, his crew had slunk off to their cots to sleep off the night's revelry. But he'd been unable to sleep, his spirit as restless as the sea in a summer squall.

Above him, clouds drifted across a velvet sparkling sky that seemed to go on forever. Eternity. Was there such a thing? He twisted the Ring and thought of King Solomon, the wisest and most powerful ruler who'd ever lived. The old Jew said the Ring received its power from God Almighty. Blake had never given much thought to God. If He existed, He certainly hadn't given much thought to Blake either. Still, the Ring did possess power, but from whence did such power hail?

Wind blasted him, tossing his hair behind him. He closed his eyes. 'Twas not only the Ring that kept him astir, but the lady below deck. A genteel lady by all accounts and yet one who wielded a cutlass with the skill and courage of any pirate.

"I see I'm not the only one who couldn't sleep." The deep voice that could only be Sam's drew Blake's gaze to the aged surgeon as he shuffled close and gazed over the black sea.

"'Tis been a busy day." Blake tipped the bottle to his lips once again.

Sam leaned on the railing. "No more than usual."

"You did not join us to celebrate."

"You know I don't indulge in such folly."

Aye, Blake expected as much. Though Sam rarely disclosed anything of his past or even spoke of himself at all, Blake had learned he'd once been a professor of Natural Philosophy at Oxford. His downfall had something to do with a lady—as downfalls usually did—a betrayal and a sentence aboard a Royal Navy Frigate. Which was where he and Blake had crossed paths. Blake a prisoner and Sam a deserter. Sam needed to disappear from society. Blake needed a surgeon. A deal was made, and Sam aided in Blake's escape. They'd sailed together ever since, and Blake relied on the elder man's wise words, for he'd never had a father who offered him such counsel. Still, the man could be rather gloomy at times, often gainsaying Blake's plans.

"Perhaps 'tis the lady that causes your soul unease," Sam offered.

Blake twisted the Ring, wishing he could disclose its power to Sam and get his opinion on recent unexplained events. "Nay. I have no time for silly feather-brained females."

"That pleases me. I intended to warn you against such madness, for she seems quite unlike your prior wenches."

"Aye, she is remarkable, is she not?" He spoke the words before he realized how true they were. "But never fear, my friend. I intend to put her ashore at the next port."

"Then why bring her on board in the first place?"

"She had something I wanted. Now that I have it, she is of no further use." Even as he said the words, he cringed at their cruel ring.

Silence spanned between them for quite some time, as it often did when they were alone together. The *Summons* continued its gentle curtsey over the dark waters. Blake continued sipping his rum.

Finally, that rum emboldened mind could keep quiet no longer. "What do you know of magical or perhaps godly powers that inhabit ancient artifacts?"

Sam uttered a rare chuckle and glanced at Blake. Moonlight sparkled humor in his eyes. "I'd say there is no such thing. Neither magic. Or God."

Back in his cabin, Blake pondered Sam's words as he stood in the dark, staring out the stern windows at the black rolling sea. A heaviness settled on his shoulders at what the wise surgeon had said. If there was no magic, no otherworldly powers...no God, then there was no purpose to any of this. No hope, no reason to go on, save to spend one's life seeking one's own pleasure. Yet wasn't that precisely what Blake had been doing? Chasing power, wealth, revenge? He gripped the black cross around his neck, a symbol of his lack of faith in the God his mother worshipped, a God who led her to cast Blake out onto the street.

Evil laughter spun him around. He peered through the dark cabin but saw no one.

There is no God. There is no God. The black specters returned, shadowy figures billowing in a hellish dance of death.

No hope, no purpose. No joy. No God, they repeated over and over.

Blake fingered the Ring. "Begone!"

The shadows disappeared, but their chanting remained, haunting him through what was left of the night until, by daybreak, his head pounded, his mouth was as dry as a dead sailor's bones, and even Bandit cowered in a corner, staring at Blake as if he were a ghost.

He hailed Pedro and ordered him to bring the lady at once.

Chapter 8

The ghouls returned—demons or whatever they were—drifting in and out of Blake's vision, hovering against the bulkhead, shapeless figures with dark, malevolent eyes. The old Jewish pirate had told Blake that the Ring could command demons. Yet when Blake ordered them away this time, they remained.

Perhaps he didn't know the proper commands. Perhaps he needed to send them on a mission.

Perhaps he was merely going mad.

He rubbed his throbbing temples when Pedro knocked and entered the cabin with Miss Hyde in tow.

Even in her wrinkled gown and hastily pinned-up hair, she was a vision of light and beauty, a *natural* beauty devoid of most women's spurious attempts to enhance what nature provided.

She halted in the middle of the cabin, hands clasped before her, eyes locked upon him.

The demons instantly vanished.

Not only in sight, but their ceaseless chanting dissipated into silence. *Pure, peaceful silence.*

Even Bandit leapt from his corner and dashed toward the lady.

Surprised, she caught him in her arms, the force of him nearly knocking her over. He clung to her as a babe would his mother and, though clearly startled, she caressed his fur.

"Shh now, has the captain been mean to you?" She glanced up at Blake. "Should we add torturing small animals to your list of crimes, Captain?"

Bandit jabbered at the lady as if answering her, and the oddest thing happened. Blake could have sworn he understood the monkey saying something about ghosts in the cabin.

Aye, definitely going mad.

"Do have a seat, Miss Hyde." He gestured toward a chair.

"I'd rather stand." She set Bandit down and lifted her pert little nose. "Unless you have summoned me with the intention of setting me free, I find myself loathing your company."

Blake chuckled. "Indeed? I should have you flogged for your brazen tongue."

A spark of terror flashed across her eyes. Regardless, she stood her ground. "I am not one of your crew, Captain, who cannot speak their minds freely. Nor should any real gentleman threaten a lady with such barbarity."

"A gentleman, am I?" Oddly, the ache in Blake's head lessened, and he found himself smiling at their banter. The heaviness that had weighed upon him all night lifted, and he felt refreshed…hopeful, even.

"Nay, do not flatter yourself, Captain. A gentleman you will never be."

Blake laughed. "Nor do I wish to be a goose-witted dandy who cowers for the favors of the opposite sex."

"You deceive yourself if that is your assessment of a gentleman." As if taxed by the conversation, she moved to sit in the chair. Bandit leapt into her lap.

"Do regale me, Miss, with your understanding of the role."

"'Tis no role, but qualities that make a *true* man— Godliness, honor, integrity, courage, and being a champion of the weak."

"Humph." Blake poured himself a sip of rum. "I have found none of those qualities in any gentleman I have met."

"Then you have not met a true gentleman."

He tossed the rum to the back of his throat, then set the glass down and studied her. Rays of sunlight shifted over her cheeks in streaks of glittering gold. Thick lashes circled her luminous golden eyes. Spirals of chestnut-colored hair dangled over her shoulders as she gently petted Bandit.

The traitorous monkey leaned his head against her breast, smiling, and Blake suddenly wished he could do the same.

He shook off the sentiment. What was wrong with him? "Quite impressive the way you set Maston in his place."

She smiled and the entire cabin seemed brighter. "I could hardly allow him to harm Charlie."

"You and she have become friends."

"I wouldn't call it that." Sorrow tainted her tone.

"Regardless, I wouldn't have expected…" He sighed, unsure he wished to insult the lady, for he was enjoying their conversation.

"Me to point a cutlass at anyone?" She arched a brow. "You forget who my father is."

Hardly. 'Twas because of *precisely* who her father was that he could not keep her. He frowned. Too bad, for he found the idea of having this lovely sprite around appealing. He gripped the black cross around his neck, balancing his feet on the deck as the ship heaved over a wave.

Placing Bandit down, she rose, her jaw tightening. "He will find me. He is not one to give up. And when he finds this bucket of imbeciles you call a pirate ship, he will sink you to the depths."

Emeline had no idea where her sudden courage sprouted from. Nor her brazen tongue. She'd never been fearless like her parents and siblings. She knew all too well that she was at this pirate's mercy, a man who had proven himself to be anything but a gentleman. And nothing like her father.

Instead of his eyes narrowing in fury. Instead of charging toward her with the intent to do her harm, he laughed.

Laughed?

Bandit joined him, hopping up and down and squeaking like a mouse.

"You find me amusing, Captain?"

"Very." He contained himself and poured more rum into his glass.

"I have seen naught that pits your skill above my father's at sea battling." She gestured toward his hand. "Save for this Ring you say has power."

He touched it, grinning. "Indeed. And it has more than proven itself."

"Then what need have you of me? Release me, I beg you." She hated the tinge of fear in her voice.

"Beg? Somehow that does not become you."

"You mistake me again for your crew, Captain, for, unlike a pirate, I harbor no exaggerated opinion of myself that forbids me to grovel for my freedom."

He sipped his rum, studying her with interest. "Hmm. I sense I have been insulted."

She would insult him further if she had the courage. As it was, she tightened her lips and assessed him. A leather jerkin hung over a cream-colored shirt that spanned across broad shoulders. Wavy dark hair drifted over his collar, matching the stubble on his chin and thin mustache. But 'twas those almond-shaped green eyes, staring at her with such intensity, that sent a quiver through her. The stern rose and fell, shifting light over the black pearl in his ear and odd emblems dangling around his neck. He was an imposing man who displayed confidence and leadership and evoked loyalty among the crew. But she sensed an emptiness in his soul.

He walked steadily toward her.

Her heart quickened. Her breathing came hard. Still, she refused to cower before this man.

He halted inches from her, his gaze traveling over her face, not in anger, rather as someone studying a curiosity. The scent of rum, leather, and the sea flooded her nose.

"You don't fear me?" he asked.

"Should I?"

A vision. An older man with a sword wound. Accusations, hatred, and violence all tangled into a web of evil in her spirit. She dared stare into the captain's eyes. Darkness swirled in their depths.

He cocked his head…lifted a hand.

She didn't flinch.

Then, ever so gently, he ran the back of his fingers over her cheek. Not in a harsh way, nor a sensuous way, but…tenderly.

He drew closer, his lips hovering over hers.

Her pulse raced. She closed her eyes.

Warmth spiraled through her. Warmth… *and* terror.

"As soft as it looks," he whispered so close, she felt his breath on her cheek.

Was he to ravish her? Moisture filled her eyes. She opened them. "Please let me go. I will bring you no pleasure, I assure you."

One side of his lips quirked. "I doubt that."

Her pulse pounded so loud, she feared it could be heard over the rush of water against the hull.

The monkey leapt onto the captain's desk and squealed loudly as if attempting to draw his master's attention away from her.

"But 'tis good to see that you are indeed afraid of me." Turning, he sauntered away.

Emeline took a moment to settle both her breathing and her heart. "Why is that good? Is it your goal that all, men, women, and animals"—she gestured to Bandit—"tremble before your majesty?"

"Hmm. Something like that." He leaned back against his desk and crossed arms over his chest.

"Tactics no gentleman should employ."

"Again with the gentleman."

Sorrow claimed her heart for this man. Something terrible had happened to him. "You could be, you know."

"Too late for that, I'm afraid." He gripped the golden emblem hanging around his neck.

"Someone betrayed you." She sensed it, though she knew not how.

He snapped his gaze to her. "An easy guess, Miss. Everyone has been betrayed by someone."

"I have not."

He studied her, then pushed from his desk and walked to look out the stern windows.

Bandit followed and settled into a patch of warm sunlight.

"Then you are most fortunate," he said, still gazing out upon the sea. "But why should I expect otherwise when you have been raised by parents who love you and have a family who cares for you?"

His words floated through the cabin in a dark mist of sorrow and anger. She swallowed a lump of emotion. This man had been terribly hurt. She knew it. But what to do? How to reach him?

He spun to face her. "I saw you in the market with them. You were giving food and clothing to the poor. Why? Why would a dreaded pirate give anything away for free?"

Shock buzzed through Emeline. "To help the unfortunate, of course. To give them hope."

"Pish!" He snorted. "You give them food for a day or two and then leave. How is that hope?"

The deck heaved and shouts echoed from above. Emeline gripped the edge of the desk to steady herself, debating whether to bother telling this volatile man about Jesus. "We give people hope by telling them there is a life beyond this one, an eternal paradise, and a God who offers them a way there through His Son." There, she'd said it. Come what may.

Instead of the fury and disgust she'd endured from many people she'd witnessed to, this man merely stared at her as if a halo had appeared atop her head. Bandit, however, leapt up and down on the window ledge with glee. Smart monkey.

Blake frowned. "I didn't take you for a fool, Miss. Only fat wits believe in myths. For even if this God of yours exists, He takes no care for His creation."

Emeline raised her brows and gestured to the Ring on his finger. "This from a man who believes a Ring has magical powers. And I'm the fool?"

Fury stiffened his jaw. He rubbed the stubble on it, eyes narrowing.

She swallowed hard. Perhaps she'd finally overstepped.

Hang it! This woman and her brazen tongue. She dared call him a fool! The man who held her life in his hands. How utterly surprising...completely baffling...*and* quite refreshing. Not once had she used her feminine wiles to seduce him. Not once had she played the coquette in order to gain her freedom. If he were honest, it might have worked, for he found himself completely enchanted by her—a rather foreign sensation.

And that must never be. He touched the Ring, studying her. Too much was at stake for him to be distracted by a woman—*any* woman.

"I will set you free on the first civilized island we encounter, Miss." He poured more rum, finding he needed its numbing effect at the moment. "Until then, please remain in your cabin where your needs will be provided."

He could tell from the look in her eyes she didn't know whether to believe him or not. No matter. The sooner he was rid of this mystifying woman, the better.

Emeline emerged from below deck to a glorious salty breeze that caressed her skin and ran cool fingers through her hair. She'd felt the brig slowing, heard the orders to lower and furl sail, then detected the mighty splash of the anchor. Yet she'd been unable to determine where they were from the limited scope of her porthole. Now, closing her eyes, she raised her face to the warm sunlight, relishing the feel of it—of being outside once again. Until Finn all but shoved her from behind.

"Quit dawdling, wench."

She stumbled across the deck, only then seeing that they had anchored in Basseterre Bay of St. Kitts Island. She recognized the port immediately, for she'd been there before with her family. Hope sprang in her bosom, a hope that had long since dwindled from spending two days alone in her cabin. Loneliness had done a dire work on her, torturing, taunting, and filling her head with thoughts of never seeing her family again. Yet now...perhaps Captain Keene intended to keep his promise, after all. If so, a surprising turn of events.

Speaking of the captain, she lifted her gaze to the quarterdeck where Rummy, who stood by the helm, gave her a cursory glance before looking away. The captain was nowhere in sight. No doubt she'd surpassed his tolerable limits of insults from a woman and intended to send her ashore without a farewell.

For some reason, the thought saddened her. During her long hours alone, she'd realized she had failed him somehow. Here was a tortured man, and she had the means to help him. Instead, she'd used her tongue for evil and not good. No doubt her siblings would already have had him on his knees in repentance, devoting his life to serving God and man. She blew out a sigh as Pedro bounded over the deck and halted before her.

"I'm goin' to miss you, Miss." He ran a hand through his thick reddish hair and grinned. "It's nice havin' a real lady on board."

Finn nudged her to the railing. "Stay put till the cap'n sees ye off." Trudging away, he shouted orders for the boat to be lowered, sending pirates rushing to unhook the craft from its moorings.

"Don't mind him, Miss. He don't care for women much." Pedro leaned on the railing and gazed over the bay.

Turquoise waters, sparkling in the morning sun, led up to the city where citizens, slaves, wagons, and carriages hastened down the cobblestone streets. Wooden docks reached into the bay toward several anchored merchant ships unloading goods into boats. Beyond the row of buildings, mountains rose, some capped with billowy clouds and all covered with lush greenery. The chime of bells, clank of wagon wheels, shouts, and the squawk of pelicans as they dove for fish in the water was music to Emeline's ears. At least on land she'd have a chance to send word to her father.

She turned to Pedro. "I shall miss you, too, Pedro." A speck of innocence still sparkled in the lad's eyes, a speck that would fade if he continued this life. But how to help him? "You could come with me. Turn away from a life of thievery and debauchery."

"Ah, nay, Miss. I ain't good for much else. At least here the captain can teach me to be useful."

"Why do you think you would not be useful elsewhere in a goodlier endeavor?"

Maston directed the men as they lowered the jollyboat over the side of the ship, casting occasional glances her way.

The lad chuckled. "I ain't smart enough, Miss, nor good enough. Leastways my parents didn't think so." His countenance fell. "They left me to rot at a monastery in Cartegena."

Emeline bit her lip, forcing back tears. So many orphans wandered the streets of Caribbean cities, hungry, without hope, feeling worthless. Clasping the boy's shoulder, she leaned to stare into his eyes. "Never rely on anyone's opinion of you, not even your parents', to determine your worth. Every soul is highly valued by God."

The boy seemed to ponder this for a moment but then shrugged. "I don't know about God, Miss. All I know is I ain't nearly as smart as most."

Emeline released a sigh and faced the city again. "Never compare yourself to others, Pedro."

"Get back t' work, ye half-masted rodent!" Finn's shout straightened Pedro's shoulders, and he smiled at Emeline and sped away.

Emeline watched the boy leave, only then seeing Charlie standing by one of the nine-pounders, staring over the city of Basseterre, a forlorn look tugging on her features.

Emeline inched closer. "Do you hail from here?"

She shook her head and sniffed, turning her face away, though not before Emeline saw moisture in her eyes. "Nay. It's jist good t' see land again." The slight crack in her voice spoke otherwise.

"Thank you for befriending me, Charlie. I shall never forget you."

Surprise lit her expression, followed by a rare smile. "I will be coming ashore, Miss."

"With me?" Emeline allowed a moment of comfort to soften her fears.

"Aye, but not wit' you. I have business t' attend, and the cap'n granted me a few hours leave."

Finn grabbed Emeline's elbow and dragged her away. "Time t' go, wench."

She attempted to jerk from his grasp, but to no avail. Ship of misfits, indeed. All in need of hope. And all in need of the love of God.

The pirates seemed surprised when she navigated the rope ladder with ease. Once settled on the thwarts of the teetering boat, she glanced up in search of the captain, but he was nowhere in sight. Charlie soon followed, taking a seat at the bow away from Emeline. Odd.

She'd no time to ponder it when Bandit clambered down the ropes and bounded into her lap.

Startled at first, Emeline scratched his head. "Well, hello, little one. I shall miss you as well."

"Get back t' the ship, ye slimy vermin!" One of the pirates headed toward them, balancing in the boat. "The cap'n will have me 'ide if ye get lost."

Bandit grabbed Emeline's hand, placed something hard against her palm, then leapt back onto the rope ladder and clambered above.

The pirate vomited a mound of curses on the monkey, the place of his birth, and his equally repugnant relatives.

Ropes were freed, men settled on thwarts, and oars were clamped in oarlocks as they shoved off from the *Summons*.

Emeline waited until no one paid her any mind, then slowly opened her hand.

The Ring of Solomon sparkled in the sunlight.

Chapter 9

"**C**ap'n says to go 'ere an' give the woman what lives there this note." Finn handed Emeline a torn piece of parchment and a small pouch, but his eyes were on a pub house across the street. Licking his lips, he shoved his pipe back into his mouth.

Beyond him, Charlie marched down the walkway, weaving around citizens and slaves.

"Why does your captain not join your debauchery ashore?" Emeline asked.

Finn reached beneath the stained bandana covering his head and scratched what had to be flea-infested hair. "None o' yer business, Miss, wit' yer fancy words. Now, get on wit' ye." He waved her away like a stray dog. And with that, he joined the other pirates who'd come ashore and headed for the tavern.

Leaving Emeline all alone with a note, a bag of coins, and a terror that threatened to consume her.

What sort of man with a speck of decency left a lady alone in a nefarious port town without benefit of escort?

Tears threatened to burst. She stomped her boot in the sand. Nay! She must be strong like her family. She must trust that God had a plan. She touched the Ring she'd stuffed in her pocket and wondered how long before Captain Keene noticed it missing. More importantly, why had Bandit given it to her? Of a truth, he was a thieving little monkey. But why her? She smiled. Regardless, it gave her some satisfaction that after all his trouble acquiring it, the devious captain had lost it again. Served him right.

Her eyes latched upon Charlie, her unusual attire causing a stir amongst the crowd through which she confidently strode.

Why did she not join the other pirates for a drink? A sudden urge to follow the woman swept away Emeline's dire circumstances.

'Twas easy to keep from being seen amidst the bustling morning crowd of citizens shopping, servants hurrying to do their master's bidding, and the poor slaves, hauling heavy loads on their backs. Wagons filled with goods brought ashore rumbled over the cobblestones, followed by beribboned carriages from which peered gentlemen and ladies in their finery. Such a contrast between those privileged with wealth and those who lived and breathed at the pleasure of their masters. But life was full of contrasts, wasn't it? And injustices. For here she was, the granddaughter of an earl, but as poor as any slave on the island.

Charlie rounded the corner of a mercantile and started down a narrow dirt road that ascended a hill. Finally, just as Emeline's breath began to heave from the exertion, the woman turned down a pathway to a group of houses clustered together and entered one of them on the far right.

Emeline crept closer for a better view. A pub? Brothel? Store? Nay. None of those things. The woman, no doubt, had a paramour here in town, which would explain her emotion earlier on board the ship.

Whatever the case, 'twas none of Emeline's affair, for Charlie had made it quite clear she would ne'er defy her captain. With a sigh, she spun on her heels and headed back toward the main part of town.

The note read Cayon Street. Three houses on the right. The red one.

The rest of the note was in French, but Emeline knew enough of that language to guess at the words.

Prenez soin d'elle. Mot envoyé à son père. Il vous récompensera. Signé

Vôtre, Blake

Take care of her. Word sent to her father. He will reward you. Yours, Blake. Yours, indeed. Emeline huffed. No doubt one of the captain's many mistresses spread across the Caribbean.

She bit her lip. But he *did* say he'd sent word to her father. She glanced up from the note to see a group of men staring at her from across the way. Pirates or sailors from the looks of their garish attire, feathered tricorns, and myriad swords and pistols strapped on their hips. One of them doffed his hat, bowed slightly, and winked.

Oh, my. Heart slamming against her ribs, she hurried to get off the streets posthaste. A woman alone was sure prey for these ruthless libertines.

The red house was easy to find. Hands trembling, she knocked on the wooden door, casting a glance behind her. Thankfully, her admirers had given up following her.

A woman with hair as red as her door answered. A would-be beauty if not for the paint on her face and lips and the overtight bodice that pushed her bosoms up near her chin.

Her gaze traveled over Emeline with suspicion. "*Oui?*"

Captain Keene had sent her to a brothel! Fury boiled in her veins as she stood there, unable to speak, unable to move. Laughter brought her gaze down the street where another group of slovenly men sauntered past.

She handed the woman the note.

Her painted brows lifted as she read. Then, blowing out a grunt, she held out her hand, palm open.

Confused, Emeline shook her head.

"The coins." The woman gave an incredulous snort.

Hence, the money Emeline thought the captain had given her, the only generous thing he had done, she now handed over to this slattern.

At least the slattern led her inside.

"You are acquainted with *Capitaine* Keene, *non*?" The woman sashayed down a dark hallway past a brightly colored receiving room and another cozier parlor with stuffed chairs, woven rugs, and a large dog that lifted his head at their passing.

"Not in the way you assume, mademoiselle."

The woman merely huffed in reply. Gathering her lavish skirts, she ascended a set of curved stairs onto a landing lined with a railing on one side and three closed doors on the other, one of which she opened.

"You may tell the...how do you say...rakish scoundrel...that I do not want his castoffs." Anger darkened the woman's red-painted cheeks.

Castoffs? Indignant, Emeline eased past her into the room. "I beg your pardon. I am not one of his doxies."

The woman flattened her lips, studying Emeline with suspicion. "Hmm. Certainly not like his usual." She shrugged. "Very well. You will be comfortable in here, *Mademoiselle*." Untying the pouch, she opened it and glanced within, a wide smile forming on her lips. "And provided with one meal a day until your papa arrives. Turn around." She spun her hand in the air. "Let me see you."

Unsure what to do, Emeline slowly pivoted.

"*Oui*, you could make a good deal of money while you are here." She jingled the pouch of coins. "Why rely on the generosity of *capricieux* men like Blake when you can take care of yourself, eh?"

Heat swamped Emeline at what the woman suggested. Yet despite the air fleeing her lungs, she managed to choke out, "I thank you, madam, but I...but I..."

"Ah, I see." She smiled, not a cruel smile, nor one that indicated displeasure, but one of understanding. "Very well. I'll send Miss Catherine with some food and"—her nose pinched—"perhaps a clean gown and underthings. *Oui, oui,* you are about the same size. You may thank me later."

With that, she closed the door before Emeline could utter another word.

'Twas a nicely decorated chamber, complete with a four-poster bed, a carved chest of drawers, a tall wardrobe, and a single upholstered red chair. A colorful woven rug graced the wooden floor, while heavy damask curtains framed the window. Emeline moved to look out upon the city. Beyond the many roofs, a strip of turquoise water sparkled in the sun. Bare masts poked into the sky, idly rocking like a maestro's baton in some deranged orchestra. She wondered which one was the *Summons*, but what did it matter? She was free. And safe for the time being.

Thank you, Lord.

Retrieving the Ring from her skirt pocket, she held it up to the sunlight, admiring how the rays sparkled off the crimson gem in the center. Did it possess the power Captain Keene claimed? For there was no denying the unusual mist and then the change in wind and tide that had given him the advantage. Either way, Emeline knew of only two forms of supernatural power in the world—good and evil, God and Satan. God no longer worked through objects as in the days before Jesus. Nay, He worked through His children filled with His Spirit. Hence, the Ring's powers must come from the enemy of mankind.

Which was why she must get rid of it immediately. Hide it where no one would ever find it. Toss it into the depths of the sea. Or perhaps throw it into the fire where all the evil it possessed would burn.

"Where is my Ring, you dung-soiled traitorous beast?" Blake darted for Bandit, but the fiendish monkey jumped onto the desk, screeching as if he were about to be skinned alive—which he might very well be once Blake got ahold of him.

If Blake got ahold of him.

He lunged, but the little weasel whisked off the desk and sped across the cabin, squealing like a baby.

The door opened. "You all right, *Capitaine*?" Maston poked his head in.

Bandit raced out the door in a blur of brown fur. Growling, Blake fisted his hands. "Now I'll never catch him!"

"Your wee monkey?" Maston glanced over his shoulder. "What has he done to you?"

Blake rubbed the back of his neck. "He stole something of mine. A Ring."

Maston waved a hand through the air, the torn lace at his cuffs fluttering. "With the last haul we took, you can buy another."

If only that were true. He ground his fists until his fingers ached. He had but one recourse.

An hour later, he emerged onto the quarterdeck and approached the railing. Beneath him on the main deck, his crew awaited his command. Some stood, a few sat on barrels, others leaned on the bulwarks. All cursed, chortled, and squawked like a flock of preened hens—hens he knew would stab him in the back if he didn't keep their pockets lined. Above them, white sails glutted with wind pulled the ship over the mighty swells of the Caribbean. Off the starboard rail, the sun touched the sea, flinging ribbons of maroon and tangerine over the horizon. A warm breeze whipped his hair behind him as he leveled his boots on the deck and crossed arms over his chest.

Chattering brought his gaze up to Bandit, hanging from the ratlines, grinning at Blake in victory. Devilish hound! The monkey was the only one who knew where Blake put the Ring when he wasn't wearing it. It must still be on the ship, for the monkey never went ashore before they'd left St. Kitts at midday.

"I have lost a Ring!" Blake's shout rose above the wind and waves, snapping all gazes in his direction. "It is of no value to anyone save myself." He went on to describe the Ring and ordered the crew to search the ship from stem to stern. "Whoever finds it will receive a bag of gold equal to twenty pound and a case of rum." He hoped such a huge reward would keep the pirates from merely pocketing the Ring should they find it, for they would surely determine the trinket to be of lesser value.

At first the men looked shocked that he offered such a large sum, but then "huzzahs" rang through the air and the crew scattered like rats to cheese. All except his surgeon, Sam, who seemed disinterested as he dropped down the hatch back to his quarters.

Blake smiled and pointed a finger of warning at Bandit, but the monkey only climbed higher. 'Twas best, for in Blake's current temperament, he'd dismember the varmint and hang his parts from the masthead.

Yet by the time the majestic sun dared peek above the dark sea after a tortured night, no Ring had been found.

Finn plucked his pipe from his lips and shrugged. "Sorry, Cap'n. I ne'er seen pirates work so hard in all me life. Most o' 'hem stayed up all night, tearin' the ship apart."

As if to offer proof of Finn's statement, Rummy dragged himself into Blake's cabin, his remaining arm swaying by his side as if it could no longer move. Even young Pedro had shadows beneath his eyes, though he still smiled at Blake as he entered.

Charlie sauntered in, leaned back against the bulkhead, and fisted hands at her waist. "A cruel joke, Captain? There is no Ring, eh?"

"No joke, I assure you." Grabbing a bottle of rum, Blake took a swig and handed it to Rummy, who had sunk into a chair, his head dropped in one hand.

"The Ring is not on board, *Capitaine.*" Maston entered, swiping off his feathered tricorn. "If it was, it would have been found by now, *non?*"

"Perhaps someone tossed it overboard." Charlie offered the one explanation Blake did not wish to hear. He ground his teeth. *Think...think.* He pictured the Ring, remembering how it lit up in the lady's hands and not his.

Wait. Bandit gave it to Miss Hyde once.

Would he have done so again?

"Finn, turn the ship around. Rummy, have your drink, then back to the helm. Hard about. We head back to St. Kitts."

Chapter 10

"**I** have some business to attend. I shan't be long, Mademoiselle Lavigne." Emeline halted at the parlor entrance, hesitating in case the woman was *entertaining*. Thank the good Lord she was alone at the moment. Not that Emeline hadn't heard noises she'd rather not have heard during the long night, but no doubt the lady's *guests* had left by now.

Red hair the color of burgundy wine fell from Mademoiselle Lavigne's pins in a bounty of curls, a few of which draped over her shoulders onto a silk nightdress embroidered with flowers. A large dog curled up at her feet.

"Thank you, *mademoiselle*, for the meal and hot bath last night." Emeline had been pleasantly surprised by both—the meal, a delicious potato bisque, boiled oysters, fresh bread, and cheese, and the bath something she'd desperately needed.

Mademoiselle Lavigne set down her cup of steaming tea and smiled at Emeline. "Call me Delphine, *s'il vous plait*. You are most welcome, my dear." Her eyes twinkled in delight. "I see Miss Catherine's gown fits you nicely."

Emeline gripped the shawl covering her nearly bare bosoms more tightly about her neck. The gown was lovely, a peach taffeta, hemmed in lace, but the neckline was far too low and the bodice far too tight for any proper lady to wear. Yet she had no choice, for Miss Catherine was washing her only other gown.

Mademoiselle laughed. "I do see why Blake likes you. He's unaccustomed to such modesty in a woman."

"As I have tried to tell you, I am not his...his..." she could hardly say the word without blushing. "If you must know, he kidnapped me from my family, and I'm quite sure he abhors me."

"Oh, I doubt that, my dear. No pirate would pay so handsomely for the care of a woman he *abhors*, as you say."

Paid handsomely?

She shook her head. "I can hardly credit it. Perhaps he feels guilty for the monstrous way in which he treated me."

"Ha! Guilt? From a pirate? *Non*, my innocent mademoiselle." Sorrow suddenly clouded the woman's face, and Emeline knew deep inside that the captain had hurt her somehow.

"Are you his mistress, *Mademoi*...Delphine?"

Again the lady laughed, only this time a shard of pain sharpened it. "Such boldness from a lady!" Rising, she spread a hand over her nightdress and sighed. "*Non*. Though I would have it so, should he ask." She moved to the unlit fireplace. The dog lifted his head. "Blake is a battered soul, unable to love, I fear. I believe due to a woman from his past, perhaps more than one."

Indeed? Emeline suddenly found herself curious about the man. Though she could not fathom why. He'd done naught but cause her harm. "I perceive that he wounded you. I am sorry."

Delphine's gaze snapped to Emeline, both shock and agony pooling within her striking blue eyes. "How...?" She swallowed, then flicked her hand through the air. "Be back by supper or you won't get a meal."

"I will. Thank you."

Outside, Emeline drew a deep breath of sea air, feeling sorry for Delphine. She'd always been critical of women like her, looking down at them for their sin and wickedness. But this woman had suffered greatly at the hands of men, that she knew. She dove her hand into her skirt pocket where she'd hidden the Ring. Perhaps 'twas this strange artifact that gave her such knowledge? Nay, impossible. Its powers hailed only from dark places.

Which is why she intended to throw it into the bay the first chance she got.

First, she must post a missive to Kingston, Jamaica. Even if her father was not there, surely one of her relatives would be at the Hyde Estate and would come to her rescue. She could not trust Captain Keene to have actually sent word.

The port city of Basseterre was just as busy as yesterday. Bells clanged, ships sailed into the bay with holds full of cargo, and citizens and slaves bustled about. After inquiring of an elderly couple where she might post a letter, she dove between a wagon and a carriage rumbling down the street and entered the postmasters.

With that task completed, she emerged to a sun high in the sky and a sweltering heat that nearly sent her back inside. The scent of roasted pig, sweat, salt, and a hint of rain filled her nose. To her right, the twang of a fiddle joined the cacophony of sounds that all together created the unique symphony of the city.

A few men tipped their hats at her as they passed. More than one's gaze lingered with interest above a suggestive smile. Despite the heat, she drew her shawl tighter, not wanting to give them a hint that she was not a chaste lady.

Turning right, she wandered past shops and warehouses—a butcher, ship chandler, tailor, sugar warehouse, and blacksmith—back to the home she'd seen Charlie enter. The master gunner was no doubt back on the *Summons* and far away, but Emeline didn't wish to return to Delphine's yet. She preferred not to return to the brothel at all, but she had nowhere else to go as she waited for her father. And since she'd spent her last three pence on postage, she could not even barter passage on a ship heading to Jamaica.

More than once, she noticed a man in a suit of black camlet embellished with gold braid glancing her way. His posh attire suggested he was a gentleman and not a pirate, sailor, or one of the other miscreants who inhabited most port towns.

Regardless, she hurried along. Perhaps whoever befriended Charlie at the house she had entered would have a room to rent and would accept Emeline's promise of a generous reward when her father arrived.

So, up the hill she went, then over to the door into which Charlie had disappeared. She raised her hand to knock, hesitating. What was she thinking? Perhaps the people on the other side of this door were no better than Delphine. Mayhap even worse. She turned to leave when the door flung open.

An elderly woman in a modest cotton gown with an apron tied about her waist and a mob cap on her head stared at Emeline quizzically. "May I 'elp you, Miss?"

The kindness in her voice and the twinkle in her eyes immediately set Emeline at ease.

"Forgive my intrusion, Madam. I…I…do you know Charlie…I mean a woman named Charlotte?" It only then occurred to Emeline she did not know Charlie's surname.

The friendly gleam faded from the woman's eyes, replaced by suspicion. "Who is asking?"

A child's voice drifted from inside.

"I befriended her on the ship *Summons*. Her captain set me ashore here to wait for my father's arrival and I—"

A young child, no older than three, with a shock of brown curly hair darted over to the woman, gripped her skirts, and stared up at Emeline. Innocence not yet tainted by the evil in the world shone from the lad's wide eyes.

The woman swept him up in her arms. "I cannot help you, Miss. It's just me and my son 'ere. We 'aven't got any extra to give you."

Her son? The woman was far too old to have a child so young. "Perhaps you have a room to rent? My father will more than compensate you. Charlie can vouch for me."

The woman studied her a minute. A salty breeze fluttered the gray hair springing from her cap. "Charlotte is gone, and I 'ave no rooms, Miss. Now if you don't mind."

The lad reached a chubby hand toward Emeline and grinned. She grabbed it and shook it in greeting. "Nice to meet you, kind sir."

"He likes you." The woman smiled. "But I still cannot 'elp you." Something caught her eye over Emeline's shoulder and her posture stiffened. "Good day to you, Miss." With that, the door slammed in Emeline's face.

Drawing a deep breath, she turned to see the same posh gentleman in black attire strolling across the dirt street. Was he following her or was she being overly fearful?

Nay. He was most definitely following her.

To what purpose? She was no one of import. She had no money.

Clutching her shawl to her throat, she lowered her gaze and hurried down the street past him. One glance over her shoulder told her he had pivoted and was fast approaching from behind.

Lord?

Blood racing, she turned down Bank Street, weaving around passersby and moving as fast as she could without drawing undue attention. She glanced over her shoulder to see if the man was still following her and…barreled into something large, solid, and warm.

"Oh my, forgive me, Sir!" She leapt back, only then noting the man wore the same black camlet suit as her pursuer, same lacy cuffs, same gold epaulets on his shoulders. His tricorn held a bright purple feather that waved in the salty breeze. An odd emblem pinned to his black cravat sparkled in the sunlight.

He said naught, only grinned as she attempted to move past him. His grip on her arm imprisoned her.

"I beg your pardon! Release me at once!" Pain etched up her arm.

The man who'd been following her appeared beside them.

"Good day to you, *signorina*." The accent was strong yet unfamiliar. His clasp on her arm overpowering, resisting all her attempts to free herself.

"Allow me to be on my way, or I will scream for help." She scanned the crowded street, wondering if anyone would come to her aid, for naught but pirates, sailors, slaves, and workers hastened about.

"Of course, *signorina*." The man grinned and held out his hand. "As soon as you give me the Ring."

Alarm buzzed through her. She dared to meet the man's gaze. Pools of darkness bubbled in his gray eyes. Within them visions appeared, undulating in the thick black, apparitions of murder and chaos that turned her blood to ice. Her stomach soured. Her mind raced. And she knew one thing. This man must never possess the Ring of King Solomon.

"Ah, but where are my manners?" Removing his hat, he swept it before him in a flourish. "I am Signor Arturo Della Morte. You may address me as Father Morte if you wish."

"You are no priest, Sir." She spat back, wondering at her courage. *Jesuits.* These were the men Captain Keene said were after the Ring.

As if disgusted by the happenings below, dark clouds rolled in and gobbled up the sun. Wind whipped in from the sea, fluttering the feathers atop the two men's hats.

Again the man called Della Morte held out his hand. "The Ring?"

Lord, help me!

Emeline shook her head. "I have no knowledge of any Ring, Signor Morte." Her stomach clamped at the lie. "Now, if you please." Quite an appropriate name for a man whose eyes held naught but death.

Those ghostly eyes scanned her from head to toe with such intensity she wondered whether he could see the Ring in her pocket. Then with a huff of impatience, he started on his way, gesturing to his friend to bring her along.

Panic curdled in her belly. She could not allow them to take her! Gathering her breath, she screamed with all her might. At that same moment, a deafening roar of thunder shook the skies, along with the ground beneath them, drowning out her appeal for help and stunning all the inhabitants of the small port town. Including the Jesuit villains.

Whispering a quick, "forgive me, Lord," Emeline kicked the man in the groin. Immediately releasing her, he bent over in agony. And before Signor Morte could react, she grabbed her skirts and tore down the street, her shawl flying off behind her.

A torrent of pounding rain unleashed from the dark skies above. Large drops pelted her, stinging her skin and creating a gray curtain that obscured everything in sight. Including her, for when she dared to glance behind her, the Jesuits were gone.

People dashed for cover. Carriages sank in the mud as the *rap-tap* of the rain on the cobblestones mimicked soldiers marching down the street.

Lightning flashed an eerie silver over the scene. Emeline blinked water from her lashes and turned down Bay Street toward Delphine's. She had nowhere else to go and no one else to trust. She could only hope the Jesuits had no clue where she was staying.

Her rain-sodden gown dragged in the mud. Saturated curls dripped onto her shoulders, but thank the good Lord, no one followed her. Heaving a deep breath, she slowed, spotting Delphine's up ahead.

Hefting her heavy skirts, she plodded toward the two-story home, trying to settle her nerves.

When strong hands gripped her shoulders and dragged her into the garden beside the house.

Chapter 11

The woman turned into a wild cat, clawing, scratching, and kicking. It took all of Blake's strength to avoid getting mauled. Slamming her back against his chest—to avoid her deadly feet—he pinned her arms and leaned to whisper in her ear. "Shh, shh, little tiger. 'Tis I."

She ceased her struggling. For but a second. Before she elbowed him in the gut.

Grunting, Blake loosened his grip. "'Tis me, Captain Keene," he repeated, foolishly thinking his identity would calm her.

"Let me go, you fiend!" She attempted to kick him backward, but her legs became entangled in her sodden skirts.

"Your word you will not run, Miss," he ground out.

Heaving a deep breath, she finally nodded.

The *tap-tap* of raindrops drummed an ominous cadence on the roof of an overhang above them that stretched from Delphine's house to what was once a stable.

He freed her, and she took one step and spun to face him, anger blooming red over her moist face. A single saturated curl dangled across her cheek. He neither expected nor saw the slap that stung his jaw.

Repressing a grin at her tenacity, he rubbed it, studying her.

Her eyes sparked fire. "What do you want with me? Have you not done enough harm?"

Rain glistened in her lashes and dripped from her hair, down her neck and onto….He forced down a burst of desire.

She slapped him again. "Stop looking at me like that!"

He arched his brows. "That's the last strike that will go unpunished, Miss."

Her body stiffened—with anger or fear he couldn't tell. Either way, it drew his gaze once again to her chest. He'd not thought the lady possessed such curves. "When I left you with Delphine, I had no idea you would take up the trade so quickly," he teased.

"Very amusing." The lady's eyes became slits of fury as she attempted to cover her chest with her hands. A blush exploded across her cheeks, pushing aside the anger. She lowered her gaze. "'Twas the only gown she had to replace mine."

Adorable. Her rare innocence had a curious effect on him.

She swallowed hard as moisture filled her eyes. And he suddenly felt like the cad he was.

"What is it you want?" she muttered.

Thunder rumbled in the distance. Raindrops fell from the roof and splashed into puddles below. The storm was heading out. The one within this lady had only just begun.

A sudden urge to take her in his arms and comfort her sent a tumult of confusion through him. Hang it, what was wrong with him? He stiffened his jaw. "I want what is mine."

Burning arrows fired from her eyes. "Is that the only reason you came?"

"Should there be another?"

She stomped her foot in the mud, splashing his boots. "Perhaps leaving a defenseless lady alone in a brothel far from home would be enough reason for a gentleman to reconsider his actions and return to make amends."

She said the words so matter-of-factly, so honestly, that they brooked no argument, save the only one he had. He *was* no gentleman. Yet that she considered it a possibility made something inside him suddenly want to be.

"I left you in good hands, provided for your care, and sent a post to your father." He huffed. "'Tis more than any other pirate would do." Then why did he feel so ashamed?

Chilled, Emeline hugged herself, doing her best to cover her low neckline, and gazed toward the street. A rivulet of water streamed over the muddy cobblestones, lit by a single ray of sunshine that pierced the departing clouds. *A single ray of light in the darkness.* A ray of hope from her Father above? She would cling to that, for 'twas quite obvious this pirate took no care for her welfare—for anyone's but his own.

She faced him. His black hair hung in strands about his face, dripping water onto his leather jerkin then onto the white cambric shirt he wore. Saturated, the cloth clung to firm rounded muscles across his chest and ripples of strength down his belly. An odd warmth spiraled through her. She thought of the Jesuits. This man had the strength to protect her. He could be her champion, just like her father had been for her mother. But heroes were made of more than sinew and strength.

He drew an impatient breath and glanced onto the street where more rays of the sun broke through the clouds, creating rainbows in the puddles. The black pearl in his ear glistened, and she wondered at its significance, along with the cross and emblem he always wore around his neck.

He faced her again and for a moment she thought she saw remorse, even shame in his eyes, giving her hope that perhaps he would protect her and take her home.

Instead, he rubbed his knuckles over the stubble on his jaw, then gripped the hilt of his sword with one hand and held out his other, palm up.

Did he intend to run her through if she refused him the Ring? Huffing, she flattened her lips and shoved her hand into her skirt pocket. The cold, wet fabric sent a chill across her shoulders. Why had she not thrown the hellish thing in the bay as she'd planned? She dropped it into his hand. "Take your cursed Ring and be gone, Captain. May our paths never again cross, for you are an insolent sot, a scoundrel of the worst kind!"

He closed his fingers over the artifact and chuckled. "The worst kind, you say? Nay." He raised his hand toward her. Flinching, she started to back away, but then he eased a strand of hair behind her ear before running the back of his fingers over her cheek. Ever so gently, ever so softly, as a lover would do. "If I were, I would do with you what every ounce of me longs to do."

Her breath caught in her throat. Fear flooded her at both his words and the simmering look in his eyes—eyes that examined every inch of her face.

He slipped the Ring onto his finger. Then before she could stop him, he leaned in and kissed her…full on the lips. Quick, gentle, and sensuous, leaving her so stunned she could neither move nor utter a word.

Or ignore the heat that flooded her.

Then turning, he dashed onto the street and disappeared from sight.

Emeline touched her lips.

'Twas her first kiss.

Delphine was *entertaining*, so Emeline quickly slipped into her chamber and took off her wet skirts. Thankfully, Miss Catherine had laid out her clean gown, chemise, petticoats, stockings, and stays on the bed. Still, as Emeline dressed, she could not tear her thoughts from Captain Keene. Her emotions spun in a cyclone of rage, frustration, and shame one minute to an odd desire and sorrow at never seeing him again the next.

"Oh, pah!" She plopped onto her bed as moisture filled her eyes. "What is wrong with me?" Why such strong sentiments for a man who had proven himself to be naught but a beastly cad? Surely, she was merely missing her parents, her family. She had been through a terrifying ordeal, and now she had Jesuits in pursuit. Any lady would be out of sorts. In truth, any interest, any affection shown by anyone would cause hope to stir, even if that *anyone* had the decency of a bilge rat.

She swiped moisture from her eyes and rose to move to the window. Dark clouds retreated on the horizon, leaving the wet city glistening in the sunlight. 'Twas as if God Himself gave the wicked place a much-needed cleansing. If only it would last.

The bare tops of masts swayed in the bay, and she wondered which one was the *Summons*. Certainly the captain would set sail as soon as he returned to his ship.

Leaving her alone and defenseless.

Would it have mattered if she'd told him about the Jesuits? Most likely not. He had his Ring. Naught else mattered to him.

Which is precisely why she must get the churlish pirate out of her thoughts completely.

Moving to the looking glass, she yanked pins from her sodden hair and did her best to sift through the tangles with her fingers.

The sounds drifting from downstairs transformed from soft lovers' moans to rising voices.

Doing her best to ignore them, Emeline stared at her reflection and sighed. Why had the captain kissed her? She was no raving beauty, at least not like her sister and mother. Her hair was the color of dull wheat, her face too round, her chin too pointed, and though they had drawn the man's gaze, her breasts were far too small for her body. Besides, no doubt the handsome pirate had his choice of females wherever he went.

Pressing fingers on her lips, she could still feel his touch, smell his musky scent of the sea and rum. *Oh, Lord, why did the first man to kiss me have to be a vile pirate?* When all she ever wanted was a hero like her father or brother.

More importantly, why was she still thinking about him?

The voices from downstairs grew louder. Curses and accusations trumpeted up the stairs. Emeline moved to the door and listened, hugging herself.

Glass shattered. A woman screamed, *"Non, non, arrêtez!"*

Emeline's heart raced. Flinging open her door, she barreled down the stairs, past the front parlor and into the receiving room. A bull of a man slammed Delphine against a wall, pinning her arms beside her and spitting obscenities in her face. Her hair hung in disheveled waves, and a trickle of blood spilled from the corner of her mouth. Eyes full of fear snapped to Emeline.

So, Emeline did the only thing she thought to do. She grabbed a vase from the table, charged the man, and slammed it over his head.

He folded onto Delphine, but the woman quickly shoved him away, sending him toppling to the floor with a thud.

For several minutes, Delphine stared at him, her chest heaving as an odd silence invaded the room. Finally, she looked up, took Emeline's outstretched hand, and stepped over his unconscious body. She trembled as Emeline led her to the settee.

Miss Catherine appeared at the door, her eyes wide as they scanned the man and then her mistress. Shrieking, she flung a hand to her mouth.

"Catherine, please get a rag, a bowl of water, and some honey or comfrey ointment if you have any," Emeline ordered.

The woman sped off as Emeline eased beside Delphine, who was still breathing hard.

"How can I thank you?" she finally muttered, drawing the corners of her robe over her silk nightdress.

"'Tis all right now. You're safe," Emeline said, but Delphine's gaze sped to the brute of a man who had attacked her.

"We must get him outside before he wakes." The urgency in her tone caused Emeline's own nerves to tighten.

"We will." Emeline squeezed her hand as Miss Catherine entered with rags, a bowl of water, and a jar.

She set them down. "What else can I do for you, mistress?" Worry tainted her voice.

When Delphine did not answer, Emeline glanced up. "Some tea would be lovely, Catherine." Nodding, the woman sped off.

Dipping a rag in the water, Emeline dabbed at the blood on Delphine's lips.

Wincing, she tried to push Emeline away. "I'm all right. There is no need."

"At least allow me to put some honey on it. It will stop the bleeding and heal it nicely."

Delphine's blue eyes met Emeline's, fear and shame drifting across them. "We really must remove him."

"Do you have a footman or butler? Anyone who could lift him?" Emeline dabbed the honey on the small cut.

"*Non*, just me and Catherine. I had a groomsman, but I could no longer afford him." Moisture filled the lady's eyes.

"Then we will do it ourselves. Just gather your strength for a moment." Finishing her ministrations, Emeline put down the rag and jar and took Delphine's hand in hers again. "You're still trembling."

"I thought he would kill me." She swallowed hard, her lovely forehead crinkling.

"What happened?"

"*Je ne sais pas*. He's a new client." She pursed her lips, then winced at the pain. "Sometimes they are angry at women, perhaps due to the rebuke of a wife or lover, and they take it out on me."

What a terrible way to live. "I'm so sorry, Delphine. I'm glad I was here."

"I am, as well." Delphine attempted a smile.

But what if Emeline hadn't been there? Would Miss Catherine have rescued her? Or would Delphine now be lying in a pool of her blood with the villain roaming free, for who gave a care for a harlot?

"You told me I could be free from the control of men," Emeline said, "from needing them to protect and provide." Pausing, she lifted a quick prayer for the right words. "Are you not doing the very same thing? Where would you be without men and their wealth?"

At first, she thought she had angered the lady, for Delphine said naught for several minutes. Then she let out a painful sigh and pulled her hand from Emeline's. "Of course you are right, *ma chérie*. I hadn't thought of it in that way. *Mais oui*, I am as much a prisoner of men's power as any woman."

"I know a way to freedom," Emeline blurted out.

Delphine frowned. "Is there such a thing in this world?"

"'Tis found in the Son of God, who died for you, who loves you, and longs to set you free."

"Bah!" Rising, Delphine waved an arm through the air. "There is no freedom found in religion. Only more slavery."

"I quite agree. I don't speak of religion. I speak of a relationship with God Himself. He forgives. He loves. He gives purpose and meaning to your life."

Delphine met Emeline's gaze, suspicion and…perhaps a hint of interest within it? A vision appeared. A man and a young Delphine alone in a darkened room, the man advancing, Delphine cowering. And Emeline knew this poor woman had been ravished when she'd been but a young girl.

"I perceive that something horrible happened to you when you were young, did it not? A man attacked you."

Shock fired from Delphine's eyes. "*Mon dieu*, how…?" She stared at Emeline in confusion, then quickly looked away. "It matters not. It was a long time ago."

Emeline stood. "It matters a great deal, for it has set the course of your life. A life you do not have to live anymore."

Delphine swallowed, then stiffened her jaw. "I will never be beholden to a man again."

"Yet you make yourself so every day." Emeline gestured toward the beast, who thankfully remained unconscious on the floor.

Sorrow and pain spilled from Delphine's eyes before they suddenly hardened again. "*Dépêchez-vous*! We must get him out of here."

It took all three of them to drag the bully out of the house and down the street, lobbing his body over moist cobblestones and through mud puddles. Finally, they deposited him in a muddy heap in front of the physician's home. Even though she was grateful the man didn't wake, Emeline felt a twinge of guilt at the bloody gash on the back of his head.

"Doctor Crenshaw will tend to him," Delphine announced as they walked back to her home.

"'Tis more than he deserves," Catherine added, rubbing the muscles in her arm.

"*Oui.*" Delphine sighed. "But I want no blood on my hands."

"'Twould be on *my* hands," Emeline said, raising her brows, as they mounted the steps to the red door that marked Delphine's house. "However, I do think you need to hire a groomsman for protection. I shudder to think what would have happened if I hadn't come home when I did."

Smiling, Delphine nodded. "I fear you are right. For now, let us all forget this horrid event and enjoy our evening."

An evening that consisted of a cold supper of cheese, bread, salted fish, and an early retirement to each of their beds. Beyond exhaustion, Emeline fell deep asleep despite the frightening events of the day.

Nightmares crept into her mind—the creak of her door opening, the pad of footsteps on the floor boards, the scent of bergamot, a man's whisper.

Then the slam of a hand over her mouth. A rag was stuffed within it. A cloth covered her nose. A sweet, smoky scent filled her lungs. A peace she didn't feel threatened to drag her into unconsciousness. Nay! Flailing her arms, she tried to rise. Muscular arms hefted her up from her bed.

This was no dream. This was real!

Chapter 12

Once again, the familiar sounds and sensations of being out to sea drifted past Emeline's ears—the creak and groan of a ship, the gentle purl of water against the hull, the rolling movement of waves. And the shouts of sailors going about their duties.

Only these shouts were in a foreign language.

Terror seized her, attempting to pull her from the fog that coated her mind. Prying her eyes open, she blinked in an attempt to clear the blurry scene. A cabin. A ship's cabin. The bulkhead and door oscillated in her vision…grew smaller, then larger…then smaller again. Pain thundered in her head. She slammed her eyes shut and spread fingers over the cot beneath her. A soft quilt. An odd scent of bergamot stung her nose.

She pushed to sit up. The cabin spun. Nausea churned in her stomach. Gripping it, she forced it down, trying to remember what had happened.

The last thing she recalled was falling asleep in Delphine's house.

Someone had come into her chamber!

Her head felt as though an anchor had embedded itself into it. Moaning, she dropped it into her hands.

The ship bucked over a wave, and she grabbed the cot to keep from falling. Shouts grew louder above her. Spanish? Nay, Italian.

Jesuits.

Fear clenched her belly, resurrecting her nausea. *Lord, where are You? Why is this happening?*

No peace came. No gentle voice assuring her all was well. Nothing made sense anymore. What could she have possibly done to be worthy of such punishment? She opened her eyes again and examined the cabin. An Italian chest of drawers was bolted to the wall beside a tall looking glass. A pitcher and basin sat atop it, along with two rather large books. Across from her, a brass-buckled mahogany trunk perched in the corner while a silk-woven rug graced the floor. Not an ordinary seaman's cabin.

Lord, what do they want with me?

She remembered her father's words. *Whenever you don't understand some tragedy that has befallen you, you must trust that God has everything under control. There is a purpose for everything. Our job is to obey and have faith.*

At the time she had thought it wise advice from a godly man. Today, it seemed nigh an impossible task.

Alone. Alone again. She hugged herself. Whenever she'd been frightened, whenever she'd felt alone, she would seek out her mother or father or siblings. And her fear and loneliness would dissipate. But now? The cabin spun again. The bulkheads rippled in her vision and seemed to close in on her, shrinking the already tiny space. Was she to be crushed alive?

Heart racing, she gulped in deep breaths in an effort to calm her breathing. She'd been given a drug of some kind. That was it. She was not going mad.

A grinding clank sounded. The door burst open to a blast of salt-laden wind and a tall, lithe man dressed in black. Narrow eyes set too close together undressed her with their gaze above a grin reminiscent of a crocodile's. Without saying a word, he grabbed her arm, hoisted her onto her feet, and yanked her out into a long hall. Lanterns perched onto walls mocked her with gruesome shadows as he dragged her behind him and then shoved her through an open door into a much larger cabin.

A captain's cabin. Signor Arturo Della Morte set down his quill pen and rose from his chair behind an elaborately carved wooden desk. He flicked bejeweled fingers at the man behind her, and within seconds, the door slammed shut. A jolt of fear shrieked down Emeline's spine, as dizziness spiraled through her head.

"Please, sit, *Signorina*." He gestured to a chair upholstered with red velvet before the desk.

Normally, she would not obey a command from such a deviant, but she feared she would fall to the deck if she didn't. The cushion was soft, the chair arms carved and hard, but she gripped them nonetheless, doing her best to stay conscious. "What did you do to me?"

"Do?" Grinning, he circled the desk, tugging at his lacy cuffs.

"I am ill."

"No. Not ill. We merely gave you a bit of opium to assure your cooperation."

Of course. The reason for the nausea and dizziness. Straightening her spine, she faced him. "It will take more than a drug to gain my cooperation, *Signor*."

His lips tightened. "Father. You will address me as father."

"I cannot do so, for I only have one earthly father and one heavenly One."

He stroked his pointed beard. "I see the rumors are true. English dogs have little control over their women's idle tongues."

Rays of sunlight rose and fell over the hideous Jesuit, glinting off the gold epaulets on his shoulders and bold cross around his neck. Beyond him, rich velvet curtains framed paned windows through which waves of a cobalt sea frolicked as if naught was wrong with the world.

But everything was wrong.

Emeline shifted her shoes across the richly woven damask rug, lifting a silent prayer for God to protect her from this man.

"Where is the Ring, *Signorina*?" He gripped the hilt of his jeweled saber, studying her.

"I do not have it. Which I'm sure you discovered when I was, no doubt, violated whilst I was unconscious." The thought of these men's hands groping her brought nausea back to her belly.

He laughed. "We searched you, though not the entirety of your person, for we are men of the cloth, after all."

Men of the pit was more like it. "As I said, I do not have it."

"But you know where it is."

"I threw it in the bay at Basseterre." She winced at her lie, but how else to gain her freedom?

"I do not believe you. You see, you were never out of our sight."

Such intense darkness pooled in his lifeless eyes that she averted her gaze to a large wooden trunk. Birds and flowers were carved in gold along the sides. Quite exquisite work for shipboard furniture.

"Why do you seek it?" she asked. "'Tis just an old relic."

His smile was wide and predatory. "You are quite full of lies for one so young."

She feigned a chuckle she did not feel. "Are you foolish enough to believe a fable, a mere myth, that it holds power?"

His jaw tightened at her insult, and for a moment she thought he'd strike her. But then he drew a deep breath and fidgeted with a silver chalice atop his desk. "If it were not true, then why does Pope Clement XI, the vicar of Christ, demand I bring it to him?"

She wanted to tell him that no man was a vicar of Jesus, no man could ever represent God Almighty. But why anger him further? "I suppose he will reward you greatly for your mission."

"To serve him is enough reward."

Now 'twas her turn to laugh.

Sharp eyes, full of malice and hate, speared her. Then swerving away, he moved to a cabinet, opened it, and retrieved a bottle. "Care for some Chianti?"

"Nay. I prefer to keep my wits about me."

"And you will need them." He poured the wine into the chalice, then spun to face her. "For if you are wise, you will tell me where the Ring is."

She studied him, his insolent stance, his posh attire, the authority he shielded himself with. In his place, a young lad appeared, thin, boney, dressed in rags, running through a small village. She blinked the vision away. Why was God showing her these things? What did they mean?

"You grew up poor, *Signor*, did you not? I see you as a young boy, hungry and cold."

He sipped his wine, but not before she saw a flicker of shock cross his eyes and a wrinkle form on his brow. He laughed. "As you can see, *Signorina*, I am quite wealthy and powerful. Both of which would be to your credit to realize, for your very life is in my hands."

"My life is in God's hands alone." She raised her chin. "Your god is power and money, and I assure you, he will only disappoint."

Without warning, he threw his chalice at her. She ducked. It struck the bulkhead with a loud *thump*. Rage mangling his features, he charged her. She slammed her eyes shut, awaiting his strike. The scent of bergamot flooded her.

Strong hands lifted her from the chair and hurled her against the bulkhead. He clutched her throat and squeezed. She couldn't breathe. Was this to be her end?

Lord?

Struggling for air, she attempted to pry his hand off her neck, but his fingers were stronger than a ship's gasket. She kicked, but her feet met only air.

"I tire of your insolence! Tell me where the Ring is, or I'll kill you right here."

He released her. Gasping, Emeline melted to the floor, gripping her throat. She heard him walk away, pour more Chianti. She had underestimated this man's hatred, his need for power.

"I regret my outburst," he said, "but your vicious tongue is not to be borne. You will find me a gentleman if you cooperate."

Finally able to breathe, Emeline struggled to rise and stared at him. More than anger, more than fear, she felt pity for him. Though a grown man now, attired in velvet and lace, and bearing the mantle of the Pope's authority, he was still that little boy, hungry and cold.

"I do not have the Ring you seek, *Signor*," she coughed out. "It was stolen from me."

Cocking his head, he let out a sigh of frustration. "Ah." He flung dark curls over his shoulder as his face lit. "Captain Blake Keene. I saw his ship in the harbor."

She thought to deny it, but what good would it do? This man was no fool.

"Since you have claimed to be a gentleman, *Signor*, I beg you to set me free. I am of no use to you."

"Ah, but you are, *Signorina*." He grinned. "Are you not Captain Keene's paramour? Surely when he hears you are in grave danger, he will give me the Ring in exchange for your safe return."

Standing upon the quarterdeck under a brisk wind, Blake stared aloft at a moon mocking him from above. Sails trimmed to tops and gallants for the night fluttered in the breeze. Below him, pirates lulled about the deck, drinking their ration of rum. Some played cards, others told fables of great heroics, a few sung an old sailor's chanty.

He rubbed the Ring tight about his finger. It had been a week since he'd taken it from Miss Hyde...*Emeline*. Thus far, it had proven its power over wind and wave, saved him from battle with a Jesuit frigate, and gained him the fortunes of two unsuspecting merchant ships. His crew was happy. Their wealth was amassing, their fame spreading. His plans were coming to fruition.

Then why did he feel like his world was being ripped apart? With the Ring, he could control God's nature, defeat ships in battle, and, if need be, bring naval admirals to their knees. But he could not control his own demons. Each night they rose to haunt him, taunt him, flaunt their putrid damnations, their never-ending blasphemous slurs. Worse when his father appeared. Would the man not leave Blake be, even in death?

Maston slid beside him, bottle of rum in hand. "The crew are restless to spend their coins at port, *Capitaine*. Perhaps we should make for the nearest anchorage. Is not your island close?"

"They are happy enough." The *Summons* leapt over a wave, and Blake gripped the railing, smiling at his bosun. "Perhaps 'tis you who longs to go ashore?"

Maston sipped his rum and snorted. "You know me well, *Capitaine*. I could use some female company."

Aye, Blake *did* know Maston. They had much in common. They both had endured brutal childhoods, both sought all they could out of life, grabbing for every bit of wealth and happiness. But they differed as well. More than wealth, Blake needed control. He would never grant anyone the power to hurt him again.

"Very well. We'll make way for Keene Island. I need to offload my portion of the treasure." *Home.* At least the only home he'd known. "If the crew remains restless after that, I'll find some debauched port to satisfy their lusts."

Maston handed him the bottle. "I will inform them."

Grabbing it, Blake took a sip and gave it back.

"I'll be takin' some o' that," Rummy called from the wheel behind them and, laughing, Maston headed his way.

Jabbering brought Blake's gaze to Bandit swinging down the ratlines. The traitorous monkey landed on the bulwarks beside Sam Goode, who stood in his usual spot at night, brooding over the inky sea.

Blake had a question for the only man on board with half a brain. Leaping down the quarterdeck ladder, he eased beside him at the railing. Wind, ripe with the scent of salt and fish, tore over him, and he breathed it in like a familiar elixir.

Bandit screeched and leapt onto Blake's shoulder.

"Good eve to you, Captain," Sam said, though his tone indicated anything but pleasure at having his brooding interrupted.

"You are a man of philosophy and science," Blake began, hoping the flattery would get the man talking. "What do you know of nightmares? Are they merely fabrications of one's deepest fears? Or do they come from some outside source?"

Silence, save for the rush of the sea and the drunken shouts of pirates, answered him.

Finally, Sam leaned further upon the railing and clasped his hands. Moonlight glistened off his short-cropped gray hair. "What possible force outside of one's own mind could they hail from, Captain? I fear these superstitious cullions you call a crew have befuddled your mind."

Indeed. A fortnight ago, Blake would have agreed and dismissed the dreams. But he'd never had nightmares, even during the worst of times. Not like those since he'd acquired the Ring. "I do believe there are powers beyond what we mere humans can know."

The wind shifted, flapping the sails above, and blasting over Blake, tossing hair into his face. He snapped it aside.

At the risk of his surgeon thinking him mad, he continued. "But what if nightmares become real, visible to one's sense of sight and hearing?"

Grunting, Sam gripped the leather baldric strung across his chest and gave Blake a look of censure. "I'd say you've been overindulging in rum, Captain. Perhaps 'tis the woman that has driven you mad. You abandoned her on St. Kitts?"

"Aye." Though Blake bristled at the term *abandoned*.

The old man's gaze locked upon Blake. "Good. Beware of losing yourself to feminine devices, for they are only illusions."

"Never fear, I have not thought of her since," Blake lied. The enigmatic Emeline Hyde had oft been on his mind this past week. No matter how hard he tried to scatter all memory of her. Yet...he studied his friend, only then recalling that 'twas a woman who had ruined him. "Are you never to seek the company of a good woman, Sam?"

He gave a sad laugh. "Is there such a thing?"

Bandit, silent until then, let out a screech as if answering the man. Oddly, it sounded as though the monkey had said yes! Blake shook his head. This wasn't the first time he thought he understood the little beast, nor the first time it seemed Bandit understood him. He twisted the Ring on his finger. Either he was going mad, or this was another power the Ring possessed. But to what purpose?

Blake chuckled. "Perhaps next time, choose a woman who is not already married?"

"I admit to the mistake." Sam stared out to sea. "But 'twas her betrayal to her husband, the admiral, that enslaved me upon a ship of the line."

Blake nodded. So he'd heard.

"Was it not a woman who nearly ruined you?" Sam asked. "You would be wise to learn from that mistake."

Blake ground his teeth. *Josephine Arnaud.* 'Twas the French vixen's betrayal that set him on his present course. "*Nearly ruined*, being the prudent phrase, for I learned much from the encounter." *And* the heartbreak. "As should you. You are free now, Sam. You have wealth. You can choose more wisely and live out your days in happiness."

"Bah." Sam shook his head. "'As for man, his days are as grass: as a flower of the field, so he flourisheth. For the wind passeth over it, and it is gone; and the place thereof shall know it no more.' That is the lot of all men."

As if confirming his words, a gust of wind tore over them, forcing Bandit to grip Blake's neck to keep from falling.

Scripture? Sam Goode quoting the Bible? Surprising. 'Twas even more surprising that Blake recognized it from the times his mother would read to him the Holy Writ. So many years ago. He gripped the cross around his neck. He'd always thought the passage morbid. Why ponder one's fate when there was still life to live?

"Then I leave you to your musings." Pushing from the railing with Bandit still atop his shoulder, Blake mounted the quarterdeck ladder and nodded at Rummy as he leapt down the companionway. As soon as he approached his cabin, the madcap monkey leapt from him and rushed back down the hall, screeching as if he'd seen a ghost. Blake could swear he heard the word evil within the beast's shrieks.

Perhaps he had. Ever since Blake had returned to the ship, Bandit refused to enter his cabin. It made no sense, but then again, many things didn't make sense at the moment. Like the darkness he felt in his cabin. More than a sense of evil. A palpable presence. Eerie cries and moans that burned his ears, sights that turned his blood to ice. Not only when he was in his cabin. He'd seen and heard the specters throughout the ship. Yet when he pointed them out to his crew, no one else could see them.

Pouring himself a shot of rum, he perched on the stern window ledge and stared upon the dark sea where faint moonlight sprayed white glitter over select waves. He rubbed his eyes. He'd not slept in a week. The Ring warmed his finger, and he closed his hand over it and braced for what was coming.

The black creatures returned, swaying, undulating, filling his cabin with a weight Blake felt pressing against his soul. Then the voices came, all muttering together, anguish and agony in their tones. He could make out only a few phrases in their demonic babble.

Doomed. Murderer. Worthless.

He closed his eyes, trying to shut them out, hoping his father would not join them as he so often did.

Emeline Hyde. Hadn't the dark figures vanished in her presence? There was goodness in her. Purity. She kept the evil part of the Ring at bay. He craved its power, but he could not go on like this. He found no joy in his recent victories, no peace in his sleep, no happiness in the pleasures he once enjoyed. He must find a way to control these demonic forces, and he had but one recourse.

Aye, no matter what, he must find Emeline and get her back.

Chapter 13

"She is no longer here." Delphine Lavigne stood in the doorway, her shoulders back, her eyes full of more pain than Blake had ever seen. She also wore a more modest gown, which was odd.

He knew he'd hurt her, but there was naught to be done for it now. She could hardly expect him to make a commitment to a strumpet, despite the promises he'd whispered to her in the night. Though a rather beautiful strumpet at that, as his gaze took her in, remembering fondly their time together. Only a small cut on her lip and a fading bruise on her cheek marred her beauty.

"What do you mean? Where is she?" He gripped the hilt of his cutlass, glancing down the street.

"I have no idea, Blake. She disappeared in the middle of the night without a word. Though…" Delphine pursed her lips.

"Though…?"

"It seems she may have been taken against her will." Fear quivered in her voice.

Alarm shot through him. "By whom?"

"I do not know, but she mentioned being followed."

Blake hung his head. Who would have cared to take an unknown woman with nigh a penny to her name?

"Now, if you please, I'm soon to set sail." Delphine started to shut the door.

Only then did he notice the portmanteau and bags perched in the foyer. "Where are you going?"

She gripped the edge of the door, leaning her head against it. "I'm going to live with my sister on Martinique." Both sorrow and a strange determination filled her eyes. "I'm out of the business, Blake. Starting over."

Shocked, Blake shook his head. "Why? What happened?" He reached up to touch her bruise, but she slapped him away before he could.

"Find her, Blake. She's a good woman, decent, kind. Though you don't deserve her."

That much was true. He didn't deserve Emeline, but he needed her. And at the moment, she might need him *if* she was in trouble. For he doubted word would have reached her family so soon.

"Take care of yourself, Delphine." Turning, he descended the steps.

"Did you ever love me, Blake?" Her voice followed him, tugging on his heart.

Halting, he faced her, an odd guilt twisting his insides. "I'm incapable of loving anyone. You know that." Before he witnessed more pain on her face, he walked away, full of more confusion and angst than he cared to admit.

Back on board the *Summons*, Finn approached him, pipe in his mouth and scrap of parchment in his hand.

"Message came fer ye, Cap'n."

"From whom?" Blake took it as his men hauled the cockboat on deck.

"Dunno. Sailor rowed it over t' us after ye left. Said some men paid 'im t' deliver it t' the *Summons* if he sees it make anchor."

The wax seal bore an unusual crest but one he'd seen before, one which turned the blood in his veins to ice. Breaking it, he opened the missive.

The Ring for Miss Hyde. Sail Northwest toward San Juan Bautista. You'll find a small island south southeast off the coast of St. Thomas. Sail into the bay. I'll find you.

Use the power of the Ring and she is dead.
Father Arturo Della Morte

Boom! Boom! The cot shook beneath Emeline. She sprang up in bed, heart pounding. *Boom*! A cannon blast! At least a twenty-pounder, from the sound of it. Who were they firing upon? She had no window to peer through. No way to know if it was day or night. Several days must have passed—how many, she had no idea. In her loneliness and despair, she'd lost track of time. She'd lost track of her sanity. And if not for the presence of Almighty God, she'd surely have lost her life as well.

She'd not seen Senor Della Morte again. Not since he'd called her Captain Keene's paramour. Not since he'd nearly choked her to death. In fact, she'd seen no one, save the same skinny man who had first come to her cabin. Each day he came only once—with food and to empty her chamber pot. Each day, he responded to her questions with a single sneer before he left.

She asked him to relay a message to his captain—that she was most definitely not Captain Keene's mistress, and that the knave would *definitely not* give a care whether she lived or died. All truths which needed to be explained. Still, she had no idea whether the messages reached the vicious Jesuit captain at all.

Were they now engaging in battle? With her below deck where a shot could blow her to bits? What did it matter? She had made her peace with God.

Well, she hoped she had, anyway. During the long days and nights, she'd appealed to Him for help and comfort, and she'd felt His warm, loving presence. She knew He was with her and there was a reason for all of this madness. What she didn't know or understand was what that reason could possibly be.

Thus far, she'd been kidnapped twice, spent days in a brothel, discarded like so much refuse by one man, then nearly killed by another. If God sent her on this mission to spread the good news of the Gospel, she'd done her best. She'd witnessed of the love of God to a pirate and a trollop, but neither had paid her any mind.

Lord, you should have sent my sister or brother on this mission, for I am certainly failing in every way. In her loneliness, she'd finally realized that God was the One who had granted her words of knowledge, visions of understanding her enemies, but what good had it done? Surely in the hands of someone more worthy, this gift would do its mighty work.

Another thunderous blast rang, but this one from another ship. A nearby ship.

Dropping to her knees, she began to pray for the safety of all involved.

"Land ho!" The expected shout came down from the crosstrees, prompting Blake to raise the spyglass to his eye. There, less than a mile off their starboard bow, the small islet burst from the sea like a cork floating atop a bottle of azure wine.

Blake knew that spit of land, for he'd careened there often. The Jesuit had chosen well. The shallow bay would allow only the *Summons* to enter, whereas its narrow inlet could easily be guarded by the Jesuit's Venetian Frigate, preventing their quick escape. Which was exactly what Blake would need—a quick escape. *If* his plan were to work.

That *if* had been scraping away at his soul for a day. 'Twas a huge *if*, one that relied on too many variables for his comfort, even for his normally crazed ventures. But what choice did he have? Even with all its power, the Ring was useless to him if wearing it sent him to the madhouse.

Scanning the area, he spotted the bare masts and furled sails of said frigate coming into view hugging the leeward side

of the island. *Hang it*! The Jesuit captain had positioned his
ship so that should Blake decide to fire upon it, he'd have to
sail within range and scope of the frigate's twenty eighteen-
pounders. All of which were run out and ready to fire.

And fire they did. *Boom*! One of them belched its load,
jetting black smoke in the air and flinging a shot into the sea
just yards off the *Summons'* starboard quarter.

A greeting, no doubt, but still Blake groaned and focused
the glass onto the frigate's deck. A man in black—not Della
Morte—stood amidships, his arms crossed over his chest,
spouting orders to the crew, none of whom rushed around in
the usual frenzy of battle. Certainly Della Morte had not
ordered them to sink the very ship that carried the Ring he so
desperately craved.

Two more shots erupted, both landing in the sea.

Blake's crew cursed and dashed about. Lowering the
scope, he found Maston staring up at him with a scowl.
"Orders, *Capitaine*?"

"Warning shots," Blake said. "Charlie!" he shouted to the
master gunner, "return our greeting if you please." Nodding,
she promptly directed her crew to fire one of the guns into the
open sea.

The *Summons* crested a wave, sending foamy water over
her bow. Blake gripped the railing as Finn uttered a string of
foul curses beside him and ran a sleeve over the sweat on his
forehead.

"All this fer a wench! Have ye lost yer mind, Cap'n? I
says it's a trap an' we's outgunned an' outmanned. We'll be
sunk t' the depths fer sure."

Behind them at the helm, Rummy belched his agreement.

Blake frowned. They were right, of course.

After completing her task, Charlie gazed at Blake with
skepticism.

Even Maston, who loved a wild adventure, raised
incriminating brows at him as he ordered the topmen to lower
sails.

Movement brought Blake's gaze to Bandit swinging down the backstay. He landed on the starboard railing, his little monkey eyes spearing Blake as he screeched and shrieked as if the world were coming to an end.

Perhaps it was. Perhaps Blake was the biggest fool of all to risk his crew, his ship, and, quite possibly, all their lives. All to save Emeline. *And* regain control of the dark side of the Ring. Of course, he couldn't tell his crew that last part. All they knew was he traded a Ring for the woman, and though there'd been complaining and grumbling and even calling for a vote, one reminder of the fortune he'd recently acquired for them shut their mouths.

He finally answered Finn. "Do you know what the Jesuits will do to Miss Hyde if I do not at least attempt her rescue?"

"Scupper me, Cap'n! Wha' business be it o' ours?" Rummy chimed in with disgust. "The woman got 'erself into trouble. Let 'er get out o' it."

Blake swept stern eyes to the helmsman. "*We* got her into this trouble, and we are going to get her out. You take me?"

The helmsman grimaced but quickly looked away, keeping his one hand on the wheel.

Cursing, Blake rubbed the back of his neck, attempting to stifle his rising doubts. But the ghoulish demons had only grown more intense, the nightmares more frightening. Even worse, his father kept appearing, each time more grotesque in form and more enraged with hatred. He hadn't slept in over a week and he was truly starting to wonder if he'd lost all sense. He needed Miss Hyde...*Emeline*. She was a ray of light in a dark world. A goodness and innocence the world desperately needed. *He* needed. In truth, he could not get the kiss he'd stolen from her out of his mind. Nor the sensations it stirred.

Besides, he had the Ring. He'd not gone to such lengths to acquire it only to back down from the challenge of a mewling muckrake.

Pedro hopped on deck from the hatch amidships, hauling a bag of gunpowder for Charlie, along with some matchsticks.

After handing them to the master gunner, he leapt up the quarterdeck and approached Blake.

"We're rescuin' Miss Hyde, Cap'n?" His blue eyes sparkled with excitement.

Finn groaned.

"That is the plan," Blake said then shouted to Maston to take in fore and main. The bosun promptly brayed further orders to the crew, sending more men scrambling aloft.

"Hard a starboard, Rummy. Watch your luff. Bring her in nice and easy."

Finn scratched beneath his bandana. "We're headin' into the bay? We'll be prime fer the pickin', like fish in a net!"

Rummy growled.

Pedro gazed at the island. "But we gotta rescue Miss Hyde. She's a good lady."

Stunned, Blake stared at the lad. He had no idea the woman had made such an impression. "Never fear, Pedro. I'll do my best to keep her safe. Now, run along. Bring up more gunpowder in case we need it."

Smiling, the boy sped away.

After casting Blake a look of scorn, Finn stuffed his pipe back in his mouth and ambled off to attend his duties. Blake, however, was not granted a moment's peace as Maston eased beside him.

"The crew's none too happy, *Capitaine*," he whispered over the rush of wind. "There's no treasure to be had and no reason to risk our lives."

Squinting in the noonday sun, Blake scanned his raucous crew spread across the main and foredeck and those up in the yards. Fifty filthy, ill-mannered souls, bloodthirsty men who'd just as soon gut him like a fish if he didn't keep them floating on gold. Aye, he supposed a few of them were loyal, but most he dared never turn his back on. "Will they obey for now?"

Removing his tricorn, Maston ran a hand through his damp hair. "*Oui*, but only because you've gained them much coin. Though none can quite grasp why you engage in this devil-may-care rescue."

Wind tore over Blake, cooling his sweat and tossing his hair behind him. Devil-may-care, indeed. For if there was a devil, he'd definitely not want Miss Hyde rescued. The thought gave him some satisfaction.

"Janson!" Maston yelled aloft. "Ease the sheets, brace yards to larboard!" Then turning to Blake, he said, "You have your magical Ring. What need have you for the woman? There are wenches aplenty across the Caribbean."

Suspicion rose as Blake studied his bosun. He hadn't remembered telling him about the Ring, and especially not that it possessed power. Perhaps Emeline had spoken of it, or an unintentional mention had slipped through Blake's inebriated lips. He would have to be more careful. "What now? A magical Ring? Have you taken to your cups early, Maston? And I do not rescue the lady to become my mistress."

"*Mon Dieu*, what other reason could there be?" His brow furrowed as he shook his head at the utter ridiculousness of the thought. "But you are the *capitaine, non*?" He shrugged.

"I am. Now enough of this." He waved him away, and planting his hat atop his head, the bosun marched off.

Taking a deep breath, Blake gazed at the island. The fronds of palm trees lining golden sand waved at him in greeting. Through the narrow inlet, calm turquoise waters beckoned him. To victory or to death?

"Crank, take the soundings," he ordered, and the man grabbed the log-and-line and flung it over the railing. 'Twould not do for Blake to run aground. Not only would he look a fool, but he'd be completely at the Jesuit's mercy.

As Crank shouted out the measurements, the *Summons* eased through the inlet of the bay, passing the frigate off their starboard side. The ship's guns winked at them in the sunlight as the eyes of the Jesuit crew followed his every move. Where was Della Morte? No doubt already on land.

Wind whipped off the turquoise waters, bringing the scent of earth and tropical flowers, normally pleasant odors that meant a break from the perils at sea.

He fingered the Ring. His plan relied on two critical things. One, this ancient jewel—a capricious relic that possessed both evil and good. And two, an even more capricious monkey. Would either of them obey him today? If not, they'd soon all be dead at the bottom of the sea.

No sooner did Emeline's feet touch the sand than her legs turned to pudding. They would have folded beneath her if not for the two brutes gripping her arms. Their fingers clamped tighter as they dragged her from the water through a thick section of sea grape and mangroves out onto the shore of a small bay. They all but shoved her down onto the sand and ordered her to stay as one would order a dog. Other Jesuits emerged from the foliage behind them, including the infamous Father Della Morte, dressed in attire so fine one would think he attended a coronation rather than a savage parlay, save for the myriad weapons strapped about his waist. A string of Italian spilled from his lips as he ordered his men to hide amongst the greenery, weapons at the ready. At least that's what Emeline assumed as she watched them scramble away.

Blinking, she continued adjusting her eyes to the bright sun overhead and her legs to being on land again. Stretching them out before her, she rubbed them and attempted to stand. Thankfully, Della Morte paid her little mind as he spoke to one of his Jesuits a few yards away. The palms that lined the shore danced in her vision, but finally the world around her settled and her legs grew firm.

Her heart was another matter. A light breeze stirred her skirts and slapped hair into her face. Flipping the strands away, she inhaled the sweet fragrance of fresh Caribbean air and lifted her head to the warm sun. Though 'twas truly wonderful to be out of that tiny cabin, she had no idea why she'd been brought here. But she *did* know the reason could not be good.

At least not for her.

A ship sailed slowly into the bay. The *Summons*? Aye, 'twas Captain Keene's brig! There he stood on the quarterdeck, poised tall and strong as if he sailed into port victorious after battle. To say she was shocked would not describe the jolt that nearly sent her tumbling back to the sand. Why would he come? He had the Ring. He had proven himself to be no hero, no defender of the weak or needy. There had to be something else he wanted from the Jesuits.

Either way, she allowed a speck of hope to settle in her heart as she whispered a prayer,

Lord, let Your will be done and no lives lost.

Chapter 14

B lake wanted to vomit at the look of impertinence on the hawkish princox's face. Gripping the hilt of his cutlass, his fingers ached to draw it and put an end to the Jesuit captain's miserable life. He'd do so if not for the lady standing just yards behind the odious beast, a look of terror twisting her lovely features.

He'd spotted her as soon as they'd sailed into the bay, kept his eye on her as they brought the brig to a halt and dropped anchor, and felt her eyes lock upon him as he, Finn, and Maston, along with Bandit, rowed the jollyboat to shore.

Now, as he approached Arturo Della Morte, the Ring warmed on his finger. Odd, that. 'Twas as if it knew what he intended to do. Perhaps reading minds was another of its powers, for he had yet to discover all its secrets.

The Jesuit cocked his hip, grinning as Blake and his men approached. On either side of him, two fellow Jesuits eyed the proceedings as if bored, both dressed in the same black suits with golden insignia, pearl-colored Venetian hose, and doublets with sleeves stitched in silver. Over Della Morte's shoulder, Blake dared a glance at Emeline. The tangled strands of her hair waved across her waist in the light breeze. Her gown was wrinkled and stained, but he could see no wounds on her skin. Only the ones in her gaze as she stared his way. Still, she stood tall and sturdy, her chin out, her jaw stiff, her lips flat. No wilting flower here.

Movement amongst the trees alerted him that Della Morte had hidden men for a possible ambush. As Blake expected. Also, as he expected, the bow of the Jesuit frigate peeked around the inlet and floated across the entrance, blocking their exit.

But Blake had a few surprises of his own. Halting before the Jesuit, he studied him. Ringlets of dark hair danced about his shoulders as he fingered a pointed beard sprouting from his chin with one hand and gripped the hilt of a jeweled saber with the other. A breeze drifted in from the sea, stirring the purple plume atop the man's hat.

"What need of all this?" Blake waved a hand toward the frigate and then the men hidden in the forest. "Seems my reputation precedes me of being a formidable foe. You are right to fear me."

Finn chuckled.

"Ha!" Della Morte snorted, while his greedy eyes latched onto the Ring on Blake's finger. "The only reputation you have is one of a thief and swindler. Therefore, I took precautions. Now, let us be done with it." He held out his open palm. "The Ring, if you please."

Blake gestured toward Emeline. "The lady first, if *you* please."

Della Morte blew out a huff and gestured for her to be brought forward. "Despicable how you Englishmen are domineered by your women. Ergo, under the circumstances, I counted on your doting infatuation."

One of his men retreated and dragged Emeline forward.

Blake ground his teeth. Maston gripped the hilt of his blade.

Against every impulse to run the insolent bawcock through, Blake gave a tight smile. "I count on your honor, Signor, since you present yourself as the Pope's man."

The Jesuit's slit-like eyes dropped to the cross around Blake's neck. "It is a blasphemy for you to wear our Lord's cross."

"No more than you, Signor," Blake returned.

The accusation hit its mark as Della Morte grimaced and once again stroked the hilt of his blade.

His man brought Emeline to stand beside the Jesuit fool.

Blake met her gaze—a longing, along with terror, in her eyes and a confidence he hoped he was conveying in his.

Della Morte held out his hand once again. Sunlight reflected off the jewels already adorning his fingers as wind fluttered the lace of his wide, embroidered sleeves.

Out of the corner of his eye, Blake spotted Bandit perched upon the branch of a nearby tree. Everything relied on the monkey's undying infatuation with two things—Emeline and the Ring. Along with the power of the relic to communicate with animals, for he'd divulged Bandit's part of the plan to the creature earlier, trusting the beast could understand Blake as well as he seemed to understand him. Or so he hoped.

"Don't give it to him, Captain." The lady finally spoke up, her voice strong yet trembling. "He will use it for much evil."

Of that Blake had no doubt.

One of Della Morte's brows arched as he gave an impatient sigh. "I could order my men to shoot you right here. Not to mention"—he gestured toward his frigate blocking the entrance to the bay—"one signal from me, and my crew will blast your paltry brig to splinters. Ergo, only by my grace do you stand here unscathed."

"I believe it has naught to do with your grace, as you say, but the rules you've no doubt heard about the Ring." Blake cocked a brow.

Della Morte scowled. "If you refer to the myth that I cannot pry it off a dead man's finger, I am aware, though not entirely convinced."

"It must be given or found alone without a body. That includes a corpse. 'Tis no myth," Blake said. "Dare to test it?"

From the look twisting Della Morte's face, he found the challenge hard to resist. "Hand it over at once or she dies!" His loud outburst scattered birds from a nearby tree.

Yanking it from his finger, Blake held it in the air between them, just out of the Jesuit's reach. "The woman?"

At one nod from Della Morte, his man pushed Emeline toward Blake. Catching her, he quickly handed her to Maston beside him, but not before he felt her warmth, heard the slight intake of her breath. Against his will, an odd joy swirled through him that he had the power to rescue this sweet flower. The first decent thing he remembered doing in quite some time.

"Don't, Blake," she protested.

He dropped the Ring into the puckish wastrel's hand.

Della Morte examined it, a huge grin stretching his mouth wide before he uttered a yelp of victory.

Blake gestured for Maston to take Emeline and retreat.

"You are a bigger fool than I thought," Della Morte crowed.

Blake grinned. "Am I, now?"

Shrieking startled the Jesuits. Bandit dropped from the tree, dashed across the sand, leapt in the air, and snatched the Ring from Della Morte's hand before the Jesuit captain knew what happened.

Cursing, he plucked the flintlock from his belt, cocked it, and pointed it at the monkey. "Give that back to me, you bedeviled beast!"

Emeline screamed. The shot missed Bandit as he scrambled to the woman and gave her the Ring.

Perfect! Spinning, Blake raced across the sand, pulling Emeline along with him. Timing was everything now.

"After them! Shoot them!" Della Morte roared as he reloaded his flintlock.

Clutching Emeline, Blake dove into the brush behind a group of boulders he'd spotted earlier. Maston and Finn, pistols drawn, followed as they'd been instructed. Twenty of his crew, whom he'd snuck ashore on the other side of the *Summons*, came grunting and shouting from the jungle, blades and knives drawn like the pack of savages they were.

Shots echoed across the water, wind, and sand.

Blake took the Ring from Emeline. "Get behind me!" He nudged her back.

Della Morte and his crew charged toward them, kicking up sand, shouting obscenities, pistols loaded, and blades drawn. Nothing stopped them, not even when they spotted Blake's men heading toward them. Instead, they shouted all the more ferociously and quickly engaged the oncoming horde.

Finn and Maston fired, striking two of them.

Blake slipped the Ring back on his finger. "Hurricane, rise now!"

There would either be a deadly battle on this island today, or the power of the Ring would save them all.

"Stay here!" he shouted to Emeline, then leapt over the boulder, drew his cutlass, and swept the blade down on the first Jesuit he encountered. His blade met flesh, and the man held his side and stumbled away.

Turning, Blake found Della Morte marching toward him, fire in his eyes.

Raising his cutlass, he met the man's first blow with force, the clank of metal screeching through the air. He forced him back, but the Jesuit recovered quickly and drove his saber toward Blake's legs. He leapt out of the way and swept his blade in from the right.

Above them, the sky grew thick with black, rolling clouds. Wind whipped up sand, stinging Blake's eyes. Wavelets turned into mighty rollers crashing ashore.

Thunder bellowed. Chest heaving, Della Morte glanced toward the sea where his frigate lurched over incoming waves.

The Ring was working!

The *Summons* would be safe in the shelter of the island. But not the Venetian Frigate. Too big to seek safety in the bay, it would surely be driven into rocks and reefs and damaged beyond repair. Unless they raised sails and scudded out to sea before the wind. Which was exactly what Blake counted on.

Saber still raised, Della Morte glanced up at the angry sky, now black and churning like a witch's cauldron. The wind grew fiercer. Sand spun in cyclones, buffeting Jesuits and pirates alike, both of whom had ceased fighting and were bumbling about.

Della Morte made one more attempt to slice Blake, but the wind plucked his saber from his grip as if it were made of parchment. His desperate eyes latched upon the Ring on Blake's finger. He struggled to reach it, wrestling against wind and sand, but both shoved him back.

With a mighty growl, the black clouds above them released bucketfuls of rain, drenching everything in sight.

"Back to the *Guerrieri Della Croce*!" Della Morte howled above the torrent.

Straining to stand upright, Blake could barely distinguish the Jesuits' blurry figures fading into the sand.

"Take cover, men!" Struggling to walk, he finally found the boulder and dropped behind it. Emeline lay curled in a ball, and he covered her with his body against the raging wind and rain.

Emeline had wanted to watch the battle. Had wanted to make a dash for it into the jungle should it appear the Jesuits were winning. But the storm Blake had unleashed with the Ring not only forbade her to move, it ripped the breath from her lungs. She covered her head with her hands and did her best to shield herself from the sand that stung like grapeshot and the wind punching her from every side.

When Blake covered her with his body, an odd stillness settled on her heart. She felt protected, not merely from wind and rain, but from other dangers as well. Which of course made no sense, for the man had proven himself naught but a depraved pirate. Yet his warmth and unique scent soothed her, giving her a reprieve from the storm raging from within and the one from without. No doubt this strange sensation was only because his presence meant he and his men had been victorious over the Jesuit band. Whether that was a good thing for her, she could not know. Though if given the choice, she'd much rather be in the company of these pirates than Jesuits, for she'd sensed an evil, an insidious darkness about them that was absent even from the bloodthirsty buccaneers.

Raindrops bounced off the boulder, then poured down in rivulets, forming a puddle beneath her, soaking her skirts. To her right, a thousand drops pummeled the sand like the deafening march of a demonic army. Sand became silt. The pounding turned to splashing as a surge of seawater crashed over them. Waves were overtaking the tiny island!

In an instant, Blake's warmth was gone. Strong hands gripped her arms and hauled her to her feet. Flinging an arm around her waist, he dove into the wind and dragged her to a band of trees. Others joined them, blurry, shifting figures. Somewhere she heard Bandit screeching.

In moments, her gown grew heavy with rain, dragging behind her. She tried to open her eyes, but the rain and sand forced them shut again.

"You are safe!" She thought she heard Blake shout, but it seemed a mere figment of her imagination. She *felt,* rather than saw the trees swaying around her, giant monsters coming to life by the power of the storm. Their creak and groan reminded her of a ship at sea, the clamor of their buffeted leaves near deafening. Still, their towering presence offered a limited fortress against the elements. Finally, she was able to open her eyes. The first thing she saw was Blake's concerned expression as he lowered her to sit beside the sturdy trunk of a calabash tree. Water dripped from strands of his dark hair as it billowed about him. Rain glistened over his neck and chest and glued his shirt to muscle and sinew. The cross and sun emblem dangled before him.

"Stay here," he shouted. Then gripping the Ring still around his finger, he struggled to stand against the wind and peered toward the shore.

Several of his crew surrounded them, hunching against the storm as Bandit leapt into her lap and clung to her for dear life.

What was Blake waiting for? Why did he not use the Ring to stop this madness before they were all swept away? *Lord, please help us*!

The eerie whine of the wind lessened. The trees slowed their raucous dance. The torrent of rain became droplets. 'Twas as if the storm had spent its fury, satisfied its anger, and now drifted off to lick its wounds. Within moments, golden daggers of sunlight cleaved through dark clouds and speared the canopy.

Emeline wiped water from her eyes and glanced up at Blake standing before her, rubbing the Ring. He shook his head, scattering rainwater over her before uttering a yelp of victory.

His men rose like sodden skeletons from their graves, shaking off moisture and grinning with exhilaration at simply being alive. A few bore bloody gashes, but most looked well enough.

Sweeping off his tricorn, Maston tipped it and chuckled at the stream pouring from it to the ground. Finn fished out his pipe from inside his waistcoat and sniffed the sodden tobacco with a scowl. Shoving it back into his pocket, he tugged off his gray bandana and wrung it out, his bald head glistening in a shaft of sunlight. Rummy drew a flask from his drenched coat, uncorked it, and took a sip.

Bandit finally released Emeline, but instead of skittering away, he wrapped his hairy arms around her neck and hugged her. At least she had one friend she could count on in this mad adventure. Still, he made it difficult for her to stand, especially with her heavy skirts that were now hopelessly tangled around her legs.

Water *plip-plopped* from leaves onto muddy puddles, but thank God the wind had lessened into a light breeze. She attempted to stand again.

A hand appeared in her vision—a large hand with the Ring on one finger. She followed it to find Blake's handsome face smiling at her from within a frame of wet dark hair.

Smiling?

He had rescued her. At great risk to his ship and crew. *And to the Ring.* When there was no need, no reason to take such a gamble. Why?

For a moment she allowed herself to hope that perhaps, just perhaps, there was a bit of gallantry lurking beneath the surface of the shallow, vainglorious pirate—that perhaps he was the hero she'd sought all her life.

Clinging to Bandit with one hand, she gripped Blake's with her other, and he swooped her to her feet. Unfortunately, her saturated web of skirts upset her balance, and she fell against him. His torso was rock-hard, his shirt cold, his breath warm, and his smile salacious.

Shoving from him, she looked away, confused at her body's reaction.

"Yer plan worked." Finn was the first to speak up, drawing Blake's gaze. "Leastwise wit' a little 'elp from a storm."

"Did you have any doubt?" He raked back his damp hair, grinning.

Maston chuckled. "Impossible. Only you could have pulled it off, *Capitaine.*" He gestured toward the Ring on Blake's finger, an odd gleam in his eye as he winked. "But that squall? Odd that it came upon us so suddenly. Seems we are the luckiest bunch of cutthroats who ever sailed the Spanish Main."

Struggling to rise, Rummy raised his flask. "Scupper and sink me, 'ere's to madcap plans an' hurricanes."

The other pirates laughed as Blake started forward.

Still clinging to Emeline, Bandit jabbered on and on as she followed the pirates. For what other choice did she have? Ahead she spotted the *Summons* through the trees, looking none the worse for the storm's impact. No doubt knowing what he'd intended to do, Captain Keene had braced all yards, bound all sheets, battened all hatches, and securely anchored the hull.

Within minutes, his crew rowed the jollyboat to the ship, and Emeline found herself once again on the main deck, standing amidst a crew of depraved miscreants. Ignoring her, Blake shouted orders to check for damage and ready the ship to set sail.

"There's no telling how far the storm took the Jesuits," he spoke to Finn beside him. "Best to get underway as soon as possible."

"Aye, Cap'n." Nodding, Finn ambled off, shouting commands to unfurl sails, cast off lines, and man the capstan.

Charlie approached, winked at Emeline, and stood before Blake. "Quite the storm, Cap'n."

"Good work handling the ship." He glanced at Emeline once again as one would a prisoner. Any affection or concern she thought she'd sensed earlier dissipated with the storm. "Take the woman to her cabin. Get her some dry attire."

Bandit leapt from Emeline's arms into the ratlines and scrambled above while Charlie escorted her below to the same cabin she'd been imprisoned in before.

"Glad you're safe, Miss." Charlie headed out the door. "Take off your gown, an' I'll find you something t' wear."

Emeline longed to ask the woman about the young child she'd seen in Basseterre, but exhaustion and fear consumed her, and all she could say was, "Thank you."

Once the door slammed shut, loneliness crowded in again. Here she was in the same prison as before, feeling much like a ragdoll snatched back and forth by two spoiled brats. A chill overtook her, and she hugged herself, shivering.

Lord, what am I doing here again?

She plopped onto the bed. Things only seemed to be getting worse. "Oh, Papa, where are you?" Even if her father received her missive and sailed to St. Kitts, she was no longer there. And he'd have no idea where to search next.

Now she was once again at the mercy of this insolent rogue. Why had he risked so much to kidnap her again when he could have his pick of women in the Caribbean? There were only two reasons she could think of. One, he intended to steal her maidenhood merely for the fun of it, or two, he thought to gain a heavy ransom from her father for her return. Perhaps both. Which terrified her all the more.

Chapter 15

B lake lowered the spyglass and grinned. They'd been underway for more than an hour and not a speck of canvas—in particular, *Jesuit* canvas—appeared on the horizon. Above him, sails thundered in the stiff trade winds as the creak and groan of timbers and splash of the sea filled the air with a far more pleasing harmony than any orchestra he'd ever heard.

"Tack to larboard, Rummy," Blake hollered over his shoulder at the one-armed helmsman. Then, gazing up at the location of the sun, he added. "Four points, south by southeast."

"Aye, aye, Cap'n."

"Maston, standby to tack! Ready about!" Blake's order sent his bosun marching across the main deck, issuing further orders to adjust headsails and brace yards in preparation for their turn.

The smell of sweet tobacco preceded his quartermaster as Finn slipped beside him, balancing his feet on the heaving deck.

"Headin' fer yer island, Cap'n?"

Blake nodded. "To lighten the load in the hold and give the crew a much-needed break."

"Good thinkin', says I." Wind blasted over them, and Finn tugged his bandana tighter. "We've taken in quite a haul under yer command, no denyin' it."

Finn never offered a compliment without a complaint. "But...?"

"Wells, there be word 'bout the woman, sayin' she's bad luck an' that yer infatuation could cost all our lives."

Blake ground his teeth. Keeping these limp-brained maggots he called a crew happy was becoming quite the tedious task. Unfortunately, he needed them for now—until he could build his kingdom. "Yet they are all safe with their pockets full of doubloons. You'd do well to remind them of that."

The brig rolled over a wave, and Finn gripped the railing and leaned closer to Blake, his gaze landing on the Ring. "Jist be careful, Cap'n," he whispered over the wind. "If word got out 'bout the power o' that Ring, I wouldn't put it past 'hem to pry it off yer dead finger." He shrugged. "Even if it don't work that way."

The sinister tone in his quartermaster's voice gave Blake pause. Spreading his boots out for balance, he crossed arms over his chest, uneasy at the look of desire in Finn's eyes as he stared at the Ring. "They are welcome to try. Now, back to work."

Tearing his gaze from the Ring, Finn ambled away as the *Summons* completed its tack.

Thus far, only Maston and Finn had a clue about the Ring's power. And Blake intended to keep it that way.

"Sheet home and belay!" Maston shouted.

"Steady as she goes," Blake added. If only he could order his life to continue on a steady path as easily. But as he glanced over Maston, Finn, Charlie, Rummy, and the rest of his crew, he wondered if he could trust any of them. Nay. There was no one in this world he could trust. Not even himself, for he could not deny he'd felt something stir within him when he'd rescued Emeline...when she'd looked at him with hope and perhaps a bit of admiration?

Hang it! He must not fall for her womanly tricks! He'd learned the hard way with Josephine Arnaud that no woman could be trusted. Not even comely ones with hearts of gold.

When the sun sank beneath the horizon in a glorious array of maroons, tangerines, and gold, Blake relinquished command of the helm and retreated to his cabin. Soon a supper of salted pork, ship biscuits, and peas was brought in, but he took little pleasure in dining with his officers, most of whom overindulged in drink, save Charlie and Pedro. And all of whom inquired as to why he'd not invited Emeline.

In truth, he had no idea, except he preferred not to address the discordant emotions she caused whenever she was near. Which made no sense. Hadn't he brought her on board to chase away his demons? She couldn't very well do that locked up in a cabin down the hall.

Thus the reason he poured himself another glass of rum, hoping to settle his mind. All it did was increase his confusion. Instead, he dismissed his officers, ordered the crewmen to clean up the mess, and waited for the door to slam, granting him silence at last.

Outside the stern windows, a myriad of stars lit the ebony sky, some clustered together, others alone yet just as bright as their grouped companions. Much like Blake. He needed no one. 'Twas those with power who ruled the world, the taskmasters, not the workers, the decision-makers not the order-takers, those who were outside the reach of the world's heartaches, betrayals, and disasters. Blake twisted the Ring on his finger. With this relic, he was well on his way to achieving such power.

Indeed, he needed no one. Especially not a woman. Tossing the last of his rum into his mouth, he stumbled to his cot, tore off his shirt, and lay down. A good night's sleep would certainly erase all his uncertainty and set him back on course.

"*Blake....Blake...*" The oily voice, distant yet vibrating like a band of insects, emerged from another world. Blake waved it away, mumbling, ignoring...

More voices joined, prodding, jabbing, poking at his consciousness. Grabbing the long knife he kept by his bed, he jerked to sit, stabbing the air before him.

The dark shadows returned. Only this time, they were larger, thicker, swaying with the movement of the ship...yet not with any worldly movement. Their bodies twisted, breaking in half, shrinking, growing, and then coming together again like no human's could.

"Get rid of the woman. Get rid of the woman. Kill her. Kill her..." the voices chanted.

Blake heard his father's distinct tone before the man even appeared, that harsh cadence that had always sent Blake cowering as a boy. Shoving through the specters, he limped, holding his belly. Blood bubbled between his fingers. "Why? Why, son?"

Nay! He could not face him again!

Leaping from his bed, he raced out of his cabin and down the hall, grabbing the first crewman he saw and handed him a key. "Get the woman and bring her to my cabin at once!"

Then making his way back, he left the door open and paced through the misty shadows, covering his ears. Air, cold and frosty bit his skin. "Kill her. Kill her."

He knew the moment Emeline entered the room. The soothing sounds of water gushing against the hull and the creak of timbers replaced the hellish howls. He opened his eyes.

The demons were gone.

The door to Emeline's cabin swung open, striking the bulkhead. She leapt from her cot, heart thundering. "Who is it?" she yelped, peering into the darkness. A shadow approached, grabbed her by the arm and dragged her into the hallway. 'Twas one of the crew she'd not met.

"Cap'n wants ye," was all he said as his foul stench stung her nose.

Her blood froze. So, this was it. The moment she feared most of all. A quick *Lord, help?* was all she managed to pray before the pirate shoved her through the captain's door and slammed it behind her.

Moonlight trickled in through the windows, shifting over the captain's desk to the deck and back again. She heard rather than saw the captain standing not three feet from her. His breath came loud and fast. An unusual chill gripped her, and she hugged herself.

"Are you ill?" she dared ask, wondering why he stood in the dark and why she sensed naught but turmoil surrounding him.

Perhaps because he knew what he was about to do.

"Nay," he finally said, moving to the desk where he struck flint to steel and lit a lantern.

Golden light spread a blanket over the room, chasing away the shadows and revealing Captain Keene, shirtless, gripping the edge of his desk as if it held the answers to all his questions. The cross and golden emblem dangled before him. Without glancing her way, he grabbed an open bottle and poured himself a shot of rum. Sipping it, he finally faced her.

Terror spun so violently in her head, Emeline feared she'd faint. But she stood her ground. If this monster intended to ravish her, she'd not make it easy.

Then, as if a dark cloud swept from his face, he smiled and gestured to her attire. She'd forgotten that Charlie had given her a pair of clean trousers, shirt, and waistcoat to wear while her gown dried.

"I find nothing amusing, Captain, about summoning me in the middle of the night in order to ravish me." She despised the quiver in her voice.

His brows raised, but his smile remained. "I'm merely admiring your new garments, Miss." Setting down his glass, he moved toward her, examining her like one would a fresh baked pie he was about to devour.

She swallowed...*hard* yet maintained her stance.

He halted before her, the muscles of his bare chest glistening, the scent of rum and male overpowering.

His eyes scanned her. "Alas, I have no intention of ravishing you, Miss Hyde." He cocked his head and gave her a curious look. "But believing so, you still asked if I was ill?"

Confusion ripped through her mind, her heart pounding. She had no answer for his question, no reason that would satisfy a man devoid of a heart. Still, if he had no desire to steal her maidenhood…why had he commanded her here? "Why did you rescue me from the Jesuits?" she blurted, wishing he didn't stand so close. His warmth, his very breath, wafted over her, his presence paralyzing.

Rather than answering, he ran the back of his fingers down her cheek, softly, gently, not in the salacious way she expected. Who was this man? Vicious pirate or noble champion? She sensed both battled within him.

Then, as if the tender action upset him, he pivoted and strode away. Back to his rum.

"You had the Ring. Why?" she pressed.

He tossed the remainder of his drink to the back of his throat. Dark hair hung down his back just below his shoulders as his muscles rolled beneath his skin, displaying a strength she'd only sensed when near the man.

He could snap her like a twig, have his way with her, and there would be naught she could do. Instead, he'd caressed her cheek tenderly and walked away.

"Have a seat, Miss Hyde," he said as he strode to the stern windows and gazed out.

"You did not answer my question, Captain, nor why you have summoned me in the middle of the night." Against her better judgement, she did as he asked and slid onto the velvet stuffed chair.

"As to the first," he began, "I simply cannot allow any man, Jesuit or not, to gain the victory over me." He shifted those mysterious, almond-shaped eyes her way, a twinkle of mischief within them. "As to the second, perhaps I do feel a need for female company." The twinkle turned licentious as his gaze scanned her again.

Though she knew his words were meant to frighten her, to keep her compliant, she sensed they were not true. Nay, a deep cut of pain sliced across this man's heart. More than one. Deep and festering—unhealed. 'Twas what drove him. She knew that now.

Sitting up straight, she clasped her hands in her lap. "Then either send me back to my cabin or get on with it, Captain. I grow weary of the exchange."

His eyes narrowed. "'Twould not be prudent, Miss, to tempt me."

Fear sent her breath heaving in her throat.

He studied her. "You will stay here tonight."

She pushed to her feet. "I will do no such thing!"

Shock, followed by admiration, flitted across his gaze. "You have no choice."

"Then you *are* to ravish me."

"Nay." He shrugged. "Not tonight." He nodded toward his cot. "You may sleep on my bed. You'll find it quite soft. I will lie on the floor."

Surely it was a trap of some sort. "I don't understand."

"'Tis not too difficult, Miss." He gestured to the bed. "Now, if you don't mind, it grows late and I'm weary."

"If you wish to ravish me, be done with it. I cannot stand these games." She forced back the tears burning in her eyes.

"If I wished to ravish you, I would have already done so. Off to bed with you!" He strode to his cot, grabbed one of the coverlets from atop it, and promptly blew out the lantern.

Darkness swept across the cabin. Emeline didn't move. "You are no gentleman, Captain. You may have rescued me, but that doesn't mean you have an ounce of honor."

She heard him drop to the deck, saw his shadow stretched out on the Persian rug.

"As I have told you," he mumbled.

"This is madness. I'm going back to my cabin." She started for the door

"I wouldn't do that if I were you. Your cabin is no longer locked. You are safer in here than at the mercy of my crew."

Frustrated, Emeline skirted him and sat on his bed to think until he fell asleep. All her instincts screamed to dash back to her cabin, but without an escort and with nothing to keep the crew away, perhaps he was right. Plus, the bed *did* feel comfortable. Heaving a sigh, she laid her head on the pillow and curled into a ball, thanking the Lord for keeping her safe. Within minutes, snoring rumbled from the captain, serenaded by the wind whistling against the stern windows.

Perhaps he had no plans to harm her this night. Then why keep her here? The man was an enigma.

Wind battered Emeline, shoving her down, booting her back. Thick blackness surrounded her. She couldn't move. Couldn't get up. Couldn't breathe. With great effort, she rose to her elbows and began crawling. She had to escape! She had to get out of here! Darkness. Black everywhere. So heavy it pressed on her even more than the wind. The darkness moved, breathed, was alive. *Evil.* Where was she? She inched over the cold steely ground, heart pounding. The wind ceased. Arturo Della Morte's hideous face appeared before her, spinning in her vision. He tossed back his head and laughed, then raised his hand. The Ring shone from his finger as a devilish twinkle flashed from his eyes. She tried to scream, but no sound emerged.

Help me, Lord!

The scene changed. She stood on the shore of a lush island. Turquoise waves stroked creamy white sands. Colorful birds chirped as they flitted from tree to tree. In the distance atop a hill stood stone turrets of a fortress. Had she gone from hell to heaven?

Della Morte sauntered from the jungle, his sardonic gaze upon her. A ray of sunlight struck the Ring on his finger and nearly blinded her. She squinted.

Dozens of birds dropped from the trees onto the sand, dead. Above her, the sky rolled up like a scroll, replaced by a black void that stretched across the sky, sucking all light and love from the Earth. The turquoise waters faded to gray. Blake appeared within them, splashing through the surf toward her, a smile on his face. He reached for her, his fingers extending toward hers.

Della Morte held up the Ring. The waters in the bay spun in a circle, round and round, faster and faster until a funnel appeared in the center.

Before she could grip Blake's hand, the force of the waves dragged him back, pulling him down into the water, tugging him toward the hole in the midst of the funnel. To what or where it led, she had no idea, but it couldn't be good.

"Blake!" Emeline rushed toward him, pounding through the surf, reaching for his hand before he was sucked beneath the waves.

Della Morte gave a sinister cackle. "Ha! You are both doomed!"

Water tore at her skirts, imprisoning her feet, as she desperately tried to reach Blake. His head disappeared beneath the waves. Only his hand remained above.

Emeline grabbed it. The water knocked her off her feet. With both hands holding fast to Blake, she dug her heels into the sand. Water filled her nose and mouth. *Lord, help*!

"Blake! Blake!"

Blake's name blared through his mind. Someone hailed him. Demons? His father? But Emeline was here. Wasn't she?

"Blake!"

He shot up from the floor, instantly plucking the knife from his belt. Blinking, he peered into the darkness. The shadows of his cabin came into view.

"Blake!" a woman screamed.

Emeline! He rushed toward the bed, expecting to find one of his crew molesting her, but she was alone, thrashing back and forth and reaching one hand into the air in desperation.

Lowering to the cot, he grabbed her shoulders. "Hush now, Emeline. Hush. 'Tis all right."

She gave a start, uttered a scream, and began punching him over and over. Snatching her wrists, he held them down. "You're having a dream, Emeline. Just a dream."

Her breathing lessened. Her arms went limp. He released her as a slight moan escaped her lips. He sensed rather than saw her eyes open and lock upon him.

Blake was quite familiar with his own nightmares. Not with those of other's. Yet, oddly, he wanted nothing more than to take this woman in his arms and comfort her.

He didn't have time to ponder it when she wrapped her arms around him. Tight. "I thought you were lost," she whispered. "Della Morte... the Ring," she muttered.

No doubt she was still lost in the nightmare, devoid of her wits.

Or surely she would not have embraced him.

Still, he would enjoy it while he could. Her curves molded against his chest so perfectly, 'twas as if they were made for each other. Her sweet scent filled his nose, her soft whispers music in his ears. He closed his eyes and rubbed her back. "Della Morte is far, far away by now. He will do you no more harm."

A strange sensation sped through him. The desire to protect this woman, to keep her safe, to be the hero she longed for...

Until she jerked away and shoved him from the bed. "What are you doing? How dare you?"

The lady's senses had returned.

So did Blake's as he landed on the hard deck.

The first glow of dawn drifted in from the windows as Blake growled and rose to his feet. "You were screaming like a wounded bird, Miss. I only meant to silence you so I could sleep." Plowing a hand through his hair, he retrieved the coverlet from the floor.

"Is that your excuse to accost me, Captain?" Her incredulous tone dwindled beneath the tremble in her voice.

"Do I need one?" He winked at her, then regretted it when she frowned and swept her legs over the side of the bed.

"Am I free to go?"

Surf and thunder, the lady was a rare beauty in the morning, even with her sleepy eyes and bedraggled hair. So unlike most women he'd woken up to.

Angry, more at himself than her, he opened the door and gestured for her to leave. In bounded Bandit, grinning and babbling as he made straight for the lady and leapt into her lap.

Astonishing. The feral monkey had not entered his cabin since he'd retrieved the Ring.

Yet as he watched the beast wrap his hairy arms around Emeline's neck, he could hardly blame him, for Blake's body still reacted from their embrace just moments ago.

This must never do.

"Get out!" He shouted a bit too loudly. "Both of you!"

Chapter 16

Two things rampaged through Emeline's mind as she stood at the bulwarks amidships. One was the horrid nightmare she had last night. The other was the tender way Blake held her, caressed her back, and whispered words of comfort in her ears. She could not shake the pleasurable sensation of his strong arms around her, the warmth of his body, the salty scent of his hair. She'd felt safe, protected, and cared for. Something she desperately needed after her nightmare. *And* after her ordeal of the past two weeks.

But then the honorable hero became the heartless pirate again. A transformation so fast and unexpected that she was on tenterhooks as to which one she would meet moment to moment. Which made it nigh impossible to deal with the man.

Though deal with him she must, so long as he kept her imprisoned on his ship.

Shielding her eyes from the sun, a handbreadth above the horizon, she gazed across the aquamarine sea, relishing the beauty of it, yet its wildness, its fickleness. Things her father said he loved most about the Caribbean. Having been raised on a ship, Emeline felt a kindred attachment to the foamy waters. Yet now they seemed naught but a formidable expanse, an impenetrable fortress between her and freedom, her and her family.

Wind whipped her hair behind her, forcing her to close her eyes momentarily as memories of her nightmare surfaced. *What does it mean, Lord? Am I supposed to save Blake from Della Morte? From the Ring?* She nibbled on her lip. Was he doomed to die and she along with him? How was she supposed to battle such evil? She was only one woman, alone and with no talents to speak of.

"I'm surprised to see the captain allows you on deck." The female voice snapped Emeline's eyes open to see Charlie approaching from her left.

Emeline glanced over her shoulder at Blake up on the quarterdeck talking to Finn. After she and Bandit had returned to her cabin, Pedro arrived with coffee and a biscuit to break her fast, informing her that the captain gave her leave to wander the ship.

Either he thought her safe from the pirates during the day, or he no longer cared what happened to her. Either way, she braved the salacious glances from the crew for a much-needed breath of fresh salty air and warm sun on her face.

Emeline smiled at Charlie. "He's full of surprises."

"That's one way t' put it." The master gunner gripped the railing as the brig mounted a large wave. "He fancies you, you know."

Emeline laughed. "Ludicrous. He needs me for something, 'tis all." 'Twas the *what* he needed that had her nerves on edge.

"Mebbe. But I ne'er seen him order the crew's hands off any female before. An' aye, he's had women on board more'an once."

So he *did* care if she were harmed. She shook off the spark of hope that rose at Charlie's words. "As I said, he wants me for something."

One of Charlie's brows arched as she scanned Emeline's breeches, shirt, and waistcoat. "The garb suits you, Miss. We may make a pirate out o' you yet."

Chuckling, Emeline balanced her shoes on the heaving deck. "No offense, but I don't wish to spend my life in thievery."

"You don't know what you're missing. But very well. Your dress is dry. I'll bring it t' your cabin later."

"Thank you." The *Summons* dipped into a trough, sending foamy spray over them. A familiar sensation, a good one. Emeline wiped her face. "Do you know where we are heading?"

"Aye. The captain's island."

"He has an island?" Emeline asked, baffled. Of course the pompous pirate would have his own island.

"You'll see," Charlie responded, leaning forward on the railing.

Emeline longed to keep the woman talking. 'Twas nice to have female company. "How did you become one of the best master gunners in all the West Indies?"

"One of? You mean *the* best." Winking, Charlie flung her long hair behind her.

"Your confidence does you great credit, Charlie." A quality Emeline sorely lacked. Her father and mother always told her she was special with unique talents, but they could never voice precisely what those talents were.

"A fearless certainty in my skills along wit' a cocksure attitude is the only thing these thieving toads respect." Charlie's eyes snapped to Maston across the deck, shouting orders to topmen. "It is the only way a woman can earn wealth wit'out a man's help."

Emeline thought of Delphine and wondered how she fared. "Surely you weren't always this confident."

Charlie stared over the sea for several moments. "Believe it or not, I used to be a decent woman raised by good parents. My father were a blacksmith. I were taught that if I behaved an' married well, I'd be happy an' fulfill my place in society." She blew out a snort.

Wind blasted over them as the captain's shouts to trim sheets bellowed across the deck. Still Emeline waited for Charlie to continue, not wanting to press her.

"I learned the hard way that life don't always work out like we plan. In the end, I'd much rather be a master gunner than some man's subservient wife."

Emeline pondered her words. In her family, she'd seen naught but happy marriages with love and respect flowing equally between husband and wife. Still, she wasn't naïve enough to believe that all marriages were so.

Sails flapped and thundered as the *Summons* tacked slightly to starboard.

"Truth is," Charlie continued, "I dressed like a man an' joined a merchant ship pretending t' be a lad. The master gunner took me under his wing, treated me like a son, an' taught me everything I know. I kept getting better an' better. We was captured by a pirate, an' I were given a choice t' join or walk the plank. I joined."

Emeline stared at her friend, amazed. "They still didn't discover you were a woman?"

"No. Stupid blokes." She chuckled.

"Then when the master gunner got cut in half by a Royal Navy twenty pounder, I was put in charge. The captain liked what he saw an' made me master gunner in his place."

"Captain Keene?"

"No, a different captain, though he had a bit of gentleman in him." Sorrow tugged on her features, and Emeline knew deep inside that this pirate captain had treated Charlie cruelly.

"What happened?"

"Nothin'. I escaped while at port an' a year later joined up wit' Captain Keene."

"I'm sorry that captain mistreated you." She laid a hand atop Charlie's, but the master gunner jerked away, her eyebrows colliding.

"How do you…?" Anger sparked in her eyes. "You proper ladies think you know what it's like for the rest o' us women. I have work t' do." Shaking her head, she marched away, leaving Emeline baffled as to what she'd said that upset her.

Blake downed yet another glass of rum, ignoring the voice within him that said he'd been overindulging of late. But how else was he to endure the excruciating temptation of Miss Emeline Hyde sleeping in his bed for the past three nights? Nay, she was not the fairest of the women he'd been with, nor the most sensuous, and certainly her tongue was not at all flattering to his ego.

But he found every ounce of him drawn to her like none before. She was everything he was not. Humble, kind, generous, *at peace.* She was light and love, and, like a moth to a flame, he was lured to her, unable to stop himself. Also like a moth, her light would surely kill him should he get too close.

Even worse, her presence brought unusual sensations of guilt and regret over the wicked life he'd chosen. Hang it! He'd never entertained such ridiculous notions before. He did not need this distraction. Not now when he was so close to achieving his dreams.

But he needed *her.*

She kept the demons and nightmares at bay. He twisted the Ring on his finger, staring out the stern windows at ribbons of sparkling sunlit waves.

"Cap'n." Finn's voice at his door spun him around. "We's approachin' Keene Island."

Blake nodded. "I'll be up shortly." He faced the windows again. Finally home. Things would be better where he was not only captain but king. Where, with this Ring, he would maintain his power and protect his kingdom from all enemies.

Up on deck, he drew the spyglass to his eye. His island sat sturdily upon the sea, her mountain peaks reaching for the clouds, her lush greenery and creamy sands inviting him home. If only his father—*and* his mother—could see him now. Could see the fortune and land he'd amassed for himself. He huffed. Along with Josephine Arnaud.

Lowering the scope, his eyes latched upon Emeline standing at the starboard railing, her lustrous hair tumbling down to her waist, her blue skirts flapping in the wind. She stood tall, chin raised, facing the sea like a regal princess. Bandit leapt from the ratlines to the railing beside her and began jabbering as if telling her a story. Her laughter reached Blake, doing strange things to his insides.

"Fire when ready!" he shouted to Charlie stationed by one of the nine-pounders, matchstick in hand. *Boom*! The gun thundered, sending a smoky haze back over the deck and announcing their arrival.

He was not the only one staring at the lady. Several of his pirates cast lecherous glances her way, along with Maston, who stood amidships ordering the topmen. He would have to watch the libertine closely.

Better yet, he must discover what power the lady held over demons, acquire it, and then send her back to her father. The sooner the better before her holiness infected him and ruined all his plans.

Emeline could only stare in horror at the same bay she'd seen in her recent nightmare, down to the coconut palms swaying in the breeze, the snowy white color of the sand, and the oblong shape of the bay. She tightened her grip on the railing as her heart squeezed. What could this mean?

The stone turrets of a small fortress gleamed in the setting sun upon a nearby hill. Beyond them, a gabled roof and white walls of a large house rose above the trees. So, this was Blake's kingdom, as he put it. The man's hubris would put any king's to shame.

Kingdom or not, land or sea, she was still his prisoner. But to what purpose? It must have something to do with that infernal Ring, but what she could not say. He'd hardly spoken a word to her in two days. She'd been given her meals in her cabin and only summoned to his when the sun sank below the horizon. After three nights, she'd stopped fearing he would ravish her, for he seemed not the least bit desirous of her in that way.

Oddly enough, she took it as an affront to her feminine allure. Was she not attractive enough to even elicit the lust of a pirate? Yet no sooner did the thought enter her mind, then she repented, for she'd rather be considered the ugliest of women than to be ravished.

Still, as the soundings were called, the commands issued to lower sails, and finally the anchor dropped with a mighty splash, she wondered what the captain had in store for her on this island. She wondered what her family was doing and where they were. Did they miss her? Were they looking for her?

As if sensing her loneliness, Bandit jumped into her arms and clung to her neck. His familiar monkey scent brought an odd comfort.

"You are my only friend, Bandit." She scratched beneath his chin, and he lifted his head and grinned.

"I'm yer friend too, Miss!" Pedro appeared beside her and tore off his floppy hat, his red hair tossed this way and that by the breeze and his smile beaming. "He says I'm t' take ye ashore an' show ye t' yer chamber."

The *he* must be the captain. But a chamber? That sounded more inviting than a jail cell. Besides, Emeline couldn't think of a better escort.

Hence, within an hour of anchoring, she found herself ashore with Pedro and two pirates, trunks hoisted on their shoulders. The captain remained behind, managing the offloading of his precious stolen goods. All the while, the beach flooded with Caribs and other natives who hailed Blake as if he were a god returning from the skies.

"This way, Miss." Pedro headed toward the jungle where a path broke through the leaves.

She started forward but felt a strange inkling and turned to see the captain's unwavering gaze upon her from the ship. Though she could not make out his eyes nor his expression in the distance, a uniquely powerful sensation stretched between them. What could it be? What did darkness have to do with light? A chill scoured over her as she shifted her gaze to the soft sudsy wavelets of the bay, remembering how she'd tried to save him from the deadly funnel in her dream.

Turning, she followed Pedro into the web of green. Perhaps her mission was to save Blake. But from what, and more importantly, how?

The mansion, for that's what it was, was not at all what she expected. For one thing, 'twas much larger than it appeared from afar, with several wings spreading out from a central large parlor that opened up to a massive ballroom. Fully armed, native guards stood before the gate, granting them entrance when they spotted Pedro.

To say she was impressed would be an understatement, for the home looked more like a king's palace than a pirate haven. She spotted paintings hanging on walls and longed for a tour, but Pedro led her up a set of curved stairs, down a long hallway decorated with carved crown molding, to a room toward the back.

The chamber was small but well-appointed. The walls were paneled in fine wood with gilded moldings and decorative cornices. A window, framed by blue damask curtains, let in a modicum of afternoon light onto the Turkish rug gracing the floor. A four-poster bed centered the room, draped in a rich velvet coverlet. Two gilded chairs, a dressing table beside a framed mirror, a porcelain tub, and a large ornately-carved wardrobe filled the rest of the room. Oddly, a closed door stood off to her right. Perhaps leading to a dressing closet. She stared in shocked delight. 'Twas a far cry from the tiny cabin she'd been stuffed in for the past several days.

"Cap'n says t' stay in here, Miss." Then, as if sensing she didn't want him to leave, he added, "Don't worry. You'll be safe."

"You're very kind, Pedro. You must have been raised well in that monastery. You said your parents left you there?"

"I got no parents, Miss." Shrugging, he gazed out the window, longing in his eyes.

"Everyone has parents."

"Natural ones, I suppose." He faced her. "But not ones who love you. I were only five, Miss. I don't remember them."

Five? Sadness weighed on her heart. "Why would they do such a thing?"

"I were a bastard, Miss." His voice started out high-pitched, then grew deep, reminding Emeline he was fast becoming a man. "The nuns told me Francisco de Taboada were my father, an' me mother were a chamber maid in his estate on Panama."

Emeline drew a deep breath. Such sad stories. Did anyone on board the *Summons* have a normal, happy childhood except for her? She'd never considered how blessed she'd been. Oh, how the enemy loved to kill, steal, and destroy every life…and the younger the better.

"I'm sorry." She could think of nothing else to say.

"Don't be, Miss. Some people are just born t' be nothin'. Others are born t' be great. The sooner we accept our lot in life, the happier we will be."

What foolish wisdom was that?

Emeline sensed a deep sorrow in the lad, far too deep for one so young. A sorrow he often hid behind his childish grin. Approaching, she reached for his hands.

"That is not true, Pedro. God never creates rubbish. Every single person is valuable to Him *and* has a purpose in this world."

He took a step back. "I gots t' go now." He flipped his hat atop his head, smiled, and left, closing the door behind him.

No sooner did Blake's feet land on his island than the Caribs he paid to protect it gathered around him, bowing and greeting him like the king he was. Two dozen of them to be exact. He'd built homes for them, gave them clothing, food, weapons, and the freedom to live on the island in whatever way they chose. In return, they were loyal to him and protected his home when he was away. That was what power and money provided—loyalty, fear, and lifelong service. All of which put Blake at the top of society and *not* the bottom. A place he would never be again.

He greeted them in return, uttering his appreciation and thanks in their native tongue, a bit of which he had learned. Then, with one last glance at the *Summons,* where he'd left a small crew as first watch, he plunged into the jungle.

As much as he loved the sea, he looked forward to coming home to a warm bath, a meal that wasn't hard tack and fish stew, and to a place where he could enjoy the finer things in life—music, dance, art. He was most anxious to show Miss Emeline his art collection, though why, he couldn't say, except that she might be the only one on the island who would appreciate it.

Emeline. He wondered at her impression of his home, picturing her surprise and astonishment at how cultured he was, how wrong she'd been in thinking him a barbaric, unlettered brute. He would prove to her that he could be a gentleman when he wanted to be.

Scads! He instantly cursed himself for those thoughts. It had been a long time since he'd cared what anyone thought of him, and he wasn't going to start now. Especially not for some highborn, virtuous, nose-in-the-air female.

However when that nose-in-the-air female sashayed into the banquet room later that night, dressed in satin and lace and with her hair pinned up in a bounty of curls, Blake found he *did* care what she thought. A great deal.

Chapter 17

When servant girls entered her chamber with pails of hot water for a bath and one of the most beautiful gowns she'd ever seen, Emeline had stubbornly refused both. She would be loath to accept the captain's trifling gifts, for no doubt a nefarious purpose lurked behind them.

Yet...

After the servants left and steam rose gently from the tub, along with the scent of the rose petals scattered across the water, she couldn't resist. It had been a least a month since she'd soaked in a hot bath, not since she'd been home at the Hyde Estate on Kingston, Jamaica. Yet, the mere thought of that safe abode flooded her with longing...*and* sorrow. She missed her parents. She missed her grandparents, Captain Merrick and Charlisse. She even missed her sister and brother. Still, the bath felt beyond wonderful as she washed the sweat and stink from her skin and hair. If only she could wash away Captain Keene and this horrible nightmare as easily.

After her bath, she sat on the bed, drying her hair and staring at the gorgeous attire the servants had laid so carefully across the coverlet. It made no sense to put on her old gown when a new—and much prettier—one was available. She fingered the pearls embedded amidst the gold thread of the stomacher, then caressed the green silk skirt, richly embroidered in woven silver designs.

What harm would it do to at least try it on?

Pah! Of course, it fit perfectly.

She had stood admiring herself in the looking glass when the servant girls returned, smiling and giggling as they assisted her with buttons and ties she could not reach. One of them pinned up her hair in a most alluring style. She had tried to engage them in conversation, but it seemed they didn't understand her.

The thought that she was being prepped and primed, dressed and basted, for some elaborate main meal niggled at the back of her mind, but she ignored it. For now, at least. Especially when she saw her reflection in the looking glass, and the woman staring back at her was just as lovely as her sister or mother. But that couldn't be.

Nay! Blast her feminine vanity! She had just begun to remove the gown when a knock on the door preceded Charlie's face peeking through the opening. Instantly her brows shot up and she whistled. "Whoa. Is that you, Emeline?" She entered the chamber, dressed in her usual breeches, shirt, and leather waistcoat. Though they appeared cleaner.

"Nay. 'Tis not me." Emeline continued unlacing the stomacher.

"Stop. I'm to take you to the banquet." Charlie grabbed her hand, halting her in her task, then cocked her head. "Better to go fully dressed, Miss, than exposing anything to those besotted leches, eh?"

Emeline frowned. "Do I have a choice? Can I not remain here?"

"You know the captain. Now come along."

And that was how Emeline now found herself walking into a large hall, complete with a long, white-clothed table in the center, lined on both sides by richly upholstered chairs. Livered servants scrambled about, placing steaming bowls and platters across it, while the captain's crew stood in clusters, yammering and partaking of drinks offered by native servant girls on platters. Most of the pirates remained in their normal buccaneer attire, though some had donned more colorful vests and had run a comb through their hair. Their presence, however, was starkly at odds with the opulent room.

Richly embroidered damask tapestries decorated most of the walls, while oil paintings depicting ships and the sea were hung in gilded frames throughout. A chandelier of cut crystal hung from the ceiling, casting a golden glow over the room. Beyond the long table, a marble fireplace took up most of the wall, and she wondered whether it ever grew cold enough to use. To its right, a raised platform held various instruments in anticipation of a concert, causing a twinge of excitement within Emeline at the prospect. Elegant side tables lined the room, holding bowls of wine, punch, and sweet meats. A breeze, scented by wildflowers and the sea, drew her gaze to two large doors on her left, leading out to what appeared to be a portico overlooking a garden.

Several eyes pinned on her like falcons to their prey. Only one set of eyes made her heart race. Captain Keene broke off from a group of his pirates and headed her way.

Emeline glanced over her shoulder, looking for Charlie, feeling a sudden need to run back to her chamber as fast as she could. But Charlie had abandoned her and was helping herself to a plate of cheese on the sideboard.

Leaving Emeline frozen in place, unable to enter the lions' den alone, unable to even move as the king of the lions approached, a hungry grin on his lips. He'd traded his pirate attire for a fine linen shirt with lace at the cuffs, covered by a black silk jerkin over which his necklaces dangled. Tight black breeches were stuffed into leather boots that clapped across the tiled floor as he moved. His dark hair was slicked back and tied behind him, but stubble still peppered his jaw. A silver dagger winked at her from his belt while his cutlass hung at his side, an ever-present symbol of danger that always hovered about the man.

Penetrating eyes swept over her in appreciation before they locked onto her face.

She swallowed down a burst of both excitement and fear.

Halting before her, he took her hand and placed a kiss upon it.

"Emeline." He spoke her common name softly, sensuously, the sound of it on his lips making her blood heat. "You look lovely."

Against her will, her traitorous breath fled her, and she uttered a tiny gasp. Which only made him smile all the more.

He knew his effect on her, the cad!

She must not play into his charm. Jutting out her chin, she jerked her hand from his. "I am not a doll for you to dress up for your pleasure."

His smile grew even wider. "On the contrary, my little sugar bird, it seems that's exactly what you are."

"Sugar bird?" She stared at him, indignant.

"'Tis a bird native to this island, quite small in size yet armed with a powerful chirp." He extended his elbow, still grinning. "It suits you."

Frowning, Emeline turned to leave, but he clutched her arm.

"Forgive my impertinence," he said. "Please,"—He seemed to choke on the word—"join us for dinner. You must be famished."

The scent of roasted pork wafted beneath her nose, eliciting a growl from her belly. She needed to eat. She needed her strength if she was to escape this madman's clutches. And escape she must. A better chance of that on land than at sea. Though how she would accomplish such a feat on an island, she had no idea.

She gave a tight smile, and ignoring his outstretched elbow, pushed past him.

'Twas Maston who pulled out her chair for her, his appreciative gaze scouring her gown and, in particular, the curve of her chest peeking above her décolletage.

"You look quite alluring tonight," he said, then took a seat beside her, whilst the captain sat at the head of the table on her other side.

His pirates sat around them. Other members of his crew, along with those who surely ran the estate while he was gone, sat further down the table.

The dinner was uneventful. The food beyond delicious. In truth, Emeline had not seen such a feast in quite some time— roasted pig, lobster in cream sauce, turtle soup, yams, Cassava biscuits, guava, papaya, and pickled vegetables. Even the conversation did not bear the usual curses, drunken slurs, and ribald boasts. 'Twas as if the elegant surroundings leeched some of the vulgarity from the men. Finn had even manicured his overgrown beard for the occasion, and Rummy, who still drank more than he ate, seemed to have at least washed the grime from his skin. The surgeon, in his fine attire, looked out of place amongst these buccaneer fools, saying very little, as was his way, yet she sensed he observed everything around him in great detail. Then there was Charlie two seats down from her, conversing, laughing, and eating with these men as if she were one of them. Though weaker in physical strength and of a gender kept in subjection to men, her confidence astounded Emeline, and she found herself longing to have a smidgeon of the woman's tenacity.

Emeline slipped a spoonful of turtle soup into her mouth and once again found the captain's eyes upon her, assessing her reaction.

"My chefs are quite good, are they not?" he asked.

"Best food I 'ad in a long time," Finn answered with a belch before she could respond, but his eyes were on the Ring gleaming from Blake's finger.

Maston leaned toward her, the scent of his rosemary cologne overwhelming. "You must ignore his barbaric manners, mademoiselle. He's unaccustomed to such fine dining and good company."

"An' ye are?" Rummy chuckled. "Don't let 'im fool ye, Miss. Maston's usual fine dinin' consists o' a bevy o' whores in 'is bed."

Finn chuckled.

A heated blush rushed up Emeline's neck at the lewd discussion, and she silently chastised herself. Having grown up around pirates, she should be accustomed to such bawdy remarks.

"At least I have the use of both my limbs and can attract the attention of females," Maston retorted, seemingly unaffected by Rummy's insult.

Rummy slammed down his bottle, stood, swayed uncontrollably, and then plopped down to his chair again. "Out to swords, ye French toad! But when I'm sober."

"Then never," Charlie interjected, eliciting chuckles from the men.

"Enough!" Blake's shout brought all gazes his way. "When you are on the *Summons*, you may act like the ill-bred, vulgar louts that you are. Here, I expect you to make an attempt at civility."

Tension tightened down the table like a taut line, and Emeline sucked in a breath, praying a fight would not ensue.

Maston must have sensed her nervousness, for he laid a hand on her arm and smiled. Normally she would have been touched by the gesture, but a hunger lingered beyond the grin that sent a chill through her.

The exchange did not go unnoticed by the captain, who glared at Maston before ordering the footman to remove his plate and serve dessert.

By the time the rum-soaked cake and candied fruit were served, Emeline's stomach had twisted in a knot. All the elegant surroundings, the fine attire, and scrumptious food in the world could not make gentlemen out of pirates. Only God could do that. She'd seen it happen more than once. Still, she had foolishly allowed herself a moment's reprieve from the horror of her situation, allowed herself to be overcome by the lavish surroundings. But these men had brought her crashing back to reality.

With the meal completed and everyone's bellies full of food and wine, Emeline rose, feeling her strength already returning. With it came a desperation to retire to her chamber to pray and plan her escape.

But the captain quickly took her by the arm. "The evening is young, Miss Hyde. I have provided music and dancing."

Surely, he jested. Confused, she met his gaze, stunned to find sincerity in his penetrating eyes. "If you please, Captain, I have a headache and wish to retire." She turned away.

"Nonsense." He held her in place and smiled. "Music is the best healer, wouldn't you agree?"

She would, for she could easily get swept away during a good concert. "I see I have no choice since I am your prisoner, Captain."

"I prefer disinclined guest." He gave a slight bow.

"You mock me and my grisly situation."

"Grisly?" He jerked back in feigned shock. "Come now, is it so bad?" He waved his arm over the room and the table still laden with sweet fruit and cake.

Frowning, Emeline refused to answer.

"Then allow me to make your situation more pleasant." He led her to the side as liveried servants cleared the table. "At least for tonight."

"If you wish to make my situation more pleasant, then I beg you, send me back to my father."

His eyes narrowed. "In good time, Miss. For now, a little music should soothe your soul." He urged her to sit in one of the chairs lining the walls as servants moved the table aside and several musicians began tuning their instruments.

Once the captain's attentions were elsewhere, Emeline made her way to the open doors where a light breeze stirred the curls at her neck and filled her nose with the scents of earthy loam and flowers. One peek outside revealed a long porch overlooking gardens too dark to see in the slim moonlight.

The most delightful sound turned her around. Was that Handel's Rinaldo? One of her favorite operas by the talented composer. To her added surprise, the men playing it were quite good.

Blake must have noticed the approval on her face as he marched toward her. "Ah, you recognize Rinaldo?"

"Of course." She studied him, the strength of his jaw, those piercing green eyes—all pirate captain, and yet this night for some reason he played the part of a gentleman. Real or a charade? Truth or lies?

He must have read her thoughts, for he snorted. "You wonder how a lowbrow thief and blackguard could possibly appreciate the finer things in life."

A traitorous smile lifted her lips. "I admit to being surprised."

He extended his elbow. "When they play an Allemande, I will surprise you even further."

Against her better judgement, she slipped her hand onto his arm and allowed him to usher her back inside.

The rest of the pirates seemed disinterested in the musical selection and more interested in the fresh bowl of wine punch on the sideboard. Charlie, Pedro, and two other pirates sat at a small table in the corner playing cards, while Finn with pipe in his mouth, Rummy, and a dozen others stood staring at the orchestra as if they'd flown in on wings.

'Twas such an odd sight that Emeline began to wonder if she was still asleep on the *Summons*, dreaming the entire event. It had to be a dream, for none of it made sense. Though why would she dream such an outlandish night? Perhaps her longing for a hero had perverted her thoughts into thinking Captain Keene could be that man. Preposterous!

Therefore, when the gentle, melodious notes of the Allemande filled the room and he asked her to dance, she agreed. If this was all but a figment of the frivolous imagination her father always teased her about, why not enjoy it?

Blake swept the lady onto the floor, bowed, and began the steps of the dance he'd learned a year past. It involved quite a bit of hopping and shifting of his feet, but he was intent on conquering it. If some dandified nobleman could do this, then hang it all, so could he!

The lady maneuvered the steps with grace and precision. Of course she did. She came from noble stock, her grandfather an earl—a man of power and culture. Both of which Blake would soon gain for himself.

When they finally met together and entwined their arms, her shocked expression, tainted with delight, warmed him.

"You are quite the dancer, Captain. Wherever did you learn?"

They spun around, still clung together. "There is much you do not know about me."

"Nor do I wish to as long as I am your prisoner," she spat back.

Her curt statement broke his jovial mood. Still, he finished the dance with as much flourish as he'd been taught, aware of how his crew gaped at him. He could only hope that seeing their captain behaving the coxcomb would not give them the false impression he was any less ruthless and commanding as always.

If so, they would find out the hard way.

He led Emeline to the side table and handed her a glass of punch. She hesitated at first, casting a suspicious glance his way before taking it. Did she think he would drug her?

The thought saddened him. Then again, how could he blame her?

To be honest, he'd been quite surprised at his own reaction to the lady when she'd entered the banquet hall. Quite surprised, indeed. 'Twas not so much the elegant silk gown and bejeweled stomacher, nor the delightful curve of her breasts peeking above it. Nor even the way her hair was swept up in a bouquet of curls, bedecked with glistening jewels. Nay. 'Twas the way the lady floated into the hall like a princess and not a prisoner, the way light and goodness entered with her and chased away the dark depravity that always hovered around him and his men.

Now, as he watched her take a sip and her striking gold eyes met his, he wondered why he'd ever thought her anything but stunning.

Shaking off the thought, he searched the table, found a bottle of port, and poured himself a large glass. He needed a drink. A strong one. The sweet, potent wine lit a fire in his belly and sent torrid waves throughout him. Alack, what spell had this lady cast upon him? For he had vowed to himself and to any God who was listening that he would never give any part of his heart away again. He fingered the Ring. Perhaps 'twas the relic that caused his enchantment. If so, he must be more careful to resist.

The orchestra struck up a harmonious tune, drawing Emeline's gaze. The dulcet sounds of a violin rose above the melody, and she closed her eyes, seemingly lost in the music, delight written on her face.

"You enjoy the violin?" he asked.

She smiled before she opened her eyes. "Yes, my mother plays. She taught me."

His brows shot up. "You play? I should like to hear you." And he meant it, for the sound of a violin always soothed him.

In an instant, her joy fled her as she tightened her lips. "As I have said, I'm not here for your entertainment, Captain. Either I am your prisoner or you must set me free."

Downing his port, he took her by the arm to a nearby chair, where he all but forced her to sit. She had broken the spell, thank the stars, for he found his anger rising.

She gazed up at him, moisture glistening in her lustrous eyes. "What is it you want from me, Captain?"

"For now, to stay here whilst I arrange for Pedro to return you to your chamber."

'Twas for the best, Blake told himself as he marched across the floor, seeking the cabin boy and cursing himself for a complete buffoon. There was no other explanation. For some idiotic reason, he'd wanted to impress the lady this night. Ludicrous. How could a prisoner be impressed with her captor?

Pedro was nowhere in sight.

Scads! Grabbing a bottle of rum from a table, he drew it to his lips and took a large sip, propriety be hanged. He needed some air, needed to clear the woman from his thoughts. Out on the porch, he found Sam staring into the darkness.

Blake slid beside him. The old surgeon spoke few words, but when he did, they were oft full of wisdom. And oh, how he needed some wisdom at the moment. As fortune would have it, he didn't have long to wait for the man to regale him.

"Your infatuation with the lady grows." Sam leaned on the railing, glass of punch in hand, staring at the strip of moonlit sea in the distance.

"Hardly." Blake cursed.

"Then why keep her?"

Blake shrugged and took another sip of rum. "Let's just say she keeps my demons at bay." 'Twas not a lie after all.

"Women *are* demons." Sam gave a rare chuckle. "Naught but trouble, Captain. I sense this one is more dangerous than she seems." He drew a deep breath. "I foresee she will disrupt all your plans, should you continue this dalliance." Then glancing over Blake's shoulder back into the ballroom, he gestured with his drink. "My point is made."

Pivoting, Blake found Maston dancing with Emeline, though 'twas not like any dance Blake knew, for the man's hands were all over the poor woman.

"Hang it!" He charged the couple.

Chapter 18

When Maston approached Emeline and asked for a dance, she flatly refused. The man may have cleaned up nicely and had shown a tad bit of sophistication, but he was naught but a libertine. She would find no hero in this pirate, no rescuer from any of the men on the *Summons* nor on this island of fools.

Maston did not take no for an answer. The scent of rum and wine flooded her nose, overpowering his rosemary cologne, as he dragged her onto the floor and began a minuet. Though 'twas no minuet she'd ever danced, for he fumbled through a series of steps before simply clutching her waist and spinning her around.

The audience of pirates chuckled and encouraged Maston with coarse jests.

"Now, that be the way t' treat a wench, Maston!"

"Grab 'er tighter, mate. Tell us, is a true lady as soft as them wenches ye frequent?"

Emeline struggled to free herself. She pushed from him, but he clutched her all the closer. She tried kicking him, but he twirled her so fast, she found no leverage. Fear, along with anger, buzzed through her. And the oddest thought blared in her mind. Where was Blake? She needed Blake! Of course that was ridiculous. Why would he care that she was being molested?

But he *did* care. At least that's what she saw on his face as he marched toward them, grabbed Maston's arm, and wrenched him around.

He didn't say a word, offered no reprimand, no insult. He merely swung back and struck Maston so hard across the jaw that the man flew backward and landed on the floor.

The pirates hooted and hollered like a pack of wolves.

The orchestra ceased...an odd final note floating in an eerie chime of shame.

The bosun struggled to rise on his elbows, blinked, and shook his head before glaring at his captain, hatred in his gaze.

"Touch her again and die," was all Blake said before taking her arm and leading her from the room.

Down a long hall and up two flights of stairs, he continued, not saying a word, his breath puffing like a dragon's. Golden light from perched lanterns flickered over his stiff mouth and tight jaw. A strand of hair had loosened from his tie and dangled over his cheek. She sensed his fury, but she also smelled wine, which meant the man was more than volatile at the moment.

Ergo, she kept her tongue. Wise, since she had no idea whether to thank him or ask him why he was so angry. A terrifying thought sent her blood racing. Perhaps he finally intended to have his way with her. Perhaps Maston's salacious dance had given Blake the impetus he needed.

He barely stopped to open the door to her chamber as he led her inside, struck flint to steel and lit a lantern. When he finally faced her, the rage in his eyes had abated, replaced by something else...something she could not name, but something which vanquished her fear.

"Lock your door and stay here, Emeline. You'll be safe."

Before she could utter a word, he left and closed the door behind him. She stood there, her heart thrashing, her breath raging, listening to his boots thunder down the hall.

It took her what seemed like hours to calm her nerves. No servants arrived to help her disrobe or bring her tea. Hence, with a great deal of struggle, she finally managed to remove her gown and stomacher, along with all its fripperies. After carefully laying them across a chair, she allowed herself one last chance to run her fingers over the soft silk and admire the beauty of such exquisite attire. Oddly, a nightdress and robe had been left for her, which she quickly donned before she knelt beside her bed and prayed.

"Lord Jesus, I don't know where You are or why this is happening, but I thank You for keeping me safe, even amongst these vile rogues. You have showered Your favor upon me, even in the darkest of places, even in the shadow of death, in which I now find myself. Help me to fear no evil and know You are with me. Help me to find Your purpose in all of this. Bless my father and mother and Esther and Caleb. Keep them safe and help them to find me soon. Amen."

Feeling more at peace than she had in a while, she crawled under the coverlet and tried to fall asleep. She must have drifted off, for she woke suddenly, her heart racing. She glanced around the dark room but saw no movement. Had she heard something? There it was again. A howl, an agonizing howl, like a wounded animal.

Pulling the covers up to her chin, she stared into the darkness, eyes wide open, waiting…listening.

Noises filtered through the wall. A groan sounded. Then footsteps. The door she had assumed led to a dressing closet flung open.

Emeline shot up in bed, terror gripping her. A shadow came through the door. She heard it breathing…hard. "Who is it? What do you want?"

"'Tis me, Emeline." The captain's pained voice responded.

"What is it? Why are you here?" Though she could guess…yet…nay. He'd had many other opportunities.

"Come with me." The deep tenor of his voice echoed through the room like a doleful ballad, prompting her to swing her feet over the edge of the mattress and hop to the floor. He disappeared into the next room, and without hesitation, she flung her robe over her shoulders and followed. Perhaps because she sensed no danger. Perhaps because the desperation in his voice tugged on her heart. Perhaps because she was the biggest, most gullible fool in the Caribbean. Either way, she entered a bedchamber similar to hers but much larger and more elaborate. The light from a single lantern flickered over the muscles on Blake's bare back as he moved to drop into one of the stuffed chairs by his bed.

Halting just inside the doorway, Emeline hugged herself, the pounding of her heart ringing in her ears.

He leaned forward, elbows on his knees, sending the cross and emblem around his neck dangling before him. "Play for me."

At first Emeline had no idea what the crazed pirate meant, but he gestured to another chair at the foot of the bed where a violin perched, leaning against the back.

"Now? In the middle of the night?" She retreated a step. "Can it not wait until morning?"

"Nay." Then several seconds later. "Please." An appeal from the heart. Not a command.

Well, how can I turn down a 'please' from my captor? She wanted to retort sarcastically but decided against it. Something was wrong, evil even. She felt it in the chamber just like she'd sensed it in the captain's cabin when he'd summoned her at night.

Thus, she picked up the violin, relishing the feel of the instrument in her hands. Memories flooded her, happy memories of her and her mother performing a duet for the crew of the *Ransom*, her father's ship. Had that only been a month ago?

She slid onto the chair and placed the bottom of the violin on her shoulder and her chin in the rest. Then, positioning the bow, she started with a simple but soothing tune she'd learned recently.

Blake hated his weakness, his need for anyone. He'd hoped the demonic nightmares would cease once he was on land, but they only got worse. No sooner had he drunk himself into a rum-induced stupor and laid his head on his pillow, desperate for sleep, than the dark shadows returned. Larger, stronger, greater in number, their incessant mocking and threatening voices blending into a hellish chant that scraped over his soul. Blaring through it all came his father's fiendish howl.

The howl of both shock and pain that would forever haunt Blake.

It faded the moment Emeline entered the chamber. Even the shadows retreated. Now, as the sweet notes from the violin spiraled through the air, all darkness fled. Peace settled on Blake. His head ceased throbbing, his heart calmed. He closed his eyes and leaned his head back on the chair.

Emeline played the instrument as well as any musician he'd heard. Such soothing tones, such exquisite notes, all expertly woven into a tapestry of wonder by the angel sitting in the red velvet chair. She looked every bit an angel in her white robe with her hair tumbling over her shoulders in a waterfall of chestnut waves. Her eyes were closed as she eased the bow over the strings in a seductive dance that mesmerized Blake.

And he hated himself for it.

Hated his growing attraction to the lady, his growing admiration, and worse, his *need* for her.

When he'd decided long ago never to need anyone ever again. Need led to want and want led to dependence and dependence led to naught but disappointment and heartache.

Still, he must keep her for now. Until he could figure out how to use the Ring to send the demons that haunted him back to hell where they belonged.

The music stopped. He opened his eyes to find the lady approaching slowly, hesitantly. He leaned forward on his knees, gripping the amulet hanging about his neck. "Please continue, Emeline."

She knelt before him, her night dress circling around her like a cloud of purity. "Something horrible happened to you. What was it?"

Snorting, he raked back his hair. "I couldn't sleep is all."

"Nay, 'tis something deeper."

Could the blasted woman see into his soul? Perhaps she was trained in the dark arts…a witch? He studied her, but the light reflecting in those glimmering golden eyes revealed only sincerity and…care?

"You cannot deny you have nightmares, see shadows. I've heard you speak of them in your sleep."

Hang it. He'd exposed too much to this woman.

"'Tis the Ring." She nodded toward the jewel on his finger. "It's evil. Legend says it summons demons."

He blew out an incredulous sigh. "If it can summon them, it can send them back to hell."

"There's only one power that can send demons scurrying away in fear."

The woman herself 'twould seem. "And what power is that, for you seem in possession of it." If he could harness it, he would have no further need of her.

"The power of God. His Holy Spirit dwells within those who confess Jesus as Lord."

"God, bah! He has naught to do with this or with me."

"Can you deny it?"

"I cannot deny that your goodness casts them away." Her skin looked like shimmering silk in the lantern light. Her lips moist and full. Her sweet smell drifted around him, taunting him. Raising his hand, he ran a finger down her cheek, then pressed it on her lips.

She didn't flinch, didn't retreat. Instead, her eyes searched his as if seeking answers before dropping to the cross dangling about his neck. "You wear the cross of Christ. Why?"

The spell broke. Blake grabbed the small crucifix, pressing it between his fingers. "'Twas my mother's. Like you, she believed in a benevolent God." *As did my father.*

"Then you know of the love of our Savior." She smiled. Such promise, such joy filled that smile that Blake hated to make it vanish. But vanish it must.

"The only love I learned was the kind that cast me from my home at sixteen."

Her lips parted slightly as sorrow claimed her features. "I'm sorry, Blake."

"She did me a favor." He leaned back in the chair and folded his hands across his bare belly.

"What of the other emblem?" Emeline pointed to his chest, then averted her gaze as if his state of undress bothered her. Or perhaps attracted her? Nay. She was too pure for that.

He fingered the lion emblem. "As the lion is king of the beasts, so will I be king of my own kingdom. The sun speaks of the dawn of my new life."

"And the dove?"

"Peace when I have achieved my goals."

She seemed to ponder his explanation, then added, "And the black pearl in your ear?"

"'Twas a gift," he mumbled. "Enough with your questions!" His outburst came out louder and more forceful than he'd wanted. But the effect was the same.

The lady shrank back, chest pumping, and eyes wide as she scrambled to her feet.

"More music," he commanded.

"And if I don't wish to play?" Her voice trembled.

He allowed his salacious gaze to scan her. "Then we will find something else to play."

Chapter 19

Emeline leaned her face toward the rising sun, relishing its warm caress and praying it would wipe away the darkness and foreboding that had consumed her during the night. After the captain fell asleep, she'd carefully laid the violin down and returned to her bed. But her mind and heart found no peace. One minute she sensed a tenderness in Blake, a humility even. The next, the steel returned to his eyes. One minute he opened his heart a crack and allowed her entrance. Then the next, he slammed it shut. One minute, he caressed her cheek gently as one would a lover. The next, he threatened to ravish her. Which man lurked beneath his pirate exterior? Hero or villain? Gentleman or rogue? He was a man of mystery. A mystery she honestly had no desire to solve.

Therefore when Charlie knocked on her door in the morning and offered to give her a tour of the gardens, Emeline gladly accepted. They broke their fast with papaya and freshly brewed coffee before leaving the big house through one of the French doors in the dining room. When Emeline inquired after the captain, Charlie said he had risen early and was attending business on board the *Summons*.

Good. Emeline had no desire to see the man after his lewd threat. She glanced over the well-maintained gardens, filled with manicured bushes and tropical flowers in every color of the rainbow—hibiscus, jasmine, ginger lilies, and bougainvillea. Their sweet scent filled the air with God's best perfume, and Emeline couldn't inhale enough of the aromatic fragrance. In the middle of the garden, birds of every color imaginable fluttered about an ornate stone fountain filled with water sparkling in the sunlight.

"It's truly beautiful," she said as they proceeded down a stone pathway that wove through the tropical paradise. "Who would have thought a pirate would own such an elaborate mansion and lavish gardens."

"Aye, surprised me as well when he first brought me here." Charlie drew a deep breath, quieter and more pensive today than usual.

They continued walking past a row of Ackee trees, the sweet fruit dangling from branches. "I'm sorry the captain assigned you to watch over me. No doubt you have better things to do."

Charlie flashed her a smile. "Not watch. He asked me t' show you around is all. An' no, I do not have duties at the moment. I use these visits here t' rest."

"Hmm. Am I free to wander about, then?"

Charlie cocked her head. "Well, you *are* on an island, Miss. With no chance of escape."

"Call me Emeline, please." The woman had a point. Unless, of course, Emeline could find a small fishing boat or shallop to steal. She knew how to sail, and her father had taught her to navigate by the sun and stars. Even so, sailing on the open sea was dangerous in so small a craft.

Female giggling tickled the air as they turned another corner to find Maston, one arm on a post, leaning over a comely servant girl who stared up at him adoringly.

Emeline's stomach soured.

The pirate's eyes lit with surprise when he saw them, and he gave a mock bow. "Ladies."

"Don't you *lady* us, you witless barracuda," Charlie spat out, then faced the young girl. "If you know what's good for you, girl, best get as far away from this puckish princox as you can."

Emeline frowned. Wasn't it just last night Maston had fondled her on the dance floor, whispering flatteries in her ears? And here he was already onto his next conquest. Weaving

her arm through Charlie's, she led her away before she and
Maston drew swords again.

"Come, let's go dip our feet in the sea, shall we?" Emeline
said. That way she could get the lay of the land, see how big
the island was and more importantly, if there was any possible
way to escape.

"I'd think you'd be sick o' the sea, Miss…Em. I'm goin' t'
call you Em." She shrugged. "But why not?"

The gardens opened to a narrow path lined by thick jungle
and riddled with tree roots and vines. Air, heavy with moisture,
grew abuzz with all manner of insects. Colorful birds flitted
through the canopy as Charlie navigated the winding trail,
Emeline on her heels.

Finally, they emerged from the tangled web of leaves and
branches to a narrow strip of sand. A single-masted fishing
boat had been pulled up from a tidal pool onto shore and tied to
the trunk of a tree.

A boat! The perfect size for a single person skilled in
sailing. Why had Charlie brought her here? There was barely
enough sand to sit upon, a mere ribbon of water in which to dip
their toes, and a thick canopy overhead blocking the sunlight.
Emeline stared at Charlie quizzically, while trying to hide her
excitement. "Not exactly what I had in mind. Is there not a
better beach?"

An impish smile sat upon the master gunner's lips as she
nodded toward the boat.

Emeline raised her brows. "Are we sailing somewhere?"

"Nay, but *you* could if you needed to." Understanding
sparked from her eyes. "See that speck o' land?" She pointed
out to sea where Emeline could barely make out a brown dot
upon the blue waters.

She nodded.

"That be Bear Island. Wit' calm seas, someone wit'
knowledge of sailing could make it. Word is there is a fishing
village there an' a small port."

Emeline swallowed a lump of emotion at the woman's kindness. Quickly followed by suspicion, for she well knew that Charlie's loyalty to the captain could not be questioned. "Even should I dare attempt such a feat and make it to shore, with what shall I book passage?"

A burst of salt-laden wind spun Charlie's long hair behind her as she offered a sly grin. "Aye, I thought of that, an' when no one were looking, I put a pouch of coins and a flintlock in the bottom drawer of the dressing bureau in your chamber. You do know how to fire it?"

Confusion joined Emeline's suspicion. "Of course, but I do not understand. Why…why would you help me?"

"You saved me from Maston at great risk t' yourself. We women must help each other in this world run by men, eh?" She winked. "An' also because you didn't do nothing deserving of your fate."

Emeline forced back the moisture in her eyes, still unsure whether she should trust the woman. "I don't know how to thank you."

"No need." Pivoting, Charlie headed down the narrow strip of sand.

Mind spinning with both renewed hope and joy at Charlie's kindness, Emeline followed. Within minutes, they entered the same shore upon which Emeline had first set her feet. 'Twas even more beautiful than she remembered. The perfect bay, deep enough for a brig, yet hidden from passing ships by the embracing arms of a wooded inlet. Turquoise water lapped ashore in glittering waves as Charlie plopped to the sand and began removing her boots.

In the distance, the *Summons* sat like a regal prince upon the calm waters, and Emeline could make out men on its deck and hear muffled shouts. If the captain was indeed on board, the last thing she wanted was to face him.

"Is there no other shore we can enjoy?"

Charlie squinted up at her in the sunlight. "Nay. Not wit' a beach this nice." Then rolling up the hems of her breeches, she leapt to her feet and headed toward the waves.

Grinning at the woman's childlike playfulness, Emeline removed her shoes, hiked up her skirts, and joined her.

The warm water tickled her feet as her toes sank into the silty sand. Just offshore, fish in a myriad of gorgeous colors darted here and there without a care in the world. The words of Jesus swelled in her mind.

Behold the fowls of the air: for they sow not, neither do they reap, nor gather into barns; yet your heavenly Father feedeth them. Are ye not much better than they?

No doubt that applied to fish, as well. Then why was *she* worried? God was in control. He knew exactly where she was, even if her parents didn't.

A spray of salty water splashed her. Shocked, she looked up to see Charlie wearing a devilish grin and about to dip her hand in the surf again.

"Oh no, you don't!" Emeline teased as she leaned over and flung foamy droplets over her friend.

They continued splashing and giggling as if they were little girls enjoying a day at the beach…instead of the master gunner of a pirate ship and the prisoner of its captain.

Still, it felt good to laugh, good to pretend that all was well with the world. If only for a moment. Finally, with their attire damp and their moods much improved, they both lowered to the sand once again.

"You're not at all like I first thought, Em." Charlie laughed. "I thought you were one o' them shrewish hoity-toity ladies who look down their regal noses at the rest of us."

Emeline smiled. "Then I thank you for the compliment."

No sooner did Charlie stretch out her legs, than the jovial mood from only moments before slipped from the woman.

"Is something wrong?" Emeline asked.

Shaking her head, Charlie leaned back on her hands.

Emeline sensed a loss, a longing in the woman. "You are missing someone."

Charlie snapped a suspicious glance her way.

"A child, perhaps?" Emeline pressed.

"How do you know such things!?" Charlie's shout startled Emeline, reminding her that this woman was as hard and tough as any man. Anger flared in her eyes before she huffed and looked away.

Emeline proceeded with caution. "I think God shows me things. Gives me knowledge about people." Her father had called the gift a word of knowledge. She should be excited, happy that she, too, possessed a special talent. But she'd yet to see its value. Other than angering those she told.

The sun peeked over the tall palms of the cove, spreading rays of warmth over Emeline. She closed her eyes, longing for the carefree moments she'd only just shared with this volatile woman, longing for a friend amidst the enemies who surrounded her. The gentle lap of waves and trill of birds caressed her ears but brought no peace to her soul.

"There *is* a child," Charlie finally said. "Michael." Such love, such longing rang from the sound of his name on her lips that a lump swelled in Emeline's throat.

Charlie gave a sad smile and picked up a shell.

"Aye," Emeline said. "I think I met him. In Basseterre."

"What? How? Why?" Charlie leapt to her feet, planting fists at her waist.

"I'm so sorry. I followed you." Looking down, Emeline ran her fingers through the sand. "I was so alone and lost. I thought perhaps you could help me."

"You saw him?" The master gunner's voice squeaked with emotion.

"Aye. For a moment, but the woman at the house sent me away."

Dropping to the sand, Charlie clutched Emeline's arm. Tight. "You must never tell anyone. No one."

"You have my word. You can trust me."

Her brown eyes flitted between Emeline's before she turned to face the sea. "Aye, I believe I can."

"May I ask what happened?"

Charlie dug her feet deeper in the sand and glanced over the waters, rubbing the shell between thumb and forefinger. "The usual sad tale. I fell in love. Believed every word he said. Allowed him to seduce me, an' then when I announced I was wit' child, he got on his ship an' sailed away."

The words spilled from her lips so fast and devoid of emotion that they seemed but a fabrication. Emeline had heard far too many similar stories from the poor women begging for scraps in the streets. "Who was he?"

"Captain Marcus Hanson or Sir Marcus Hanson, as he likes to be called. Baronet, merchantmen, plantation owner. Rich an' powerful." She drew a deep breath and stared out to sea. "He swept me away on wild adventures, treated me like a princess, a precious thing to be cherished."

Exactly what Emeline always longed for. A hero, a romance like her parents. "I understand. I truly do. What woman wouldn't have fallen for such attention?" Would she? *Was* she? Her gaze landed on the *Summons*, seeking a glimpse of the captain.

"I am a fool, Em. A complete fool." Charlie pasted on a hard smile. "But I learned. I grew stronger. I know what men are now. What liars they are. Not a one to be trusted."

Emeline longed to tell the woman that not all of them were like that. The men in her family, those who had turned to God, were honorable, trustworthy, *true* heroes. "Yet look at you now. You're a master gunner aboard a successful pirate ship. A man's job, to be sure. And you do it well."

Finally, the lady smiled again. "Better!"

"Indeed." Emeline laughed as a tiny crab skittered across the sand and dove into a hole.

Minutes passed in silence before Emeline dared to ask, "Who is the woman who cares for Michael?"

"My mum."

"And you support them with the treasure you earn?"

"Aye, the only way I can. That's why I joined wit' Cap'n Keene. I could not provide for Michael doing anything else. Nor my mum. We would be begging on the streets."

Taking a risk with the capricious woman, Emeline laid her hand on Charlie's. "You are so brave and strong. I admire you immensely. You entered a man's world, even dress like them, and you possess more courage and strength than them all." So unlike Emeline, who had the confidence of a gnat. Even more shameful was this woman did not even rely on God.

Charlie gave her hand a squeeze. "You are kind. I see why he likes you."

Emeline had no doubt to whom she referred. "He likes only himself."

Charlie laughed. "Well, they do say opposites attract."

Emeline couldn't help but join in her laughter.

"You know, my family and I help people in situations like yours. There are other opportunities for women on these islands. Thievery is no decent life. God *can* help you."

Charlie tossed the shell into the water with a *plunk*. "If God were gonna help me, He'd a done it already."

Emeline longed to say more, to help this lady see how much God loved her, but movement caught her eye, and Bandit came darting across the sand and barreled into her arms, nearly knocking her over. Behind him, Captain Blake Keene marched toward them.

Looking none too happy.

Chapter 20

"I want every sheet checked for rips, every rope, block, and pulley inspected. Caulk the seams, tar the rigging, scrub the deck, polish every spit of brass, and pump the bilge from the hold." Blake spouted a string of orders to Finn as they stood amidships. His quartermaster nodded, sending his pipe bobbing up and down in the morning light.

Blake continued, giving further instructions, though his friend no doubt knew what to do. He'd sailed with Blake for five years, since Blake had first set out as a buccaneer. "I want the brig cleaned from stem to stern, guns cleaned, supplies checked and replenished, and ready to set sail at a moment's notice."

Finn pulled the pipe from his mouth. "Aye, aye, Cap'n. Ye knows ye can trust me." His grin, which was rarely so wide, revealed two missing teeth on the bottom and a gold one on top. Yet when he lowered his gaze again, 'twas to the Ring on Blake's finger.

Blake clapped him on the back, hoping he could trust him, but remembering his vow to put no faith in anyone again, not a man or, especially, not a woman.

Finn pointed his pipe at the Ring. "Are ye tellin' me that this Ring were the same Ring King Solomon wore?"

Blake nodded, fingering the relic. "Aye, that's what I hear."

"Well, I'll be the son o' a sea urchin. No wonder ye stole it from ole Slippery Crock." He licked his lips. "And it 'as power! Mystical power. Blind me, but were it what made the storm on the island that 'elped us escape?"

As much as Blake would prefer to deny it, how could he? "So it would seem."

Finn whistled and scratched beneath his bandana. "Wit' that kind a power, ye'd be undefeated on sea an' land."

That was the idea. Still, the hungry gleam in the quartermaster's eyes gave Blake pause. Friend or not, what man on earth wouldn't want to possess such power? And who could blame him?

Chattering rang across the deck, and Bandit leapt from the ratlines onto Blake's shoulder. He'd wondered where the monkey had run off to. Most likely swinging through the canopy, chasing birds, and enjoying the abundance of tropical fruits. Now, he screeched into Blake's ear and put his spindly little hand on the Ring on Blake's finger.

He could have sworn he heard Bandit say, "The Ring is hers." But that couldn't be.

Finn chuckled. "Seems even yer monkey wants the Ring."

Blake shook his head. "Did you hear him say something?"

"The stinky varmint?" Finn's brows crossed. "Nay. Are ye feelin' well, Cap'n?"

"Never mind." Blake grabbed Bandit and set him on the deck just as female laughter floated on the morning mist. Making his way to the railing, he could hardly believe his eyes. Charlie and Emeline frolicked in the surf like little girls, splashing each other over and over and laughing as if they hadn't a care in the world. Amazed, he envied them, watching their childish play for several moments, finding it hard not to smile.

Joining him, Finn snickered. "Well, fire an' flame. Ne'er saw Charlie act like a girl afore."

"Aye, 'tis a strange sight, indeed. Now, quit dawdling and get to work." Blake regretted his harsh tone, but he must prove his authority with his crew, even those he considered friends. Besides, he suddenly remembered that last night he had disclosed things to Emeline he'd never told anyone, and his anger burned.

What was it about the silly female that caused him to open his heart, a heart he vowed to keep safe behind a fortress of indifference and self-interest?

Shoving his pipe back into his mouth, Finn ambled away, grumbling, just as Bandit leapt onto the bulwarks. The traitorous monkey spotted Emeline and Charlie and wasted no time scrambling up the ratlines onto the forward yard and leaping from it onto a palm branch reaching for the brig. From there, he darted across the sand to the ladies.

Blake double-checked his Ring just in case, then cursed and ordered a pirate to row him ashore.

Emeline looked none too happy to see him, though how could he blame her? He must not show weakness, must not show that what happened between them last night troubled him in the least. Hence, he put on his most authoritative expression, ordered Charlie to the brig to aid Finn with the repairs, and told Emeline to accompany him.

Sighing her displeasure, the lady slipped her shoes back on, stood, brushed sand from her skirts, and gave him a pointed look. "Am I to run the gauntlet, Captain?"

Blake couldn't help but grin. "Tempting. Unless you've done something to warrant it?"

"The look on your face. 'Tis the same one you give your crew when they've done something to incur your wrath."

"Ah, you think you know me so well, my sugar bird."

"Stop calling me that! I am not made of sugar, nor am I your little bird."

Her face flushed in such an adorable way, Blake smiled again, something he was doing far too often for a pirate captain. "Follow me." Turning, he started for the jungle, listening for her footsteps behind him. Would she obey?

Moments passed, but finally the sound of shuffling sand along with grumbling brought his assurance.

Pushing aside a large fern, he held it back for her as she entered the tangled wood. Bandit darted for her but leapt into a tree instead.

"How long are we to be on this island?" She brushed past him. Her sweet scent blended with the smell of earth and greenery, defying her earlier declaration that she was not made of sugar.

A sugar he would love to sample.

"I haven't decided." He slipped beside her. "Are you bored already? Prefer the tiny cabin on the *Summons*?"

Clutching her skirts, she stepped over a thick vine traversing the path and frowned. "What I prefer is to be home with my family."

"Hmm. I doubt they have such a fine estate since I've heard they give away quite a bit to the impoverished."

Halting, she glared at him. A strand of her chestnut-colored hair dangled over her moist cheek, and he longed to slip it behind her ear. "What does it profit a man if he gains the whole world but loses his soul?"

Now 'twas Blake's turn to frown. "You quote the Bible to a pirate?" He started forward again.

"Then you know the Word of God."

A lizard skittered across the trail and disappeared into a shrub. "My mother read it to me when I was a child. As you can see, it made little impact."

"Obviously."

They walked in silence for several minutes, listening to the birdsong and buzz of insects. Along with Bandit's occasional babbling above them as the monkey followed them through the canopy. Though Blake preferred the sea, there was something magnificent about life that teemed thick in the jungle.

"What *will* make an impact on you, then, Captain?" she asked.

A pungent question, indeed. One he did not wish to answer at the moment, for it had much to do with the lady herself.

Soon, they emerged into a large clearing full of rows and rows of all manner of crops. If he admitted it, he enjoyed the way Emeline's eyes widened at the sight.

"What is all this?"

"I cleared the land for the Caribs who live here. They were already good at growing some crops, but I introduced others. Over there,"—he pointed to their left—"they grow yams and peppers. Then here, you see the lines of corn. Toward the jungle to the south,"—he gestured to the right—"are bananas and Cassava. On the other side of the island, we planted coffee and sugar cane."

Fisting his hands on his hips, he gazed over the vast farmland, still amazed at what he had accomplished. Several natives worked among the rows, tending the plants, while others loaded wagons with fresh produce. Surely the lady would find such a large farm impressive.

"They are your slaves?" she finally asked, her tone disapproving.

He frowned. Not the reaction he'd hoped for. "Nay, they are welcome to eat whatever they grow as long as they provide for me and my crew when we are here and my staff when we are at sea. You see, we are self-sufficient. With fish and wild boar aplenty, we have all we need to survive."

Her eyes swept to his, nary a hint of the amazement and admiration he expected to see within them.

"Is that what you seek most? A kingdom of your own?"

"Who wouldn't want that?" He clutched the lion emblem around his neck, frustration bubbling in his gut. "Surely you find something here worthy of your approval?"

Wind tore over them, fluttering her loose curls behind her. "What does my opinion matter? You forget I am your prisoner."

Blake ground his teeth. "And yet you have your freedom to roam as you please."

"It is still a cage, is it not?"

The ungrateful wench! "If that is what you prefer, it can be arranged."

There it was. The first speck of fear crossed her eyes. The first speck of the respect he deserved. Though for some reason, he instantly regretted it.

As if angry at his censure of the lady, Bandit leapt from a branch onto his shoulder and scolded him. Unfortunately, Blake understood the monkey's harsh castigation well enough. Shoving him from his shoulder, he hoped he would leave, but the treasonous beast vaulted into Emeline's arms.

Drawing the monkey close, she lowered her gaze. "I am appreciative of the comforts you have provided, Captain."

He wanted to add, *as you should be,* but thought better of it. Instead, he led her past the fields and down another trail, past the Carib village, the sugar and gristmills, and storage barns. All of which engendered not a speck of her admiration.

In fact, her jovial mood from only moments ago grew dour, and he longed for their joyful banter to return.

He plucked Bandit from her arms. "I trust this may quite astound you." As it had astounded Blake when he'd first discovered this particular power of the Ring. "Bandit," he spoke with authority, drawing the monkey's gaze. "Go fetch the lady a ripe mango."

Grinning, Bandit flew from his arms onto a branch above them, then swinging through the canopy, made his way to a mango tree Blake had spotted. Within minutes, the monkey returned, a ripe green and orange fruit in his hand, which he quickly gave to Emeline.

She stared at it, her delicate brows scrunching, as her eyes shifted between the mango and Blake. "He does your bidding. He understands you?"

"Aye." Blake rubbed the back of his neck. "I can hardly believe it as well." He scratched Bandit on the head. "You mentioned one of the powers of the Ring was communicating with animals, did you not?"

"Aye." She blew out a sigh. "I thought 'twas only that the wearer understood what the animal said, not the other way around." Her eyes widened. "That was why Bandit stole the Ring from Della Morte on that island with the hurricane. You instructed him."

Blake nodded, enjoying this brief glimmer of approval from the lady.

Smiling, she plopped the mango into her skirt pocket and caressed Bandit's cheek. "Thank you, little one."

The monkey's grin couldn't have been wider.

Finally, back at the great house, Blake ushered her into the dining hall and ordered a light lunch of fresh bread, cheese, and plantains. Against all reason, he wanted to spend more time with the lady, found her company challenging and enjoyable like none other.

But 'twas obvious the lady did not return such sentiments. "I fear I am not hungry. May I retire to my chamber, Captain?" She stood before him, eyes and jaw like steel.

"Forgive my earlier outburst, Emeline." He approached, enjoying her flinch at the sound of her Christian name on his lips. He quite enjoyed the sound of it as well.

"An apology?" A spark of playfulness flitted across her eyes. "Are you feeling well?"

He knew she meant it in jest, but he was not in the jesting mood. "Will you at least admit that I have accomplished more than most lads tossed from their homes at only sixteen?"

Her eyes met his, sorrow and sincerity burned within them. "You have done well, Captain. I merely wonder to what purpose?"

To what purpose? The woman muddled his brain. Any normal woman, anyone, in fact, regardless of their approval of his lifestyle, would be more than impressed with what he had accomplished in so short a time. Storming to the window, he stared out upon his island, *his* kingdom. Why did he care what this feeble missionary woman thought?

Emeline stared at Blake. A man of intense conflict and deep sorrow. Much like the funnel she'd seen in her dream, confusion, pain, loss, and betrayal all spun around him in a desperate need for power and control that would eventually pull him under. Worse, he was volatile. She never knew what would set the man off like a matchstick to a cannon.

He snapped an angry gaze her way. "You baffle me, Emeline."

Thankfully, before she could respond in kind, Pedro entered the room, a wide grin on his face.

"Cap'n, can I go t' the stables an' ride one o' the horses?"

Blake gave a disgusted grunt. "If you want to be a pirate captain someday, you need to quit wasting your time in idle pursuits. Pish! You should be on board the *Summons* helping Finn with repairs. But what do I expect from the likes of you? At your age I was working from dawn to dusk on my father's plantation!"

Emeline's body stiffened at the demeaning words pouring out like bilge water over the innocent lad. Pedro's cheerful countenance sank to the floor. His shoulders slumped. All life and sparkle fled his eyes.

"I have work to do." Blake marched to the door, the slam of his boots on the tile echoing his fury through the room. "Pedro, take Miss Hyde to her chambers and then report to Finn on the *Summons* immediately!" he shouted over his shoulder before he disappeared down the hall.

Forcing back her own fury, Emeline approached Pedro, who remained frozen in place, staring out the window like a pirate who'd just been keelhauled. Though he tried to contain himself, his bottom lip quivered.

"He didn't mean what he said, Pedro. He's angry with me, not you." She tried to pull him close for a hug, but he jerked away.

"He's righ', Miss. I'm not much good for nothing."

She gripped his shoulders and made him look at her. "That is not true. You are a smart, capable young man, and you will make something great out of yourself someday."

His lips slanted, but he shook his head. "If my own father didn't want me, Miss…" His voice trailed off into a sob.

Sorrow gripped her heart so tight, she slumped into a nearby chair. How does a child recover from such rejection? *Why, Lord? Why do you allow so much pain in this forsaken world?* "Come sit with me a moment." She gestured to a chair beside hers.

"Nay, Miss, I best do what the cap'n ordered." He ran a hand through his shock of red hair and smiled. Always a smile on this boy, no matter his pain.

"You must believe in yourself, in who God made you to be. And know that whatever task is set before you, He will equip you to do it well." Even as she said the words, she realized she needed to hear them as much as this lad. Wasn't she just as much an accident as this boy? She'd been only seven years old when she'd overheard her parents saying they'd not wanted another child after Caleb, how upset they'd been when her mother had found out she was with child again. How they wanted to spend their time and money helping orphan children, not having more of their own. It devasted her at the time. She was an accident, an unforeseen tragedy, a burden to her parents.

"Thank you for your kindness, Miss." Pedro interrupted her thoughts. "You're the only one ever been nice to me."

Emeline smiled, then allowed the lad to escort her back to her chamber. Once there, she checked the bottom drawer of the dressing bureau and found the coins and pistol just where Charlie had put them. Astounding. She closed the drawer and spent the afternoon praying for Pedro, for Charlie, for the captain, and for all of them.

"I must be here for a reason, Lord. All these people desperately need to know You, to know they are loved and that You have a better plan for their lives. But am I doing any good at all?" For it seemed to her, she was wasting her time. "Perhaps You should have sent my sister... or better yet, my brother." Surely, they would have the entire island bowing their knees to the Almighty by now.

Feeling every bit the failure that Pedro felt earlier, she paced her chamber throughout the afternoon, one minute glancing out the window onto the gardens below, the other resting upon her bed, the next counting the steps from wall to wall.

All the while thinking of that fishing boat Charlie had shown her and plotting her soon escape.

Chapter 21

Blake's frustration only grew through the afternoon, an afternoon of dealing with a series of trifling issues in the management of the estate and farmland. All of which made him long to be out to sea again. In due time. First, he must plot his next conquest, his next step toward enlarging his kingdom. In addition, he needed a plan to deal with that infernal Jesuit, Signor Arturo Della Morte, who was no doubt still in pursuit of the Ring.

After cleaning and putting on fresh attire, he passed by Emeline's door, ignoring the yearning to see her. Instead, he made his way downstairs, heading for his gallery, where his estate manager had recently hung a new painting. Something about the masterpieces always soothed his nerves. With the addition of a little rum, of course.

No sooner did he enter the large gallery, the walls of which were covered with paintings, than he saw Emeline standing before his newest acquisition, gazing up at it with admiration.

Finally, there was something the lady appreciated. He took a moment to admire her as he headed her way. Though she was of a more petite stature than most women, she held herself tall and regal as if she were royalty. She wore the same azure gown that gathered at her small waist and spread out in a voluminous overskirt, revealing a silk petticoat underneath. A lacy fringe that matched the cuffs on her half sleeves lined her modest neckline. 'Twas the same gown she'd worn since he'd first seen her, but he still found it quite appealing. She'd pinned up her hair in a bundle of curls from which several had escaped and dangled about her neck.

Hearing his approach, she glanced his way. He longed for a smile but received a mere frown instead. In truth, his presence seemed to leech all the joy from her face.

But what did he expect? He slipped beside her and gestured toward the painting. "What are your impressions of Jan Vermeer? I quite admire this one, *Girl with a Pearl Earring.*"

"I adore his work." She nibbled on her lower lip. "However, I am quite astonished to find any of it here."

Ignoring her disapproving tone, he waved an arm around the gallery. "You'll find more of his work, along with several pieces by Diego Velázquez. Most are reproductions, of course, but I do have one original. Would you like to see it?"

"How on earth would you have acquired an original?" Her tone was incredulous.

He raised one brow and grinned.

"Ah. How could I forget?" She looked away. "You are a pirate and a thief." Her sharp rebuke cut him. "All of these are stolen, then?"

"Nay. Not all. I purchased one or two." Why did he always feel like he needed to defend himself with this woman? He'd never been ashamed of his chosen profession before. Quite the opposite.

They moved to look at the next piece, one of his favorites—a naval battle by Willem van de Velde the Younger.

She gazed up at it in wonder.

"I see we not only share a love of music but of art, as well." As he knew she would. None of his pirates or staff had a care for the fine arts, leaving him lonely in his admiration. "Is it not majestic?"

"It is truly stunning. I do admire your taste, Captain," she said, then faced him, studying him in that invasive way of hers before adding, "You should not have scolded him so. You belittled him."

At first Blake merely stared at her, confused, his mind searching for who the *him* was. Ah…so that was it. He snorted in disbelief. "Pedro is a cabin boy, not a prince."

She shook her head, sending her curls dancing. "And you are so much better than he?"

"Aye, as you can see," he said, waving his hand around the opulent room—the paintings, the sculptures, the Persian rugs gracing the floor, and the lanterns perched on walls between pieces of artwork, casting a royal glow over everything.

"So a man is measured by his possessions?" She cocked her head, frowning.

Blake gripped the lion amulet dangling around his neck. "And power."

She studied him. Lantern light sparkled across her eyes—eyes that dove deep into his as if searching for treasure. "What do you intend to do with your power? Are you content with your island kingdom, or do you have other conquests in mind?"

"Many other conquests, Miss. Why would I need the Ring to do what I have already accomplished without it?"

"Then you are to rule the world?" A sparkle of playfulness lit her eyes.

"Perhaps not the entire thing." He joked but then grew serious. "But 'twould be nice to rule the Spanish Main, send the power-hungry European powers back home, and take the land for myself. As you see, I am quite benevolent to the natives."

She moved to the next painting. "What of the African slaves already here?"

"I would set them free to work for me."

At first she nodded, no doubt pleased with his charity, but then she released a heavy sigh. "Such ambitious plans, Captain."

They moved on to view two paintings by Diego Velázquez. Silence spanned between them as she examined the portrait of a young Spanish princess, *Infanta Margarit Teresa in a Blue Dress*.

"I will admit you surprise me, Captain. I have never met a pirate with the taste of a nobleman."

"A compliment?" Blake laid a hand on his heart. "I find myself quite taken aback."

"Even more surprising"—she shot an angry look his way—"is that you expect your prisoner to regale you with *said* compliments."

He smiled, longing to touch one of her curls. "Honestly, I do not think of you as such."

She frowned. "Then what am I doing here?"

He fingered the Ring, and against every desire within him, answered her, "Teach me to control the demons from this Ring, and I will set you free."

Emeline had already informed him that demons only fled in the presence of God's Holy Spirit. "As I have said, 'tis not me, Captain, who chases evil away. You speak of power. The ultimate power comes from the Almighty and presides in those who trust His Son. That is where real power in this life lies. Not in ruling your own kingdom."

"Hmm." He glanced back at the painting, seemingly unfazed by her homily. "'Tis not been my experience."

"It could be, should you wish it."

He lifted his hand toward her as if he intended to caress her cheek yet again, then dropped it. "Are you trying to convert me, my little missionary?"

"Nay, I'm trying to save you."

One brow arched. "It appears, however, 'tis you who needs saving at the moment."

She could not deny it. Though she could not resist adding, "Appearances can be deceiving, Captain."

At this he smiled. The banter between them, while tense at times, she found oddly enjoyable. The man was not dull by any means. He had an intelligence about him, a sharp mind and quick wit.

When he was sober, that was, and not angry.

He walked ahead of her to another painting of a tall ship amidst a raging storm at sea, and she took the opportunity to study him. He looked every bit the pirate captain with his tight breeches stuffed in Hessian boots, his embroidered leather jerkin covering a white cambric shirt, open at the collar where his necklaces hung. The ever-present cutlass at his hip swung as he walked. Today, he had tied his dark wavy hair behind him, while matching stubble lined his jaw and perched upon his lips in a thin mustache. But 'twas those eyes that mesmerized her—that had mesmerized her from the first time he looked at her on Nassau—almond-shaped and much like the stormy sea in the painting he gazed upon, turbulent and restless.

He caught her staring at him and smiled, not the smile of a pirate, nor a kidnapper, but the smile of a courtier, a gentleman toward his lady. Their eyes locked for several moments, and she wondered if he could indeed become the hero she so desired.

Later at dinner, as she sat around the table with his crew and staff and watched him drown himself in rum and curse as well as any of them, she withdrew her former question. What was wrong with her to even consider such a thing? For some reason unbeknownst to her, he had her emotions in a spin. Surely she was the silliest of all women to ever think anything honorable existed in such a man who thought naught of stealing from others and kidnapping women.

A truth that further came crashing down upon her when he burst into her bedchamber hours later, deep in his cups, and demanding she play the violin for him. He wore naught but his breeches, and despite the moonlight drifting in through the window landing on his powerful chest, reminding her he could crush her with one blow, she denied him.

"Find someone else to play. I'm tired."

He drew close, halting just inches from where she sat on her bed. The smell of rum and spice and Blake surrounded her. His heavy breaths filled the air. He was a panther on the prowl, a man accustomed to getting what he wanted. She was a fool to deny him.

"You *will* play for me, Miss, or I fear I will have to remain in your chamber with you all night."

"To what purpose?" Her voice quivered.

"Let us not find out." His tone was not threatening, but rather one of desperation.

Still, the threat remained. The one that reminded her she was naught but a prisoner in this crazed pirate's dream of power.

So, she played for him as he sat in a chair, his head leaning against the cushioned back. A single lantern revealed a face that at first looked tortured but now relaxed into an almost peaceful repose.

Perhaps the Ring did summon demons, as the myth implied. Or rather it called forth demons already at work within this man. Regardless, she could hardly spend the rest of her nights in his bedchamber. Either he must get rid of the vile Ring or give his life to God. Unfortunately, she saw neither as a possibility.

Which meant she must make her escape as soon as possible.

Yet as she stared at Blake, his muscular chest rising and falling beneath the deep breaths of sleep, a melancholy overcame her. If he remained on this path, he would end up dead, not only in spirit but in body. She knew it deep inside. Could see it in his future—a future full of crushed hopes and sorrow, ending in hellfire.

Oh, Lord, she prayed silently while she began a softer tune on the violin. *You said to pray for Your enemies, to bless those who curse You. Hence, I'm praying for Blake. He needs You. He needs to know You. Please help him. Please tell me how I can help him.* Why she cared, she could not say, but something about the man stirred her soul.

Finishing the song, she removed the violin from beneath her chin and laid it in her lap. Wind *whished* across windowpanes where ribbons of moonlight streamed into the room. Distant laughter echoed from somewhere in the house. Intending to return to her chamber, Emeline gently laid the violin in its case and rose.

"Don't stop." Blake's deep voice rumbled as he lifted his head from the back of the chair.

"I thought you were asleep." Emeline took a step toward him, clasping her hands.

He leaned forward, resting his forearms on his knees, his hair hanging around his face, but said naught.

"I'm weary, Blake. May I return to my bed?"

Rising, he moved toward her, his shadow so large, his movements so predatory, that she swallowed down a lump of fear. Yet she remained in place.

He halted mere inches from her. Lantern light swept over his face, revealing an exhaustion she could not fathom and a humility she never expected. Raising his hand, he eased the back of his fingers over her cheek, so softly, so gently...she closed her eyes beneath the sensation.

The heat from his body flooded her, his scent, his touch. Heart pounding, she opened her eyes and took a step back, angry at her response to him.

"Good night, Captain," she blurted nervously and turned toward the door.

His firm grasp on her arm swung her about. "You are right about Pedro. I should not have been so harsh. But you must understand. I have a ship to run, men to command. I cannot tolerate laziness nor disrespect."

"I do understand. More than you know."

"Aye. You hail from a mighty stock of ship captains." He breathed out a deep sigh, released her, and dragged a hand through his hair. "But the boy. He has promise for one so young."

"You might tell him that now and then, Captain."

He nodded. "Aye."

She could leave. But something kept her in place. "I am shocked you would listen to a silly woman such as myself."

He snapped his gaze her way. "I listen to many things you say." He moved toward her again, and before she could stop him, he took a strand of her loose hair tumbling over her nightdress and fingered it as if it were made of spun gold.

"May I leave, Captain?"

He stared at her, his eyes inches from hers. "On one condition."

She waited, her nerves tight, her mind reeling, ready to defend her chastity if need be.

Before she could gather her resolve, his lips lowered to hers. Soft, sensual, moist, their touch sent powerful waves down to her toes, sensations she'd never felt before. She should kick him! She should slap him. She should run away as fast as she could.

Instead, she stood there, allowing his kiss. Nay. Enjoying it, responding to it! The shame!

He deepened it, exploring, loving. He tasted of rum and spice. Wrapping his arms around her, he drew her close, pressing her curves against his hard chest. His strength surrounded her, enfolding her in a cocoon of protection. Her legs turned to mush. He held her tighter. Warmth spiraled through her. Reason! Reason! Sanity! She begged for release from this madness!

He withdrew. "Emeline." His voice was sultry, deep, breathless.

Horror flooded her. Shame soon followed. Pushing from him, she drew a hand to her mouth. Was he to take more liberties now that she had allowed his kiss? What had she been thinking?

His eyes, brimming with desire, searched hers. He took a step back. "You may leave."

Spinning on her heels, Emeline fled from the room.

Chapter 22

The next two days passed in a blur of shame, fear, and loneliness. Save for occasional outings during the day with Pedro as her chaperone and a prattling Bandit in her arms, Emeline remained in her chamber. Even when Blake sent Charlie one night and Finn the next to escort her to dinner, she insisted she was ill and refused to come. She could not face the captain. She could not face herself. Had she forgotten all her parents taught her, what God taught her about keeping herself pure for marriage?

Moving to the window, she admired the exquisite swaths of maroon, saffron, and tangerine the Almighty painted across the horizon above the setting sun. An evening wind sent palm fronds dancing and leaves fluttering across the small island, bringing with it the sweet scent of flowers and earthy loam.

She pressed fingers onto her lips as memories returned of the unimaginable sensations Blake had evoked with his kiss. She'd never kissed a man before, save for the one Blake had stolen once before. That one didn't count. This one…this one…suffice it to say, she had no idea the power of a man's touch.

She'd already repented repeatedly of her wanton reaction and had hence decided she must avoid Blake at all costs and escape as soon as possible. Yet each night as she waited for the house to grow silent in sleep, Blake had opened the door between their chambers, drawn up a chair, and sat just inside her room. He said not a word, not a good evening, not a reproof, nor even a request for her to play the violin. He merely sat there in silence like a predator keeping watch over an unsuspecting prey. She pretended she was asleep.

Again, the man baffled her. Why did he not say something? Mention their kiss? Insist she accompany him to dinner? Why did he make no effort whatsoever to see her? Perhaps he'd found her kiss dreary. Perhaps he'd felt nothing. Worse, it disgusted him. 'Twould certainly explain why he'd told her to leave soon after.

"Lord, I'm being silly." She turned from the window and moved to sit on her bed. "Worse than silly. Why should I care what he felt? I'm grateful he dismissed me." She heaved a sigh and caught her reflection in the looking glass. The same plain woman stared back at her, the same dull hair, same ordinary features. She looked away.

One thing she *did* know. If the captain were to sit in her chamber each night, she must make her escape during the day. She must choose the time wisely, when servants and crew alike were busy with their tasks. Better, she must create a diversion—something that captured the attention of everyone.

Blake plucked a pickled oyster from the platter and popped it in his mouth. The sharp fishy taste tickled his tongue and brought a sense of satisfaction. Cook had done well. Surely, Emeline would appreciate having her choice of so fine a variety of small dishes instead of a main meal. Especially since she'd not eaten dinner the past two nights—two nights he'd kindly afforded her. But his kindness was at an end.

He glanced around the banquet hall, his gaze shifting over Charlie pouring herself a drink next to Rummy who already held a bottle in hand. Then over to Sam Goode, who appeared to be lecturing a small group of sailors about something that kept them riveted. Down the table from Blake, Pedro helped himself to potted shrimp on toast, while Finn, who had donned a clean bandana for the occasion, headed his way, pipe in his mouth. The rest of his crew lingered about the room chattering like a band of monkeys. Speaking of…where had Bandit run off to? Blake had not seen him since yesterday when he'd spotted him in Emeline's arms as she strolled about the gardens with Pedro. Yet another member of his crew appeared to be missing—Maston. Odd. The Frenchman rarely missed one of Cook's fine meals.

Finn drew up beside him and plucked the pipe from his mouth. "Quite a fancy spread ye got goin' tonight, Cap'n. What be the occasion?"

Grabbing a bottle of rum, Blake poured himself a glass. "No occasion. Just thought the crew would like one more hearty meal before we set sail on the morrow."

"Aye, Cap'n. A good idea. It'll soon be back t' nothin' but 'ard tack, salted pork, an' over-ripe fruit." Crossing beefy arms over his chest he glanced about the room. "Where be that miss you been keepin' all t' yerself? Hadn't seen 'er in a while. She still ill?"

Instead of answering him, Blake rattled off a list of tasks he'd given his quartermaster to accomplish to ensure the *Summons* was stocked and in fine shape for sailing. Regardless, his thoughts were on the *miss* that Finn had mentioned. He'd sent one of his crew, a rather imposing man, to her chamber to bring her to the banquet hall. Whether she wanted to or not. He'd have done it himself, but 'twas not his place to beg a lady for attention. *Hang it!* When it came to the fairer gender, he'd never had to plead for favors at all.

Finn poured himself a drink and began answering each of Blake's concerns, but Blake's attention shifted to the open doors at his right.

Emeline Hyde walked in. Nay, more like she was dragged in by his man, Layton. The pirate started to pull her toward Blake, but she jerked from his grasp and said something that caused the man to send a questioning look his way.

Blake gestured for him to leave her be.

There she stood, head held high, chin in the air, staring him down as if he were the Kraken himself. She was an angel perched amidst a pack of demons. A bright light in a dark world. Sweet as honey yet sour to the taste. Soft as silk yet sharp as any knife.

"There the wench be, Cap'n," Finn interrupted his list of accomplishments. He stuffed the pipe back into his mouth and took a puff, but his gaze wandered to the Ring on Blake's finger.

The woman made no move in his direction. Ignoring Finn's obsession with the Ring—for now—Blake started toward her, all the while gauging her mood. He knew he'd frightened her with his kiss, knew his reaction to it must have caused further alarm. For it had greatly alarmed him. Hence, the reason he'd left her alone the past two days. That and the fact he knew now without a doubt he must return the woman to her family posthaste. Her goodness, her purity was infecting him like a cancerous tumor spreading throughout his heart, turning the pirate into a puritan, the thief into a benefactor, the libertine into a gentleman. This was no way for a pirate captain to behave! Concerned for the feelings and chastity of a woman prisoner? Pish! He should have heretofore had his way with her and been done with it. Locked her in chains in his bedchamber to keep his demons at bay. He frowned. At best, he must avoid any and all contact with her.

Her golden eyes, sparking with both defiance and fear, locked upon his as he approached. He'd brought her here to both feed and inform her they were to set sail on the morrow. But in truth, he'd wanted to see her. Now that he did, he felt all resolve to keep her at arm's length trickle off him onto the tile floor.

"You summoned me, Captain?" Her sharp tone cut, yet he sensed a tremble course through her, and she lowered her gaze.

"You must eat, Emeline." He proffered his elbow.

Anger accused him from her eyes, but she slipped her hand onto his arm, nonetheless, and allowed him to escort her to the long table where all manner of meats, fish, cheese and pastries were elegantly displayed.

"I was sorry to hear you've been ill," he teased as he swept an arm over the buffet and handed her a plate.

Her lips flattened. "An illness borne from being your captive, Captain." She took the plate, her eyes moistening. "And from being your plaything."

He could not help a slight grin. "You speak of our kiss."

"'Twas *your* kiss…a kiss you stole."

"I am a pirate, after all." Raising a brow, he took her hand and lifted it to his lips.

She snagged it away. "You find this amusing?"

"Nay, I found our kiss…quite captivating." He searched her eyes.

They flicked between his, unsure, fearful, before she swallowed and glanced away.

He leaned toward her. "Could you not tell?"

"I could hardly think with your bold intrusion into my mouth."

He chuckled. "You are quite enchanting, Emeline."

Her brow folded in a most adorable way as she stared at him aghast. "No one has ever called me so."

"Then they are fools!" Scads! What was he doing? He was supposed to put distance between them, not lure her closer. He took a step back. "Nevertheless, we are to set sail on the morrow for Jamaica."

Hope, followed by suspicion, traveled across her moist eyes. "What of your demons, Captain?"

"I'm the captain of the pirate ship, *Summons* and the king of this island. I can handle a few demons." He attempted a smile, the joy of which languished within him, for he had no idea how to do such a thing. Perhaps if he acquired a Bible, a flask of Holy Water? There were many things he could attempt. None of which involved either this precious lady or her God.

The look she gave him was rife with doubt, but she said naught for several moments. "I pray you do not trifle with me, Captain, and give me hope where there is none to be found. Will you, indeed, take me home?"

Blake poured more rum into his glass, and, against everything within him, answered her, "You have my word. Now, eat."

After casting him a dismissive glance, she turned and moved down the buffet, placing morsels of shrimp, cheese, pickled vegetables, and bread onto her plate. Instead of returning to him, she joined Charlie and Pedro, who were engaged in a game of dice along with a few of his crew.

He tossed the rum into his mouth and poured another glass, frustration brewing in his gut. Wasn't this what he wanted? For her to keep her distance? Finally, the rum took effect, relaxing his nerves and numbing his agitated thoughts. Still, he could not take his eyes off her.

Light followed her, along with the eyes of many of his crew and staff. And he found himself jealous of their attentive stares. Forcing his gaze away, he located two musicians and ordered them to play something…anything…to liven his mood.

Soon the hall brimmed with the dulcet sounds of strings, bassoons, and a harpsichord as more staff and crew entered to partake of this final feast—a soirée he typically held before they set out to sea once again. Laughter, music, chattering, and even a shout or two filled the air as pirates and servants alike enjoyed the food and companionship. Blake prided himself on including everyone, no matter their status. He would not be like his father, who had belittled and berated those beneath him. Especially Blake.

He sipped his drink, scattering thoughts of the man, and glanced at the Ring. The crimson jewel in the center glistened in the candlelight. Nay, not candlelight. It possessed light all its own, shining from within. *Power*. Ultimate power. With his new venture to begin tomorrow, he'd be on his way to more conquests. Soon his name would be on every trembling lip in the Caribbean—a name that would evoke respect and fear.

After he returned Miss Hyde to her home, that was.

Against his will, his gaze found her again, laughing with Charlie, who apparently had won a pouch of coins. The master gunner excused herself and left the hall, passing Maston as he entered and giving him both a wide berth and a threatening look. Ignoring her, the Frenchman waltzed into the room in a flourish of silk and lace, his sharp gaze scouring its occupants. Upon spotting Emeline, he started for her.

Fury boiled under Blake's skin. Did the man not see him standing here? Did he think he could accost the lady again and not pay for it with his life? Gripping the hilt of his cutlass, Blake charged toward him just as the Frenchman halted before Emeline, took her hand, and planted a kiss upon it. Disgust flared on Emeline's face. Tugging from his grasp, she started to turn when Maston must have said something that upset her, for she raised her hand to slap him. But before she could, he caught her wrist and grinned.

All this, Blake saw in the seconds it took for him to reach them. Seconds in which his rage flamed as hot as a furnace. He thought to draw his sword and run the man through, but that would be too quick a death.

Instead, he flung his body against Maston's, sending him reeling across the floor. Before he recovered, Blake slammed his fist across his jaw. Maston tumbled backward. The music halted. The chattering ceased as all eyes landed on the battling duo. Blake nudged Emeline behind him.

Instead of outrage, the Frenchman grinned, rubbed his jaw, and started for Blake.

Movement lured Blake's gaze to the doorway. Not just any movement, but a familiar movement, a familiar visage. One that sent a whirlwind of confusion, desire, and anger through him.

All eyes swept to the intruder, including Maston's, who halted, placed one hand on his hip, and smiled.

Dressed in tight leather breeches and a jerkin, both of which molded to every curve, a flowing rose-colored linen shirt, and a cutlass strapped to her side, the woman marched into the hall with the authority of a captain. Hair the color of black silk cascaded over her shoulder down to her waist, while eyes as sharp, lustrous, and as deadly as a leopard's locked upon Blake. And just like a cat who'd caught her prey, she grinned.

Josephine Arnaud.

Emeline had barely recovered from Maston's salacious insult and Blake's heroic rescue when a woman caught the attention of everyone in the room. Including Blake's. Not just any woman, but a rare beauty, an *exotic* beauty. The kind of beauty men only dreamed about and women envied. Despite being dressed in pirate attire, or perhaps because of it, she exuded a feminine charm, an allure that even set Emeline's heart beating a bit faster.

Whispers sped about the room. Blake seemed unable to speak, and Maston, along with most of the men, grinned at her as if they'd captured a ship full of gold.

She sashayed toward Blake, her gaze shifting between him and Emeline, before she halted and gave him a seductive smile. "Blake, *mon cher*, I have missed you," she said in a sultry French accent. "You are looking more handsome than I remember."

"What are you doing here, Jo?" Blake's tone was one of disdain.

She cocked her head. "As I said, *mon amour*, I missed you." Her gaze shifted to Emeline and the sparkle in her eyes from only moments before turned to dust. "*Mais* I see you have found another?" She scanned Emeline from head to toe. "Hmm. Rather plain for your tastes, *non*?"

Anger welled at the insult, anger *and* shame. Emeline took a step back.

The woman gave a disgusted snort. "Run along, little mouse, back to your hole." She flicked jewel-adorned fingers at Emeline before looping her arm through Blake's and dragging him away.

Mind spinning and emotions in a whirl, Emeline stared after them, expecting Blake to turn about, defend her honor, castigate the woman for her affronteries. Was it not just moments ago he dashed in like a hero to protect her?

Yet as the minutes sped by and Blake, with the woman on his arm, moved farther away, forgetting that Emeline existed, she realized she'd been a fool to ever think she mattered to him.

Grabbing her skirts, tears burning in her eyes, she dashed from the hall, more determined than ever to make her escape tonight.

Chapter 23

"I should lock you in irons," Blake seethed. "How did you get past my defenses?" He allowed Jo to pull him aside, if only to get her away from Emeline. He'd learned from experience that the woman's tongue was sharper and deadlier than any blade. Her disdain for all living creatures—save for herself—would no doubt inject poison into Emeline's pure heart. And he could not allow that to happen.

"Why, Blake, *chéri,* put away this bad humor. I know you are happy to see me."

Halting, Blake faced her. "Again, how are you here? How did you find my island?"

She leaned toward him, her familiar scent of rosewater invoking memories he'd long tried to forget. Memories of pleasures he'd not known existed, a love and bond he'd thought unbreakable, and an unbearable torment that had nearly destroyed him.

"All the brethren know about your island, Blake. You forget who taught you about defenses." She smiled sweetly, seductively, and gave him a look that once had sent him to his knees, groveling for favors and willing to do anything she wanted.

Instead, her smile fell flat onto the floor beneath them.

Frustration brewed, and he turned, intending to escort Emeline back to her chamber to safety so he could deal with this vixen.

But the lady was gone. And all light and life abandoned the room with her.

Or perhaps 'twas Jo's presence that leeched all joy and goodness away.

Even so, the banquet hall had grown unusually quiet as every eye remained upon them.

He gripped Jo's arm. Tight. Happy when he saw her flinch, he dragged her from the room, out the open French doors, and onto the portico.

Releasing her to face him, he gripped the hilt of his cutlass. "How did you get onto my island undetected? Tell me now!" For he had every inch of coastline well-guarded.

With a snort, she flung her silky hair over her shoulders and gazed over the dark jungle. "There is but a sliver of a moon, and I rowed in a small skiff by myself." She shrugged. "No doubt your men merely missed me."

"Where is *La Sorcière*?"

"Anchored not far off the southeast corner of your little paradise." She gave a devious grin. "Never fear, my crew have orders to stand down."

"Stand down? Pish, woman! My gunmen will sink her before she could fire a shot." Something about her story bristled, for the lady had never been on good terms with the truth.

Crossing arms over his chest, he studied her. Even ten years older than he, she was still the comeliest woman he'd ever seen. Or was she? No doubt 'twas her exotic beauty that had first attracted him. That and her promise to teach him how to fight, captain a ship, become a formidable pirate. And, as she had so enticingly put it—transform the boy into a man. Yet as she stood smiling at him now, with starlight transforming her ebony hair into silver-kissed silk, her full lips, high cheek bones, and striking eyes, not to mention the crests of her bosoms peeking at him above her tight jerkin, he oddly found all desire he'd once felt for her melting into a forgotten puddle.

"Why are you here?" he demanded, keeping his harsh tone.

"I told you." She pouted and gave him sad eyes. "I missed you. I wanted to apologize—"

"For leaving me stranded on that spit of land? Without a morsel of food or drop of water?"

Shrugging, she waved her jeweled hand through the air. "I knew you would survive."

"Did you?" At the time, Blake hadn't been sure whether he'd die of starvation or a broken heart. Both equally deadly.

"Well, here you are, *non*?"

"I want you off my island forthwith." Stiffening his jaw, he narrowed his eyes. "I'll have my men escort you to your boat—if that is even true—and you will row out to your ship and sail away. Do you take me?"

"I'd love to *take* you. Do you not remember those many nights…?" She sidled up to him and whispered, "That one night when we…"

Blake shoved her away before she could finish the salacious memory. Even so, his body reacted to her words, and he hated himself for it. She'd found him a young man of only sixteen working at the docks, barely surviving, and she'd seduced him into her web of licentious wickedness. At the time, he'd been more than eager to partake of her fruits, more than eager to learn everything about pirating, about being a man and commanding a ship.

She'd promised they'd be together forever, sailing the world's seas, hoarding all its gold, and living like a king and queen.

Until the day she grew bored of him and found another young man to play with.

"Don't be so cruel, Blake. I have come to regret leaving you." She pouted. "I have not found your equal in all the Caribbean."

He gave an indignant huff. "I am not the innocent fool you once knew."

"*Non.* I don't believe you are." She gestured toward his ear. "You wear the black pearl I gave you. You still think of me, *non*?" A sly grin curved her lips.

"Never."

Sighing, she cocked her head. "*Alors*, I have a proposition for you, Blake."

"I want naught to do with you." He started away to summon his men.

She grabbed his arm. "Hear me out. Why not join forces? Word is you are set to conquer more lands, gain more wealth and power."

Was it his imagination or did her gaze flicker over the Ring on his finger?

"You'll need more than one ship for the task, *non*? You'll need a fleet. Therefore, I am offering a partnership."

He shook his head, jerking from her touch and eyeing her suspiciously. "I recall how our last partnership ended."

"As I said, I have come to regret that. Will you not forgive me?" Her mesmerizing eyes shifted between his.

"Nay. I will not. Nor do I need you or your ship." He rubbed the Ring, wondering if he could use it against her. "Now, I insist you leave."

She took a step back, defeat finally tugging upon her beautiful features. "In the middle of the night? Do allow me to stay. I promise to leave in the morning." She drew close, rubbing against him. "For old times' sake? You owe me, Blake." She drew her full lips into another pout.

"For what?" he spat back.

"You would not be the captain of a ship, nor have wealth, nor this island, nor any hope of power without my—how do you say?—tutelage. You'd still be working at the docks in Barbados, dousing your sorrows with rum each night."

Blake swallowed. Her words were true enough. But he'd more than paid that debt long ago. The only thing left to her credit was the lesson she'd taught him to never love or trust anyone ever again.

"Come now, Blake. What can one woman do against an island full of men? Put a guard on me if you want."

'Twas like locking a tiger in a cage made of parchment. "Very well. One night. If you dare defy me, Jo, I'll not hesitate to have you drawn and quartered."

One side of her lips quirked in a charming grin. "Oh, you do know how to stir a lady's heart."

Emeline paced her chamber. Back and forth, back and forth over the lush Turkish carpet, onto the polished wooden floor, up to the mahogany wardrobe, then spinning, retracing her steps to her bed. She had waited for the sounds of revelry to fade, waited for the island's inhabitants to sneak off to their beds, waited for naught but the sound of wind and wave and an occasional whippoorwill to grace her ears. Nerves aflame, all she needed to do now was wait until well past the usual hour that Blake would enter her chamber. Once that passed, as she was sure it would since the brigand had the ravishing dark-haired lady to attend to his needs, she could easily slip out of the house and find her way to the fishing boat.

At least she hoped she could do so in the dark. Still, 'twas the perfect time to make her move with this unforeseen distraction entering the equation.

Boot steps pounded the tile in the hallway. A door creaked open, then slammed moments later, the thrust of it shaking the walls. Blake had returned, no doubt besotted and, from all indication, angry.

Inching up to the door between their chambers, Emeline listened for the sound of a female voice, a murmur, a lover's whisper. Nothing aside from a groan and the creak of a bed made its way to her ears. If Blake was alone, it wouldn't take long for the demons to begin their torment and him to require her presence. Pah. She'd have to wait a while longer.

"You wish me to seduce him?" Josephine set the lantern on a table in her chamber—the one where Blake had imprisoned her with a single guard outside. A single guard! Pff! An insult.

It hadn't taken Maston long to find her, send the guard off on some duty, and enter the room.

Drawing her close, the popinjay kissed her neck, inhaling her perfume with an intoxicating groan. "That should be no trouble. I see the way he looks at you. The way every man looks at you."

Josephine smiled at the compliment. "But I only want you, *mon amour*."

Maston wrapped his arms around her. "After this, we will be together forever."

Or until she grew weary of him, which was fast approaching now that he'd served his usefulness. How fortuitous to have run into the fool, Maston, on Basseterre. Even more fortuitous had been to lure him to her bed and discover he was the bosun on board Blake's ship, the *Summons*. Imagine her surprise at hearing that the young cockerel had survived being deserted on an island, and even more surprising was his success, his island, and the tale Maston told about a mysterious Ring Blake had gone to great lengths to acquire in a card game. All information the French fop happily conveyed in the throes of passion. *Solomon's Ring*! The ancient artifact coveted by all who dabbled in the mystical arts. It must be the one. Rumors had circulated throughout the Caribbean that it had been found. And though her powers as a witch were great, she must possess it. She must!

Thus, she expressed her undying love for Maston, along with her interest in the Ring, and he leapt and yapped and groveled at her feet like a puppy willing to do her every bidding.

Reaching up, she wrapped her arms around his neck and caressed his hair. "How am I to get it from him?"

"Do you have the laudanum I gave you?" he asked.

"*Oui*, in my pocket." Little did the fool know she'd added a potion of her own.

Excitement with a hint of desire sparked in his dark eyes. "Put it in his rum. Insist he drink it before he beds you. Then, wait until he drifts off to sleep, and you'll have your chance."

With a feminine sigh, she pushed from him, turned, and sashayed away, a move she'd made dozens of times with dozens of admirers. She must never appear too eager, too forward. Men like Maston enjoyed a challenge. His strong arms curled around her waist from behind, and he leaned to kiss her neck once again.

"I'm mad with love for you, Josephine."

"Then let us get the Ring and rule the world together."

Hot! Why was it so hot? The crackle of flames pressed against Blake's ears as searing tongues licked his skin. His eyes popped open. He stood on the edge of a jagged cliff. A black cloak blanketed the sky where nary a star could be seen. One peek over the side revealed yellow and red flames leaping and cavorting into the night from a molten lake bubbling like a boiling pot of crimson stew.

Horrified, he backed away. Into something solid. Reaching for his cutlass, he spun. No hilt met his fingers. No human met his gaze. At least not a living one. A black skeleton stared at him from hollow gaping holes where eyes once had been. Flesh began to grow over bone, slowly at first, like tar over oakum, then faster, filling in gaps with muscle and veins.

Blake started to dash around the horrifying figure. Dozens of gray shifting specters appeared, moaning obscenities, forcing him back. Behind him, the molten lake, before him loathsome ghouls. More flesh took form over the bones, eyes filled sockets, nails on fingers, and finally hair appeared.

"Hello, little mongrel." His father smiled wickedly.

"Leave me alone!" Blake roared, charging past the man toward the demons. Better them than his father. Or the lake of fire.

His father clutched his arm, digging nails into his skin. "You sent me to hell! Now you will join me!" He dragged Blake to the edge of the cliff. Fighting with all his strength, Blake punched, kicked, and clawed, but to no avail against his father's otherworldly power. One final push sent Blake careening over the side...falling...falling toward the searing flames.

"Nay!"

Blake sat up in bed. Sweat moistened his forehead and neck. Breathing hard, he swung his legs over the side and dropped his head into his hands.

He needed Emeline. Hang it. He needed her!

Pushing to his feet, he raked back his hair and started for her chamber when his own door creaked open. With lightning speed, he plucked his cutlass from the table and charged forward. "Who goes there?"

"Only me, *mon amour*." The feminine French accent scraped over him. A sour taste rose in his mouth.

His door shut, and the curvaceous figure slithered his way. "Do put down your blade, Blake. I have not come to fight. Quite the opposite."

Groaning, Blake set down his sword and lit a lantern. Josephine stepped into the light, a tiger on the prowl, a rather scantily dressed tiger wearing naught but a sheer night dress that left little to his imagination.

He narrowed his eyes, limiting his gaze to her face. "Did you seduce my guard?"

She fingered a strand of her silky black hair. "Did you truly believe one little guard could keep me from you?" Her smile was bawdy, predatory.

Snorting, he looked away, searching for his rum. Indeed, he should have known. "Go back to your chamber, Jo."

She inched toward him and slithered a finger down his arm. "The desire in your eyes defies your words."

Jerking from her touch, he found his rum and poured a glass. Was the vixen right? Did he still desire her, even after her betrayal? Nay, even though much time had passed since he'd enjoyed female company, even though a most alluring one stood before him, even though admittedly, his body reacted slightly to her touch, he found that his heart, his soul felt naught but repulsion.

He faced her. "You no longer captivate me, Josephine. Return to your chamber, or I'll have you locked in the guardhouse."

Frowning, she fluttered her long lashes like she used to when she wanted something from him. "Very well, Blake. I'm not one to beg. However, let us have one last drink together." She nodded toward an empty glass beside his full one. "For the times we once shared?"

Suspicion etched down his spine. Still, what harm would it do? A quick drink and she'd be gone and then he could open the door to Emeline's chamber. *Emeline.* Even with this half-naked woman standing beside him, 'twas Emeline who invaded his thoughts.

Only one sip remained in the bottle. He moved to the sideboard and grabbed another. Yet when he turned around, he thought he saw Jo slip something into the pocket of her nightdress. No matter. There was nothing of value here to steal.

Emeline leaned her ear against the door, clearly hearing Josephine's accent. Heart folding in on itself, she backed into the darkness. What did she expect? Blake was a pirate with the morals of a goat and Josephine was the most beautiful woman Emeline had ever seen. Besides, 'twas obvious from their encounter earlier that she and Blake knew one another—had no doubt been intimate in the past.

Ignoring the twinge of jealousy, Emeline moved to the window where a night breeze swept in, cooling her skin and sifting through her hair. It did naught to assuage the fear, heartache, and anger bubbling in a tumultuous brew in her belly. In the distance, dark clouds gobbled up the moon, casting gloomy shadows over the land—just like her fading dreams for a true gentleman, a hero to sweep her off her feet.

Every time she thought there was hope for Blake to become that honorable man, he shifted back into his old ways. When would she learn? Hadn't her father always told her she was far too naïve, too trusting, and always kept her head in the clouds?

She must take this opportunity to leave. Blake would be occupied for quite some time, and the rest of the house was fast asleep.

Turning, she gathered the money and gun from the drawer, stuffed them in a small sack she'd found, and started for her door. She'd already mapped the best way out of the house unnoticed and the most unguarded way through the jungle to the fishing boat.

She reached for the door handle when a crash sounded from Blake's chamber and a chilled mist enveloped her. Halting, she shivered, staring at Blake's door. Why had the air suddenly grown so cold on such a balmy night? Not only cold, but a heaviness fell upon her, a malevolence that nearly shoved her to the floor.

Breath heaving, she flung a hand to her throat and crept toward Blake's chamber door, listening for voices or movement from within.

Pray.

The unspoken voice blared within her. A command, an urging she could not deny.

Pray.

A dark mist slithered underneath the door into her chamber, snaking around her shoes, winding up her legs. Air seized in her throat. When she glanced down, it was gone. Yet the icy cold remained. And she had no doubt. Evil was present on the other side of this door.

Pray.

Emeline obeyed. Taking a step back, she closed her eyes and appealed to Almighty God for His protection over Blake, over her, and for victory over the evil presence.

Chapter 24

J osephine took both glasses and handed the one with the potion to Blake. With an impatient huff that more than annoyed her, he took it and lifted it in the air. "For old times' sake."

She put on her most charming smile. "Those were good times, *non*?" Sipping her drink, she stared at him over the edge of the glass.

He didn't answer, merely tossed the rum into his mouth and slammed down his glass as was his way when it came to drink. Now all she had to do was wait for him to collapse to the floor, and she would slip the Ring from his finger. Easy.

A slight creak, barely discernible, drifted from the chamber beside Blake's. Odd. Who would be up at this hour? Even more odd, who would be housed right beside their captain? No doubt it was that frightfully drab girl he'd been fawning over when Josephine had first arrived. The mere sight of them together still heaved bile into her throat. But what did it matter? Upon spotting Josephine, he had quickly discarded the little mouse.

"Now leave." Blake's tone was angry, hostile even, as he gestured for the door.

How dare he treat her as if she were nothing but a common wench? "I haven't finished my drink." She gave him a pleading look. "Just another moment?"

He crossed arms over his chest and waited. Churlish bore! He used to be quite entertaining, but apparently the drab prude had leeched all the fun out of the man. What a shame.

A glaze crept over his eyes. He blinked, wobbled, and gripped the table beside him.

Josephine smiled.

A minute later, Blake fell, struck his head on the edge of the table, and collapsed to the floor. Finally.

Setting down her glass, Josephine knelt beside the unconscious pirate and ran the back of her hand over the stubble on his jaw. He'd grown even more handsome in the past five years. Pity. With the addition of the potion she'd concocted, he wouldn't wake for days. By then, she'd be long gone on her way to conquer everything and everyone in her path.

Lifting his limp hand, she admired the Ring. Lantern light penetrated the crimson jewel, ricocheting out in copper beams. Solomon's Ring! Could it truly be? The one ancient artifact every witch, warlock, and sorcerer craved above all else. Now it would be hers!

She tugged on it. It wouldn't budge.

She twisted it and yanked again. Nothing.

Cursing, she glanced around the chamber for some salve, anything with which to loosen it. That's when she felt it. Light, virtue, goodness. Her skin prickled. A foul taste rose in her mouth. It was the enemy! His power sifted through the walls and marched toward her like a legion of holiness. Hurriedly, she tried to twist the Ring, desperate to remove it. But the light enveloped her. She couldn't breathe. Her blood became ice. Rising, she gripped her throat, gasping for air, and darted from the room.

Emeline allowed her eyelids to close. For just a moment. Just a moment in which she could give in to the exhaustion beckoning her to drift into oblivion. To a place where she was not a prisoner of a mad pirate captain, where she was not sitting beside said captain's bed, wondering if he would live or die.

Instead of, at this very moment, rowing herself to safety and freedom.

But when she'd burst into his chamber and found him unconscious on the floor, blood oozing from a gash on his forehead, she did the only thing she knew to do, the right thing. She called for help. The French lady was nowhere to be seen, though the chill that had struck Emeline in her chamber was even more present in Blake's—a sharp, icy chill that penetrated flesh and bone and speared straight for the soul.

Finn answered her call for help, and soon they had Blake in his bed and Sam tending his wound. Still, after several hours, the infernal pirate had not woken up despite Sam's many attempts waving smelling salts beneath his nose. "The blow to his head was not hard enough to cause such a long sleep," Sam had said, frowning with confusion before he and Finn finally left to return to their beds.

Emeline refused to leave. Something was wrong, dreadfully wrong, and she didn't feel right about leaving Blake alone and unable to defend himself.

"Lord, please heal this man. You told us to pray for our enemies." Leaning over, she placed a hand on his arm. "So, I'm praying for Blake. Heal him and deliver him from this illness and evil."

A swath of gray light floated through the window, looping over the sill, easing across the floorboards and over the rug before spreading out, chasing away the gloom of night. Hugging herself, Emeline glanced around the room, still feeling the chill of the night. "In the name of Jesus, I command all evil to depart this chamber!" She spoke the words with the authority and faith her parents had taught her to use when wielding the weapons God had given those who love Him.

Thunder rumbled as a breeze wafted in and cloaked Emeline in instant warmth. "Thank you, Lord." Why had she not realized until now the source of the icy oppression she'd felt? 'Twas no doubt due to evil spirits brought in by…she glanced at the Ring on Blake's finger.

He moaned, his lips moving. His breathing heightened, and he reached up and touched the wound on his forehead.

"Blake," Emeline said, drawing his gaze.

Oddly, he smiled before confusion wrinkled his brow.

"You fell and hit your head."

Heaving an aggravated sigh, he pushed to sit and swung his legs over the edge of the mattress, shaking his head and uttering a curse.

Emeline backed her chair up. "Perhaps not as much rum next time?"

"I didn't fall," he barked a bit too loudly. When she stood to leave, he reached for her hand. "Forgive me, Emeline. My head feels like it has been fired from a cannon."

She stared at him, unsure whether or not to leave. Certainly she was not in the mood to endure his ill temper when she'd given up a night's sleep to tend him.

"Josephine," he mumbled.

So, Emeline *had* heard the French woman after all.

"I will summon her, Captain," she said curtly before grabbing her skirts and turning to leave.

"Nay!" His shout spun her around. "She must have put something in my drink."

Whether 'twas true or not, Emeline found her gaze traveling to the Ring again. "You've encountered naught but evil since you acquired that Ring—nightmares, demons, and now this unforeseen illness." She would add to that the unnatural chill and oppression she'd felt earlier, but she knew he wouldn't believe her.

Thunder rumbled, shaking the walls.

"I implore you, Blake, remove the Ring. Hide it away if you must and see if things do not improve."

He stared at her for several minutes as if she'd asked him to dance a jig on the roof. "Never." Struggling to rise, he gripped the bedpost to steady himself. "This Ring is the answer to all my dreams."

"Only if your dreams are to die young."

As if confirming her statement, a torrent of rain unleashed outside the window, pounding the roof and the garden below like the march of a thousand demons.

Emeline darted from the room.

"Toads and lizards!" Josephine plucked a book from her bag and slammed it on the desk in her chamber.

"Come now, *ma très chère*." Maston's sickly sweet tone caused nausea to gurgle in her belly. "We shall get the Ring, never fear."

"We?" she quipped with a snort, then planted fists at her waist. This was not going to be as easy as she thought. Not only could she not remove the Ring, but the sleeping potion she'd put in Blake's drink had not worked, for she'd seen the man as chipper as ever in the dining hall for the noonday meal. The pompous ninny!

If a storm had not enveloped the island, that *pompous ninny* would have set sail already, putting far too much distance between her and the Ring.

Now what to do? She bit her fingernail, cursing. "I forgot what the legends said—that the Ring cannot be removed from the finger of whoever wears it. Blake must take it off. But how to get him to do that?"

Opening the book of spells, she flipped through the pages, seeking anything—a hex, a spell, a potion that would force Blake to do whatever she asked of him.

"Why not get the girl to do it?" Maston adjusted his stained cravat.

Josephine swung to face him. "Don't be a fool, Claude. She's a simpleton, a daft twit."

Maston quirked a brow. "She has more power than you think. Come, my sweet." He gestured toward the bed. "Let me love you as you deserve. Perhaps it will clear our minds and help us discover a way forward."

"You will not so much as touch me, *mon cher*, until I am in possession of the Ring." She held up one of her hands and wiggled her fingers. "*Comprendre*? Therefore"—she turned and sashayed toward the window, gazing at the rain pouring from dark skies—"it would be in your best interest to aid me in whatever plan I decide upon."

Which was the only reason she tolerated his slobbering presence.

"Of course. I am here to help."

Moving back to the book, she continued to flip through it. "I must find a curse, a hex. The perfect one that will turn Blake into my slave."

Standing on the portico outside the banquet hall, Emeline released a heavy sigh. It had rained for two days straight, and one look at the dark, roiling sky told her it had no intention of quitting any time soon. Movement snagged her gaze just in time to see Bandit barreling toward her. He leapt into her arms and proceeded to regale her with some tale of the wild. Which, no doubt, he'd been enjoying until the relentless storm had forced him inside.

"Now where have you been, little one? I've missed you." Against all propriety, she leaned her face against his, inhaling his moist animal smell.

"You and that little beastie." Charlie laughed as she approached. "He's ne'er taken t' anyone but Blake before." The master gunner stared out over the gray, dripping scenery and shook her head. "Blast this storm. Like the rest o' the crew, I'm anxious t' be at sea again."

"Truly? I would think you'd enjoy such a luxurious respite on land."

"Aye, it has been nice, but I can't make the fortune I need resting an' reveling like some fat spoiled monarch, now, can I?"

Emeline nodded her understanding. The lady had a son and mother to support. "Seems I am stuck here as well," she said.

Charlie gave her a knowing look. "I'm sorry, Em."

Bandit leapt onto the railing and began a long-winded, screeching rant, complete with hand gestures pointing toward the rain. Emeline hoped his scolding would, indeed, scare the storm away. She wondered why Blake hadn't used his Ring. If it could create storms, surely it could dissipate them? But she hadn't seen him since she'd dashed from his chamber, not even during the past two nights when he normally interrupted her sleep. She could only assume he'd found solace elsewhere.

'Twas one of the reasons she'd taken her meals in her room. If he was so foolish to continue a dalliance with a woman, evil or not, who'd left him unconscious on the floor, then they deserved each other.

In truth, if not for the blasted storm, she would have set sail at the first opportunity. As it was, her loneliness finally overcame her judgment, and she decided to come down for supper.

"Look!" Charlie exclaimed, tossing her long hair over her shoulder. "Sky!"

Following her gaze, Emeline spotted a small speck of blue in the distance and a brightening of the clouds around it. The rain lessened slightly.

"Thank God," she said. Even Bandit grinned and leapt back into her arms.

Maybe now she could leave this godforsaken island once and for all.

Apparently not until she suffered through one last dinner with the crew of the *Summons*, including their captain, who entered the hall looking no worse the wear for his illness. His eyes immediately latched upon her, and a grin lifted his lips. But no sooner did he start toward her, than Mademoiselle Josephine Arnaud, or should she say Captain Arnaud—as Finn had informed Emeline—swept into the room, this time wearing a stunning gown and very tight stomacher which accentuated every one of her abundant curves.

All male eyes snapped in her direction as she looped her arm through Blake's and halted him in his tracks. Was it Emeline's imagination, or did the lady cast her a look of spite over her shoulder?

The meal passed like many others, with the sounds of burps and grunts and the slapping of lips, reminding Emeline of cows chewing their cud. Add to that an overindulgence of rum along with the pompous boasting of men who felt the need to bloviate on their petty accomplishments. Though Blake sat to her right at the head of the table, 'twas Josephine on his other side who demanded his attention. Yet from his reaction, he seemed none too pleased. Odd, that. More than once, she heard him tell her in no uncertain terms that since the storm had dissipated, she was to leave.

On the contrary, whenever he faced Emeline, his manner softened as he inquired whether she liked the food, how she fared, and told her that he'd missed her violin playing.

"Quite an accomplishment, *ma chère*."

Emeline continued to study the painting while cringing at the French voice that interrupted her quiet enjoyment. She'd come into the gallery to escape the drunken revelry in the hall and to enjoy one last look at the exquisite artwork Blake had collected. Now that the storm had passed, she hoped to make her escape tonight. What she hadn't expected was to see Josephine moving toward her with a catlike grin on her comely face.

Even before the lady stopped beside her, a heaviness permeated the air. More than a heaviness, 'twas a wickedness Emeline had oft felt when in the presence of a voodoo practitioner.

"To what do you refer, *Mademoiselle*?"

"Call me Jo. Everyone does." She cocked her head and studied the painting. "Blake does have such odd taste in art."

Emeline made no comment.

"I refer, of course, to the way you captivated him," Jo continued. "It is quite obvious he is infatuated with you." Her grin belied the slightest hint of spite in her voice.

Emeline stifled a laugh. Ridiculous notion. "I hadn't noticed."

Jo sighed. "It is that Ring, you know, causing all his recent trouble. It is evil, pure evil, and despite the fables that surround it, it will only cause Blake pain, heartache, and possibly death."

Though Emeline gave the lady a suspicious glance, she quite agreed. Still, how did the woman know about the relic—or its power?

"I only bring it up," Jo continued, "because, regardless of what you may think of me, I do care for Blake. He and I were quite close once."

The sultry tone of her voice sent a shard through Emeline's heart. "You may be right, *Mademoiselle*, as I suspect the same, but there's naught to do about it. The captain refuses to relinquish it nor even remove it from his finger."

Spikes of pain, like pinpricks of fire, stabbed Josephine's back. They began the moment she'd drawn close to the repugnant prude and only grew worse the longer she spoke with her. She shifted her stance uncomfortably, but the pain only increased. With it, fear gnawed her belly. *Fear?* Something she hadn't felt in quite some time. At least not until she came to this island. And more specifically near this strange woman.

She glared into Emeline's golden eyes and did what she must, what she'd done a dozen times with a dozen people who grated her nerves. She invoked a silent curse upon her.

The lady didn't react at all, merely shifted her gaze back to the painting. No sickness invaded her belly, no fever rose to consume her, no confusion muddled her thoughts. *Non.* The woman seemed impervious to the evil flung her way, almost as if there were an invisible shield around her.

Jo silently cursed. Of course. She belonged to the enemy! That would explain the pain and fear in her presence, the bright light that made Josephine want to run for the shadows. *Devil's blood!* She must limit her time with the righteous snod, or surely the God she served would expose Jo for what she was.

"I'm told you have a measure of influence on Blake," she interjected, angry that the woman continued to ignore her.

Emeline gave a ladylike snort. "Foolishness! I am his prisoner."

"Hmm." Jo tapped one of her long fingernails on her chin. "Regardless, I do believe if anyone can get him to remove that dastardly Ring, it is you, my dear."

Instantly, the woman's features softened. Jo smiled. That imbecile Maston had been right. This prig cared for Blake and, from what Jo had seen, he returned the sentiment. The suggestion had been planted. Now it was up to the woman, for it would be far easier to merely steal the Ring when off Blake's finger than put a hex on him and hope it worked this time.

Chapter 25

Furious, Blake pounded on Josephine's chamber door. He'd sent two of his fiercest pirates earlier that morning to escort her to her boat and ensure she rowed back out to her ship. He'd also ordered the men manning the cannons on either side of the bay where the *Summons* was anchored to be on high alert should the vixen be foolish enough to attempt an attack after she boarded her ship.

But she hadn't boarded her ship. Hadn't even left the house. Instead, he'd found the two pirates wandering about the garden, laughing and smelling the flowers like flighty butterflies. When questioned, they had no remembrance of any orders to do much of anything. Blake had locked them in the guardhouse to enhance their memory.

Yet he began to wonder at his own memory, for he'd not slept in two nights. Not since the rain started and Emeline had dashed from his bed chamber. She'd been the only one to stay with him, care for him, after he'd injured his head. In return for her kindness, he'd been rude, harsh even, when she'd asked him to remove the Ring. But he couldn't do that. Wouldn't do that. Not for anyone. Hence, ashamed and feeling like the knave he was, he'd left her alone, didn't demand she play her violin or keep him company during the night. And for that, he'd suffered terribly in her absence.

"Josephine!" He pounded the door again.

It cracked to reveal an insolent grin beneath a seductive gaze. "*Oui?*"

"What did you do to my pirates?"

One dark brow rose as she opened the door. "Whatever do you mean?"

"You turned them into goose-brained ninnies."

"*Moi?*" Pivoting, she sashayed back into the chamber, perhaps to hide her smile. "You give me too much credit. I am a mere woman."

Blake's jaw tightened. He knew she dabbled in the dark arts, had seen books of spells and chants in her cabin long ago. Yet he'd never put much weight in such fanciful fables of otherworldly power.

Until the Ring. The odd thought struck him.

She spun, her long silky hair twirling about her. A few strands splayed gracefully upon the exposed crests of her bosoms above her leather jerkin. He shifted his gaze away.

She must have noticed and mistaken it for interest. "If you close the door, Blake, we can—" she glanced at the bed— "enjoy the afternoon together. Like old times, *oui?*"

Oddly, his body did not respond to the notion. His stomach did, however, as a bitter brew simmered within it.

Grunting, he gripped the hilt of his blade. "Gather what you brought. I'm taking you to your boat if I have to hoist you over my shoulder and drag you there."

Seemingly unruffled, she chuckled. "Oh my, that does sound like fun." She moved toward him, eyeing him up and down like one would assess a purchase.

Her scent of rosewater and the sea wafted around him, choking him. Halting, she lowered her gaze to his lips and licked her own. A slight moan of desire spilled from them as she leaned in for a kiss.

Blake shoved her back. "I am not the naïve lad you seduced into your web. You have no power over me anymore, Jo. Now gather your things."

Stumbling, she caught her balance and glared at him with eyes that grew darker and more malevolent by the second.

"*Très bien.* I see you have made your decision." She walked toward a desk in the far corner where a candle burned beside a dish, several bottles, and a large book.

Blake grew impatient while she fumbled with the objects, pouring liquid from one to another, and then capping and placing others in a pouch. Rays of afternoon sunlight streamed through the windows, along with a salty breeze, but neither helped chase away the heaviness in the air.

Jo began mumbling something, almost singing, but without a tune.

"Let's go!" he shouted. "I'll not wait another moment."

She continued chanting as she placed her items in the pouch and blew out the candle.

"Ready." Turning, she raised both arms and then dropped them, flinging her fingers in his direction.

He stared at her, confused. "Have you gone mad? Let's begone."

But she remained in place, eyes locked upon his. Darkness swirled in her gaze. Nay, worse than darkness, a throbbing blackness sparked with fire. Then it was gone.

All strength drained from Blake, and he gripped the doorframe lest he fall. What was happening?

"You don't look well, Blake." Jo approached. "*En fait*, you have gone quite pale."

Hang it! Gathering all his strength and quickly fading wits, Blake stumbled into his bed chamber. He'd be damned if he would faint like some timid female in front of Josephine, for the lady pounced on any sign of weakness like a shark to blood. Hence, when his vision began to spin and his legs wobbled, he quickly excused himself and ambled down the hall, bumping into side tables and walls before he gained the privacy of his room.

"Cap'n!" The startled voice belonged to Finn, standing at Blake's open wardrobe. At least he thought 'twas Finn through the haze that now covered Blake's eyes.

"What are you doing in here, Finn?" Blake managed to shout as he dropped into a chair.

"Nothin', Cap'n." Clearly flustered, his quartermaster continued in a nervous tirade. "Jist admirin' yer attire, were thinkin' I might ask ye if I can borrow one o' yer fancy suits. There's a serving wench I've got me eye on, you see, an'—"

"Silence!" Blake held up a hand to halt the incessant chattering, which was wreaking havoc on his already chipped mind. "Cease your babbling, or I'll shoot you where you stand."

Finn approached, peering at Blake curiously. "Are ye all right, Cap'n?"

Conspicuously absent was Finn's pipe, but Blake supposed if he intended to steal something, 'twould not be wise to leave the smell of tobacco in the room.

"Get out, Finn. Leave me be." Blake should punish him for such an affront, but at the moment, he could hardly form two thoughts. "Out!"

Grumbling, Finn started away.

"Wait." Blake rubbed his temples where an agonizing pain rose. "Gather ten of the crew and take Josephine to her boat. Make sure she rows out to her ship at once!"

"Aye, Cap'n."

Slivers of moonlight broke through clouds and drifted into Emeline's chamber, luring her outside to make another dash through the jungle, as she had done the night before. The fishing boat had still been there! And ready to set sail. But the seas had been too rough. The retreating storm had left a wake of surging whitecapped waves far too large for her small fishing boat to navigate safely. So, she had returned to her chamber, pleased when she'd been able to leave and come back undetected.

She'd not seen or heard Blake the entire day, though whispers floating about the house spoke of how he'd finally sent Josephine Arnaud back to her ship. Other whispers ensued, particularly when Emeline had ventured down for a light supper with Charlie and Pedro.

"Cap'n's ill." Charlie had answered Emeline's inquiry as to his whereabouts.

Emeline had settled in her mind that she would never see him again. That she didn't wish to see him again. Though now that she found him absent, it worried her. "Again? But he'd recovered so nicely."

"Don't know what it be, Miss." Pedro plucked a banana from the buffet and began peeling it. "But it has him in a foul mood."

"Perhaps I should check on him," Emeline said, glancing at pirates and servants alike stuffing their faces with the fine fare Cook had laid out on banquet tables.

"I wouldn't bother, Miss." Sam Goode slid beside her, plateful of collared beef and pickled cucumbers in one hand and a drink in the other. "He merely needs his rest."

"What do you think is the source of this second illness?"

"Nothing serious, I assure you. Most likely exhaustion from overwork. He needs rest is all."

Bandit dashed into the hall, leapt atop the table beside Emeline, and began screeching and squawking something fierce.

Charlie waved him away. "Wonder what's gotten into him?"

"Filthy beast," Sam exclaimed as he grabbed his food and hastened off.

Whatever it was, Bandit would not cease his frantic diatribe until Emeline picked him up and brought him to her chamber. Even then the monkey seemed unusually agitated and jittery, pacing in front of the door that led to Blake's chamber until finally, when evening shadows stole the sunlight, he fled out the window.

Afterward, Emeline had taken up her own pace, waiting…waiting…for the house to quiet, its occupants to take to their beds, and to ensure Blake would not burst through her door. Minutes passed like hours, as one by one, ever so slowly, the sounds of music, laughter, conversation, and the footsteps of servants skittering to and fro all ceased. Replaced by the katydids, flutter of leaves in the breeze, lap of waves, and the call of night herons outside.

It was time. Halting at the window, she glanced over the island. A half-moon painted strips of silver over palms and mahogany leaves as they waved in the light breeze. Beyond them, the sea glistened like ink, ribboned in pearls.

Drawing a deep breath, she glanced one last time toward Blake's chamber and then started for her door.

A moan sounded. So light, she barely heard it. Against her better judgement, she slowly opened the door between their chambers and peeked inside. The normally virile pirate sat slouched in one of his velvet stuffed chairs, his chin on his chest, his legs stretched out before him, looking like a doll that had lost its stuffing.

"Captain?" She crept inside.

Lifting his chin, he peered in her direction, squinting, and finally offering her a smile. "Emeline."

Dashing toward him, she knelt at his feet and touched his forehead. Hot, but not too hot. Still, all color had fled his skin, his breathing was shallow, and his limbs appeared limp and frail. Not at all like the great Captain Blake Keene. Her heart grew heavy, and she hated herself for it. She'd longed for a hero, a warrior, a gentleman—a man of God. What did she get? A greedy, selfish pirate with the manners of a camel and the faith of a reprobate.

But she cared for him. She knew that now. She might even love him. Which was why she must leave, and the sooner the better.

A glitter caught her eye, drawing it to the Ring. It had to be the source of his illness.

"Blake." She slid her hand into his and squeezed. "'Tis the Ring that causes you to be so ill." Wasn't that what Josephine had said? That it would do naught but cause him pain and suffering.

"Bah!" He shook his head.

"You must take it off. Just for a little while."

His reply was a mere moan.

"Why don't you give it a try?" She pleaded.

He pried his eyes open a mere slit, staring at her as if he could barely see her.

"What harm could it do? Take it off. Hide it somewhere if you must, then let's see if you recover."

Releasing her hand, he moaned again and, with great effort, drew up his legs and leaned forward. Strands of his dark hair slid over his cheek, and she resisted the urge to brush them away, to feel the stubble on his jaw, to ease his pain.

He twisted the Ring…round and round…until finally, he tugged it off his finger and handed it to her.

Surprised, she stared at the wicked thing, wishing she could destroy it.

Struggling to stand, Blake wobbled, then promptly dropped back to his chair, gesturing to a table against the far wall. "Put it in that lockbox, lock it, and bring me the key."

She did so. Unwillingly. Silently asking God whether she should take it and be rid of it forever, for she wanted naught to do with the cursed thing.

"That should keep Bandit away, at least." Blake took the key and attempted a chuckle as Emeline hoisted him up as best she could and with one arm around his waist, helped him to his bed.

Coughing, he sank into the mattress as if the effort drained him of any remaining strength.

"You are a kind woman, Emeline," he whispered, his eyes closed. "Too good for the likes of me."

That much was true. For she had no idea why she was tending to her captor when she should be making her escape from his clutches.

Foolish woman!

She stood back, staring at him, memorizing his face, the steely cut of his jaw, his thin mustache, dark brows, and the ever-present necklaces lying atop his chest. If her plan succeeded, she'd never see him again. Oddly, that thought saddened her most of all.

Soon his breathing deepened as he drifted off to sleep. Good. No doubt that meant 'twas the Ring, indeed, which caused his illness. He should recover quickly now, and with Josephine gone as well, this pirate, this man who had captivated her heart, would soon continue on his quest to rule the world. Or at least the Caribbean.

Before she changed her mind, she darted from his chamber into hers and slipped out her door. The house was silent save for the sound of distant snoring, the chime of a clock, and the wind whisking over windowpanes. Retracing her steps from the night before, she descended the stairs and tiptoed past the banquet hall, then through the gallery where dark paintings mocked her as she passed. She crept into the quiet kitchen, then the pantry, next through the storeroom beyond until finally she exited the house out the servants' entrance. Keeping to the north side, where no guard stood watch due to the impenetrable jungle, she avoided the gardens and entered the maze of green unnoticed.

Without a lantern, the darkness made it difficult to navigate the winding trail. More than once she tripped over rocks and roots. More than once, she fell to the mud. Twigs and vines scraped her neck and arms. But finally, she heard the lap of waves and emerged onto the tiny inlet. Her gaze glanced over the boat and out to sea where naught but calm, starlit swells gave her the nod of approval to embark on her journey.

Drawing a deep breath, she lifted a prayer for God's will and her safety. Then, moving to the boat, she checked to ensure the sailcloth was intact and the oars were locked in place before she started shoving it from the sand.

Leaves swished. Footsteps padded, and a breathless pant tore hope from her heart. Still, she refused to give up. She had to leave. This was her chance! She had the boat nearly in the water now.

"Miss! Miss!" Pedro's voice halted her.

She glanced up at the lad as he broke from the dark greenery onto the shore. Even in the dim light of the moon, she saw panic on his expression.

"What is it? How did you find me?"

"Charlie sent me, Miss." He placed hands on his knees, breathing hard. "Said you'd be here."

Frustration bubbled in her stomach. "What do you want?" Perhaps the boy wished to escape with her? Nay, he was no prisoner.

Finally, Pedro drew himself up. "It's the cap'n, Miss. He's dying."

"I just left him. He will recover." She faced the boat again. "Now, leave me be, Pedro."

"He got worse, Miss. Much worse. The surgeon's wit' him now. Says he don't have much time. Ye've got to come!"

Chapter 26

M aston was not good at waiting. He'd never been good at waiting. Especially when great rewards were at stake, when he would finally acquire everything he deserved. Footsteps alerted him, and he slid into the shadows at the end of the hallway as that imbecile Finn ambled by, leaving a trail of putrid tobacco in his wake.

Shadows. This would be the last time Maston would be in the shadows. With Josephine Arnaud by his side and the Ring on his finger, they would rule the Spanish Main, not that fathead Blake. *Non*. Maston would be second to no man. If only his father could see him now. He'd be sorry he'd allowed his shrewish wife to cast Maston from their home, calling him names no child should hear.

Smiling, he adjusted his cravat, picturing his aged father crawling to bow before Maston, begging forgiveness and favors. Justice would be served when Maston dismissed him like so much refuse…

Just as he had done to him.

Voices rumbled down the hallway. Sam's and Charlie's.

"Nothing we can do for him," Sam said.

"Nothing at all?" Charlie asked. "What is ailing him?"

"I have no idea. Never saw anything come upon a man so quick and fierce."

The two walked past Maston.

"Will he die?" Charlie asked, a slight tremor in her voice.

"I don't know."

"Someone should stay with him."

"I'm returning. I need to get opium and willow bark from the cabinet."

Their voices muffled into whispers as they disappeared in the shadows.

Good. Blake was alone. At least for a few moments. Enough time for Maston to get in and steal the Ring. Before Jo had been escorted back to her ship, she'd instructed him to get the powerful artifact and meet her on the south side of the island just past the mangrove swamp.

"Then we shall be together forever, *mon amour*." She had kissed him so fervently, with such passion, he thought he'd left the tethers of this world and entered paradise. At that moment, he would have done anything for her.

Pushing from the wall, he crept toward Blake's chamber, fingering the knife stuck in his belt.

"I hope that pious sprite managed to get him to remove the Ring," Jo had said, offering him a wicked smile. "If not, cut off his finger."

Which is exactly what Maston would do. And he'd enjoy it. He'd been under Blake's dictatorial thumb for too long. Cutting off one of his fingers seemed more than adequate payment.

The door creaked open a little too loudly, but his task should not take long. The great Captain Blake Keene sprawled over his bed like a puppet whose strings had been cut. He neither stirred nor opened an eye when Maston approached. Stooping by his bed, he reached for his hand but nearly dropped it due to the heat radiating from the captain's skin. No Ring sat upon his finger.

Odd. Maston groaned. *Bon sang*! What to do now? It must be here somewhere. Blake would not keep it far. After groping through Blake's pockets—to which his captain remained oblivious—Maston combed through the room, opening drawers, flipping through books, lifting up vases and trinkets. That's when he found the lockbox. Of course.

Voices in the hall alerted him. Grabbing the box, he did the only thing he could do. He opened the door to the chamber beside Blake's and dashed inside, closing it after him.

Emeline was the most foolhardy, naïve, bird-witted woman ever to live. Over and over, she chastised herself as she followed Pedro through the jungle back to the great house. More than once, she nearly halted and dashed back to the boat. Yet something pressed her onward—empathy, concern? More likely a stupidity for which there was no cure.

Now, as she slipped inside Blake's chamber, drawing a glance from Sam Goode, a shudder overcame her, along with a stench that spoke of more than mere illness.

"There's naught you can do, Miss." Sam leaned back in his chair. "Might as well go back to your bed."

Drawing close, Emeline studied Blake. Pedro had said he was worse. The lad had not exaggerated. With pale, flaccid skin, dark circles beneath his eyes, blue lips, and shallow breathing, Blake looked as close to death as a condemned man at the noose. Despite her attempts to the contrary, her heart shrank within her.

A quick glance told her the Ring had not been returned to his finger. Another glance told her the lockbox containing it was gone. Odd, that. Why was Blake now at death's door?

"I'd rather stay, if you don't mind," she said quietly.

The surgeon studied her, then closed the book he'd been reading. "Your choice." He glanced at Blake. "But I don't know if you're up to it. Death can be an ugly thing."

Death?

Alarm fired every nerve. She steeled herself. "I have seen much death in my life, Sir." 'Twas true enough. Though she had not seen anyone die whom she…she…she could not even bring herself to think the word.

"Very well. Come get me if there is any change. I'm three doors down on the left." With that, the surgeon closed the door behind him.

Oh, Lord, what do I do? Have I returned only to watch him die?

Emeline drew up a chair and sat. The Ring was gone, but whatever illness it had caused remained. Or was it the Ring that had done this? She took one of Blake's hands in hers and winced at the heat emanating from his skin.

Pray.

Aye. Of course. This was no ordinary illness. Instantly she knew that, could sense it deep inside. This was a spell, a hex, a wicked device cast upon Blake. And she also knew where it had come from. Josephine Arnaud. She had pushed aside the sense God had given her about the woman, not wanting to believe such an evil thing about anyone. Now there was no doubt.

Rising from her chair, she knelt beside the bed and laid both hands on Blake's feverish body. He didn't flinch...was barely breathing. She had to move fast. She'd seen her parents pray against spells on many occasions. She'd just never executed such power herself.

Drawing a deep breath, she closed her eyes and spoke in her most commanding voice, which trembled at the moment. "In the name of Jesus, I command any spell, hex, or wicked curse cast upon Captain Blake Keene to be broken and leave his body at once."

Her words seemed to drift upon the air and float out the open window, as powerless as the woman who spoke them. Or were they? She must have faith. She knew the power of her Lord's name, had seen it in action many a time. Now she would wait....*and believe.*

An hour passed and nothing changed.

Another hour and—was it her imagination, or did Blake's breathing grow steadier?

His moan snapped her eyes open just moments after she'd given in to exhaustion and allowed them to close.

She knelt by his side and laid the back of her hand over his forehead. Still warm but not as hot as before.

More elation than she should feel soared through her.

"Emeline," he mouthed.

"Aye, 'tis me." She reached for a glass of water on the table, dipped a cloth into it, and dribbled it over his parted lips.

He licked it up, then attempted to speak. "Wha...? Wha...?"

"Shh, now, rest. You've been ill, but you are getting better."

Thank You, Lord. She couldn't help but smile as she sat back, watching him drift off to sleep again.

An hour later, the clock chimed four, and Emeline popped open her eyes to find Blake staring at her from his bed.

Blinking, she shook off her sleep, embarrassed. "I must have drifted off."

"You are beautiful when you sleep." His voice emerged muffled, yet stronger than before.

Ignoring how his compliment warmed her, she was more astonished to see that the color had returned to his face. "No doubt you are still delirious with fever."

He smiled. "I'm feeling much better." His brow wrinkled. "You healed me, didn't you?"

"Me? Nay." She shook her head. "God healed you. I prayed for you, 'tis all." Moving close, she laid a hand on his forehead. Warm. "You still have a fever. Now rest. 'Twill be light soon."

"A drink?" He struggled to sit, rubbed his head, and then dropped back to the mattress. With a mighty groan, he attempted it again. This time, she gripped his arm and helped him until he sat and swung his legs to the floor. His necklaces dangled over his bare chest, the skin of which still glistened with sweat.

Grabbing a glass, Emeline handed it to him, and he took it, his hand shaking.

"Easy, Blake." She helped him drink, then took the glass. "You should lie down. You almost died last night."

"Did I?" He leaned forward on his knees, drawing in deep breaths as if to stave off any further visits by the grim reaper.

Moments passed in silence with naught but the rush of wind outside the window and the distant call of a gull.

Emeline should leave. With Blake improving, she need not watch over him, and being alone with the man, being this close to him, was not good for her heart.

"I killed my father."

He said the statement as if he were announcing the weather—emotionless, sober.

Taken aback, Emeline stared at him. "What did you say?"

"I sliced him through with my blade," he added, not looking her way.

Clearly the man was still overcome with fever.

"Shh. You must be dreaming." She nudged him back, but he resisted.

"Would that it was a dream." He sighed, his gaze finally snapping to hers. "Does that frighten you, my little sugar bird?"

She studied him, wondering why he divulged such a secret. A pain she could not fathom burned in his eyes. "Why would you do such a thing?"

"He deserved it." He lowered his gaze once again. "He beat my mother. Over and over. Year after year. Treated her as he did one of his slaves on his plantation on Barbados."

Emeline nodded. 'Twas more common than one would think for men to treat their wives thus.

Raking back his hair, Blake dropped his head into his hands. Dark strands fell across his jaw that rolled and bunched tight with anger. "Many nights as a child, I'd hear his drunken shouts, hear her screams, and finally her endless sobbing."

He rubbed a finger over the black cross around his neck. "As I told you, she was a religious woman, believed in the God you espouse. Lot a good it did her."

"Then why do you wear it?"

"To remind me that God comes to no man's rescue." His tone was full of spite.

"He came to yours this night," she dared to say.

~ 244 ~

Which only got her a disbelieving grunt. "I could not defend her. Could not help her at all. Not for many years. But then I grew tall and strong, and by age sixteen, I was as large as my father."

Emeline swallowed down a lump of emotion, guessing the rest of the sad tale.

"As usual, he was deep in his cups and angry at the world. He began arguing with my mother about what"—he shook his head—"I don't remember. All I remember is the rage I felt as he started slapping her without mercy."

Emeline could not imagine such a thing. The men in her family, the fathers, brothers, and uncles, were kind, loving, and gentle with every woman.

Blake glanced at her, and the unfathomable agony and sorrow in that one look nearly tore her heart from her chest. "I dashed for him, pulled his blade from his scabbard and leveled it at him, demanding he leave her be." Frowning, he shook his head. "After the shock wore off at seeing his son behave like a man, my father began taunting me, calling me names no father should call a son. He charged me, swiping at the sword as if it were naught but air."

Blake rubbed his temples. His breathing grew heavy. Emeline placed a hand on his arm. The fever remained. "Please, Blake, lie down. You are still sick. There's no need to tell me these things."

"Aye, there is. I need to." He swallowed hard.

She nodded, waiting, her heart growing far too heavy.

"The blade trembled in my hand. My mother screamed for me to drop it and leave him be. But I couldn't. I wouldn't. He continued barreling toward me. I swept the blade down in an effort to keep it from his grip....at the last minute he swerved to the left and the sword plunged into his belly."

Emeline flung a hand to her mouth.

"He died in agony." Blake's words carried no sorrow, no pity, no remorse.

Emeline remained quiet, moisture filling her eyes.

"She cried for him." Blake's tone was incredulous as he snapped his gaze to her, shock and horror written on his tight expression. "Not merely cried, but she ran and fell on him, sobbing in horror." He growled. "I saved her, and she cried for him."

"He was her husband, Blake."

"And I was her son," he spat back, fury screaming from his face. "She threw me to the wind. Tossed me from the house that very night and told me never to return."

Emeline could only stare at him. Only then did this man's pain, this man's need for control, for power, begin to make sense.

"No boy should have to suffer as you did," she finally said. "What did you do?"

He shrugged. "I survived." He grabbed his other necklace, the emblem of the lion, the sun, and the dove. "I *more* than survived. Found work down at the docks."

"Where did you get that from?" Emeline gestured toward the amulet she'd always assumed had been stolen from some conquered merchant.

"An aged captain gave it to me. I was mopping the floors of a punch house in the wee hours of the morning, one of my many jobs. All the patrons had left except one old sailor who sat at a table in the corner staring at me. I thought he was drunk, but when I came close, he called me over." Blake held the pendant up to the lantern light. "Said he saw something in me. Said I would do great things. Then he pulled this over his head and handed it to me." Blake dropped the amulet, sending it banging against his chest.

"What else did he say?" Emeline asked.

He gave her a skeptical look. "Only that I was chosen."

Precisely. She couldn't help but smile. She'd heard countless tales from countless people of similar encounters with beings who pronounced a special destiny, a *chosen* destiny on their lives. *Angels.* The man who spoke to Blake must have been an angel. Dare she tell him that or would he think her mad? "What do you think he meant?"

He shrugged. "Perhaps chosen to rule the Caribbean." A sardonic gleam crossed his green eyes, and she knew he must be feeling well again.

"You're impossible."

"So I've been told." He smiled, and in his gaze she saw a burning, a longing, and an affection that both elated and terrified her. Lifting a hand, he gently caressed her cheek as was his way.

Clutching it, she lowered it back to his knee before the effect of his touch caused all reason to abandon her. "You are feeling better. I should leave." She glanced out the window where the faintest glow of light announced a new day. "You need to rest." Emeline rose.

"Stay." From the look in his eyes, 'twas more a request than an order.

"No need. The demons are gone, are they not?" For she no longer felt the oppression in the room.

Instantly, his gaze dropped to his finger, then up to the chest of drawers. Pushing from his bed, he leapt to his feet, teetered for a second, then marched to the place where he'd left the lockbox, rage fisting his hands. "Where is my Ring?"

Chapter 27

D id you take it?" Blake faced Emeline, who, even with her hair in disarray and her gown wrinkled, looked more beautiful than he remembered. Sudden embarrassment swamped him that he'd disclosed such intimate details of his life, stories he'd never told a soul.

She shook her head. "It was gone when I got here, Blake. I'm sorry."

Should he believe her? When everyone else in his life always betrayed him? "You hated it. You wanted it gone."

She folded her hands in front of her. "True enough. Nonetheless, I did not take it."

Blake growled. He must not trust her. Must not trust anyone. "Finn! He was here in my chamber searching for something. He's always had his eye on the Ring."

She took a step toward him. "Blake…forget the Ring. The evil it brought you is gone. Get some rest."

"Where's Bandit?" For he wouldn't put it past the smelly beast to steal it again.

"The lockbox was far too heavy for a monkey to carry," she countered.

He eyed her with suspicion, unsure of her motives. Unsure of his own. Without saying a word, he tossed a shirt over his head, slipped on his boots, strapped on his weapons, and slammed out the door. He would find the Ring. And when he did, he'd kill the man, woman, child…or monkey who took it.

Three hours later, after waking and interrogating every member of his crew and staff—all while ignoring their shock at finding him alive—he ordered every chamber, hall, kitchen, library, and gallery to be searched. Still no Ring was found.

The pirates who escorted Josephine back to her ship reported she had, indeed, rowed out to *La Sorcière* and set sail soon after. However, lookouts on the south side of the island told him her ship had been spotted hugging the coast for several hours before she had set off to sea. Odd.

If anyone had the courage to defy him and steal the Ring, 'twould be her. Yet how did she even know about it? She had made no mention of it to him. Still, she'd returned to her ship long before Blake had removed it from his finger. And Emeline was right about Bandit. He did not have the strength to heft so large a box.

Therefore, only two of his crew remained high in his suspicions. One of whom he assumed was off on some dalliance with a native girl, and the other he'd just summoned to the library where Blake conducted his inquisitions.

"Do you really think it was Finn?" Emeline spoke from her seat on a nearby settee, Bandit in her arms.

Blake turned from the window. "I can think of no one else who both knew about the Ring and has enough reckless greed to dare defy me." He crossed arms over his chest. "Rummy is always besotted, Sam cares not for his own life, Pedro is just a lad, and Charlie is too smart for such a defiant feat that would surely get her keelhauled or worse. Besides, though they may have had their suspicions, I don't believe any of them knew about the Ring."

"What of Maston? Is he not missing?"

Oddly, at the mention of the man's name, Bandit flapped his hairy arms in the air and screeched.

Ignoring him, Blake blew out a sigh. "Perhaps, but his greed extends toward women and wine, not power."

Movement brought Blake's gaze to the doorway where Finn entered, wide-eyed and looking like a mouse about to be caught in a trap.

"Where's the Ring, Finn?" Blake ground out.

Swallowing hard, Finn tugged at the bandana around his head. "I didn't take it, Cap'n. I swears."

"You were in my chamber right before I got sick. You were looking for it, were you not?"

Finn cast a pleading glance at Emeline.

"Were you not?" Blake's shout caused Emeline to flinch and Finn to take a step back.

"Aye, I were lookin' fer it, Cap'n. But I didn't find it. I didn't take it."

Blake fingered the hilt of his blade. "If you had found it, you would have stolen it. Defied me! Betrayed me!"

Squealing, Bandit began shaking his head, drawing a glance from Blake, and he suddenly wished he could still understand him. What was wrong with the infernal varmint?

Finn shrank back, terror streaking his eyes. "I can't say fer sure, Cap'n. I…I wanted to see it, touch it, try its power. 'Ard to resist, eh? But take it?" His breathing heightened. "I don't think I would've, Cap'n."

Blake studied him. He'd known Finn for five years, and he'd never seen him so frightened, not even when they'd been chased by a fleet of French frigates a year past, not even when one of said frigates had pummeled the *Summons* with a broadside that had nearly sent her down to Davey Jones' locker.

"If you have it, Finn, give it back to me at once, and I vow to let you live."

"But I don't 'ave it, Cap'n. I swears on me mother's grave."

Blake approached his quartermaster… slowly… methodically, the thud of his boots sounding out the man's demise. With his gaze locked upon Finn and his hand itching to pull his cutlass, Blake halted before him. "If I discover you took it, you'll be pleading to join your mother in that grave."

Lowering his eyes to the floor, Finn nodded.

A servant rushed through the door, a piece of parchment in hand. "Captain Keene, you told us to search Claude Maston's chamber more thoroughly."

Looking up, Blake nodded.

"We found this missive. Don't know how we missed it before." He handed the parchment to Blake.

By the time you read this, my dear Capitaine, I will be long gone with both your Ring and your woman. You took me for a docile popinjay, but now you discover I am far more shrewd and courageous than you'll ever be.

Au revoir, mon Capitaine. See you in hell.

With as much grace as she could gather, Emeline swung her legs over the bulwarks and planted her feet once again on the deck of the *Summons*. Whatever the note had said, it thrust Blake into a rampage so swift and hard that she feared his health would relapse. Yet now, as she watched him mount the quarterdeck ladder, issuing orders to his crew, he seemed more stalwart than ever. Whatever had nearly killed him had been of a spiritual nature, which the name of Jesus had evicted. Yet at the moment, it seemed he'd been taken over by an equally deadly demon, one that filled his eyes with bloodlust and his heart with darkness.

He had stormed through the house, shouting orders to his crew to ready the *Summons* and to his staff to maintain and protect the island in his absence. Chaos ensued with servants running hither and thither and supplies being gathered and sent to the ship. Hence, within the hour, Blake escorted Emeline to the cockboat, barely uttering a word.

And once again she found herself a prisoner on board his ship.

No one ordered her below. No one paid her much mind as she wove through the dozens of pirates scurrying across the deck and made her way to the starboard railing overlooking the bay. A humid breeze stirred the tendrils of her hair as rays from a rising sun warmed her and spread golden fingers over turquoise waters. Beyond the white sand of the shore, the turrets and gables of Keene House poked above the verdant web of the jungle, defiant and strong like the arms of the dead rising from a grassy grave. Oddly, sorrow draped over her at leaving this place. Which was ridiculous, of course. Still, so much had happened here. She'd learned a great deal about Blake, his mournful past, what motivated him—much of which had gripped her heart, her very soul, and refused to let go. Which was also ridiculous. Foolish, foolish girl.

"You're a dreamer, my sweet darling," her father would say. "Always have your head off in some adventure."

Squealing turned her just in time to see Bandit swinging from the ratlines and taking one final leap into her arms. Thankfully, she caught him in time as the monkey nestled his cheek against hers.

"Where have you been, you naughty monkey?"

To which he only grinned.

"Hands to stations!" Blake brayed. "Unfurl sails, loose topsails, man the capstan!"

Finn added a few commands of his own, sending men leaping into shrouds and others dashing here and there, gathering lines, and gripping the spokes of the capstan.

Blake stood on the quarterdeck, more authority and determination riding on his face than most admirals facing battle. Wind tossed his dark hair behind him as he and Rummy studied a map spread across the binnacle. He'd donned his usual pirate attire, with tight breeches stuffed in knee high boots, a white shirt open at the collar and covered by a leather jerkin. A myriad of weapons stuffed in his baldric winked at her in the sunlight.

For one brief moment their eyes met, and a look of understanding passed between them. Interrupted by a shout from the shore.

"Cap'n! A body."

Emeline spun about. There on the shore stood two pirates, pulling a bloated corpse from the water.

With much grunting and groaning, Blake's men finally hauled the body up the rope ladder and dropped it upon the deck with a disrespectful thud.

Claude Maston.

Several pirates gasped at the sight. Charlie drew a hand to her mouth. Rummy cursed. Finn stared at the body of his friend, a numb look on his face, and Pedro said in a trembling voice, "Poor Maston."

Poor Maston, indeed. Blake had a good idea what had happened to him, and it only incensed him more.

"We should bury 'im, Cap'n." Finn drew the pipe from his mouth, not yet willing to look Blake in the eyes.

Though Blake no longer believed he had anything to do with the missing Ring, the fact that he had even considered betraying Blake proved the man's loyalties did not stretch beyond his own desires. Hence he could no longer trust him. Ever.

One glance at Emeline standing at the railing revealed the horror on her face. Hang it. He should not have allowed her to witness such a frightening sight.

He glanced back at Maston. "Nay, I do not wish him to remain on my island. We'll bury him at sea. Holland, Duarte, take the body below and wrap it in sailcloth. The rest of you"—Blake scanned his crew—"back to work! We set sail immediately!"

Grumbling, his crew skittered away as Blake turned to Finn. "Escort Miss Hyde to my cabin, then return here to your duties."

"Aye, Cap'n," Finn said, staring at the deck. "Where we be headin', if I may ask?"

"We are pursuing *La Sorcière*, and after I retrieve my Ring, I'm going to sink her and her captain to the depths."

More tired than he'd been in a long while, Blake entered his cabin, unbuckled his baldric, and laid his weapons on his desk with a heavy *clank*. Heaving a deep sigh, he stared out the stern windows as the sun dragged the last ribbons of orange over the edge of the horizon, pulling a dark quilt upon the sea in their stead.

Emeline. Only then did he remember that he'd sent her to his cabin. He turned. There she was, fast asleep on his bed. He couldn't help but smile. She looked so peaceful, like a little lamb without a care in the world. However, he knew better. She was no lamb nor a little bird as he so oft called her. She was wise and strong and brave. And good. He longed to protect her from this evil world. Trouble was, *he* was the evil in her world at the moment.

Moving to the cupboard, he uncorked a bottle of rum and took a big swig. He'd spent the day searching the seas for any sign of Josephine's ship. She could not have gotten too far in only a day, but she might as well be at the other end of the world, for he'd not spotted a single sail skimming upon the turbulent blue waters.

A soft murmur brought his gaze around to Emeline, who was just rising to sit on his bed. Looking embarrassed, she rubbed her eyes. "My apologies, Captain."

"None necessary. You were awake all last night." Resisting the urge to draw near to her, he wove around his desk and leaned back against it, crossing his boots at his ankles. "On my account."

She smiled. "As were you."

He rubbed his chin. She had forfeited a night's sleep for him and yet, her thoughts were for his exhaustion.

The ship rolled over a wave and Emeline gripped the bedframe, her eyes widening as if she just realized where she'd slept. Jumping up, she attempted to brush the wrinkles from her skirts, red blooming over her cheeks.

Blake grinned.

"Maston," she whispered, her voice edged in sorrow. "What happened?"

Blake sipped his drink. "Josephine happened."

Her confused look prompted him to continue. "The note I received? 'Twas from him, informing me he'd taken the Ring and was running away with Josephine."

Shock flashed in Emeline's eyes. "Oh, my." Her brow wrinkled. "So, they were…they were..."

"Lovers, aye. I should have seen it. Maston chases after every skirt he sees, and Josephine needed a little pigeon to do her bidding." Setting down his glass, he crossed arms over his chest. One would think Blake would be so accustomed to betrayal that it no longer surprised or pained him. This recent betrayal had done both. Further proving his weakness. He silently cursed.

"He must have entered your chamber when you were ill," Emeline said, "when Sam had stepped out for a moment."

Nodding, Blake felt fury string tight across his jaw.

Emeline approached, the swish of her skirts accompanying the dash of the sea against the hull. Her gaze drifted over his ear. "Wherever is your black pearl earring?"

Absently, Blake touched his earlobe. "I tossed it overboard. Should have done it years ago." In truth, he had no idea why he'd kept it.

She studied him curiously. "'Twas a gift from her."

Shaking his head, he snorted. "How do you know such things?"

"I'm sorry, Blake," she said, her tone melancholy. "I know you've suffered from much treachery."

"I don't want your pity," he said a bit too harshly. "I want my Ring."

He frowned at the disappointment in her eyes, then chastised himself for caring what this female thought.

The *Summons* pitched over a wave, and he reached out to steady her.

She jerked from his touch as if it burned her skin. "Do you think Josephine killed him? Is she capable of such a horrific act?"

Blake raked back his hair. "More than capable. She used him to get the Ring, no doubt promised to love him forever"—as she had done with Blake—"and after he was of no further use, she did away with him."

"Heartless," Emeline breathed out.

"Now you understand her."

"I believe she is a witch." Emeline hugged herself. "I have no doubt your illness was a result of some vile spell she cast upon you."

"A witch?" He shook his head. "Indeed, that makes more sense than I care to admit."

"Poor Maston." Moisture glazed her eyes. "I am sorry he was willing to betray you."

Grabbing his glass, Blake pushed from the desk and went to refill it. "Maston lived for himself. He was driven by a lust for every pleasure he could find."

"Hmm. Similar to your lust for power," she countered sarcastically.

Blake faced her, drink in hand. One of her adorable brows quirked in jest. Yet was it a jest? More truth than jest, for her words pricked his heart. Was he no different than Maston? They both sought things in this life that would satisfy and protect. Maston yearned for love in the arms of women. Perhaps because, like Blake, he'd been tossed to the streets by one. And Blake sought power to prevent such a tragedy from occurring again.

As the last vestiges of light dipped over the horizon, shadows crept out of hiding. Blake could no longer see the exquisite details of her face. After taking a gulp of rum, he set down his glass, then struck flint to steel and lit the lantern on his desk. Threads of golden light spread outward, landing on Emeline and circling her in a golden glow—a heavenly glow. He wouldn't be surprised if she didn't hail from that eternal city, sent down to Earth to set him aright.

Her eyes searched his, a look in them he'd not seen before. A look that stirred his heart, making him want to promise her the world if she'd only continue gazing at him like that.

"I should leave." She backed away. "Am I to lodge in the same cabin?"

He reached for her hand and stayed her. "Don't go."

She faced him but said nothing.

"Pedro told me what you did," he said.

The slightest catch of her breath sounded, barely noticeable, and she lowered her gaze.

"That you were about to escape, indeed, *could* have escaped. But when you discovered how ill I was, you forsook your only opportunity and returned." He still could not believe it…that anyone would put the needs of others ahead of themselves. Scads! The needs of her captor! What kind of creature stood before him? Angel? Saint? A true lady with the heart of a queen.

She gave him a tender smile. "I couldn't very well allow you to die, could I?"

"Why not? I've kept you prisoner against your will for nigh a month. There's not a person on Earth who would not have taken the chance to get away. But not you." Reaching up, he brushed the back of his fingers over her cheek. Always so soft.

At first, she closed her eyes at his touch, then snapped them open and took a step back, her breathing coming fast. "Human life is far more important than my freedom."

"Any human life?" He longed to hear that she cared, that she had returned because she felt affection for him.

"Any." She would not meet his gaze.

"I don't believe you."

Confusion wrinkled her brow. "Why would I lie?"

"Because you feel something for me. I see it in your eyes. I felt it in your kiss."

Red flushed across her face. From anger or shame, he couldn't tell. "You insufferable, lecherous toad! Do you think every female fawns over your affections?"

"Perhaps." He grinned. "But I care that only a particular one does."

With a humph, she turned to leave.

"A wager, then?"

She spun, eyes aflame.

"A single kiss. One kiss, merely to discover if you harbor any affection for me at all."

"A gentleman would never suggest such a thing! I will not engage in such licentious play."

Yet she made no move to leave. Blake drew closer. "What are you afraid of?"

"Ridiculous!" She whirled around, but Blake grabbed her hand and pulled her close. When she made no move to resist, he wrapped an arm around her and drew her against his chest. Her soft curves molded against his firm muscles, and still she remained. In truth, she seemed to weaken in his embrace.

Slowly, gently, he put his lips on hers.

Chapter 28

E meline wanted to resist. She did! She wanted to slap the rogue pirate and storm from his cabin. She wanted to....

But chains wrapped about her heart...her body, holding her a prisoner in his arms. The bulkheads, the deck, the furniture, the windows all faded away as if they'd been but a dream, and she'd finally entered reality.

Heavenly sensations swirled down to her toes, then spun back up again, sending her heart leaping, her breath heaving, and resurrecting an urge within her to become a part of this man, spirit, soul and...body.

Pressing her closer, he explored her mouth with such tenderness, such desire, her legs grew weak. He caressed her back, ran fingers over her cheek, then encased her in his arms once again. She'd never felt so safe, so cherished as she did in that moment.

And so out of control!

She sensed his need for her growing, and planting her palms on his chest, she nudged him back.

Withdrawing, he leaned his forehead against hers, their heated breaths mingling in the air between them.

"I'd say that settles it, don't you?" His voice was coarse with desire.

What was she thinking? She wasn't thinking. This had naught to do with thoughts or logic or reason. This had everything to do with her heart and the waves of pleasure still flowing over her entire body. She wanted more of this man, more of every part of him. And she hated herself for it.

She wanted to say it settled nothing, but she now knew that, regardless that this man was a power-greedy, lecherous pirate, regardless he had kidnapped her and kept her captive, regardless he most definitely was not the hero in the romance she'd always dreamed of…

She loved him.

But would her love be enough? Or was he merely toying with her girlish emotions? As no doubt he had with many a female before her.

Drawing back, she raised her gaze to his.

What she saw in his eyes nearly sent her careening backward—love, care, affection. Not lust, nor playfulness, but a seriousness, a determination. He ran a thumb over her moist lips and gave her a sultry smile. "You have me quite smitten, my little sugar bird."

Smitten? No one had ever been smitten by her. But smitten was not love, and she would not settle for less from the hero in her story.

When she didn't respond, he added, "You cannot hide your affection for me, Emeline. 'Tis written on your face, burning in your eyes, and shouting from the heat of your passion."

She lowered her gaze. "Passion is not love. Perhaps you confuse the two."

He cupped her chin with his fingers and raised her eyes to his. "Perhaps 'tis you who are confused, for I have known passion. But I have not known love until this moment."

Love.

She studied those almond-shaped eyes of his, searching for insincerity, for any hint of mirth to expose his deceit. All she saw was a depth of emotion that nearly made her leap back into his arms.

"Tell me you feel the same, Emeline. I know you do."

She hesitated, unsure whether the truth would help or hurt. But how could she deny it? Finally, she whispered, "I do."

His grin was wide as he reached out and drew her close once again.

She allowed his embrace, enjoying the feel of his strength cocooning her, sheltering her. Could this man be the hero of whom she'd always dreamed?

"Blake." Pushing from him, she gripped his arms. "I beseech you, give up this mad quest for the Ring."

Frowning, he shrugged from her embrace and retreated to his desk. Picking up his glass, he took a sip.

"Don't you see?" she continued, praying their love would be enough for him to change his ways. "The power you seek is all a delusion. It will corrupt you. It will never be enough, never give you the joy and peace you seek. Neither will it shield you from the betrayal of others, as you hope." She gave him a pleading look. "Leave the Ring. Let it go. Take me home and meet my family. You'll like them." In truth, she hoped her father or grandfather could divert Blake onto a more godly path.

Tossing the rest of the rum into his mouth, he slammed down the glass. "But will they like *me*? Besides, what would a reprobate like me do with a bunch of missionaries?"

She felt as though a boarding axe had embedded in her heart. "You don't have to be that man anymore."

He turned to stare at the moonlit waves out the windows. "You fell in love with this reprobate. Or so you say. I will not change for you or anyone."

Emotion burned in Emeline's throat. She forced back tears. "Then will you keep your promise to take me back to Jamaica?" For she knew now there could be no future between them.

He faced her, the affection gone from his eyes, replaced by pain and a resolve that would not be put off. "After I get the Ring. You have my word, Emeline, and then you'll never have to see me again."

Blake planted his boots on the heaving deck and gripped the quarterdeck railing as the *Summons* crested a foam-capped swell. Morning sunlight cast swaths of golden lace upon both ship and sea, creating a masterpiece more beautiful than those hanging in his gallery. He smiled. Wind whipped over him, and he inhaled the familiar scent of brine and freedom. This was the life he'd chosen. Freedom to do what he wished and the power to rule the seas.

"Loose head and topsails!" he shouted, then gripping the lion medallion, he turned to Rummy. "Two points to larboard. Full and by."

The helmsman nodded and adjusted course, while his new bosun Layton sent men up into the ratlines to unfurl tops for maximum speed. 'Twas a vast ocean to cover in order to find Josephine, but he knew her well, knew her haunts and hunting grounds. 'Twas only a matter of time before he found her.

He grimaced, forcing down his rage for the time being, reserving it for the witch—the witch who had used and murdered Maston, among many other vile things. Yet Blake's anger at the Frenchman had abated the minute he'd ordered his body tossed overboard at dawn. 'Twas not a just fate for the simple crime of loving a woman, albeit the wrong woman, an evil woman.

However, Blake's murderous thoughts vanished the moment an angel in blue skirts emerged from the companionway and made her way to the starboard railing. Her chestnut hair blew in silken strands behind her while every ray of sunlight diverted course and landed on her, glittering in her hair, shimmering across her gown, and sparkling over her skin as if she were not from this world.

Blinking, Blake cursed himself for the ludicrous thoughts. Then why did every one of his crew stop to stare at her?

"Back to work!" he shouted over the crash of waves and blast of wind. Still, she would not look his way.

For the first time in weeks, he'd slept deep and sound. No nightmares plagued him, no phantom demons infiltrated his cabin. Just as Emeline had said, 'twas the Ring which opened the gates of hell. Was it causing Josephine the same distress? He hoped so.

With all canvas spread to the favoring breeze, the *Summons* cut through the azure sea, plunging into the rollers and sending spray back over the deck in brilliant showers. Snapping hair from his face, Blake gripped the railing and closed his eyes, listening to the creak and moan of the ship, the dash of the sea against the hull. Music as soothing as any violin.

Emeline. Only her presence had controlled the dark side of the Ring, but he could no longer keep her prisoner against her will. She deserved so much better than that.

She deserved so much better than him.

Charlie approached the lady and leaned on the railing beside her and the two women began conversing. Their laughter bubbled over Blake like a soothing elixir as Bandit dropped from the ratlines beside them. Scooping him up in her arms, Emeline nestled her cheek against his hairy forehead, eliciting a wide grin and joyful screech from the beast. And a surge of jealousy within Blake. Absurd!

He looked away. He'd kissed her. Deeply and passionately. 'Twas like no other kiss he'd ever experienced, for it touched a part of him far deeper than his flesh, a part of him no one had ever touched before. Even worse, he'd declared his love! When he'd vowed long ago never to show such weakness again, never to put himself in a vulnerable position where he could be harmed, cast away, or betrayed.

The *Summons* leapt over a mighty swell, sending a spray of salty water over him, cooling his humor. By his admission of love, he'd given her power. And what did she do with it? She tried to convince him to give up his quest for the Ring. The most alarming part was that—for a brief moment—he'd wanted to. If only to please her. Scads! Her goodness was infecting him! And he must not allow that.

Pedro eased on her other side. Tousling his wavy hair, she gave him a hug. A hug? Pirates didn't hug! Nay! As soon as he retrieved the Ring, he would honor his vow and take her home. Before his entire crew became a band of jingle-brained do-gooders.

Or worse, missionaries!

At that very moment, as if she sensed his thoughts, she glanced at him over her shoulder. The tender look she gave him, along with her gentle smile, nearly broke through his resolve to do anything but love her for the rest of his days.

Thankfully, "A sail, a sail!" trumpeted down from the lookout at the crosstrees, interrupting his dangerous thoughts.

Plucking the spyglass from his belt, Blake leveled it on the horizon, shifting it to the left when the lookout added, "Off the larboard bow!"

There, in the distance and barely discernable, were the swollen white curves of several sails. Too far to know to what ship they belonged.

"Helms alee, Rummy!" Blake ordered, then shouted down to Finn and Layton. "Stations for the stays! Rise tacks and sheets! Slow and steady."

Within seconds, the *Summons* tacked aweather, its bow plunging and rising in the foamy surf.

Balancing on the pitching deck, Blake lifted the glass to his eye, searching for an ensign, a name on the bow, anything to identify what ship it was. Pirates, merchants? Or was it the ship he sought?

Minutes passed like hours. Thus far, it appeared they'd not spotted the *Summons*. Good.

Blake shifted the glass to the hull where the crest of Jesuits came clearly into view, along with the name *Guerrieri Della Croce*. Hang it! 'Twas Della Morte's ship. As much as he'd like to engage the impudent mule and send him to the depths, he had not the time. *La Sorcière* was his target.

Swinging the scope to the ship's deck, he focused on the men rushing across it, having no doubt seen Blake by now. That's when he saw her. Hair the color of the night flailing in the wind and the black leather of Josephine's pirate attire.

Confusion tore through him, sending his thoughts into a whirlwind, seeking an answer, any answer, aside from the only one that made sense. Josephine and Della Morte were working together.

"They've all canvas to the wind and are heading our way, Cap'n!" Finn shouted from the main deck.

Blake ground his teeth. Too late to hang back and follow them, discover where they would drop anchor, and steal the Ring on land. For 'twould be far more difficult a task at sea. Regardless, he had no other recourse save the one set before him—fight or die.

Della Morte growled his displeasure. "You are quite sure, Josephine?"

"*Oui*, 'tis him. I know his paltry brig anywhere." She handed him the spyglass. "Look for yourself."

His gaze dropped to the Ring on her finger, sparkling in the morning sun. "But we have the Ring, *mia cara*. Why bother with him?"

"Because he's a swaggering princox, a rapacious whiffet!" she spat back. "I want him dead." She uttered a blasphemous curse. "*En fait*, he *should* be dead! Why didn't my spell kill him? I put my strongest hex on him, one that should have overpowered any trick of my enemy!"

The witch gave Della Morte pause. The sooner he was rid of her, the better. He took Josephine's hand and brought it to his lips. Their night together had been more than satisfying, but the woman had outlived her usefulness. She'd retrieved the Ring for him, for which he was eternally grateful. As an added benefit, she was an excellent lover. Though now it was time for her to hand over the powerful relic.

Trouble was, she was being stubborn....hesitant. Typical female. The lot of them useless except for one thing. Of course he had promised her not only his undying devotion and love, but that she could use the Ring for a few months to acquire the wealth she needed before he must take it to the Pope. In the meantime, they would scour the seas and amass such a fortune they'd never have to lift another finger. They would be together forever. Or so he'd vowed.

Trouble was, none of that was true. Goose-witted women. They were so easily duped by flatteries and tender words of affection.

She snagged her hand back. "Go after him, you idiot!"

Della Morte ground his teeth, unaccustomed to such disrespect. "Very well. If you insist. I shall enjoy this, *mia cara*. Finally, I will destroy this ill-bred pirate and his pious chit once and for all!"

Grinning, she gripped the hilt of her rapier. "This shall be fun! Our first conquest together, *mon chéri*."

"First of many." He kissed her on the cheek before uttering orders to prepare for battle.

Chapter 29

A re you mad, Blake?" Emeline stormed up the quarterdeck ladder and perched herself beside the infuriating man. "Are you forgetting the Ring?"

"That is the reason for my madness, my little sugar bird. As well you know." His eyes dipped to her lips, and she knew he thought of their kiss.

A kiss from which neither her heart nor her body had yet recovered.

She glanced toward the *Guerrieri Della Croce*, now tacking aweather and coming round on the *Summons'* starboard quarter. Even devoid of spyglass, it had been easy to spot Josephine standing beside Della Morte. After that, it had only taken her a moment to realize their troubling alliance and, hence, the formidable evil Blake set himself up against.

Why she concerned herself with the man's safety was beyond her. He'd made it clear that his love only stretched as far as his plans for world domination. Anyone daring to interfere with those plans was cast aside in favor of the power he craved. What kind of love was that? Not the love she sought, nor the hero who would win her heart.

"Extinguish the galley fire. Sand the decks!" Blake roared.

"What is your plan, Captain?" she shouted over the blast of wind as she flipped strands of hair from her face.

He gave no reply, simply cupped his hands and issued more orders that sent some men into the shrouds and others dashing across deck.

"Even if you are able to sink them, won't your precious Ring also go down to the depths?"

"I won't allow that to happen."

"Your hubris will be your death." Emeline planted hands at her waist. "And all of your crew along with you."

The brig bucked over a wave, and she stumbled backward.

Grabbing her arm, Blake steadied her. A glimpse of sorrow crossed his eyes before they glazed over again with the heat of battle. "Get below at once." His tone brooked no argument nor further discussion.

Emeline retreated. Stubborn fool. *Lord, what do I do?* Descending the ladder, she inched to stand against the quarterdeck, awaiting her fate and the fate of all aboard.

"What's all tha' about a Ring, Cap'n?" Rummy chirped from the wheel.

"None of your concern," Blake retorted, grimacing. The lady had a point—a valid point. Under normal circumstances, Blake had no doubt he could defeat the slower Italian frigate. But with the Ring? Would Jo or Della Morte know how to use it? Would the Ring obey such evil people? He laughed at his own question. It had obeyed him, had it not? Still, he had no choice. Fight or die. He only regretted that he hadn't gotten Emeline to safety beforehand.

Finn leapt up the stairs and halted by his side.

"I know what you're going to say, Finn. Stubble it. Aye, they have the Ring."

"Aye, Cap'n. We've seen what it does, is all."

"We don't know if it will work for them, and if not, we can easily defeat them." Shoving down his mistrust of the man—temporarily—he gave him a look of confidence. "Prove your loyalty, Finn. Help me lead this crew into battle and win!"

A brief gleam of joy appeared in the man's eyes before he stuffed his pipe in his mouth and sped off.

Positioning the scope to his eye once again, Blake grimaced at the oncoming ship. Even should he wish to make a run for it, he could not avoid a battle now. The real problem lay in how to cripple them enough to surrender so he could board and take the Ring. By all accounts, 'twas a suicide mission, and many would die this day.

Descending the ladder, Blake stormed across the main deck. "All hands on deck! Helm, hard a-port! Up tops and gallants!" At least he could gain the weather edge, which would grant him some advantage.

Layton bellowed further orders, sending topmen leaping into the ratlines and racing up shrouds.

"Stations for stays! Bring her about. Helms a lee!" Layton continued, and within minutes, the *Summons* tacked about, wood groaning and blocks creaking. The deck canted to port. The crew held on as the mad rush of the sea reached for the railing.

Boom!

The air quivered with the thunder of a gun. "All hands down!" Blake shouted as he crouched by the mainmast. The shot plunged into the sea, mere yards off their starboard side. Not a warning shot. Nay, they wanted him sunk and dead. Rising, he marched across the deck. "Brace up the weather yards! Shorten to battle sail!" Then turning to his new bosun, he commanded, "Bring us to windward of them, if you please, Layton."

It was then that Blake spotted Emeline, backed against the quarterdeck, eyes alert, jaw stiff with determination. *Hang it*. 'Twas safer below, but the woman was as stubborn as a pirate who smelled gold.

Ignoring her, he advanced to the starboard railing, grabbed the ratlines, and leapt upon the bulwarks. Wind, as hot and fierce as the blood coursing through his veins, raced over him, flapping his shirt and thundering in his ears. How he loved the fight, the battle. He'd become more than an expert, had brought his crew and himself a fortune beyond compare. But the fortune he sought in *this* conquest was far more valuable.

The foam-capped turbulent sea spread out before him, sunlight glinting off waves. Yet the *Guerrieri Della Croce* continued closing the distance between them. In minutes, their shot would no longer miss. But neither would Blake's.

"Ready the broadside!" he shouted to Charlie. The *Summons* was coming up on the weather gauge.

That Della Morte would allow Blake to do so spoke to his inexperience in sea battles. Of course, the man bragged of being more priest than pirate. No doubt 'twas his faith in the power of the Ring that drove him onward.

Ten portholes flung open on the *Guerrieri Della Croce's* port side, and the dark muzzles of ten guns poked through. Twenty-pounders from the look of them. They would do much more damage to the *Summons* than Blake's nine-pounders would do to their ship.

Turning, Blake cupped his hands and shouted over the wind, "Bear off! Haul your braces, ease sheets, starboard guns standby…fire as you bear!" He gazed up at Rummy. "Be ready for a sharp veer to starboard."

With a roar and belch of flame and smoke, the *Summons'* guns spoke, sending a shudder through the ship. The wind quickly swept away the stinging haze just in time to see flames shoot from the *Guerrieri Della Croce's* ten guns.

"Helm's alee!" Blake ordered the quick tack, which hopefully would present a smaller target for the incoming shots. He dashed to cover Emeline with his body.

The reverberating thunder of guns shook the sky as he spread his arms over her and leaned his head against hers. Her harried breaths filled the air between them, her sweet scent so at odds with the stench of battle. The *Summons* staggered beneath one of the shots.

Cursing, Blake pushed from her and marched to examine the damage as the ship yawed widely to starboard.

"Jist smashed our bulwarks at the waist," Finn said, gripping the railing beside the shattered wood. "No other shots hit us."

Blake nodded, relieved. Plucking the spyglass from his belt, he examined the *Guerrieri Della Croce*, bracing his boots on the tilting deck. Her foremast was shattered. Fragments of the yards hung in the waist below. Grinning, he lowered the scope and scanned the horizon. No black clouds, no advancing storms. Why wasn't Jo using the Ring?

Still, the Italian frigate persisted, completing a larboard tack and coming up on the *Summons'* starboard side.

"Ease braces, mainsail aloft. Hard a-port. Ready the larboard guns!" Blake would position a broadside against their stern. If it worked, it would certainly cripple them.

"Aye, Cap'n!" Charlie began braying orders to her gun crew as Pedro brought more shot and cartridges up from the magazine.

Minutes seemed like hours as his topmen rapidly adjusted sailcloth for the quick turn. Without the weather gauge, the *Guerrieri Della Croce* lumbered clumsily in their tack, finally presenting their stern. Blake smiled.

"On my order, Charlie," he shouted. "Hold…" Carefully, he watched the rise and fall of waves, along with the positioning of their enemy. "Hold…Fire!"

The ten nine-pounders exploded in rapid succession, pummeling the air and sending smoke over the *Summons*. Before their shots even struck the Italian ship, she responded with her stern chasers, the booms of which shook sky and sea. They were nigh yards apart. 'Twould be impossible for none of those shots to strike the *Summons*.

Emeline found herself once again encased in a cocoon of Blake. His unique scent of the sea, man, and spice filled her nostrils and brought her more comfort than she cared to admit. He said naught, but she could feel the tension of battle strung tight around him, the pressure of command, the responsibility for many lives. She'd oft seen her father and brother in battle, had watched them transform from priest into warrior at a moment's notice.

This man was no different. In truth, she'd been amazed at his skill in combat, his quick decisions, his authoritative commands, and his ability to outmaneuver and outsmart his enemy.

The whine of shot, the snap of wood, and a jarring impact forced Blake to push from her and storm across the deck. "Damage report!"

One of the pirates let out an ear-piercing scream and fell to the deck. Blake dropped beside him and hailed two pirates to bring the man below to Sam. From what Emeline could tell, a large wooden splinter had pierced his leg.

No other men seemed to be harmed. Thank God. One shot had scythed through most of the shrouds on the foremast, while another had slammed into the hull at the bow.

"Above the waterline," Finn quickly informed Blake, who ordered three of his men below to plug the hole with sailcloth.

The *Guerrieri Della Croce* had not fared as well. With expert precision, Blake and Charlie had raked her stern, sending ten shots down her length. Her mizzen-topmast was shot away. Her main gaff dangled loose from the peak halyards, and her broad sail crumpled, puffing out awkwardly in the breeze. Smoke poured from a charred hole in her stern.

Blake grinned. The pirates cheered, raising blades and pistols in the air as they tossed insults at their defeated foe.

Not *yet* defeated. For Emeline knew Blake had to board her to retrieve the Ring. That would most likely involve sword and pistol fights, which meant death to many. She shivered.

"Lord, please help Blake give up his mad quest. Please let no one die today," she whispered, but the wind swept her words away so fast, and she wondered if they ever made it up to heaven.

"Why isn't the Ring working?" Signor Arturo Della Morte raged, resisting the urge to toss the witch and the impotent Ring into the sea. If he hadn't been tasked by the Pope himself to bring it to him, he'd do just that and be done with the infernal relic.

"I have no idea!" Josephine barked back, twisting the Ring round and round on her finger. "It should work! All the wearer must do is command it!" Fear and fury etched across her once comely face.

Cursing, Della Morte turned to watch as his crew sped to repair the damage as best they could. His mainmast lay in a heap upon the deck, smoke poured from his stern, where a fire had started, his mizzen was useless, and the sea rushed in through a hole in his hull. "Infidel, heathen pirate!" He would never have engaged him without the Ring. The *Guerrieri Della Croce* listed to larboard, and without a mainsail, it would prove difficult to navigate.

With an angry roar, he turned to Josephine and extended his hand. "Give me the Ring. Perhaps it will work for me. I am a priest, after all!" The words fired from his lips, an order rather than a request. He knew the witch did not respond well to being commanded about. But what choice did he have?

She narrowed her dark eyes upon him, her long lashes nearly covering her pupils. Good thing, for he did not wish to see the hex she was no doubt placing on him.

The ship bounced over a wave, spraying them with seawater. Behind him, curses, hammers, and the grunts of labor added to the blast of wind and creak of sodden wood. His open palm remained. "You promised to give it to me, did you not?"

One black eyebrow quirked as her lips drew into a line. "Very well. But *your* promise remains. We are a team. Whatever reward you receive from the Pope, I will have my share."

"Of course, *mia cara*. I am forever yours." It would be a travesty to rid the world of such beauty, but of course he must. He could not risk having a vile spell cast on him after he defied her.

Tugging off the Ring, she slapped it in his hand.

It began to glow and heat in his palm. Excitement soaring through him, he slipped it on his finger and held up his hand. "I

command a large funnel to appear in the sea near the *Summons*
and draw the ship down to the depths!"

With the immediate danger abated, Emeline pushed from
the quarterdeck and moved to the starboard railing. Indeed,
Della Morte's ship, with a considerable list to larboard,
appeared to be drifting helplessly under the tattered ribbons of
the mainmast. Smoke still spewed from her stern.

On the foredeck, Charlie and her gun crew cleaned and
prepared the guns for more shots if needed. Topmen remained
above, adjusting sail per Layton's and Finn's orders, while
Blake strode across the ship, inspecting damage and giving
further commands for sails to be raised and a course set for the
Guerrieri Della Croce.

So, he *did* intend to board her. Foolish man.

As if Bandit sensed the end of danger, the monkey
emerged from an open hatch and scrambled to perch in the
ratlines beside Emeline. She found herself wishing she could
understand his excited jabbering, but he merely frowned at her
and climbed higher. It seemed he knew something important
she didn't. Or perhaps she *did* know. She definitely sensed
something, an evil that permeated the air around her, the sea
beneath her, and sent a shiver prickling down her spine.

A black circle appeared on the water nigh twenty yards
from the *Summons*. At first, she thought 'twas merely a shadow
from a cloud, but no large clouds passed overhead. She would
have paid it no mind, except it grew larger and larger,
expanding over the sea like a fountain of oil bubbling up from
the deep.

Bandit screeched from the tops.

The circle began to spin, slowly at first, but increasing in
both speed and size, until a hole appeared in the center. A
funnel! Blood raced from her heart. She gripped her throat,
unable to breathe, unable to think. 'Twas just like her dream,

the one in which Blake had been sucked down into a hole in the bay.

"Blake!" she shouted just as a pirate from above yelled, "Avast, over the starboard side!"

Blake, along with Finn and Layton, appeared by her side in seconds.

Finn scratched beneath his bandana. "Son o' a seadog, what be that?"

"It be the devil's work." Layton's voice edged in terror as he backed away from the railing.

"Cap'n!" Charlie pointed to the growing funnel. "We'll be drawn to the depths."

Pedro gaped at the sight, wide-eyed, as did most of the crew.

Pushing from the railing, Blake issued order after order to hoist all sails and make a hard turn to larboard.

But the edges of the funnel had already reached the *Summons*, yanking it into the current. Still Blake continued his commands, and his men soon had all canvas set to the wind, ready for a turn that would propel them out of the funnel's force.

"Hard alee!" he shouted to Rummy, and the one-armed helmsman threw his body into it and cranked the wheel as hard and fast as he could.

The pull of the funnel was too strong. Like the mighty arm of a giant, it wrenched the brig off its course. Against all power of wind, wave, and rudder, the *Summons* began circling the dark hole, wide at first, then growing closer and closer with each revolution.

Numb with fear, Emeline could hardly gather a thought. *Why are you allowing this, Lord?* 'Twas just like her dream. Yet in that dream, she had awoken before she'd saved Blake. Had that been an omen of this disaster to come? Or of her failure to save those she loved?

Blake appeared beside her and clutched the railing as the brig spun to larboard. "Is this from the Ring?" His tone was spiked with defeat.

"Aye. It must be."

"Then we are doomed. There is no power greater than the Ring."

No power greater? The *Summons* took another turn around the funnel, tilting the deck more violently this time. Emeline gripped the railing, feeling the sea spray on her fingers. Of course there was a power greater than the Ring! A power greater than everything. But who was she to wield such power? Naught but a timid girl ruled by her selfish dreams and emotions.

You are My little warrior.

She shook off the ludicrous thought. Charlie appeared on her left and cast her a look of fear? Nay. A look of resignation, emptiness, loss. Yet, if Emeline had even half of the woman's courage and confidence…

Pedro squeezed between them and gripped Emeline's hand, his bottom lip quivering. "Are we to die, Miss?"

The poor lad. Like Emeline, he compared himself with others and always found himself lacking. Hadn't she told him more than once that God didn't make refuse? That everyone had God-given talents and purpose?

'Twas time she believed that about herself. Hadn't God granted her the gift of knowledge? Hadn't God, through her faith, delivered Blake from whatever evil spell Jo had cast upon him? But this? She stared out over the swirling sea, moving faster now, spinning the *Summons* as if it were but a toy, round and round into a dark hole that grew deeper by the minute. If only her father were here, her mother and siblings! They would know what to do, how to defeat this evil.

I chose you for such a time as this.

The words from the book of Esther rang in her ears as the *Summons* jerked to starboard, nearly dipping into the sea.

"God can defeat this!" she shouted over the wind. *Help me, Lord. Grant me courage and Your power!*

No one argued with her declaration. No one laughed. But no one agreed.

With one hand clenching the railing, she raised the other to heaven. "In the mighty name of Jesus, be still." She knew not what else to say, but then again, surely God knew what she meant.

Chapter 30

Fear did strange things to people. Meeting one's fate in such a gruesome way caused even the bravest of men to cry—as evidenced by Blake's sobbing crew behind him. Apparently, it also had the effect of driving some people mad. For Emeline's declaration was precisely that. Reaching for her, he drew her close, wanting to be beside her when he breathed his last, hating that he'd been unable to save her and bring her home as he'd promised.

There was no defeating the power of the Ring. Which was precisely why he sought it for himself. Now all his efforts, all his wealth, his island and mansion, the little power he brandished was all for naught. Yet better to have tried than to remain an impotent serf, always yielding to the rules and dictates of overlords.

His only regret stood beside him, wrapping her arm around his waist and burying her face in his shirt. "I'm sorry, Emeline," he whispered in her ear.

Charlie merely stared over the sea, a numbness covering her eyes. Pedro gripped Blake's side. Tight. Blake wrapped his other arm around the lad. Finn and Layton forsook their tirades of curses and began to pray. Odd, that. He'd never expected to hear such pleadings to the Almighty from the likes of them.

The wind shifted. The mad rush of the sea softened. The *Summons* righted itself. Blake glanced over the railing to see the dark hole at the center of the funnel growing smaller and smaller as the frenzied spin of the waters diminished.

"Look!" His shout drew everyone's gazes, including Emeline, who lifted her head from his chest.

The last dark spot of the funnel disappeared. Completely. Replaced by the normal rise and fall of the Caribbean swells glittering in bright sunlight.

"Huzzah!" His crew broke into cheers and laughter, louder and more joyful than when they'd captured a prize full of gold. Charlie bowed her head, breathing heavily. Finn drew out his pipe and stuffed it in his mouth. Layton didn't move, just stared over the sea in disbelief. Pedro yipped and hollered and began dancing with Bandit, who had leapt into his arms.

In the distance, no more than one hundred yards away, the *Guerrieri Della Croce* had raised her remaining sails and was slowly drifting away, tilting beneath the blows she'd received and heading toward a spit of land in the distance.

Surely Blake was dreaming. The *Summons* and all on board had no doubt been sucked into the funnel and were now at the bottom of the sea. Though the look of shock and relief on Emeline's angelic face and her sweet smell told him 'twas no dream. "What just happened?"

Smiling, she gazed up at him, her eyes sparkling with delight. "God happened. He saved us, Blake!" She blew out a sigh and scanned the sea. "The funnel was evil, demonic." She glanced back at him. "You said there was no power greater, but I knew there was. God's power is greater than anything!"

Blake shook his head. How could he deny what he'd seen with his own eyes? The funnel had been real and about to devour them, but with one prayer from this dear lady, her God rescued them.

Excitement lit her face. "Do you not see how powerful He is and how much He loves you? He sent His Son to die for you."

A spark lit in his soul, a light, a hope that what Emeline said could be true. That there was, indeed, a Creator who loved Blake, whose power was unmatchable. Yet…wasn't that what his mother used to tell him—before she threw him, penniless, onto the streets? Regardless of what just happened, Jo and

Della Morte were getting away. And he couldn't live with himself if he allowed that.

He turned to issue orders for the chase when she grabbed his arm and squeezed it tight. "Let them go. They deserve each other and that bedeviled Ring."

He placed his hand atop hers, gently, and with his other eased a strand of hair the wind had blown across her cheek. "I cannot, Emeline. Not when it is within my grasp. Besides, with such power, think of the evil they could do in this world."

Moisture filled her eyes. "Yet you have seen there is a power much greater than theirs."

He eased the back of his fingers against her cheek. "'Tis your power, your God's power, not mine."

"It could be, if you give your life to Him." She gazed up at him with such affection, such pleading, that he almost bowed his knee to her God then and there just to see her smile. But Blake could never relinquish his power and freedom to another. He'd been betrayed too many times to trust anyone again, God or not.

He stiffened his jaw. "I'm not ready for that. I may never be, Emeline."

The pain that crossed her face nearly crushed him.

"They still have the Ring," she said. "They can still evoke its power."

"But I have you." Winking, he leaned in for a kiss on her cheek before marching away.

"Warts and lizards!" Josephine stiffened her spine as she descended the ladder onto the gundeck and crew quarters. She'd had her fill of being treated like a bootlicking fluffhead. Especially by that swaggering toad in his ostentatious Jesuit finery! Did he truly believe she would not see through his façade? That she possessed no powers to do so? *Imbécile! Oui,* she'd been enchanted by the man's Italian good looks and charming words. She'd believed that perhaps he harbored some affection for her.

Rare emotion burned in her throat, but she quickly swallowed it as her boots landed on the deck. Perhaps she hoped he cared for her, that love actually existed in the world. Perhaps she was as big a fool as he was, for now she knew, without a doubt, love was a mere powerless fable, an impotent myth, and a cruel joke among the weak and gullible. Neither of which was she! Why the Ring seemed to work for him and not her, she could not say. What she *could* say was that the Jesuit cretin had greatly miscalculated both her power and her spite toward those who crossed her. Hence, the reason she'd concocted one of her special spells just for him and any of his crew who didn't side with her. Now, to address said crew and convince them she would be the better captain, that she, along with her dark powers, would make them wealthier beyond their imagination. If that didn't work, the incantation of obedience should turn them into jellyfish in her hands.

Blake could have caught and boarded the *Guerrieri Della Croce* within an hour, yet he held back, pretending damage to his brig. The foolish Jesuit was bringing his frigate to anchor at a small island in the distance, one of the islands of the Baja Mar. No doubt he assumed he had a better chance of winning a battle on land than at sea, especially as damaged as the ship was.

Yet Blake knew the skill and ferocity of his crew, knew they'd be even more ruthless, armed with revenge for Della Morte after he'd nearly sent them to the depths. Blake also knew he'd have a better chance of retrieving the Ring from the Jesuit fiend on land, where the powerful artifact could only cause wind and rain that would pummel them both. He waited until the *Guerrieri Della Croce* lumbered into a cove before hoisting all canvas and speeding their way.

Within an hour of dropping anchor along the western shore, his crew spilled over the bulwarks like rats disturbed from their lair and rowed to the sandy beach, all manner of weapons strapped about them.

Blake slid his cutlass into its sheath and adjusted the pistols in his brace, then took one last glance at Emeline standing at the railing, Bandit in her arms. She looked his way, sorrow and disappointment lining her comely face, but there was naught to be done for it.

He would not give up his dream. Not for a woman he could never be with, a woman more angel than human. A woman who deserved a noble, honorable man—the hero she kept wanting him to be.

"Stay here," he said as he slid onto the bulwarks.

She offered him a gentle smile. "Be safe."

He nodded, resisting the urge to run and take her in his arms. Instead, he leapt over the side into the jollyboat and headed to shore. He'd wanted to ask her to call upon her God should things not go in his favor, but how could he request such a selfish thing? Besides, he was no fool. God had only saved them because she'd been on board. With her safety assured, why would God bother to protect him and his band of ruffians?

These thoughts plagued his mind as he led his men through a mangrove swamp, then through a thickly vined jungle out onto a long strip of sandy beach. Tilting heavily to larboard, the Jesuit ship sat idly in turquoise waters several yards offshore, canvas, yards, and lines strewn about her deck in a web of destruction, looking more like a defeated dragon than demon. He'd expected an ambush in the jungle, but instead Della Morte had assembled the remainder of his men on the beach. At least forty of them stood behind the vile Jesuit, fully armed and grimacing in the hot afternoon.

The sun, now high in the sky, reflected off water and sand, nearly blinding Blake as he and his men marched toward their enemies. Dragging a sleeve over the sweat on his forehead, he wondered what devious plan brewed in the evil man's mind. Standing behind him, two Jesuits dressed in similar attire as their leader glared at Blake. And beside Della Morte, wearing her usual black breeches and waistcoat, Josephine placed a hand on her hip and smiled his way. He supposed she could cast another spell upon him, but didn't that require potions and cauldrons and such? He hoped so.

Della Morte reached up to stroke his beard, ostentatiously flaunting the Ring which sparkled in the sunlight. Ringlets of black curls danced about his shoulders, joining the purple plume quivering from his hat.

Only when Blake drew closer did he see the bloody bandages, cuts, and bruises marring the Jesuit's crew. At least half of them were in no shape to fight.

He halted before the man. "Since you are clearly defeated, allow me to set terms which will ensure the lives of you and your men."

"Terms, you say? Bah!" Della Morte waved a hand through the air, the lace at his cuffs fluttering.

Josephine took a step toward Blake, her eyes ablaze with hatred. "How are you alive, *mon amour?*" She fisted hands at her waist. "How did you defeat the funnel?"

"Ah, ha, so you do admit defeat?"

"We admit no such thing." Della Morte stretched his neck.

"How did you do it?" Josephine spat through clenched teeth. "I demand to know the source of your power."

He barely afforded her a glance. "'Tis God's power. One you will never possess."

Her eyes widened and, for the first time since he'd known her, real fear sparked within them. She glanced behind him as if looking for someone before she uttered curse after curse over land, sea, air, and water. "My enemy. My *only* enemy." She ground her fists together.

Della Morte released a sigh of boredom and waved her away. "Go back to your potions, *mia cara*. We men have business to discuss."

She speared the Jesuit with a gaze that would surely wake the dead before she took a step back. Odd. The woman never cowered before any man.

"We have no business other than my terms." Blake grew bored as well. "Give me the Ring, and you and your men will live. 'Tis really quite simple."

"You shall not have the Ring while I live!"

"Then I shall take it when you are dead."

"Ah, but you cannot. It will go to hell along with me. I must give it to you, or you must find it apart from a body. I believe those are the conditions, no?"

"I'd rather you go to your grave with it on your finger than for you to remain alive and wield its power."

A momentary flash of unease crossed the man's confident gaze. "*Sì,* I do believe you. Therefore." He twisted the Ring on his finger and uttered a string of Italian with the authority of a king.

Blake didn't need an interpreter to know what he'd said, for dark clouds instantly crowded out the sun above them. Wind thrashed through the leaves of palms and pimentos lining the shore, adding a cacophony of sounds to the crash of waves and buzz of insects. Sand swirled around his boots.

Della Morte smiled.

"Fight us like men!" Blake shouted. "'Tis a coward's way to use the Ring."

"Is it? Then you are as much a coward as I."

Blake was about to draw his blade and order his men to battle when the wind suddenly lessened, the waves stopped raging, and the sun broke through the dissipating clouds.

A screech akin to a dying pig emerged from Jo, who bent over, gripping her belly as if she were ill.

Blake knew what had happened before he turned around. Emeline stood at the edge of the jungle. Too far to make out her expression, but he found himself suddenly glad she'd not obeyed his order to remain on the ship. Bandit flew from her arms into a nearby tree.

He faced Della Morte again, pasting a cocksure grin on his face. "You were saying?"

The sneer on the Jesuit's face transformed into a wicked grin. He flung a hand in the air. "I propose a challenge."

Blake bunched his fists, longing to run the man through and be done with it.

"A fight. A sword fight between you and me. If I win, you and your crew set sail immediately with no harm to me or my men."

Blake huffed. The man's overinflated opinion of his skill would be his downfall. "And if *I* win?"

"Unlikely, but if so, I will give you the Ring, and you will leave me and my men unscathed."

"Why would I agree to so ludicrous a challenge when you are so clearly outmanned?"

"I quite agree, though you should know my crew are trained to fight to the death. Therefore, should we battle, there will be many deaths on both sides. And, *sì*, perhaps I will be counted among them. Or perhaps you? But I will still have the Ring. What a waste, do you not think? At least if you accept my challenge, you have a chance of winning the Ring."

Unfortunately, the Jesuit made sense. Blake studied him. That the man had been well trained at swordplay was evident from their last encounter. Yet they'd been interrupted before Blake could prove himself the master. To fight Della Morte and win would be the only way for Blake to own the Ring. To fulfill all his dreams.

Even if the fiend would not honor his bargain, they'd end up in a battle, one which Blake's men would surely win.

"Then I accept."

Cheers bellowed from both his men and the Jesuit's crew as Blake backed away, removed his baldric, tore his shirt over his head, and plucked the cutlass from his sheath.

Chapter 31

Della Morte shrugged out of his coat, pulled off his neckerchief, and drew his jeweled saber. His victorious grin as he shuffled toward Blake bespoke of confidence in his skills and an assumption of Blake's lack thereof.

He would soon discover his error.

Leveling his cutlass at his opponent, Blake pasted a bored look on his face. "Are we to fight or dance?"

The man's eyes narrowed. He dashed forward, thrusting his blade toward Blake's heart.

With ease, Blake snapped it away with a mighty clank. Cheers from his men clapped his back while Della Morte's crew shouted encouragements to their captain.

Twirling his saber in the air, Della Morte cleaved it down toward Blake. Leaping out of the way, Blake snapped his cutlass upward and caught Della Morte in the thigh. A red line marred his dark velvet breeches. Fury marred his features. Flinging back his long black curls with one hand, he swooped his sword down upon Blake with the other.

Their blades met in a resounding clank that echoed over sand and sea.

"That be the way of it!" one of Della Morte's men shouted.

Back and forth they parried. With expert skill, Della Morte drove Blake back, forcefully slashing this way and that so fast, Blake had difficulty fending him off.

But fend him off he did, meeting each blow with one of his own. Jarring *clanks* and *clings* rang across the shore. The muscles in his arms ached. Sweat stung his eyes.

The Jesuit raised his sword for a mighty blow. Blake swung about and drove his cutlass in from the left, hoping to catch the man off guard and wound him again.

Della Morte dipped his sword in defense just in time, then quickly brought it up, catching Blake's side.

A woman screamed.

Emeline flung a hand to her mouth. She hadn't meant to scream, but when Della Morte's blade struck Blake, she thought he was done for.

And that thought frightened her more than anything ever had.

Blake gripped his side, but did not fall to the sand. Nay, rather the wound seemed to give him renewed strength.

"Ah, ha! You do bleed," Della Morte cackled. "For a moment, I thought you might be part reptile."

"'Tis you who are the snake." Blake paced before the fiend, cutlass extended, breath heaving.

In an action almost too quick to see, Della Morte rammed his blade at Blake.

With ease, Blake slashed it away and charged the monster head on.

Leaping out of the way just in time, Della Morte brought his sword across Blake's blade arm.

Emeline gasped, her heart pounding.

Moans and curses flew from Blake's crew, mingled with cheers from Della Morte's.

Blood spilled down Blake's arm onto the hilt of his cutlass. He gripped it tighter.

Oh Lord, please help him. Help him win. Don't allow him to die.

An odd realization struck her. Her fears did not hail from fear of becoming a prisoner of the Jesuits yet again, nor even that they would still have the Ring. Nay, 'twas more the thought of losing the man she loved. Even if he wasn't the hero of her dreams.

Raising his cutlass, Blake swooped down upon Della Morte, who met his blade with a roaring *clang* that sent birds flapping from a nearby tree. Hilt to hilt they battled, growling and grinding their teeth, pushing and shoving this way and that.

Emeline had witnessed many a sword fight in her short life, witnessed the exquisite skill of her father, brother, and grandfather. Blake possessed that same skill, albeit a bit less refined. Which could prove to his advantage over Della Morte's more polished approach.

Sweat streamed into Blake's eyes. Blinking it away, he freed his blade from the monster's and shoved him backward. Then, before Della Morte could recover, Blake lunged, thrust, and slashed toward the man with more rapidity and strength than he should possess after being wounded. The rounded muscles in his arms and chest glistened in the sunlight as they bunched and rolled beneath the exertion.

Hugging herself, Emeline swallowed a lump of fear.

A flicker of uncertainly danced across the Jesuit's face as he fumbled to defend himself and bring his sword to bear.

Before he could, Blake chopped it with his cutlass. Della Morte lost his grip. His sword flew out of his hand and landed in the sand a few yards away.

Emeline breathed a sigh of relief.

Someone grabbed her arm. *Tight.* Pain etched up to her shoulder as the person spun her around and yanked her into the jungle.

Della Morte made a dash to retrieve his sword. Blake leveled his cutlass at the man's throat. A drop of blood joined the sweat dripping onto his shirt as one of his eyes began to twitch uncontrollably. He glanced at something behind Blake and gave a nod before his nervous gaze returned to Blake.

Shouts of glee from Blake's crew circled around them whilst Della Morte's crew moaned and cursed. The other two Jesuits drew their sabers as if they would take up where their captain let off.

"Ah, ah, ah," Blake warned them. "I'll gut him, and you'll never have the Ring to bring to your Pontifex Maximus."

Terror twisted Della Morte's features as he gestured for his men to stand down and lifted both hands in surrender, a supercilious sneer on his lips. "A bargain is a bargain. Lower your weapon, and I'll hand you the Ring."

Never would Blake lower his guard in this lying snake's presence. Not until he had the Ring on his finger.

A scream echoed in the distance. *Emeline!* A wild glance told him she no longer stood at the edge of the jungle. Where was Jo?

"What have you done with her?" Blake thrust his cutlass at the man again.

"Nothing, I assure you." He twisted off the Ring and held it up to the sunlight. Rays glimmered off the crimson center, setting it aflame.

It was so close. A foot or two and Blake could reach out and grab it. The power he sought. The freedom. Everything he'd worked for, shining like a beacon right before him.

Then, with a grin of victory, Della Morte pulled back his arm and tossed the precious relic into the tangle of trees and brush lining the shore.

Another scream echoed over the sand.

Horror turned Blake's blood to ice. "What have you done?"

"You have a choice, *Capitano*." Della Morte placed one hand on his hip. "I will not stop you—and *only* you"—he glanced at Blake's crew and then his own men standing behind him—"from retrieving the Ring. Should you foolishly elicit any help, a battle will ensue and many will die." Wincing, he shifted to stand on his uninjured leg "I swear on the most holy Pope's life. But if you do search for the Ring, I fear it will be too late for your dear love. For even now, she sinks in the silt of the mangrove swamp."

Before the Jesuit's words assembled into a rational thought in Blake's mind, Jo sauntered up. "I'd say she has less than a minute or two before she goes under."

The Ring or Emeline? The Ring or Emeline? Blake stood beneath the searing rays of the hot sun, sweat streaming down his chest and back, stinging his wounds. The gentle caress of waves on shore and swish of wind-blown leaves created a peaceful cadence he felt none of inside.

There was *no* decision. No choice to make. He knew that. But a cyclone of confusion filled his mind, empowered by demonic whispers.

It's what you've wanted your entire life. You can have the power, the freedom, the control you've always sought. It's only a few feet away.

The woman is nothing. She will eventually betray you like all women do.

With the power of the Ring, you can have any woman you want.

Go get it!

Nay! He knew those shadowy voices. They hailed from a dark world he no longer wished to be a part of. An evil, power-greedy world of strife, jealousy, and betrayal. He'd seen a power mightier than the Ring or anything else on Earth. A good power, a holy power. 'Twas the power of Almighty God, the power of His love for mankind, for Blake—a love he'd never known but always longed for.

Emeline had been the one to show him that love, along with God's power for all who believed. A sensation floated down upon him like none he'd ever felt. It encompassed him in a blanket of love, power, purpose…and joy, indescribable!

God?

Spinning around, Blake raced across the sand, shouting orders for his crew to stand down unless attacked. Sheathing his cutlass, he burst into the jungle, shoving aside branches, vines, and leaves.

Lord, help me find her! Please!

Another scream sounded, this one weaker, muffled. He headed in that direction. "I'm coming, Emeline! I'm coming!"

He leapt over a fallen tree, racing down the sandy path. Birds squawked and took flight, disturbed from their nests. Insects buzzed in his ear.

"Blake!" A faint shout turned him to the left. His boots landed in water. He slogged through the silt, weaving around the tangled web of mangrove roots.

"Emeline!"

"Here…"

She was close. Yet he couldn't see her. The metallic taste of terror filled his mouth. There! A hand stretched between two massive roots. He slogged toward her, waist deep in the water now. "Emeline." He grabbed her hand and squeezed.

"Blake, you came," she whimpered.

He peered between the thick roots. Her radiant face smiled up at him. But only her face. The rest of her was beneath swamp water that reached her chin. How had Jo trapped her in this maze?

"I'm sinking…" she managed to say.

Blake was, too. The heavy silt had already swallowed up his boots. "How did you get in there? Is there no way to swim out?"

"Nay. She moved something heavy over the only outlet."

"Hold on." He tried to release her hand, but she gripped him so tight he could not.

"Let go, Emeline. Trust me."

Even as he said the words, he wondered why she would. He'd given her no reason to ever trust him. Still, her hand slipped away.

The water was up to her nose.

Freeing his boots from the silt, he crawled up on the roots as far as he could and swung his cutlass at the thick vines, chopping, hacking. All the while taking care to not strike the dear lady. Within minutes that seemed like hours, he created a hole large enough to pull her through.

"Grab ahold, Emeline." Laying chest down on the web of roots, he lowered both arms.

Dark water swallowed her face.

"Nay!" Blake reached for her, groping for a grip on her arms, gown, anything.

Finally, she gripped his hand. He pulled with all his might. She wouldn't budge.

Growling, he tugged harder, ignoring the bite of roots on his bare skin.

Her shoulders appeared. Then her other arm emerged from the water and clamped onto his hand. With a groan that would wake the dead, Blake pulled her from the swampy silt and yanked her through the hole, laying her atop the roots.

Their heavy breaths mingled in the humid air as she fell against his chest and wrapped her arms around him. "You came."

"Of course, my little sugar bird." Nudging her back, he brushed a spatter of mud from her cheek. Love and admiration spilled from her eyes as she continued gulping in air. What joy there was to be found in that one look. More joy than he'd thus experienced with all his power and wealth.

He wanted to tell her he loved her, wanted to tell her he was a changed man, wanted to ask if there was a chance he could be the hero she sought. But he hesitated, old insecurities and fears clambering over his heart.

"What do you say we get out of this swamp before the tide comes in?" he asked.

Josephine heaved a sigh of impatience, watching Della Morte's imbecilic crew scour the jungle for the Ring.

"Whatever possessed you to toss it into such a thick web?" She shook her head and cast a look of disdain at the Jesuit idiot.

He fingered his beard. "I thought it would be easy to find. I hardly tossed it very far." He cupped his hands over his mouth. "To the left, Gershown. Move to your left."

Cursing him and his crew under her breath, Josephine stormed into the greenery herself. After several minutes of poking through sand, prying around leaves, being stabbed by thorns, and getting mud underneath her fingernails, she was ready to turn Della Morte and every one of his men into toads.

"It's gone," she announced as she emerged from the thick shrubbery, wiping her hands on her breeches.

Della Morte's face flamed. "It cannot be! I will not give up."

"I tell you, it is gone." She speared him with a torrid gaze. If *she* couldn't find it with her powers, then it wasn't there to be found. Besides, the frivolous artifact had proven useless in her hands, powerless, really. This way, Blake would not have it either.

"What do you know, you callow wench?"

Now was the time to rid herself of this peevish cur. She'd far too long endured his insolent remarks and demeaning insults.

Reaching into her pocket, she pulled out a pouch and took out a vial of the potion she'd concocted the day before.

"What is that?" Della Morte dabbed his neckerchief over his sweaty forehead.

"It is your death, *mon amour*."

Chapter 32

Emeline's hair hung to her waist in a tangled sticky mass, and her salt-encrusted skirts grated upon her stockings with each step, but she couldn't be happier as she emerged from the jungle arm-in-arm with Blake.

Despite the wounds on his chest and arm, he'd told her he had won the sword fight. Even so, before they emerged onto the shore, they halted and peered through the leaves of a thick shrub. Yet they saw no battle, no waiting enemy, and hence, no trap set for them. In truth, neither Della Morte's crew nor his frigate were in sight, while Blake's men lounged aimlessly upon the sand.

Upon seeing them, Finn leapt up from the boulder he perched upon and approached, Pedro and Charlie following behind.

Only then did Emeline see three bodies lying in the sand.

Blake followed her gaze, then released her and uttered, "Stay here" before heading toward them.

"It be Della Morte hisself." Finn slipped beside Blake. "An' 'is henchmen."

Defying Blake's orders, Emeline followed, her mind spinning with Finn's news and her heart clenching at the sight of renewed blood trickling down Blake's arm.

Halting before the bodies, Blake frowned when he saw Emeline beside him. She'd seen the dead before, but these men appeared to have suffered immensely. Their lips were blue. Their vacant eyes stared up at the sun, a mangled look of horror frozen on their features.

"What happened?"

"Dunno," Charlie offered. "That pirate lady, she sprinkled something on them, an' they all dropped t' the ground."

Pedro let out a whimper and Emeline drew him close. "'Twas most likely some evil hex."

"Death and wounds," Finn muttered, backing away. "Sweet Jesus, preserve us."

Blake frowned. "Did they find the Ring?"

"Nay." Sam's voice turned Emeline around to see the old surgeon approaching, medical satchel in hand. "I overheard them arguing. When they couldn't find it, she killed these three and left with their crew. Let me bandage your wounds."

Blake glanced at the cuts on his chest and arm as if just now noticing them. "Nay, I'm all right."

"Let him do it, Blake," Emeline appealed, drawing his tender smile. Was it her imagination or was there something different in his eyes, in his smile?

"Sure were some fight ye 'ad, Cap'n," Finn shoved his pipe back into his mouth.

Taking Emeline's arm, Blake drew her away from the gruesome scene. "Where are Della Morte's crew?"

"They went wit' her, Cap'n'," Charlie said with an incredulous snort.

"Willingly?" Blake lowered to sit on a boulder where Sam could begin his ministrations.

"Aye, after they saw what she did to their leaders."

Emeline nodded toward Blake's crew scattered across the beach. "Why didn't she harm you or take Blake's ship?"

"That be the strange thing," Finn mumbled, teetering the pipe still in his mouth. "She came right up t' us like she were going to kill us all, but something stopped her."

"Aye!" Pedro added in an excited tone. "She said somethin' about us bein' protected afore she marched away, cursin' an' hollerin', carryin' on like a beached shark."

Blake faced Emeline, and they both smiled, a look of understanding flowing between them that sent warmth to her toes. Had he finally submitted to God?

Finn tugged the bandana lower on his head. "I still can't believe ye walked away from the Ring like ye did."

Emeline blinked. Surely, she heard incorrectly. "What was that?"

"Aye." Charlie smiled at Emeline. "Della Morte gave the cap'n a choice. Save you or get the Ring."

"And he saved you!" Pedro announced proudly, as if it were him who'd done the heroic deed.

Emeline stared at Blake, stunned, almost afraid to believe 'twas true.

She hadn't time to consider it before Blake's crew headed toward them with huzzahs on their lips and bottles of rum in their hands.

Hours later, Blake paced the length of his cabin back and forth, back and forth, cursing himself for behaving a moonstruck toady. How had he gone from being a powerful—the *most* powerful—scavenger of the seas in need of no one, trusting no one, man or woman, to a sniveling sod whose heart could be crushed by a single word from one woman?

Not just any woman, but a woman who was everything he was not—an angel sent from heaven, whose very smile and goodness radiated a light that scattered all darkness. He had a question to ask her, a question burning on his heart, a question that if he did not ask her this night, he'd never have the courage.

Therefore, time was of the essence before he came to his senses and realized he had no right to ask anything of her.

But the crew had deserved to celebrate, the ship needed repairs, and Blake had orders to dispatch, commands to issue, and responsibilities to uphold as captain.

Yet now as the *Summons* glided along on an inky sea beneath a waning moon and a majestic expanse of sparkling stars, he'd requested Emeline's presence in his cabin.

Would she come? Or was she too exhausted from the day to bother? Hence the reason he paced.

Light footsteps padded, and he looked up to see her standing in the doorway, a stunning mirage of purity and light. Tendrils of loose hair hung about her long, graceful neck. Her cheeks were pink from the sun, her face glowing, her golden eyes sparkling. She bit her lip and lowered her gaze as if suddenly shy in his presence.

"Emeline." He held out his hand for her, ushering her inside before closing the door.

"'Tis hardly proper, Captain, to be alone with you." She gave him a teasing grin.

"Too late for that, is it not?"

"But now…" She ran a finger over the dust on his desk.

He approached, wanting to know what had changed between them and hoping 'twas exactly what he longed for. "Now?"

She faced him, her chest rising and falling rapidly as if she were nervous. "You forsook the Ring. You chose me over your dream." Even as she said it, moisture glistened in her eyes. "Why?"

Swallowing, Blake gripped the lion medallion, wanting to declare his love again, but…unsure of her reaction. He deserved her scorn, her disdain and disgust. After what she'd endured by his hand, he deserved naught but a slap in the face. And far worse.

Yet he'd never been one to cower from anything. He raised his eyes to hers. "I discovered that the Ring was not as important to me as you are, Emeline." Taking her hands in his, he squeezed them. "Power, wealth…Scads, should the entire world be handed to me on a platter, 'twould be empty without you. I love you, Emeline."

Confusion twisted her brow, followed by shock and…disbelief? Breathless, she stumbled backward, jerking back her hands to catch her balance on the shifting deck.

Blake grabbed her waist to steady her, his heart sinking. Not exactly the reaction he'd hoped for.

Lantern light shifted over her face, dark…light…dark…light…like the swaying of a deadly pendulum, sealing his fate.

Releasing her, he backed away. "Forgive me. I over spoke. I'll call someone to escort you back to your cabin."

"You will do no such thing!" Emeline could hardly keep up with the capricious man's moods. One minute loving, the next sad, and now an angry resignation had overtaken him.

He stared at her, those green eyes of his like daggers into her soul. 'Twas the second time he'd declared his love for her. The first she'd ignored, being on the heels of a passionate kiss. But this one? No seductive gleam shone from his eyes. In truth, neither did she see an alcoholic haze. Hence, the reason it had taken a minute for the shock to reach her heart. Lifting a coy chin, she moved to the stern windows and gazed out upon the moonlit sea. "Tell me more about this newfound love for me, Captain."

He took the bait. His footsteps followed her, and she felt the heat radiating off him across her back. He leaned forward. His warm breath on her neck sent shivers down to her toes, his masculine scent an elixir for every ill.

"Not newfound. Merely hidden beneath my prideful delusion." He wrapped his arms around her waist. "You are the most enchanting, beautiful woman I have ever met. You are good and kind and generous. I know I don't deserve you, but I could not let another day slip by without telling you of my true affections."

She swung about. No man had ever graced her with such compliments, such words of love. Were they true or merely a result of an emotional day? He stood but inches away, his closeness heating every ounce of her. "And what of the Ring?"

He shrugged. "'Tis a mere trinket and naught compared to God's power."

She smiled, hope flooding her soul. "Have you made your peace with Him, then?"

"I have." He grabbed the cross around his neck. "At that moment on the beach when given a choice between you and the Ring, I knew. I knew God was there. I felt Him. I felt His love. And you have shown me His power." He sighed. "What need have I of some Ring?"

"What of the power you crave, the control?"

His lips curved. "Perhaps I will give God control over my life. Seems He knows far better than I."

She flew into his arms. "I'm so happy, Blake. 'Tis what I've been praying for." Nudging back from him, she searched his eyes for a hint of any insincerity. *Show me, Lord. Show me.* But only love beamed from within them.

"I love you, Blake. I have for a long—"

Before she could finish, his lips were on hers. Once again, her world imploded in a pool of pleasurable sensations— loving, caressing, all-consuming. Until naught else mattered but the man whose arms encased her in a barricade of strength and warmth.

He withdrew, leaving her breathless and wanting more.

"Forgive me. I want to be the honorable man you seek. I will not take liberties with so precious a lady."

"Pah! Take liberties, I beg you." Her sultry tone shocked even her, but she did not want him to stop. Ever. She kissed him again. Passionately...deeply, wanting more and more of him, and all the while hoping this wasn't a dream.

Grabbing her shoulders, he withdrew and pushed himself back, a look of both surprise and censure on his face. "Scads, woman. Who knew such passion lurked inside..."

"Inside so virtuous a covering?" she teased. "I am still a woman, after all."

"Then you give me no choice but to make a decent lady of you." He winked above a sensuous grin, but then suddenly grew somber.

The elation of only moments before trickled away as she stood waiting.

"I do not deserve you, Emeline. You deserve a hero, a gentleman, as you've so often made clear. I am far from being that man, though I sense I am on my way." He caressed her cheek with the back of his hand.

She leaned into his touch. "Ask me, Blake."

He stared at her quizzically.

"Ask me."

He hesitated for several seconds as the swish of waves and creak of wood serenaded them while ribbons of moonlight draped them in silver. Then, dropping to one knee, he gazed up at her. "Marry me, Emeline. I promise to become the hero you've always longed for."

Her heart nearly burst through her chest. "You already are, Blake. You already are!"

Rising, he cocked a brow. "Is that a yes?"

She fell into his arms. "More than a yes. A promise."

Blake lowered his lips for another kiss when the door creaked open. Flustered and angry at the interruption, Emeline leapt back, warmth flooding her face. Thankfully, she gripped the desk before Bandit flew into her arms.

"Sorry fer the interruption, Cap'n." Finn ambled in, looking embarrassed and shifting his eyes away from the couple. "Shoulda knocked."

"Indeed." Blake growled. "What is it?"

"Jist thought ye'd want to know as soon as possible." Finn gestured to the monkey. "The varmint 'as somethin' fer ye."

With a ragged sigh, Blake faced Emeline and reached for Bandit.

Before he could grab him, Bandit extended his open paw toward the captain, squealing as if it contained a pouch of doubloons.

Lantern light flickered off the crimson jewel in the center of the Ring.

Emeline's heart dropped like an anchor. Not that dastardly trinket again! A thousand doubts crowded out her recent joy. Now that Blake had his Ring back, would he go back to his old ways?

Chapter 33

One week later, Kingston Harbor, Jamaica

Blake stood at the starboard railing of the *Summons,*
gazing over the turquoise waters of the harbor toward
the fledgling town of Kingston in the distance. Somewhere in
that city or on its green slopes was the Hyde Estate or
Redemption Manor, as Emeline had called it. And somewhere
within its walls was Emeline Hyde, finally home where she
belonged.

"Allow me to go to my family alone, Blake," she had
pleaded with him. "I will explain to them the circumstances
that caused you to kidnap me. I shall tell them you've changed,
relay the events of our adventure, tell them how you risked
your life for me."

Blake had crossed arms over his chest. "I don't like it.
Seems a coward's way to me. I should face your father man to
man."

"He will most likely shoot you." She gave a nervous
chuckle and bit her lip. "He's a godly man, but not one to
tolerate any harm done his family."

Blake's heart had shriveled. "That does not bode well for
him to accept our engagement."

"Please, Blake. I will return." A blast of wind tossed a
strand of her hair across her cheek, and Blake had eased it
aside.

"How long do you need?" His glance took in Fort Charles,
knowing it might not take long for the Royal Navy to
recognize his ship as the pirate ship *Summons.*

"A day or so."

Three days had passed. Blake's crew, nervous at being in a Royal Navy port, were itching to leave. He could hardly blame them. Hence, against everything within him, he'd finally promised to set sail on the morrow. Too much time had passed. 'Twas quite possible Alexander Merrick Hyde, the next Earl of Clarendon, had locked Emeline in her chamber until Blake would give up and sail away.

Or worse, he intended to alert the Royal Navy to Blake's presence.

Surely if it were his own daughter, he would do the same.

Charlie moved to stand beside him. "She'll return. I knows it. She loves you."

"Perhaps, but 'tis becoming clear her godly family want naught to do with me."

The smell of Finn's pipe wafted on the breeze. "I says we set sail now, Cap'n, afore we be spotted fer the buccaneers we be an' hung at the gibbet on the morrow." He gripped his neck as if he could already feel the rope.

"We *were* buccaneers, Finn. Were," Blake said. "We will find new ways to gain our fortune from now on."

Finn stared at him as if he'd grown fins and a tail. "What be this madness?"

"I'm giving up my evil ways, Finn." Blake slapped him on the back, knowing full well the declaration might cost him a knife in the gut. But he must trust God, trust that if he did the right thing, God would protect him.

"Givin' up the trade?" Straddling the bulwarks, Rummy took a swig of rum. "Scupper, sink, and burn me. The crew won't go fer it, Cap'n."

"Then they may find another pirate ship to join."

Pedro slid down the backstay and landed on the deck, a wide grin on his face. "I think it's a good idea, Cap'n."

Before Blake could respond, Bandit, clinging to the ratlines, began squealing and flinging his arm through the air, pointing across the harbor.

Squinting against the bright sunlight, Blake glanced over the sparkling waters. There, in the distance, a cockboat rowed in their direction. He plucked the scope from his belt and positioned it on the craft. Was it possible for a heart to both leap and sink at the same time? Emeline sat among the thwarts, looking like a regal princess. Right beside her sat Alexander Merrick Hyde, looking none too happy. Two other men, fully armed, from what Blake could tell, sat next to them. Along with the rowers, that made six fighting men. The only consolation was that another woman sat on Emeline's other side. Surely, Viscount Hyde would not bring his women along for a fight. Would he?

Regardless, on the promise they would not be arrested, Blake ordered his crew to stand down and offer no resistance. Not that they could do much in clear view of the fort. Still, despite their protests and grumbling, he prayed not only that he had made the right decision but that they would heed his, most likely, last command.

In moments, after the boat thudded against the *Summons* and the rope ladder was tossed, Alexander Merrick Hyde, Viscount Hyde, leapt over the bulwarks and landed on the deck with a mighty thump.

His piercing blue eyes locked onto Blake as he drew his cutlass and charged toward him. "I should have you arrested for piracy and kidnapping!"

Curses and growls flooded the deck, but thankfully Blake's pirates offered no resistance.

He swallowed. The tip of the man's blade was but an inch from his throat. "A fit punishment, my lord."

"Papa, stop it at once!" Emeline said from behind her father, where a quick glance revealed the frustration and anger on her face. Not fear, however. Perhaps the man did not intend to arrest Blake, after all.

Alexander Hyde pressed the cutlass closer. "What is your defense?"

"None. I am guilty as charged." Blake stood his ground, returning the man's forceful gaze with one of his own. "But you should know, my lord," he added, "I have made my peace with God and repented of my evil ways."

A woman sashayed forward who surely must be Emeline's mother. Sunlight glinted off golden curls cascading down her back and lit her eyes with the same purity and goodness that filled Emeline's. Only a few lines at the edges of her eyes gave away her age. Oddly, she cast Blake a smile before turning toward her husband with a frustrated sigh. "Do leave him be, dear. He seems quite penitent."

Ignoring her, Viscount Hyde kept his eyes on Blake. "You believe yourself to be worthy of my daughter, Emeline?"

"Nay, I do not. I doubt any man would be, my lord." Blake shifted his gaze to Emeline. "But if you allow it, I vow to protect and love her all her days like no one ever could."

This appeared to satisfy Viscount Hyde, for he sheathed his blade and took a step back. "Good."

The entire ship seemed to breathe a sigh of relief.

Tugging from the grasp of a man who must be her brother, Emeline dashed toward Blake, casting a look of reprimand at her father. "You didn't have to scare him so, Papa."

One brow lifted as Viscount Hyde nodded toward Blake. "I doubt this man is so easily frightened."

Blake slipped his hand into Emeline's. "I thank you, my lord, for believing me."

"You? Nay. My daughter, aye."

Bandit dashed across the deck and leapt into Emeline's arms, grinning and leaning his cheek against hers.

Emeline's mother laughed. "Who might this be?"

"This is Bandit. He's the real hero aboard this ship." Smiling, Emeline winked at Blake.

He scratched beneath Bandit's chin. "Indeed. I quite agree."

"I cannot wait to hear that story." Emeline's brother approached, the perfect image of his father with his black hair and penetrating eyes—now honed in on Blake. "So you're the man who stole my sister away?"

"Caleb, my brother," Emeline announced.

Blake glanced at Emeline. "If you'll have the truth of it, I believe 'twas the other way around." He winked at her, then faced her father again. "I made an attempt to return her to you safely, my lord. Did you receive my post?"

A gust of wind tossed a strand of Alex's black hair across his cheek, and he snapped it away, frowning. "I did. And after we received Emeline's missive yesterday, we were preparing to set sail when"—he smiled lovingly at his daughter—"by God's good fortune she appeared on our doorstep." He took a step closer to Blake. "But the next time you leave my daughter alone and undefended in a dangerous port, you'll wish you had never been born. Do you take me?"

"Quite well, my lord." Blake met the man's sharp gaze, hoping to convey his sincerity.

"Papa, cease now," Emeline said. "He's a changed man."

One of Alex's dark brows arched. "We shall see."

Emeline's mother glanced over Blake's crew, most of whom stood about with shocked looks on their faces. Others with admiration. No doubt the Pirate Earl's reputation had stunned them into silence. An unusual occurrence. Even Sam stood at a distance, eyeing the proceedings with interest. "Now where is this female master gunner you told me about?"

Emeline gestured for Charlie to approach, and the woman did so, albeit with suspicion in her gaze.

"Emeline has explained your situation, Charlotte," Emeline's mother said. "My husband and I would like to offer you employment either at our estate or, if you prefer, one of our many ships. We would move your…"—she leaned in close to whisper—"family here to Kingston so you could be close."

For the first time since Blake had met Charlie, tears filled her eyes. "I would like that very much, milady."

"And you, lad." Viscount Hyde strode up to Pedro, who was leaning against a barrel. "I hear you're a fine up-and-coming seaman. If Captain Keene won't give you a position, you may have one on my ship."

Pedro's blue eyes lit like sapphires. "You mean it? I can?" For a moment, it seemed the boy would cry, but then he straightened and gathered himself. "I'd like that very much, my lord."

"Good, then." Viscount Hyde gripped his shoulder, then turned to Rummy. "A one-armed helmsman. I admit I didn't believe my daughter when she told me."

Rummy grinned but said naught as Finn approached and withdrew his pipe. "The best helmsman in the Caribbean, my lord. But only when 'e 'as a bottle o' rum in hand."

They all chuckled.

Emeline's mother wove her arm through her daughter's, and the look of love between them sent emotion burning in Blake's throat. His own mother had cast him out, and he'd always blamed God for it. But the God he now knew as a Father would never do such a thing. He stepped forward. 'Twas the perfect time to make his announcement, to inform Emeline's family, as well as his crew, of his plans. "Emeline may have told you I own an island."

Viscount Hyde crossed arms over his chest and nodded.

"I understand part of your mission here in the Caribbean is to help the poor, the widowed, and orphans."

Emeline stared at him curiously.

"I would like to offer my island as a refuge for those in need. There is plenty of food, fresh water, and an estate that can house hundreds."

At first, Viscount Hyde merely stared at him, his brow furrowing. Emeline's mother, however, clapped her hands together. "How wonderful!"

Caleb nodded his approval while grunts of shock filtered among his pirates.

The viscount stepped toward Blake, a look of admiration on his face—an admiration he'd never received from his own father. He swallowed down a burst of emotion as the man gripped his shoulder. "I am most pleased. Most pleased."

"Wha' 'bout us?" Finn spoke up, garnering grunts from the rest of the crew.

Blake scanned his men. "You are welcome to join us in our new mission, or I'm happy to leave you on an island of your choosing. Sam," he called to the surgeon, "we could use a man of your skill and education."

To which the old pirate nodded. Was it Blake's imagination or did a smile replace the man's perpetual frown?

Emeline glanced at her father. "After we explain the truth of God's Word to them, that is?"

Viscount Hyde drew his daughter close. "So good to have you home safe, darling. And look what you have accomplished." He waved a hand over the brig. "Egad, with God's help, you have redeemed an entire pirate ship!"

At that last comment, some of Blake's crew appeared to be having trouble breathing. Yet a wave of raw emotion swept over Emeline's face at the compliment.

Then turning to Blake, her father raised an incriminating brow. "Now, where is this Ring my daughter tells me about?"

Blake flattened his lips, loathing even the sound of the foul relic. "I kept it under lock and key in my desk, my lord. I wanted naught more to do with it and would have tossed it in the sea, if not for Emeline's insistence I bring it to you. She said you'd know what to do."

"Indeed. Fetch it." He glanced at Caleb. "My son will take it and dispose of it in a place where no one will ever find it."

Lady Hyde wove her arm through Emeline's. "Enough of all this. We have a wedding to plan!"

Hours later, Emeline found Blake at the bow of the *Summons*, one hand on the hilt of his cutlass, staring out over the moonlit waters of Kingston Harbor. "Father is ready to leave."

Turning, he drew her close and kissed her forehead. "I wish you could stay on board."

"It wouldn't be proper." She glanced up at him. "But in a week, I will be your wife."

"I cannot believe it." He eased a strand of hair from her cheek. "I never thought...never thought..."

"Anyone could love you?"

"That someone like *you* could..." He drew her against his chest. His warmth and scent of oak and the sea flooded her as the beat of his heart thumped against her cheek. How she wished she could stay in his arms forever.

"When you first stole me away on your ship," she said. "I could never have imagined so wonderful an outcome."

"Me either." He chuckled.

Reaching up, she fingered the stubble on his jaw. "How often I wondered why God had allowed such a tragedy to happen to me. What possible purpose could there be? Was I doing any good at all, helping anyone?"

"You cannot be serious?" Blake huffed, then gripped her shoulders. "You radiate the love and light of God everywhere you go. 'Twas why the demons scattered in your presence. Why Delphine quit the trade."

"What?" Emeline blinked.

"Aye. She told me as much when I went looking for you." Emeline shook her head.

"Pedro and Charlie are rescued," he continued. "And even Sam is considering that God might exist."

"Now, you tease me, Captain." She gave a coy grin.

A breeze tossed a strand of hair onto her cheek, and he gently brushed it aside. "Nay. He told me so yesterday."

If Blake announced that Bandit sprouted wings and flew away, she'd believe that over Sam turning to God.

Cupping her chin, he lifted her gaze to his. "But 'tis me you saved most of all." He eased the back of his fingers over her cheek. "I promise to always be the hero of your dreams."

So much joy and love burst within her she could hardly contain it. "And I promise to never lie to you or betray you and to always love you."

Leaning down, he kissed her like he never had before. With the intensity and passion of a man who truly cherished her, a man who would protect and love her forever.

A most unexpected answer to all her prayers and dreams! But in the end, all things truly did work together for good for those who love God.

About the Author

AWARD-WINNING AND BEST-SELLING AUTHOR, MARYLU TYNDALL dreamt of pirates and sea-faring adventures during her childhood days on Florida's Coast. With more than thirty books published, she makes no excuses for the deep spiritual themes embedded within her romantic adventures. Her hope is that readers will not only be entertained but will be brought closer to the Creator who loves them beyond measure. In a culture that accepts the occult, wizards, zombies, and vampires without batting an eye, MaryLu hopes to show the awesome present and powerful acts of God in a dying world. A Christy and Maggie award nominee and two-time winner of the RWA Inspy Reader's Choice Award, MaryLu makes her home with her husband, six children, four grandchildren, and several stray cats on the California coast.

For a peek at the characters and scenes from the book, visit my The Summons Pinterest Page under mltyndall!

Look for the next book in the series coming January 2026, **The Sentinel**!

Read the books that started it all! The Legacy of the King's Pirates Series! *The Redemption, The Reliance, The Restitution, The Ransom, The Reckoning, The Reckless, The Resolute*

If you enjoyed this book, one of the nicest ways to say "thank you" to an author and help them be able to continue writing is to leave a favorable review on Amazon, Barnes and Noble, Goodreads, Bookbub (And elsewhere, too!) I would appreciate it if you would take a moment to do so. Thanks so much!

Comments? Questions? I love hearing from my readers, so feel free to contact me via my WEBSITE: https://www.marylutyndall.com/ Or email me at: marylu_tyndall@yahoo.com

Follow me on:
PINTEREST:
BOOKBUB:
AMAZON
Instagram
BLOG: https://crossandcutlass.blogspot.com/

To hear news about special prices and new releases sign up for my newsletter on my Website or follow me on Bookbub!
https://www.marylutyndall.com/
https://www.bookbub.com/authors/marylu-tyndall

Other Books by MaryLu Tyndall

THE REDEMPTION

THE RELIANCE

THE RESTITUTION

THE RANSOM

THE RECKONING

THE RECKLESS

THE RESOLUTE

THE FALCON AND THE SPARROW

THE RED SIREN

THE BLUE ENCHANTRESS

THE RAVEN SAINT

CHARITY'S CROSS

SURRENDER THE HEART

SURRENDER THE NIGHT

SURRENDER THE DAWN

FORSAKEN DREAMS

ELUSIVE HOPE

ABANDONED MEMORIES

SHE WALKS IN POWER

SHE WALKS IN LOVE

SHE WALKS IN MAJESTY

VEIL OF PEARLS

WHEN ANGELS CRY

WHEN ANGELS BATTLE

WHEN ANGELS REJOICE

TEARS OF THE SEA

TIMELESS TREASURE
THE LIBERTY BRIDE
THE HIGHWAYMAN'S BARGAIN
THE PRIVATEER'S PRIZE
BEAUTY FROM ASHES
CHRISTMAS BOUNTY

www.ingramcontent.com/pod-product-compliance
Lightning Source LLC
Chambersburg PA
CBHW062115170626
46813CB00002B/462